William Henry Davenport Adams

Witch, Warlock and Magician

William Henry Davenport Adams

Witch, Warlock and Magician

ISBN/EAN: 9783337371210

Printed in Europe, USA, Canada, Australia, Japan

Cover: Foto ©Andreas Hilbeck / pixelio.de

More available books at **www.hansebooks.com**

Historical Sketches of Magic and Witchcraft in England and Scotland

BY

W. H. DAVENPORT ADAMS

'Dreams and the light imaginings of men'
SHELLEY

London
CHATTO & WINDUS, PICCADILLY
1889

PREFACE.

THE following pages may be regarded as a contribution towards that 'History of Human Error' which was undertaken by Mr. Augustine Caxton. I fear that many minds will have to devote all their energies to the work, if it is ever to be brought to completion; and, indeed, it may plausibly be argued that its completion would be an impossibility, since every generation adds something to the melancholy record— 'pulveris exigui parva munera.' However this may be, little more remains to be said on the subjects which I have here considered from the standpoint of a sympathetic though incredulous observer. Alchemy, Magic, Witchcraft—how exhaustively they have been investigated will appear from the list of authorities which I have drawn up for the reader's convenience. They have been studied by 'adepts,' and by critics, as realities and as delusions; and almost the last word would seem to have been said by Science— though not on the side of the adepts, who still continue to dream of the Hermetic philosophy, to lose themselves in fanciful pictures, theurgic and occult, and to write about the mysteries of magic with a simplicity of faith which we may wonder at, but are bound to respect.

It has not been my purpose, in the present volume, to attempt a general history of magic and alchemy, or a scientific inquiry into their psychological aspects. I have confined myself to a sketch of their progress in England, and to a narrative of the lives of our principal magicians. This occupies the first part. The second is devoted to an historical review of witchcraft in Great Britain, and an examination into the most remarkable Witch-Trials, in which I have endeavoured to bring out their peculiar features, presenting much of the evidence adduced, and in some cases the so-called confessions of the victims, in the original language. I believe that the details, notwithstanding the reticence imposed upon me by considerations of delicacy and decorum, will surprise the reader, and that he will readily admit the profound interest attaching to them, morally and intellectually. I have added a chapter on the 'Literature of Witchcraft,' which, I hope, is tolerably exhaustive, and now offer the whole as an effort to present, in a popular and readable form, the result of careful and conscientious study extending over many years.

W. H. D. A.

CONTENTS.

INTRODUCTION.

BOOK I.

THE ENGLISH MAGICIANS.

BOOK II.

WITCHES AND WITCHCRAFT.

WITCH, WARLOCK, AND MAGICIAN.

INTRODUCTION.

PROGRESS OF ALCHEMY IN EUROPE.

THE word χημεια—from which we derive our English word 'chemistry'—first occurs, it is said, in the Lexicon of Suidas, a Greek writer who flourished in the eleventh century. Here is his definition of it :

'Chemistry is the art of preparing gold and silver. The books concerning it were sought out and burnt by Diocletian, on account of the new plots directed against him by the Egyptians. He behaved towards them with great cruelty in his search after the treatises written by the ancients, his purpose being to prevent them from growing rich by a knowledge of this art, lest, emboldened by measureless wealth, they should be induced to resist the Roman supremacy.'

Some authorities assert, however, that this art, or pretended art, is of much greater antiquity than Suidas knew of ; and Scaliger refers to a Greek manuscript by Zozomen, of the fifth century, which is entitled 'A Faithful Description of the Secret and Divine Art of Making Gold and Silver.' We may assume that as soon as mankind had begun to set an artificial value upon these metals, and had acquired

1

some knowledge of chemical elements, their combina-
tions and permutations, they would entertain a desire
to multiply them in measureless quantities.   Dr.
Shaw speaks of no fewer than eighty-nine ancient
manuscripts, scattered through the European libraries,
which are all occupied with 'the chemical art,' or
'the holy art,' or, as it is sometimes called, 'the
philosopher's stone'; and a fair conclusion seems to
be that 'between the fifth century and the taking of
Constantinople in the fifteenth, the Greeks believed in
the possibility of making gold and silver,' and called
the supposed process, or processes, *chemistry*.

The delusion was taken up by the Arabians when,
under their Abasside Khalifs, they entered upon the
cultivation of scientific knowledge. The Arabians conveyed it into Spain, whence its diffusion over Christendom was a simple work of time, sure if gradual.
From the eleventh to the sixteenth century, alchemy
was more or less eagerly studied by the scholars of
Germany, Italy, France, and England; and the
volumes in which they recorded both their learning
and their ignorance, the little they knew and the
more they did not know, compose quite a considerable
library. One hundred and twenty-two are enumerated
in the 'Bibliotheca Chemica Curiosa,' of Mangetus, a
dry-as-dust kind of compilation, in two huge volumes,
printed at Geneva in 1702.   Any individual who
has time and patience to expend *ad libitum*, cannot
desire a fairer field of exercise than the 'Bibliotheca.'
One very natural result of all this vain research and
profitless inquiry was a keen anxiety on the part of

victims to dignify their labours by claiming for their 'sciences, falsely so-called,' a venerable and mysterious origin. They accordingly asserted that the founder or creator was Hermes Trismegistus, whom some of them professed to identify with Chanaan, the son of Ham, whose son Mizraim first occupied and peopled Egypt. Now, it is clear that any person might legitimately devote his nights and days to the pursuit of a science invented, or originally taught, by no less illustrious an ancient than Hermes Trismegistus. But to clothe it with the awe of a still greater antiquity, they affirmed that its principles had been discovered, engraved in Phœnician characters, on an emerald tablet which Alexander the Great exhumed from the philosopher's tomb. Unfortunately, as is always the case, the tablet was lost; but we are expected to believe that two Latin versions of the inscription had happily been preserved. One of these may be Englished as hereinunder:

1. I speak no frivolous things, but only what is true and most certain.

2. What is below resembles that which is above, and what is above resembles that which is below, to accomplish the one thing of all things most wonderful.

3. And as all things proceeded from the meditation of the One God, so were all things generated from this one thing by the disposition of Nature.

4. Its father is *Sol*, its mother *Luna*; it was engendered in the womb by the air, and nourished by the earth.

5. It is the cause of all the perfection of things throughout the whole world.

6. It arrives at the highest perfection of powers if it be reduced into earth.

7. Separate the earth from the fire, the subtle from the gross, acting with great caution.

8. Ascend with the highest wisdom from earth to heaven, and thence descend again to earth, and bind together the powers of things superior and things inferior. So shall you compass the glory of the whole world, and divest yourself of the abjectness of humanity.

9. This thing has more fortitude than fortitude itself, since it will overcome everything subtle and penetrate everything solid.

10. All that the world contains was created by it.

11. Hence proceed things wonderful which in this wise were established.

12. For this reason the name of Hermes Trismegistus was bestowed upon me, because I am master of three parts of the philosophy of the whole world.

13. This is what I had to say concerning the most admirable process of the chemical art.

These oracular utterances are so vague and obscure that an enthusiast may read into them almost any meaning he chooses ; but there seems a general consensus of opinion that they refer to the ' universal medicine' of the earlier alchemists. This, however, is of no great importance, since it is certain they were invented by some ingenious hand as late as the fifteenth century. Another forgery of a similar kind is the ' Tractatus Aureus de Lapidis Physici Secretis,' also attributed to Hermes; it professes to describe the process of making this 'universal medicine,' or 'philosopher's stone,' and the formulary is thus translated by Thomson :

'Take of moisture an ounce and a half ; of meridional redness— that is, the soul of the sun—a fourth part, that is, half an ounce ; of yellow sage likewise half an ounce ; and of auripigmentum half an ounce ; making in all three ounces.'

Such a recipe does not seem to help forward an enthusiastic student to any material extent.

THE EARLIER ALCHEMISTS.

It is in the erudite writings of the great Arabian physician, Gebir—that is, Abu Moussah Djafar, sur-named *Al Sofi*, or The Wise—that the science of alchemy, or chemistry (at first the two were identical), first assumes a definite shape. Gebir flourished in the early part of the eighth century, and wrote, it is said, upwards of five hundred treatises on the philosopher's stone and the elixir of life. In reference to the latter mysterious potion, which possessed the wonderful power of conferring immortal youth on those who drank of it, one may remark that it was the necessary complement of the philosopher's stone, for what would be the use of an unlimited faculty of making gold and silver unless one could be sure of an immortality in which to enjoy its exercise ? Gebir's principal work, the ' Summæ Perfectionis,' containing instructions for students in search of the two great secrets, has been translated into several

European languages ; and an English version, by
Richard Russell, the alchemist, was published in
1686.

Gebir lays down, as a primary principle, that all
metals are compounds of mercury and sulphur. They
all labour under disease, he says, except gold, which is
the one metal gifted with perfect health. Therefore, a
preparation of it would dispel every ill which flesh is
heir to, as well as the maladies of plants. We may
excuse his extravagances, however, in consideration
of the services he rendered to science by his discovery
of corrosive sublimate, red oxide of mercury, white
oxide of arsenic, nitric acid, oxide of copper, and
nitrate of silver, all of which originally issued from
Gebir's laboratory.

Briefly speaking, the hypothesis assumed by the
alchemists was this : all the metals are compounds,
and the baser contain the same elements as gold,
contaminated, indeed, with various impurities, but
capable, when these have been purged away, of assuming all its properties and characters. The substance
which was to effect this purifying process they
called the philosopher's stone (*lapis philosophorum*),
though, as a matter of fact, it is always described
as a *powder*—a powder red-coloured, and smelling
strongly. Few of the alchemists, however, venture
on a distinct statement that they had discovered or
possessed this substance.

The arch-quack Paracelsus makes the assertion, of
course ; unblushing mendacity was part of his stock-
in-trade ; and he pretends even to define the methods

by which it may be realized. Unfortunately, to
ordinary mortals his description is absolutely unintelligible. Others there are who affirm that they
had seen it, and seen it in operation, transmuting
lead, quicksilver, and other of the inferior metals into
ruddy gold. One wonders that they did not claim a
share in a process which involved such boundless
potentialities of wealth!

Helvetius, the physician, though no believer in the
magical art, tells the following wild story in his
'Vitulus Aureus':

On December 26, 1666, a stranger called upon him,
and, after discussing the supposed properties of the
universal medicine, showed him a yellow powder,
which he declared to be the *lapis*, and also five large
plates of gold, which, he said, were the product of its
action. Naturally enough, Helvetius begged for a
few grains of this marvellous powder, or that the
stranger would at least exhibit its potency in his
presence. He refused, however, but promised that he
would return in six weeks. He kept his promise,
and then, after much entreaty, gave Helvetius a pinch
of the powder—about as much as a rape-seed. The
physician expressed his fear that so minute a quantity
would not convert as much as four grains of lead ;
whereupon the stranger broke off one-half, and
declared that the remainder was more than sufficient
for the purpose. During their first conference,
Helvetius had contrived to conceal a little of the
powder beneath his thumb-nail. This he dropped into
some molten lead, but it was nearly all exhaled in

smoke, and the residue was simply of a vitreous character.

On mentioning this circumstance to his visitor, he explained that the powder should have been enclosed in wax before it was thrown into the molten lead, to prevent the fumes of the lead from affecting it. He added that he would come back next day, and show him how to make the projection; but as he failed to appear, Helvetius, in the presence of his wife and son, put six drachms of lead into a crucible, and as soon as the lead was melted, flung into it the atoms of powder given to him by his mysterious visitor, having first rolled them up in a little ball of wax. At the end of a quarter of an hour he found the lead transmuted (so he avers) into gold. Its colour at first was a deep green; but the mixture, when poured into a conical vessel, turned blood-red, and, after cooling, acquired the true tint of gold. A goldsmith who examined it pronounced it to be genuine. Helvetius requested Purelius, the keeper of the Dutch Mint, to test its value; and two drachms, after being exposed to aquafortis, were found to have increased a couple of scruples in weight— an increase doubtlessly owing to the silver, which still remained enveloped in the gold, despite the action of the aquafortis.

It is obvious that this narrative is a complete mystification, and that either the stranger was a myth or Helvetius was the victim of a deception.

The recipes that the alchemists formulate—those,

that is, who profess to have discovered the stone, or to have known somebody who enjoyed so rare a fortune—are always unintelligible or impracticable. What is to be understood, for example, of the following elaborate process, or series of processes, which are recorded by Mangetus, in his preface to the ponderous 'Bibliotheca Chemica' (to which reference has already been made)?

1. Prepare a quantity of spirits of wine, so free from water as to be wholly combustible, and so volatile that a drop of it, if let fall, will evaporate before it reaches the ground. This constitutes the first menstruum.

2. Take pure mercury, revived in the usual manner from cinnabar; put it into a glass vessel with common salt and distilled vinegar; shake violently, and when the vinegar turns black, pour it off, and add fresh vinegar. Shake again, and continue these repeated shakings and additions until the mercury no longer turns the vinegar black; the mercury will then be quite pure and very brilliant.

3. Take of this mercury four parts; of sublimed mercury (*mercurii meteoresati* — probably corrosive sublimate), prepared with your own hands, eight parts; triturate them together in a wooden mortar with a wooden pestle, till all the grains of running mercury disappear. (This process is truly described as 'tedious and rather difficult.')

4. The mixture thus prepared is to be put into a sand-bath, and exposed to a subliming heat, which

is to be gradually increased until the whole sublimes.
Collect the sublimed matter, put it again into the
sand-bath, and sublime a second time ; this process
must be repeated five times. The product is a very
sweet crystallized sublimate, constituting the *sal
sapientum*, or wise men's salt (probably calomel), and
possessing wonderful properties.

5. Grind it in a wooden mortar, reducing it to
powder ; put this powder into a glass retort, and
pour upon it the spirit of wine (see No. 1) till it
stands about three finger-breadths above the powder.
Seal the retort hermetically, and expose it to a very
gentle heat for seventy-four hours, shaking it several
times a day ; then distil with a gentle heat, and the
spirit of wine will pass over, together with spirit of
mercury. Keep this liquid in a well-stoppered bottle,
lest it should evaporate. More spirit of wine is to
be poured upon the residual salt, and after digestion
must be distilled off, as before ; and this operation
must be repeated until all the salt is dissolved and
given off with the spirit of wine. A great work
will then have been accomplished! For the mercury,
having to some extent been rendered volatile, will
gradually become fit to receive the tincture of gold
and silver. Now return thanks to God, who has
hitherto crowned your wonderful work with success.
Nor is this wonderful work enveloped in Cimmerian
darkness ; it is clearer than the sun, though preceding
writers have sought to impose upon us with parables,
hieroglyphs, fables, and enigmas.

6. Take this mercurial spirit, which contains our

magical steel in its belly (*sic*), and put it into a glass
retort, to which a receiver must be well and carefully adjusted ; draw off the spirit by a very gentle
heat, and in the bottom of the retort will remain
the quintessence or soul of mercury. This is to be
sublimed by applying a stronger heat to the retort
that it may become volatile, as all the philosophers
affirm :

> ' Si fixum solvas faciesque volare solutum,
> Et volucrum figas faciet te vivere tutum.'

This is our *luna*, our fountain, in which ' the king '
and ' the queen ' may bathe. Preserve this precious
quintessence of mercury, which is exceedingly volatile,
in a well-closed vessel for further use.

8. Let us now proceed to the production of common
gold, which we shall communicate clearly and distinctly, without digression or obscurity, in order
that from this common gold we may obtain our
philosophical gold, just as from common mercury we
have obtained, by the foregoing processes, philosophical mercury. In the name of God, then, take
common gold, purified in the usual way by antimony,
and reduce it into small grains, which must be
washed with salt and vinegar until they are quite
pure. Take one part of this gold, and pour on it
three parts of the quintessence of mercury : as philosophers reckon from seven to ten, so do we also
reckon our number as philosophical, and begin with
three and one. Let them be married together, like
husband and wife, to produce children of their own
kind, and you will see the common gold sink and

plainly dissolve. Now the marriage is consummated ; and two things are converted into one. Thus the philosophical sulphur is at hand, as the philosophers say : ' The sulphur being dissolved, the stone is at hand.' Take then, in the name of God, our philosophical vessel, in which the king and queen embrace each other as in a bedchamber, and leave it till the water is converted into earth ; then peace is concluded between the water and the fire— then the elements no longer possess anything contrary to each other—because, when the elements are converted into earth, they cease to be antagonistic ; for in earth all elements are at rest. The philosophers say : ' When you shall see the water coagulate, believe that your knowledge is true, and that all your operations are truly philosophical.' Our gold is no longer common, but philosophical, through the processes it has undergone : at first, it was exceedingly ' fixed ' (*fixum*) ; then exceedingly volatile ; and again, exceedingly fixed : the entire science depends upon the change of the elements. The gold, at first a metal, is now a sulphur, capable of converting all metals into its own sulphur. And our tincture is wholly converted into sulphur, which possesses the energy of curing every disease ; this is our universal medicine against all the most deplorable ills of the human body. Therefore, return infinite thanks to Almighty God for all the good things which He hath bestowed upon us.

9. In this great work of ours, two methods of fermentation and projection are wanting, without

which the uninitiated will not readily follow out our process. The mode of fermentation : Of the sulphur already described take one part, and project it upon three parts of very pure gold fused in a furnace. In a moment you will see the gold, by the force of the sulphur, converted into a red sulphur of an inferior quality to the primary sulphur. Take one part of this, and project it upon three parts of fused gold ; the whole will again be converted into a sulphur or a fixable mass ; mixing one part of this with three parts of gold, you will have a malleable and extensible metal. If you find it so, it is well; if not, add more sulphur, and it will again pass into a state of sulphur. Now our sulphur will sufficiently be fermented, or our medicine brought into a metallic nature.

10. The method of projection is this : Take of the fermented sulphur one part, and project it upon two parts of mercury, heated in a crucible, and you will have a perfect metal ; if its colour be not sufficiently deep, fuse it again, and add more fermented sulphur, and thus it will gain colour. If it become frangible, add a sufficient quantity of mercury, and it will be perfect.

Thus, friend, you have a description of the universal medicine, not only for curing diseases and prolonging life, but also for transmuting all metals into gold. Give thanks, therefore, to Almighty God, who, taking pity on human calamities, hath at last revealed this inestimable treasure, and made it known for the common benefit of all.

Such is the jargon with which these so-called

philosophers imposed upon their dupes, and, to some extent perhaps, upon themselves. As Dr. Thomson points out, the philosopher's stone prepared by this elaborate process could hardly have been anything else than *an amalgam of gold*. Chloride of gold it could not have contained, because such a preparation, instead of acting medicinally, would have proved a most virulent poison. Of course, amalgam of gold, if projected into melted lead or tin, and afterwards cupellated, would leave a portion of gold —that is, exactly the amount *which existed previously in the amalgam.* Impostors may, therefore, have availed themselves of it to persuade the credulous that it was really the philosopher's stone ; but the alchemists who prepared the amalgam must have known that it contained gold.*

It is well known that the mediæval magicians, necromancers, conjurers—call them by what name you will—who adopted alchemy as an instrument of imposition, and by no means in the spirit of philosophical inquiry and research which had characterized their predecessors, resorted to various ingenious devices in order to maintain their hold upon their victims. Sometimes they made use of crucibles with false bottoms—at the real bottom they concealed a portion of oxide of gold or silver covered with powdered sulphur, which had been rendered adhesive by a little gummed water or wax. When heat was applied the false bottom melted away, and the oxide of gold or

* *Cf.* Stahl, 'Fundamenta Chimiæ,' cap. 'De Lapide Philosophorum '; and Kircher, 'Mundus Subterraneus.'

silver eventually appeared as the product of the operation at the bottom of the crucible. Sometimes they made a hole in a lump of charcoal, and filling it with oxide of gold or silver, stopped up the orifice with wax ; or they soaked charcoal in a solution of these metals ; or they stirred the mixture in the crucible with hollow rods, containing oxide of gold or silver, closed up at the bottom with wax. A faithful representation of the stratagems to which the pseudo-alchemist resorted, that his dupes might not recover too soon from their delusion, is furnished by Ben Jonson in his comedy of ' The Alchemist,' and his masque of ' Mercury vindicated from the Alchemists.' The dramatist was thoroughly conversant with the technicalities of the pretended science, and also with the deceptions of its professors. In the masque he puts into the mouth of Mercury an indignant protest :

' The mischief a secret any of them knows, above the consuming of coals and drawing of usquebagh ; howsoever they may pretend, under the specious names of Gebir, Arnold, Lully, or Bombast of Hohenheim, to commit miracles in art, and treason against nature ! As if the title of philosopher, that creature of glory, were to be fetched out of a furnace !'

But while the world is full of fools, it is too much to expect there shall be any lack of knaves to prey upon them !

IN THE MIDDLE AGES.

The first of the great European alchemists I take to have been
Albertus Magnus or Albertus Teutonicus (Frater Albertus de Colonia and Albertus Grotus, as he is also

called), a man of remarkable intellectual energy and
exceptional force of character, who has sometimes,
and not without justice, been termed the founder of
the Schoolmen. Neither the place nor the date of his
birth is authentically known, but he was still in his
young manhood when, about 1222, he was appointed
to the chair of theology at Padua, and became a
member of the Dominican Order. He did not long
retain the professorship, and, departing from Padua,
taught with great success in Ratisbon, Köln, Strass-
burg, and Paris, residing in the last-named city for
three years, together with his illustrious disciple,
Thomas Aquinas. In 1260 he was appointed to the
See of Ratisbon, though he had not previously held
any ecclesiastical dignity, but soon resigned, on the
ground that its duties interfered vexatiously with his
studies. Twenty years later, at a ripe old age, he
died, leaving behind him, as monuments of his persistent industry and intellectual subtlety, one-and-
twenty ponderous folios, which include commentaries
on Aristotle, on the Scriptures, and on Dionysius the
Areopagite. Among his minor works occurs a treatise
on alchemy, which seems to show that he was a
devout believer in the science.

From the marvellous stories of his thaumaturgic
exploits which have come down to us, we may infer
that he had attained a considerable amount of skill in
experimental chemistry. The brazen statue which he
animated, and the garrulity of which was so offensive
that Thomas Aquinas one day seized a hammer, and,
provoked beyond all endurance, smashed it to pieces,

may be a reminiscence of his powers as a ventriloquist. And the following story may hint at an effective manipulation of the *camera obscura :* Count William of Holland and King of the Romans happening to pass through Köln, Albertus invited him and his courtiers to his house to partake of refreshment. It was midwinter ; but on arriving at the philosopher's residence they found the tables spread in the open garden, where snowdrifts lay several feet in depth. Indignant at so frugal a reception, they were on the point of leaving, when Albertus appeared, and by his courtesies induced them to remain. Immediately the scene was lighted up with the sunshine of summer, a warm and balmy air stole through the whispering boughs, the frost and snow vanished, the melodies of the lark dropped from the sky like golden rain. But as soon as the feast came to an end the sunshine faded, the birds ceased their song, clouds gathered darkling over the firmament, an icy blast shrieked through the gibbering branches, and the snow fell in blinding showers, so that the philosopher's guests were glad to fold their cloaks about them and retreat into the kitchen to grow warm before its blazing fire.

Was this some clever scenic deception, or is the whole a fiction ?

A knowledge of the secret of the *Elixir Vitæ* was possessed (it is said) by *Alain de l'Isle,* or Alanus de Insulis ; but either he did not avail himself of it, or failed to compound a sufficient quantity of the magic potion, for he died under the sacred roof of Citeaux, in 1298, at the advanced age of 110.

Arnold de Villeneuve, who attained, in the thirteenth century, some distinction as a physician, an astronomer, an astrologer, and an alchemist—and was really a capable man of science, as science was then understood—formulates an elaborate recipe for rejuvenating one's self, which, however, does not seem to have been very successful in his own case, since he died before he was 70. Perhaps he was as disgusted with the compound as (in the well-known epitaph) the infant was with this mundane sphere—he 'liked it not, and died.' I think there are many who would forfeit longevity rather than partake of it.

'Twice or thrice a week you must anoint your body thoroughly with the manna of cassia; and every night, before going to bed, you must place over your heart a plaster, composed of a certain quantity (or, rather, uncertain, for definite and precise proportions are never particularized) of Oriental saffron, red rose-leaves, sandal-wood, aloes, and amber, liquefied in oil of roses and the best white wax. During the day this must be kept in a leaden casket. You must next pen up in a court, where the water is sweet and the air pure, sixteen chickens, if you are of a sanguine temperament; twenty-five, if phlegmatic; and thirty, if melancholic. Of these you are to eat one a day, after they have been fattened in such a manner as to have absorbed into their system the qualities which will ensure your longevity; for which purpose they are first to be kept without food until almost starved, and then gorged with a broth of serpents and vinegar, thickened with wheat and beans, for at least two

months. When they are served at your table you will drink a moderate quantity of white wine or claret to assist digestion.'
I should think it would be needed!

Among the alchemists must be included *Pietro d'Apono.* He was an eminent physician; but, being accused of heresy, was thrown into prison and died there. His ecclesiastical persecutors, however, burned his bones rather than be entirely disappointed of their *auto da fé.* Like most of the mediæval physicians, he indulged in alchemical and astrological speculations; but they proved to Pietro d'Apono neither pleasurable nor profitable. It was reputed of him that he had summoned a number of evil spirits; and, on their obeying his call, had shut them up in seven crystal vases, where he detained them until he had occasion for their services. In his selection of them he seems to have displayed a commendably catholic taste and love of knowledge; for one was an expert in poetry, another in painting, a third in philosophy, a fourth in physic, a fifth in astrology, a sixth in music, and a seventh in alchemy. So that when he required instruction in either of these arts or sciences, he simply tapped the proper crystal vase and laid on a spirit.

The story seems to be a fanciful allusion to the various acquirements of Pietro d'Apono; but if intended at first as a kind of allegory, it came in due time to be accepted literally.

I pass on to the great Spanish alchemist and magician, *Raymond Lully,* or Lulli, who was scarcely inferior

in fame, or the qualities which merited fame, even to
Albertus Magnus. He was a man, not only of wide, but
of accurate scholarship ; and the two or three hundred
treatises which proceeded from his pen traversed the
entire circle of the learning of his age, dealing with
almost every conceivable subject from medicine to
morals, from astronomy to theology, and from alchemy
to civil and canon law. His life had its romantic
aspects, and his death (in 1315 ?) was invested with
something of the glory of martyrdom ; for while he was
preaching to the Moslems at Bona, the mob fell upon
him with a storm of stones, and though he was still
alive when rescued by some Genoese merchants, and
conveyed on board their vessel, he died of the injuries
he had received before it arrived in a Spanish port.

There seems little reason to believe that Lulli
visited England about 1312, on the invitation of
Edward II. Dickenson, in his work on ' The Quint-
essences of the Philosophers,' asserts that his
laboratory was established in Westminster Abbey—
that is, in the cloisters—and that some time after his
return to the Continent a large quantity of gold-dust
was found in the cell he had occupied. Langlet du
Fresnoy contends that it was through the intervention of John Cremer, Abbot of Westminster, a persevering seeker after the *lapis philosophorum*, that he
came to England, Cremer having described him to
King Edward as a man of extraordinary powers.
Robert Constantine, in his ' Nomenclator Scriptorum
Medicorum ' (1515), professes to have discovered
that Lulli resided for some time in London, and

made gold in the Tower, and that he had seen some gold pieces of his making, which were known in England as the nobles of Raymond, or rose-nobles. But the great objections to these very precise statements rests on two facts pointed out by Mr. Waite, that the rose-noble, so called because a rose was stamped on each side of it, was first coined in 1465, in the reign of Edward IV., and that there never was an Abbot Cremer of Westminster.

Jean de Meung is also included among the alche-mists ; but he bequeathed to posterity in his glorious poem of the ' Roman de la Rose ' something very much more precious than would have been any formula for making gold. In one sense he was in-deed an alchemist, and possessed the secret of the universal medicine ; for in his poem his genius has transmuted into purest gold the base ore of popular traditions and legends.

Some of the stories which Langlet du Fresnoy tells of *Nicholas Flamel* were probably invented long after his death, or else we should have to brand him as a most audacious knave. One of those amazing narra-tives pretends that he bought for a couple of florins an old and curious volume, the leaves of which—three times seven (this sounds better than twenty-one) in number—were made from the bark of trees. Each seventh leaf bore an allegorical picture—the first re-presenting a serpent swallowing rods, the second a cross with a serpent crucified upon it, and the third a fountain in a desert, surrounded by creeping serpents.

Who, think you, was the author of this mysterious volume? No less illustrious a person than Abraham the patriarch, Hebrew, prince, philosopher, priest, Levite, and magian, who, as it was written in Latin, must have miraculously acquired his foreknowledge of a tongue which, in his time, had no existence. A perusal of its mystic pages convinced Flamel that he had had the good fortune to discover a complete manual on the art of transmutation of metals, in which all the necessary vessels were indicated, and the processes described. But there was one serious difficulty to be overcome: the book assumed, as a matter of course, that the student was already in possession of that all-important agent of transmutation, the philosopher's stone.

Careful study led Flamel to the conclusion that the secret of the stone was hidden in certain allegorical drawings on the fourth and fifth leaves ; but, then, to decipher these was beyond his powers. He submitted them to all the learned savants and alchemical adepts he could get hold of : they proved to be no wiser than himself, while some of them actually laughed at Abraham's posthumous publication as worthless gibberish. Flamel, however, clung fast to his conviction of the inestimable value of his ' find,' and daily pondered over the two cryptic illustrations, which may thus be described : On the first page of the fourth leaf Mercury was contending with a figure, which might be either Saturn or Time—probably the latter, as he carried on his head the emblematical hour-glass, and in his hand the not less emblematical

scythe. On the second stage a flower upon a moun-
tain-top presented the unusual combination of a blue
stalk, with red and white blossoms, and leaves of
pure gold. The wind appeared to blow it about very
harshly, and a gruesome company of dragons and
griffins encompassed it.

Upon the study of these provokingly obscure
designs Flamel fruitlessly expended the leisure time
of thrice seven years : after which, on the advice of
his wife, he repaired to Spain to seek the assistance of
some erudite Jewish rabbi. He had been wandering
from place to place for a couple of years, when he
met, somewhere in Leon, a learned Hebrew physician,
named Canches, who agreed to return with him to
Paris, and there examine Abraham's volume.
Canches was deeply versed in all the lore of the
Cabala, and Flamel hung with delight on the words
of wisdom that dropped from his eloquent lips. But
at Orleans Canches was taken ill with a malady of
which he died, and Flamel found his way home, a
sadder, if not a wiser, man. He resumed his study
of the book, but for two more years could get no clue
to its meaning. In the third year, recalling some
deliverance of his departed friend, the rabbi, he perceived that all his experiments had hitherto proceeded
upon erroneous principles. He repeated them upon
a different basis, and in a few months brought them
to a successful issue. On January 13, 1382, he converted mercury into silver, and on April 25 into
gold. Well might he cry in triumph, ' Eureka !'
The great secret, the sublime magistery was his: he

had discovered the art of transmuting metals into gold and silver, and, so long as he kept it to himself, had at his command the source of inexhaustible wealth.

At this time Nicholas Flamel, it is said, was about eighty years old. His admirers assert that he also discovered the elixir of immortal life; but, as he died in 1419, at the age (it is alleged) of 116, he must have been content with the merest sip of it! Why did he not reveal its ingredients for the general benefit of our afflicted humanity? His immense wealth he bequeathed to churches and hospitals, thus making a better use of it after death than he had made of it in his lifetime. For it is said that Flamel was a usurer, and that his philosopher's stone was ' cent per cent.' It is true enough that he dabbled in alchemy, and probably he made his alchemical experiments useful in connection with his usurious transactions.

BOOK I.

THE ENGLISH MAGICIANS

CHAPTER I.

ROGER BACON: THE TRUE AND THE LEGENDARY.

IT was in the early years of the fourteenth century
that the two pseudo-sciences of alchemy and astrology,
the supposititious sisters of chemistry and astronomy,
made their way into England. At first their progress was by no means so rapid as it had been on the
Continent; for in England, as yet, there was no
educated class prepared to give their leisure to the
work of experimental investigation. A solitary
scholar here and there lighted his torch at the altar-
fire which the Continental philosophers kept burning
with so much diligence and curiosity, and was
generally rewarded for his heterodox enthusiasm by
the persecution of the Church and the prejudice of
the vulgar. But by degrees the new sciences increased the number of their adherents, and the more
active intellects of the time embraced the theory
of astral influences, and were fascinated by the delusion of the philosopher's stone. Many a secret
furnace blazed day and night with the charmed
flames which were to resolve the metals into their
original elements, and place the pale student in

possession of the coveted *magisterium,* or 'universal medicine.' At length the alchemists became a sufficiently numerous and important body to draw the attention of the Government, which regarded their proceedings with suspicion, from a fear that the result might injuriously affect the coinage. In 1434 the Legislature enacted that the making of gold or silver should be treated as a felony. But the Parliament was influenced by a very different motive from that of the King and his Council, its patriotic fears being awakened lest the Executive, enabled by the new science to increase without limit the pecuniary resources of the Crown, should be rendered independent of Parliamentary control.

In the course of a few years, however, broader and more enlightened views prevailed; and it came to be acknowledged that scientific research ought to be relieved from legislative interference. In 1455 Henry VI. issued four patents in succession to certain knights, London citizens, chemists, monks, mass-priests, and others, granting them leave and license to undertake the discovery of the philosopher's stone, 'to the great benefit of the realm, and the enabling the King to pay all the debts of the Crown in *real gold and silver.*' On the remarkable fact that these patents were issued to ecclesiastics as well as laymen, Prynne afterwards remarked, with true theological acridity, that they were so included because they were 'such good artists in transubstantiating bread and wine in the Eucharist, and were, therefore, the more likely to be able to effect the transmutation of

base metals into better.' Nothing came of the
patents. The practical common-sense of Englishmen
never took very kindly to the alchemical delusion,
and Chaucer very faithfully describes the contempt
with which it was generally regarded. Enthusiasts
there were, no doubt, who firmly believed in it, and
knaves who made a profit out of it, and dupes who
were preyed upon by the knaves; and so it languished
on through the sixteenth and seventeenth centuries.
It seems at one time to have amused the shrewd
intellect of Queen Elizabeth, and at another to have
caught the volatile fancy of the second Villiers, Duke
of Buckingham. But alchemy was, in the main, the
modus vivendi of quacks and cheats, of such impostors as Ben Jonson has drawn so powerfully in his
great comedy—a Subtle, a Face, and a Doll Common,
who, in the Sir Epicure Mammons of the time, found
their appropriate victims. These creatures played
on the greed and credulity of their dupes with successful audacity, and excited their imaginations by
extravagant promises. Thus, Ben Jonson's hero runs
riot with glowing anticipations of what the alchemical
magisterium can effect.

> ' Do you think I fable with you? I assure you,
> He that has once the flower of the sun,
> The perfect ruby, which we call *Elixir*,
> Not only can do that, but, by its virtue,
> Can confer honour, love, respect, long life ;
> Give safety, valour, yes, and victory,
> To whom he will. In eight-and-twenty days
> I'll make an old man of fourscore a child. . . .
>   'Tis the secret
> Of nature naturized 'gainst all infections,

Cures all diseases coming of all causes ;
A month's grief in a day, a year's in twelve,
And of what age soever in a month.'

The English alchemists, however, with a few ex-
ceptions, depended for a livelihood chiefly on their
sale of magic charms, love-philters, and even more
dangerous potions, and on horoscope-casting, and
fortune-telling by the hand or by cards. They acted,
also, as agents in many a dark intrigue and unlawful
project, being generally at the disposal of the highest
bidder, and seldom shrinking from any crime.

The earliest name of note on the roll of the English
magicians, necromancers and alchemists is that of

ROGER BACON.

This great man has some claim to be considered the
father of experimental philosophy, since it was he
who first laid down the principles upon which physical investigation should be conducted. Speaking
of science, he says, in language far in advance of his
times : ' There are two modes of knowing—by argument and by experiment. Argument winds up a
question, but does not lead us to acquiesce in, or feel
certain of, the contemplation of truth, unless the
truth be proved and confirmed by experience.' To
Experimental Science he ascribed three differentiating
characters : ' First, she tests by experiment the grand
conclusions of all other sciences. Next, she discovers,
with reference to the ideas connected with other
sciences, splendid truths, to which these sciences
without assistance are unable to attain. Her third
prerogative is, that, unaided by the other sciences,

and of herself, she can investigate the secrets of nature.' These truths, now accepted as trite and self-evident, ranked, in Roger Bacon's day, as novel and important discoveries.

He was born at Ilchester, in Somersetshire, in 1214. Of his lineage, parentage, and early education we know nothing, except that he must have been very young when he went to Oxford, for he took orders there before he was twenty. Joining the Franciscan brotherhood, he applied himself to the study of Greek, Latin, Hebrew, and Arabic ; but his genius chiefly inclined towards the pursuit of the natural sciences, in which he obtained such a mastery that his contemporaries accorded to him the flattering title of ' The Admirable Doctor.' His lectures gathered round him a crowd of admiring disciples ; until the boldness of their speculations aroused the suspicion of the ecclesiastical authorities, and in 1257 they were prohibited by the General of his Order. Then Pope Innocent IV. interfered, interdicting him from the publication of his writings, and placing him under close supervision. He remained in this state of tutelage until Clement IV., a man of more liberal views, assumed the triple tiara, who not only released him from his irksome restraints, but desired him to compose a treatise on the sciences. This was the origin of Bacon's ' Opus Majus,' ' Opus Minus ' and ' Opus Tertius,' which he completed in a year and a half, and despatched to Rome. In 1267 he was allowed to return to Oxford, where he wrote his ' Compendium Studii Philosophiæ.' His vigorous advocacy of new methods of scientific investigation, or, perhaps, his unsparing exposure of the ignorance and vices of the monks and the clergy, again brought down upon him the heavy arm of the ecclesiastical tyranny. His works were condemned by the General of his Order, and in 1278, during the pontificate of Nicholas III., he was thrown into prison, where he was detained for several years. It is said that he was not released until 1292, the year in which he published his latest production, the 'Compendium Studii Theologiæ.' Two years afterwards he died.

In many respects Bacon was greatly in advance of his contemporaries, but his general repute ignores his real and important services to philosophy, and builds up a glittering fabric upon mechanical discoveries and inventions to which, it is to be feared, he cannot lay claim. As Professor Adamson puts it, he certainly describes a method of constructing a telescope, but not so as to justify the conclusion that he himself was in possession of that instrument. The invention of gunpowder has been attributed to him on the strength of a passage in one of his works, which, if fairly interpreted, disposes at once of the pretension ; besides, it was already known to the Arabs. Burning-glasses were in common use ; and there is no proof that he made spectacles, although he was probably acquainted with the principle of their construction. It is not to be denied, however, that in his interesting treatise on ' The Secrets of Nature and Art,'* he ex-

* Epistola Fratris Rogerii Baconis de Secretis Operibus Artis et Naturæ et de Nullitate Magiæ.

hibits every sign of a far-seeing and lively intelligence, and foreshadows the possibility of some of our great modern inventions. But, like so many master-minds of the Middle Ages, he was unable wholly to resist the fascinations of alchemy and astrology. He believed that various parts of the human body were influenced by the stars, and that the mind was thus stimulated to particular acts, without any relaxation or inter-ruption of free will. His 'Mirror of Alchemy,' of which a translation into French was executed by 'a Gentleman of Dauphiné,' and printed in 1507, abso-lutely bristles with crude and unfounded theories—as, for instance, that Nature, in the formation of metallic veins, tends constantly to the production of gold, but is impeded by various accidents, and in this way creates metals in which impurities mingle with the fundamental substances. The main elements, he says, are quicksilver and sulphur ; and from these all metals and minerals are compounded. Gold he de-scribes as a perfect metal, produced from a pure, fixed, clear, and red quicksilver ; and from a sulphur also pure, fixed, and red, not incandescent and un-alloyed. Iron is unclean and imperfect, because engendered of a quicksilver which is impure, too much congealed, earthy, incandescent, white and red, and of a similar variety of sulphur. The 'stone,' or substance, by which the transmutation of the imper-fect into the perfect metals was to be effected must be made, in the main, he said, of sulphur and mercury.

It is not easy to determine how soon an atmosphere of legend gathered around the figure of 'the Admirable

Doctor ;' but undoubtedly it originated quite as much in his astrological errors as in his scientific experiments. Some of the myths of which he is the traditional hero belong to a very much earlier period, as, for instance, that of his Brazen Head, which appears in the old romance of ' Valentine and Orson,' as well as in the history of Albertus Magnus. Gower, too, in his ' Confessio Amantis,' relates how a Brazen Head was fabricated by Bishop Grosseteste. It was customary in those days to ascribe all kinds of marvels to men who obtained a repute for exceptional learning, and Bishop Grosseteste's Brazen Head was as purely a fiction as Roger Bacon's. This is Gower's account :

> ' For of the gretè clerk Grostest
> I rede how busy that he was
> Upon the clergie an head of brass
> To forgè; and make it fortelle
> Of suchè thingès as befelle.
> And seven yerès besinesse
> He laidè, but for the lachèsse*
> Of half a minute of an hour . . .
> He lostè all that he hadde do.'

Stow tells a story of a Head of Clay, made at Oxford in the reign of Edward II., which, at an appointed time, spoke the mysterious words, ' Caput decidetur—caput elevabitur. Pedes elevabuntur supra caput.' Returning to Roger Bacon's supposed invention, we find an ingenious though improbable explanation suggested by Sir Thomas Browne, in his ' Vulgar Errors ':

' Every one,' he says, ' is filled with the story of Friar Bacon, that made a Brazen Head to speak these words, " *Time is.*"

---

* *Laches*, oversight.

Which, though there went not the like relations, is surely too literally received, and was but a mystical fable concerning the philosopher's great work, wherein he eminently laboured : implying no more by the copper head, than the vessel wherein it was wrought ; and by the words it spake, than the opportunity to be watched, about the *tempus ortus*, or birth of the magical child, or "philosophical King" of Lullius, the rising of the "terra foliata" of Arnoldus ; when the earth, sufficiently impregnated with the water, ascendeth white and splendent. Which not observed, the work is irrecoverably lost. . . . Now letting slip the critical opportunity, he missed the intended treasure : which had he obtained, he might have made out the tradition of making a brazen wall about England : that is, the most powerful defence or strongest fortification which gold could have effected.'

An interpretation of the popular myth which is about as ingenious and far-fetched as Lord Bacon's expositions of the 'Fables of the Ancients,' of which it may be said that they possess every merit but that of probability !

Bacon's Brazen Head, however, took hold of the popular fancy. It survived for centuries, and the allusions to it in our literature are sufficiently numerous. Cob, in Ben Jonson's comedy of 'Every Man in his Humour,' exclaims : 'Oh, an my house were the Brazen Head now ! 'Faith, it would e'en speak *Mo' fools yet !'* And we read in Greene's 'Tu Quoque' :

> 'Look to yourself, sir ;
> The brazen head has spoke, and I must have you.'

Lord Bacon used it happily in his 'Apology to the Queen,' when Elizabeth would have punished the Earl of Essex for his misconduct in Ireland :—
'Whereunto I said (to the end utterly to divert her), "Madam, if you will have me speak to you in this

argument, I must speak to you as Friar Bacon's head spake, that said first, ' *Time is*,' and then, ' *Time was*,' and ' *Time would never be*,' for certainly " (said I) "it is now far too late ; the matter is cold, and hath. taken too much wind." '   Butler introduces it in his 'Hudibras' :—' Quoth he, " My head's not made of brass, as Friar Bacon's noddle was." '   And Pope, in 'The Dunciad,' writes :—' Bacon trembled for his brazen head.'   A William Terite, in 1604, gave to the world some verse, entitled ' A Piece of Friar Bacon's Brazen-head's Prophecie.'   And, in our own time, William Blackworth Praed has written ' The Chaunt of the Brazen Head,' which, in his prose motto, he (in the person of Friar Bacon) addresses as ' the brazen companion of his solitary hours.'

' THE FAMOUS HISTORIE OF FRIAR BACON.'

Towards the end of the sixteenth century, the various legends which had taken Friar Bacon as their central figure were brought together in a connected form, and wrought, along with other stories of magic and sorcery, into a continuous narrative, which became immensely popular.   It was entitled, ' The Famous Historie of Friar Bacon : Conteyning the Wonderful Thinges that he Did in his Life ; also the Manner of his Death ; with the Lives and Deaths of the Two Conjurers, Bungye and Vandermast,' and has been reprinted by Mr. Thoms, in his ' Early English Romances.'

According to this entertaining authority, the Friar was ' born in the West part of England, and was sonne to a wealthy farmer, who put him to the schoole to the parson of the towne where he was borne ; not with intent that hee should turne fryer (as hee did), but to get so much understanding, that he might manage the better the wealth hee was to leave him. But young Bacon took his learning so fast, that the priest could not teach him any more, which made him desire his master that he would speake to his father to put him to Oxford, that he might not lose that little learning that he had gained. . . . The father affected to doubt his son's capacity, and designed him still to follow the same calling as himself ; but the student had no inclination to drive fat oxen or consort with unlettered hinds, and stole away to "a cloister" some twenty miles off, where the monks cordially welcomed him. Continuing the pursuit of knowledge with great avidity, he attained to such repute that the authorities of Oxford University invited him to repair thither. He accepted the invitation, and grew so excellent in the secrets of Art and Nature, that not England only, but all Christendom, admired him.'

There, in the seclusion of his cell, he made the Brazen Head on which rests his legendary fame.

'Reading one day of the many conquests of England, he bethought himselfe how he might keepe it hereafter from the like conquests, and so make himselfe famous hereafter to all posterities. This, after great study, hee found could be no way so well done as one ; which was to make a head of brasse, and if he could make this head to speake, and heare it when it speakes, then might hee be able to wall all England about with brasse.*

---

* This patriotic sentiment would seem to show that the book was written or published about the time of the Spanish Armada.

To this purpose he got one Fryer Bungey to assist him, who was a great scholar and a magician, but not to bee compared to Fryer Bacon : these two with great study and paines so framed a head of brasse, that in the inward parts thereof there was all things like as in a naturall man's head. This being done, they were as farre from perfection of the worke as they were before, for they knew not how to give those parts that they had made motion, without which it was impossible that it should speake : many bookes they read, but yet coulde not finde out any hope of what they sought, that at the last they concluded to raise a spirit, and to know of him that which they coulde not attaine to by their owne studies. To do this they prepared all things ready, and went one evening to a wood thereby, and after many cere- monies used, they spake the words of conjuration; which the Devill straight obeyed, and appeared unto them, asking what they would ? "Know," said Fryer Bacon, "that wee have made an artificiall head of brasse, which we would have to speake, to the furtherance of which wee have raised thee; and being raised, wee will here keepe thee, unlesse thou tell to us the way and manner how to make this head to speake." The Devill told him that he had not that power of himselfe. "Beginner of lyes," said Fryer Bacon, "I know that thou dost dissemble, and therefore tell it us quickly, or else wee will here bind thee to remaine during our pleasures." At these threatenings the Devill con- sented to doe it, and told them, that with a continuall fume of the six hottest simples it should have motion, and in one month space speak; the time of the moneth or day hee knew not : also hee told them, that if they heard it not before it had done speak- ing, all their labour should be lost. They being satisfied, licensed the spirit for to depart.

'Then went these two learned fryers home againe, and pre- pared the simples ready, and made the fume, and with continuall watching attended when this Brazen Head would speake. Thus watched they for three weekes without any rest, so that they were so weary and sleepy that they could not any longer refraine from rest. Then called Fryer Bacon his man Miles, and told him that it was not unknown to him what paines Fryer Bungey and himselfe had taken for three weekes space, onely to make and to heare the Brazen Head speake, which if they did not, then had they lost all their labour, and all England had a great losse thereby; therefore hee intreated Miles that he would watch

whilst that they slept, and call them if the head speake. " Fear
not, good master," said Miles, " I will not sleepe, but harken and
attend upon the head, and if it doe chance to speake, I will call
you ; therefore I pray take you both your rests and let mee alone
for watching this head." After Fryer Bacon had given him a
great charge the second time, Fryer Bungey and he went to
sleepe, and Miles was lefte alone to watch the Brazen Head.
Miles, to keepe him from sleeping, got a tabor and pipe, and
being merry disposed, with his owne musicke kept from sleeping
at last. After some noyse the head spake these two words,
"TIME IS." Miles, hearing it to speake no more, thought his
master would be angry if hee waked him for that, and therefore
he let them both sleepe, and began to mocke the head in this
manner : "Thou brazen-faced Head, hath my master tooke all
these paines about thee, and now dost thou requite him with two
words, TIME IS ? Had hee watched with a lawyer so long as
hee hath watched with thee, he would have given him more and
better words than thou hast yet. If thou canst speake no wiser,
they shal sleepe till doomes day for me : TIME IS ! I know Time
is, and that you shall heare, Goodman Brazen-face.

    ' " Time is for some to eate,
      Time is for some to sleepe,
      Time is for some to laugh,
      Time is for some to weepe.
    ' " Time is for some to sing,
      Time is for some to pray,
      Time is for some to creepe,
      That have drunken all the day.

' " Do you tell us, copper-nose, when TIME IS ? I hope we
schollers know our times, when to drink drunke, when to kiss
our hostess, when to goe on her score, and when to pay it—that
time comes seldome." After halfe an houre had passed, the
Head did speake againe, two words, which were these, "TIME
WAS." Miles respected these words as little as he did the former,
and would not wake them, but still scoffed at the Brazen Head
that it had learned no better words, and have such a tutor as his
master : and in scorne of it sung this song :

    ' " Time was when thou, a kettle,
      wert filled with better matter ;
      But Fryer Bacon did thee spoyle
      when he thy sides did batter.

‘ “ Time was when conscience dwelled
with men of occupation ;
Time was when lawyers did not thrive
so well by men's vexation.

‘ “ Time was when kings and beggars
of one poore stuff had being ;
Time was when office kept no knaves—-
that time it was worth seeing.

‘ “ Time was a bowle of water
did give the face reflection ;
Time was when women knew no paint,
which now they call complexion.

‘ “ TIME WAS ! I know that, brazen-face, without your telling ;
I know Time was, and I know what things there was when Time
was ; and if you speake no wiser, no master shall be waked for
mee.” Thus Miles talked and sung till another halfe-houre was
gone : then the Brazen Head spake again these words, “ TIME IS
PAST ;” and therewith fell downe, and presently followed a
terrible noyse, with strange flashes of fire, so that Miles was halfe
dead with feare. At this noyse the two Fryers awaked, and
wondred to see the whole roome so full of smoake ; but that
being vanished, they might perceive the Brazen Head broken
and lying on the ground. At this sight they grieved, and called
Miles to know how this came. Miles, halfe dead with feare,
said that it fell doune of itselfe, and that with the noyse and fire
that followed he was almost frighted out of his wits. Fryer Bacon
asked him if hee did not speake ? “ Yes,” quoth Miles, “ it spake,
but to no purpose : Ile have a parret speake better in that time
that you have been teaching this Brazen Head.”

‘ “ Out on thee, villaine !” said Fryer Bacon ; “ thou hast undone
us both : hadst thou but called us when it did speake, all England
had been walled round about with brasse, to its glory and our
eternal fames. What were the words it spake ?” “ Very few,”
said Miles, “ and those were none of the wisest that I have heard
neither. First he said, ‘ TIME IS.’ ” “ Hadst thou called us then,”
said Fryer Bacon, “ we had been made for ever.” “ Then,” said
Miles, “ half-an-hour after it spake againe, and said, ‘ TIME WAS.’ ”
“ And wouldst thou not call us then ?” said Bungey. “ Alas !”
said Miles, “ I thought hee would have told me some long tale,
and then I purposed to have called you : then half-an-houre after

he cried, 'TIME IS PAST,' and made such a noyse that hee hath
waked you himselfe, mee thinkes." At this Fryer Bacon was in
such a rage that hee would have beaten his man, but he was
restrained by Bungey: but neverthelesse, for his punishment, he
with his art struck him dumbe for one whole month's space.
Thus the greate worke of these learned fryers was overthrown, to
their great griefes, by this simple fellow.'

The historian goes on to relate many instances of
Friar Bacon's thaumaturgical powers. He captures
a town which the king had besieged for three months
without success. He puts to shame a German con-
juror named Vandermast, and he performs wonders
in love affairs ; but at length a fatal result to one of
his magical exploits induces him to break to pieces
his wonderful glass and doff his conjurer's robe.
Then, receiving intelligence of the deaths of Vandermast and Friar Bungey, he falls into a deep grief,
so that for three days he refuses to partake of food,
and keeps his chamber.

' In the time that Fryer Bacon kept his Chamber, hee fell into
divers meditations ; sometimes into the vanity of Arts and
Sciences ; then would he condemne himselfe for studying of
those things that were so contrary to his Order soules health ;
and would say, That magicke made a man a Devill : sometimes
would hee meditate on divinity ; then would hee cry out upon
himselfe for neglecting the study of it, and for studying magicke :
sometime would he meditate on the shortnesse of mans life, then
would he condemne himselfe for spending a time so short, so ill as
he had done his : so would he goe from one thing to another, and
in all condemne his former studies.'

' And that the world should know how truly he did repent his
wicked life, he caused to be made a great fire ; and sending for
many of his friends, schollers, and others, he spake to them after
this manner : My good friends and fellow students, it is not
unknown to you, how that through my Art I have attained to
that credit, that few men living ever had : of the wonders that I

have done, all England can speak, both King and Commons : I
have unlocked the secrets of Art and Nature, and let the world
see those things that have layen hid since the death of Hermes,*
that rare and profound philosopher : my studies have found the
secrets of the Starres; the bookes that I have made of them do
serve for precedents to our greatest Doctors, so excellent hath my
judgment been therein. I likewise have found out the secrets of
Trees, Plants, and Stones, with their several uses ; yet all this
knowledge of mine I esteeme so lightly, that I wish that I were
ignorant and knew nothing, for the knowledge of these things (as
I have truly found) serveth not to better a man in goodnesse, but
onely to make him proude and thinke too well of himselfe. What
hath all my knowledge of Nature's secrets gained me ? Onely
this, the losse of a better knowledge, the losse of Divine Studies,
which makes the immortal part of man (his soule) blessed. I have
found that my knowledge has beene a heavy burden, and has kept
downe my good thoughts ; but I will remove the cause, which are
these Bookes, which I doe purpose here before you all to burne.
They all intreated him to spare the bookes, because in them there
were those things that after-ages might receive great benefit by.
He would not hearken unto them, but threw them all into the
fire, and in that flame burnt the greatest learning in the world.
Then did he dispose of all his goods ; some part he gave to poor
schollers, and some he gave to other poore folkes : nothing left he
for himselfe : then caused hee to be made in the Church-Wall a
Cell, where he locked himselfe in, and there remained till his
Death. His time hee spent in prayer, meditation, and such Divine
exercises, and did seeke by all means to perswade men from the
study of Magicke. Thus lived hee some two years space in that

---

* Hermes Trismegistus ('thrice great'), a fabulous Chaldean
philosopher, to whom I have already made reference. The
numerous writings which bear his name were really composed by
the Egyptian Platonists ; but the mediæval alchemists pretend to
recognise in him the founder of their art. Gower, in his 'Confessio Amantis,' says :

'Of whom if I the namès calle,
Hermes was one the first of alle,
To whom this Art is most applied.'

The name of Hermes was chosen because of the supposed magical
powers of the god of the caduceus.

Cell, never comming forth : his meat and drink he received in at a window, and at that window he had discourse with those that came to him; his grave he digged with his owne nayles, and was there layed when he dyed. Thus was the Life and Death of this famous Fryer, who lived most part of his life a Magician, and dyed a true Penitent Sinner and Anchorite.'

Upon this popular romance Greene, one of the best of the second-class Elizabethan dramatists, founded his rattling comedy, entitled 'The Historye of Fryer Bacon and Fryer Bungay,' which was written, it would seem, in 1589, first acted about 1592, and published in 1594. He does not servilely follow the old story-book, but introduces an under-plot of his own, in which is shown the love of Prince Edward for Margaret, the 'Fair Maid of Fressingfield,' whom the Prince finally surrenders to the man she loves, his favourite and friend, Lacy, Earl of Lincoln.

GREENE'S COMEDY.

In Scene I., which takes place near Framlingham, in Suffolk, we find Prince Edward eloquently expatiating on the charms of the Fair Maid to an audience of his courtiers, one of whom advises him, if he would prove successful in his suit, to seek the assistance of Friar Bacon, a 'brave necromancer,' who 'can make women of devils, and juggle cats into costermongers.'* The Prince acts upon this advice.

Scene II. introduces us to Friar Bacon's cell at Brasenose College, Oxford (an obvious anachronism, as the college was not founded until long after Bacon's time). Enter Bacon and his poor scholar, Miles,

* That is, costard, or apple, mongers.

with books under his arm ; also three doctors of
Oxford : Burden, Mason, and Clement.

BACON. Miles, where are you ?

MILES. *Hic sum, doctissime et reverendissime Doctor.* (Here I am,
most learned and reverend Doctor.)

BACON. *Attulisti nostros libros meos de necromantia ?* (Hast thou
brought my books of necromancy ?)

MILES. *Ecce quam bonum et quam jucundum habitare libros in
unum !* (See how good and how pleasant it is to dwell among
books together !)

BACON. Now, masters of our academic state
That rule in Oxford, viceroys in your place,
Whose heads contain maps of the liberal arts,
Spending your time in depths of learnèd skill,
Why flock you thus to Bacon's secret cell,
A friar newly stalled in Brazen-nose?
Say what's your mind, that I may make reply.

BURDEN. Bacon, we hear that long we have suspect,
That thou art read in Magic's mystery :
In pyromancy,* to divine by flames ;
To tell by hydromancy, ebbs and tides ;
By aeromancy to discover doubts,—
To plain out questions, as Apollo did.

BACON. Well, Master Burden, what of all this ?

MILES. Marry, sir, he doth but fulfil, by rehearsing of these
names, the fable of the 'Fox and the Grapes' : that which is
above us pertains nothing to us.

BURD. I tell thee, Bacon, Oxford makes report,
Nay, England, and the Court of Henry says
Thou'rt making of a Brazen Head by art,
Which shall unfold strange doubts and aphorisms,
And read a lecture in philosophy :
And, by the help of devils and ghastly fiends,
Thou mean'st, ere many years or days be past,
To compass England with a wall of brass.

BACON. And what of this ?

MILES. What of this, master ! why, he doth speak mystically ;
for he knows, if your skill fail to make a Brazen Head, yet

---

* See Appendix to the present chapter, p. 58.

Master Waters' strong ale will fit his time to make him have a
copper nose. . . .
    BACON. Seeing you come as friends unto the friar,
Resolve you, doctors, Bacon can by books
Make storming Boreas thunder from his cave,
And dim fair Luna to a dark eclipse.
The great arch-ruler, potentate of hell,
Tumbles when Bacon bids him, or his fiends
Bow to the force of his pentageron.*. . .
I have contrived and framed a head of brass
(I made Belcephon hammer out the stuff),
And that by art shall read philosophy :
And I will strengthen England by my skill,
That if ten Cæsars lived and reigned in Rome,
With all the legions Europe doth contain,
They should not touch a grass of English ground :
The work that Ninus reared at Babylon,
The brazen walls framed by Semiramis,
Carved out like to the portal of the sun,
Shall not be such as rings the English strand
From Dover to the market-place of Rye.

In this patriotic resolution of the potent friar the
reader will trace the influence of the national enthusiasm awakened, only a few years before Greene's
comedy was written and produced, by the menace of
the Spanish Armada.

It is unnecessary to quote the remainder of this
scene, in which Bacon proves his magical skill at
the expense of the jealous Burden. Scene III.
passes at Harleston Fair, and introduces Lacy, Earl
of Lincoln, disguised as a rustic, and the comely

---

    * The pentageron, or pentagramma, is a mystic figure pro-
duced by prolonging the sides of a regular pentagon till they
intersect one another. It can be drawn without a break in the
drawing, and, viewed from five sides, exhibits the form of the
letter A (pent-alpha), or the figure of the fifth proposition in
Euclid's First Book.

Margaret. In Scene IV., at Hampton Court, Henry III. receives Elinor of Castile, who is betrothed to his son, Prince Edward, and arranges with her father, the Emperor, a competition between the great German magician, Jaques Vandermast, and Friar Bacon, 'England's only flower.' In Scene V. we pass on to Oxford, where some comic incidents occur between Prince Edward (in disguise) and his courtiers ; and in Scene VI. to Friar Bacon's cell, where the friar shows the Prince in his 'glass prospective,' or magic mirror, the figures of Margaret, Friar Bungay, and Earl Lacy, and reveals the progress of Lacy's suit to the rustic beauty. Bacon summons Bungay to Oxford—straddling on a devil's back—and the scene then changes to the Regent-house, and degenerates into the rudest farce. At Fressingfield, in Scene VIII., we find Prince Edward threatening to slay Earl Lacy unless he gives up to him the Fair Maid of Fressingfield ; but, after a struggle, his better nature prevails, and he retires from his suit, leaving Margaret to become the Countess of Lincoln. Scene IX. carries us back to Oxford, where Henry III., the Emperor, and a goodly company have assembled to witness the trial of skill between the English and the German magicians—the first international competition on record!—in which, of course, Vandermast is put to ridicule.

Passing over Scene X. as unimportant, we return, in Scene XI., to Bacon's cell, where the great magician is lying on his bed, with a white wand in one hand, a book in the other, and beside him a lighted lamp.

The Brazen Head is there, with Miles, armed, keeping watch over it. Here the dramatist closely follows the old story. The friar falls asleep; the head speaks once and twice, and Miles fails to wake his master. It speaks the third time. 'A lightning flashes forth, and a hand appears that breaks down the head with a hammer.' Bacon awakes to lament over the ruin of his work, and load the careless Miles with unavailing reproaches. But the whole scene is characteristic enough to merit transcription:

SCENE XI.—*Friar Bacon's Cell.*

FRIAR BACON *is discovered lying on a bed, with a white stick in one hand, a book in the other, and a lamp lighted beside him; and the* BRAZEN HEAD, *and* MILES *with weapons by him.*

BACON. Miles, where are you?

MILES. Here, sir.

BACON. How chance you tarry so long?

MILES. Think you that the watching of the Brazen Head craves no furniture? I warrant you, sir, I have so armed myself that if all your devils come, 1 will not fear them an inch.

BACON. Miles,
Thou know'st that I have divèd into hell,
And sought the darkest palaces of fiends;
That with my magic spells great Belcephon
Hath left his lodge and kneelèd at my cell;
The rafters of the earth rent from the poles,
And three-form'd Luna hid her silver looks,
Tumbling upon her concave continent,
When Bacon read upon his magic book.
With seven years' tossing necromantic charms,
Poring upon dark Hecat's principles,
I have framed out a monstrous head of brass,
That, by the enchanting forces of the devil,
Shall tell out strange and uncouth aphorisms,
And girt fair England with a wall of brass.
Bungay and I have watch'd these threescore days,

And now our vital spirits crave some rest :
If Argus lived and had his hundred eyes,
They could not over-watch Phobetor's* night.
Now, Miles, in thee rests Friar Bacon's weal :
The honour and renown of all his life
Hangs in the watching of this Brazen Head ;
Therefore I charge thee by the immortal God
That holds the souls of men within his fist,
This night thou watch ; for ere the morning star
Sends out his glorious glister on the north
The Head will speak.   Then, Miles, upon thy life
Wake me ; for then by magic art I'll work
To end my seven years' task with excellence.
If that a wink but shut thy watchful eye,
Then farewell Bacon's glory and his fame !
Draw close the curtains, Miles : now, for thy life,
Be watchful, and . . .   (*Falls asleep.*)

MILES.   So ; I thought you would talk yourself asleep anon ;
and 'tis no marvel, for Bungay on the days, and he on the nights,
have watched just these ten and fifty days : now this is the night,
and 'tis my task, and no more.   Now, Jesus bless me, what a
goodly head it is ! and a nose !   You talk of *Nos†* *autem glori-
ficare;* but here's a nose that I warrant may be called *Nos autem
populare* for the people of the parish.   Well, I am furnished with
weapons : now, sir, I will set me down by a post, and make it as
good as a watchman to wake me, if I chance to slumber.   I
thought, Goodman Head, I would call you out of your *memento.‡*
Passion o' God, I have almost broke my pate !   (*A great noise.*)
Up, Miles, to your task ; take your brown-bill in your hand ;
here's some of your master's hobgoblins abroad.

THE BRAZEN HEAD (*speaks*).   Time is.

MILES.   Time is !   Why, Master Brazen-Head, you have such a
capital nose, and answer you with syllables, ' Time is '?   Is this
my master's cunning, to spend seven years' study about ' Time
is '?   Well, sir, it may be we shall have some better orations

---

* From the Greek φόβος, fear ; φόβητρα, bugbears.

† Bad puns were evidently common on the stage before the
days of Victorian burlesque.

‡ So Shakespeare, ' 1 Hen. IV.,' iii.   Falstaff says : ' I make as
good use of it as many a man doth of a death's head, or a memento
house.'

of it anon : well, I'll watch you as narrowly as ever you were
watched, and I'll play with you as the nightingale with the glow-
worm; I'll set a prick against my breast.* Now rest there,
Miles. Lord have mercy upon me, I have almost killed myself.
(*A great noise.*) Up, Miles ; list how they rumble.
THE BRAZEN HEAD (*loquitur*). Time was.
MILES. Well, Friar Bacon, you have spent your seven years'
study well, that can make your Head speak but two words at
once, ' Time was.' Yea, marry, time was when my master was a
wise man; but that was before he began to make the Brazen
Head. You shall lie while you ache, an your head speak no
better. Well, I will watch, and walk up and down, and be a
peripatetian† and a philosopher of Aristotle's stamp. (*A great
noise.*) What, a fresh noise ? Take thy pistols in hand, Miles.
(*A lightning flashes forth, and a Hand appears that breaks down the*
HEAD *with a hammer.*) Master, master, up ! Hell's broken loose !
Your Head speaks ; and there's such a thunder and lightning,
that I warrant all Oxford is up in arms. Out of your bed, and
take a brownbill in your hand ; the latter day is come.
BACON. Miles, I come.   (*Rises and comes forward.*)
O, passing warily watched !
Bacon will make thee next himself in love.
When spake the Head ?
MILES. When spake the Head ? Did you not say that he
should tell strange principles of philosophy ? Why, sir, it speaks
but two words at a time.
BACON. Why, villain, hath it spoken oft ?
MILES. Oft ! ay, marry hath it, thrice ; but in all those three
times it hath uttered but seven words.
BACON. As how ?
MILES. Marry, sir, the first time he said, ' Time is,' as if Fabius
Commentator‡ should have pronounced a sentence ; then he said,

---

* So in the ' Passionate Pilgrim ':
     ' Save the nightingale alone :
     She, poor bird, as all forlorn,
     Leaned her breast uptill a thorn.'
   † A *peripatetic*, or walking philosopher. Observe the facetious-
ness in ' Aristotle's *stamp.*' Aristotle was the founder of the
Peripatetics.
   ‡ Fabius *Cunctator*, or the Delayer, so called from the policy of
delay which he opposed to the vigorous movements of Hannibal.

4

'Time was;' and the third time, with thunder and lightning, as in great choler, he said, 'Time is past.'

BACON. 'Tis past, indeed. Ah, villain! Time is past;
My life, my fame, my glory, are all past.
Bacon,
The turrets of thy hope are ruined down,
Thy seven years' study lieth in the dust :
Thy Brazen Head lies broken through a slave
That watched, and would not when the Head did will.
What said the Head first ?

MILES. Even, sir, 'Time is.'

BACON. Villain, if thou hadst called to Bacon then,
If thou hadst watched, and waked the sleepy friar,
The Brazen Head had uttered aphorisms,
And England had been circled round with brass :
But proud Asmenoth,* ruler of the North,
And Demogorgon,† master of the Fates,
Grudge that a mortal man should work so much.
Hell trembled at my deep-commanding spells,
Fiends frowned to see a man their over-match ;
Bacon might boast more than a man might boast ;
But now the braves‡ of Bacon have an end,

One would suppose that the humour here, such as it is, would hardly be perceptible to a theatrical audience.

* In the old German 'Faustbuch,' the title of 'Prince of the North' is given to Beelzebub.

† *Demogorgon*, or *Demiourgos*—the creative principle of evil—figures largely in literature. He is first mentioned by Lactantius, in the fourth century ; then by Boccaccio, Boiardo, Tasso ('Gierusalemme Liberata'), and Ariosto ('Orlando Furioso'). Marlowe speaks, in 'Tamburlaine,' of 'Gorgon, prince of Hell.' Spenser, in 'The Faery Queen,' refers to—

> 'Great Gorgon, prince of darkness and dead night,
> At which Cocytus quakes, and Styx is put to flight.'

Milton, in 'Paradise Lost,' alludes to 'the dreaded name of Demogorgon.' Dryden says : 'When the moon arises, and Demogorgon walks his round.' And he is one of the *dramatis personæ* of Shelley's 'Prometheus Unbound' : 'Demogorgon, a tremendous gloom. . . . A mighty Darkness, filling the seat of power.'

‡ Boasts. So in Peele's 'Edward I.': 'As thou to England brought'st thy Scottish braves.'

Europe's conceit of Bacon hath an end,
His seven years' practice sorteth to ill end :
And, villain, sith my glory hath an end,
I will appoint thee to some fatal end.*
Villain, avoid ! get thee from Bacon's sight !
Vagrant, go, roam and range about the world,
And perish as a vagabond on earth !
MILES. Why, then, sir, you forbid me your service ?
BACON. My service, villain, with a fatal curse,
That direful plagues and mischief fall on thee.
MILES. 'Tis no matter, I am against you with the old proverb,
' The more the fox is cursed, the better he fares.' God be with
you, sir : I'll take but a book in my hand, a wide-sleeved gown
on my back, and a crowned cap† on my head, and see if I can
merit promotion.
BACON. Some fiend or ghost haunt on thy weary steps,
Until they do transport thee quick to Hell !
For Bacon shall have never any day,
To lose the fame and honour of his Head.

[*Exeunt.*

Scene XII. passes in King Henry's Court, and the
royal consent is given to Earl Lacy's marriage with
the Fair Maid, which is fixed to take place on the
same day as Prince Edward's marriage to the Princess
Elinor. In Scene XIII. we again go back to Bacon's
cell. The friar is bewailing the destruction of his
Brazen Head to Friar Bungay, when two young gentlemen, named Lambert and Sealsby, enter, in order to
look into the ' glass prospective,' and see how their
fathers are faring. Unhappily, at this very moment,
the elder Lambert and Sealsby, having quarrelled, are
engaged ' in combat hard by Fressingfield,' and stab
each other to the death, whereupon their sons imme-

---

* This reiteration of the same final word, for the sake of
emphasis, is found in Shakespeare.
† A corner or college cap.

diately come to blows, with a like fatal result.   Bacon,
deeply affected, breaks the magic crystal which has
been the unwitting cause of so sad a catastrophe,
expresses his regret that he ever dabbled in the unholy science, and announces his resolve to spend the
remainder of his life 'in pure devotion.'

At Fressingfield, in Scene XIV., the opportune
arrival of Lacy and his friends prevents Margaret
from carrying out her intention of retiring to the
nunnery at Framlingham, and with obliging readiness
she consents to marry the Earl.   Scene XV. shifts to
Bacon's cell, where a devil complains that the friar
hath raised him from the darkest deep to search about
the world for Miles, his man, and torment him in
punishment for his neglect of orders.

Miles makes his appearance, and after some comic
dialogue, intended to tickle the ears of the ground-
lings, mounts astride the demon's back, and goes off
to ——!   In Scene XVI., and last, we return to the
Court, where royalty makes a splendid show, and the
two brides—the Princess Elinor and the Countess
Margaret—display their rival charms.   Of course the
redoubtable friar is present, and in his concluding
speech leaps over a couple of centuries to make a
glowing compliment to Queen Elizabeth, which seems
worth quotation:

'I find by deep prescience of mine art,
  Which once I tempered in my secret cell,
  That here where Brute did build his Troynovant,*

---

* An allusion to the old legend that Brut, or Brutus, great-
grandson of Æneas, founded New Troy (Troynovant), or
London.

From forth the royal garden of a King
Shall flourish out so rich and fair a bud,
Whose brightness shall deface proud Phœbus' flower,
And overshadow Albion with her leaves.
Till then Mars shall be master of the field,
But then the stormy threats of war shall cease :
The horse shall stamp as careless of the pike,
Drums shall be turned to timbrels of delight ;
With wealthy favours Plenty shall enrich
The strand that gladded wandering Brute to see,
And peace from heaven shall harbour in these leaves
That gorgeous beautify this matchless flower :
Apollo's heliotropian* then shall stoop,
And Venus' hyacinth† shall vail her top ;
Juno shall shut her gilliflowers up,
And Pallas' bay shall 'bash her brightest green ;
Ceres' carnation, in consort with those,
Shall stoop and wonder at Diana's rose.‡

So much for Greene's comedy of 'Friar Bacon and Friar Bungay'—not, on the whole, a bad piece of work.

Among the earlier English alchemists I may next name, in chronological order, George Ripley, canon of Bridlington, who, in 1471, dedicated to King Edward III. his once celebrated 'Compound of Alchemy ; or, The Twelve Gates leading to the Discovery of the Philosopher's Stone.' These 'gates,' each of which he describes in detail, but with little enlightenment to the uninitiated reader, are :—1. Calcination ; 2. Solution ; 3. Separation ; 4. Conjunction ; 5. Putrefac-

* Probably the reference is to the sunflower.
† The classic writers usually identify the hyacinth with Apollo.
‡ The rose, that is, of the Virgin Queen—an English Diana— Elizabeth. In Shakespeare's 'Midsummer Night's Dream' (Act iv., scene 1) we read of 'Diana's bud.'

tion ; 6. Congelation ; 7. Cibation ; 8. Sublimation ; 9. Fermentation; 10. Exaltation; 11. Multiplication ; and 12. Projection. In his old age Ripley learned wisdom, and frankly acknowledged that he had wasted his life upon an empty pursuit. He requested all men, if they met with any of the five-and-twenty treatises of which he was the author, to consign them to the flames as absolutely vain and worthless.

Yet there is a wild story that he actually discovered the 'magisterium,' and was thereby enabled to send a gift of £100,000 to the Knights of St. John, to assist them in their defence of Rhodes against the Turks.

Thomas Norton, of Bristol, was the author of ' The Ordinall of Alchemy' (printed in London in 1652). He is said to have been a pupil of Ripley, under whom (at the age of 28) he studied for forty days, and in that short time acquired a thorough knowledge of ' the perfection of chemistry.' Ripley, however, refused to instruct so young a man in the master-secret of the great science, and the process from ' the white' to ' the red powder,' so that Norton was compelled to rely on his own skill and industry. Twice in his labours a sad disappointment overtook him. On one occasion he had almost completed the tincture, when the servant whom he employed to look after the furnace decamped with it, supposing that it was fit for use. On another it was stolen by the wife of William Canning, Mayor of Bristol, who immediately sprang into immense wealth, and as some amends, I suppose, for his ill-gotten gains, built the

beautiful steeple of the church of St. Mary, Redcliffe
—the church afterwards connected with the sad story
of Chatterton. As for Norton, he seems to have lived
in poverty and died in poverty (1477).

The ' Ordinall of Alchemy ' is a tedious panegyric
of the science, interspersed with a good deal of the
vague talk about white and red stones and the philosophical magnesia in which ' the adepts ' delighted.

To Norton we owe our scanty knowledge of Thomas
Dalton, who flourished about the middle of the
fifteenth century. He had the reputation of being a
devout Churchman until he was accused by a certain
Debois of possessing the powder of projection. Debois
roundly asserted that Norton had made him a thousand
pounds of gold (lucky man !) in less than twelve hours.
Whereupon Dalton simply said, ' Sir, you are for-
sworn.' His explanation was that he had received
the powder from a canon of Lichfield, on undertaking
not to use it until after the canon's death ; and that
since he had been so troubled by his possession of it,
that he had secretly destroyed it. One Thomas Herbert, a squire of King Edward, waylaid the unfortunate man, and shut him up in the castle of Gloucester,
putting heavy pressure upon him to make the coveted
tincture. But this Dalton would not and could not
do ; and after a captivity of four years, Herbert
ordered him to be brought out and executed in his
presence. He obeyed the harsh summons with great
delight, exclaiming, ' Blessed art Thou, Lord Jesus !
I have been too long absent from Thee. The science

Thou gavest me I have kept without ever abusing it; I have found no one fit to be my heir; wherefore, sweet Lord, I will restore Thy gift to Thee again.'

'Then, after some devout prayer, with a smiling countenance he desired the executioner to proceed. Tears gushed from the eyes of Herbert when he beheld him so willing to die, and saw that no ingenuity could wrest his secret from him. He gave orders for his release. His imprisonment and threatened execution were contrived without the King's knowledge to intimidate him into compliance. The iniquitous devices having failed, Herbert did not dare to take away his life. Dalton rose from the block with a heavy countenance, and returned to his abbey, much grieved at the further prolongation of his earthly sojourn. Herbert died shortly after this atrocious act of tyranny, and Debois also came to an untimely end. His father, Sir John Debois, was slain at the battle of Tewkesbury, May 4, 1471.; and two days after, as recorded in Stow's "Annales," he himself (James Debois) was taken, with several others of the Lancastrian party, from a church where they had fled for sanctuary, and was beheaded on the spot.'

APPENDIX TO CHAPTER I.

The ancient magic included various kinds of divination, of which the principal may here be catalogued:

Aeromancy, or divination from the air. If the wind blew from the east, it signified good fortune (which is certainly not the general opinion!); from the west, evil; from the south, calamity; from the north, disclosure of what was secret; from all quarters simultaneously (!), hail and rain.

Axinomancy, practised by the Greeks, more particularly for the purpose of discovering criminals. An axe poised upon a stake, or an agate on a red-hot axe, was supposed by its movement to indicate the offender. Or the names of suspected persons were called out, and the movement of the axe at a particular name was understood to certify guilt.

Belomancy, in use among the Arabs, was practised by means of arrows, which were shot off, with written labels attached to them; and the inscription on the arrow first picked up was accepted as prophetic.

Bibliomancy, divining by means of the Bible, survived to a comparatively recent period. The passage which first caught the eye, on a Bible being opened haphazard, was supposed to indicate the future. This was identical with the *Sortes Virgilianæ*, the only difference being that in the latter, Virgil took the place of the Bible. Everybody knows in connection with the Sortes the story of Charles I. and Lord Falkland.

Botanomancy, divining by means of plants and flowers, can hardly be said to be extinct even now. In Goethe's 'Faust,' Gretchen seeks to discover whether Faust returns her affection by plucking, one after another, the petals of a star-flower (*sternblume*, perhaps the china-aster), while she utters the alternate refrains, 'He loves me !' 'He loves me not !' as she plucks the last petal, exclaiming rapturously, 'He loves me !' According to Theocritus, the Greeks used the poppy-flower for this purpose.

Capnomancy, divination by smoke, the ancients practised in two ways : they threw seeds of jasmine or poppy in the fire, watching the motion and density of the smoke they emitted, or they observed the sacrificial smoke. If the smoke was thin, and shot up in a straight line, it was a good omen.

Cheiromancy (or Palmistry), divination by the hand, was worked up into an elaborate system by Paracelsus, Cardan, and others. It has long been practised by the gipsies, by itinerant fortune-tellers, and other cheats ; and recently an attempt has been made to give it a fashionable character.

Coscinomancy was practised by means of a sieve and a pair of shears or forceps. The forceps or shears were used to suspend a sieve, which moved (like the axe in axinomancy) when the name of a guilty person was mentioned.

Crystallomancy, divining by means of a crystal globe, mirror, or beryl. Of this science of prediction, Dr. Dee was the great

English professor; but the reader will doubtless remember the story of the Earl of Surrey and his fair 'Geraldine.'

Geomancy, divination by casting pebbles on the ground.

Hydromancy, divination by water, in which the diviner showed the figure of an absent person. 'In this you conjure the spirits into water; there they are constrained to show themselves, as Marcus Varro testifieth, when he writeth how he had seen a boy in the water, who announced to him in a hundred and fifty verses the end of the Mithridatic war.'

Oneiromancy, divination by dreams, is still credited by old women of both sexes. Absurdly baseless as it is, it found believers in the old time among men of culture and intellectual force. Archbishop Laud attached so much importance to his dreams that he frequently recorded them in his diary; and even Lord Bacon seems to have thought that a prophetic meaning was occasionally concealed in them.

Onychomancy, or *Onymancy*, divination by means of the nails of an unpolluted boy.

Pyromancy, divination by fire. 'The wife of Cicero is said, when, after performing sacrifice, she saw a flame suddenly leap forth from the ashes, to have prophesied the consulship to her husband for the same year.' Others resorted to the blaze of a torch of pitch, which was painted with certain colours. It was a good omen if the flame ran into a point; bad when it divided. A thin-tongued flame announced glory; if it went out, it signified danger; if it hissed, misfortune.

Rabdomancy, divination by the rod or wand, is mentioned by Ezekiel. The use of a hazel-rod to trace the existence of water or of a seam of coal seems a survival of this practice. But enough of these follies:

> 'Necro-, pyro-, geo-, hydro-, cheiro-, coscinomancy,
> With other vain and superstitious sciences.'
>
> Tomkis, 'Albumazar,' ii. 3.

CHAPTER II.

THE STORY OF DR. JOHN DEE.

THE world must always feel curious to know the
exact moment when its great men first drew the
breath of life ; and it is satisfactory, therefore, to be
able to state, on the weighty authority of Dr. Thomas
Smith, that Dr. John Dee, the famous magician and
'philosopher,' was born at forty minutes past four
o'clock on the morning of July 13, 1527. According to the picturesque practice of latter-day biographers,
here I ought to describe a glorious summer sunrise,
the golden light spreading over hill and pasture, the
bland warm air stealing into the chamber where lay
the mother and her infant ; but I forbear, as, for all I
know, this particular July morning may have been
cloudy, cold, and wet ; besides, John, the son of
Rowland Dee, was born in London. From like want
of information I refrain from comments on Master
Dee's early bringing-up and education. But it is reported that he gave proof of so exceptional a capacity,
and of such a love of letters, that, at the early age of
fifteen, he was sent to the University of Cambridge, to
study the classics and the old scholastic philosophy.

There, for three years, he was so vehemently bent, he says, on the acquisition of learning, that he spent eighteen hours a day on his books, reserving two only for his meals and recreation, and four for sleep—an unhealthy division of time, which probably over-stimulated his cerebral system and predisposed him to delusions and caprices of the imagination. Having taken his degree of B.A., he crossed the seas in 1547 ' to speak and confer ' with certain learned men, chiefly mathematicians, such as Gemma Frisius, Gerardus Mercator, Gaspar a Morica, and Antonius Gogara ; of whom the only one now remembered is Mercator, as the inventor of a method of laying down hydro-graphical charts, in which the parallels and meridians intersect each other at right angles. After spending some months in the Low Countries he returned home, bringing with him ' the first astronomer's staff of brass that was made of Gemma Frisius' devising, the two great globes of Gerardus Mercator's making, and the astronomer's ring of brass (as Gemma Frisius had newly framed it).'

Returning to the classic shades of Granta, he began to record his observations of ' the heavenly influences in this elemental portion of the world ;' and I suppose it was in recognition of his scientific scholarship that Henry VIII. appointed him to a fellowship at Trinity College, and Greek under-reader. In the latter capacity he superintended, in 1548, the performance of the 'Ειρηνη of Aristophanes, introducing among ' the effects ' an artificial scarabæus, which ascended, with a man and his wallet of provisions on its back, to Jupiter's palace. This ingenious bit of mechanism delighted the spectators, but, after the manner of the time, was ascribed to Dee's occultism, and he found it convenient to retire to the Continent (1548), residing for awhile at Louvain, and devoting himself to hermetic researches, and afterwards at Paris (1580), where he delivered scientific lectures to large and distinguished audiences. 'My auditory in Rhemes Colledge,' he says, 'was so great, and the most part older than my selfe, that the mathematicall schooles could not hold them ; for many were faine, without the schooles, at the windowes, to be auditors and spectators, as they best could help themselves thereto. I did also dictate upon every proposition, beside the first exposition. And by the first foure principall definitions representing to the eyes (which by imagination onely are exactly to be conceived), a greater wonder arose among the beholders, than of my Aristophanes Scarabæus mounting up to the top of Trinity-hall in Cambridge.'

The accomplishments of this brilliant scientific mountebank being noised abroad over all Europe, the wonderful story reached the remote Court of the Muscovite, who offered him, if he would take up his residence at Moscow, a stipend of £2,000 per annum, his diet also to be allowed to him free out of ' the Emperor's own kitchen, and his place to be ranked amongst the highest sort of the nobility there, and of his privy councillors.' Was ever scholar so tempted before or since ? In those times, the Russian Court seems to have held *savants* and scholars in as much esteem as nowadays it holds *prima-donnas* and

ballerines.   Dee also received advantageous proposals
from four successive Emperors of Germany (Charles V.,
Ferdinand, Maximilian II., and Rudolph II.), but the
Muscovite's outbade them all.   A residence in the
heart of Russia had no attraction, however, for the
Oxford scholar, who, in 1551, returned to England
with a halo of fame playing round his head (to speak
figuratively, as Dee himself loved to do), which
recommended him to the celebrated Greek professor
at Cambridge, Sir John Cheke.   Cheke introduced
him to Mr. Secretary Cecil, as well as to Edward VI.,
who bestowed upon him a pension of 100 crowns per
annum (speedily exchanged, in 1553, for the Rectory
of Upton-upon-Severn).   At first he met with favour
from Queen Mary ; but the close correspondence he
maintained with the Princess Elizabeth, who ap-
preciated his multifarious scholarship, exposed him
to suspicion, and he was accused of practising against
the Queen's life by divers enchantments.   Arrested
and imprisoned (at Hampton Court), he was subjected
to rigorous examinations, and as no charge of treason
could be proved against him, was remitted to Bishop
Bonner as a possible heretic.   But his enemies failed
again in their malicious intent, and in 1555 he received
his liberty.   Imprisonment and suffering had not
quenched his activity of temper, and almost immediately upon his release he solicited the Queen's assent
to a plan for the restoration and preservation of
certain precious manuscripts of classical antiquity.
He solicited in vain.

When Elizabeth came to the throne, Dee, as a

proficient in the occult arts, was consulted by Dudley (afterwards Earl of Leicester) as to the most suitable and auspicious day for her coronation. She testified to her own belief in his skill by employing him, when her image in wax had been discovered in Lincoln's Inn Fields, to counteract the evil charm. But he owed her favour, we may assume, much more to his learning, which was really extensive, than to his supposed magical powers. He tells us that, shortly before her coronation, she summoned him to Whitehall, remarking to his patrons, Dudley and the Earl of Pembroke, ' Where my brother hath given him a crown, I will give him a noble.' She was certainly more liberal to Dee than to many of her servants who were much more deserving. In December, 1564, she granted him the reversion of the Deanery of Gloucester. Not long afterwards his friends recommended him for the Provostship of Eton College. ' Favourable answers ' were returned, but he never received the Provostship. He obtained permission, however, to hold for ten years the two rectories of Upton and Long Ledenham. Later in her reign (July, 1583), when two great nobles invited themselves to dine with him, he was compelled to decline the honour on account of his poverty. The Queen, on being apprised of this incident, sent him a present of forty angels of gold. We shall come upon other proofs of her generosity.

Dee was travelling on the Continent in 1571, and on his way through Lorraine was seized with a dangerous sickness ; whereupon the Queen not only sent 'carefully and with great speed' two of her physicians, but also the honourable Lord Sidney 'in a manner to tend on him,' and 'to discern how his health bettered, and to comfort him from her Majesty with divers very pithy speeches and gracious, and also with divers rarities to eat, to increase his health and strength.' Philosophers and men of letters, when they are ailing, meet with no such pleasant attentions nowadays! But the list of Elizabeth's bounties is not yet ended. The much-travelling scholar, who saw almost as much of cities and men and manners as Odysseus himself, had wandered into the farthest parts of the kingdom of Bohemia; and that no evil might come to him, or his companion, or their families, she sent them her most princely and royal letters of safe-conduct. After his return home, a little before Christmas, 1589, hearing that he was unable to keep house as liberally as became his position and repute, she promised to assist him with the gift of a hundred pounds, and once or twice repeated the promise on his coming into her presence. Fifty pounds he *did* receive, with which to keep his Christmas merrily, but what became of the other moiety he was never able to discover. A malignant influence frequently interposed, it would seem, between the Queen's benevolence in intention and her charity in action; and the unfortunate doctor was sometimes tantalized with promises of good things which failed to be realized. On the whole, however, I do not think he had much to complain of; and the reproach of parsimony so often levelled at great Gloriana would certainly not apply to her treatment of Dr. Dee.

She honoured him with several visits at Mortlake, where he had a pleasant house close by the riverside, and a little to the westward of the church— surrounded by gardens and green fields, with bright prospects of the shining river. Elizabeth always came down from Whitehall on horseback, attended by a brave retinue of courtiers ; and as she passed along, her loyal subjects stood at their doors, or lined the roadside, making respectful bows and curtseys, and crying, ' God save the Queen !' One of these royal visits was made on March 10, 1675, the Queen desiring to see the doctor's famous library ; but learning that he had buried his wife only four hours before, she refused to enter the house. Dee, however, submitted to her inspection his magic crystal, or ' black stone,' and exhibited some of its marvellous properties ; her Majesty, for the better examination of the same, being taken down from her horse ' by the Earl of Leicester, by the Church wall of Mortlack.'

She was at Dr. Dee's again on September 17, 1580. This time she came from Richmond in her coach, a wonderfully cumbrous vehicle, drawn by six horses ; ' and when she was against my garden in the fielde,' says the doctor, ' her Majestie staide there a good while, and then came into the street at the great gate of the field, where her Majestie espied me at my dore, making reverent and dutifull obeysance unto her, and with her hand her Majestie

5

beckoned for me to come to her, and I came to her coach side ; her Majestie then very speedily pulled off her glove, and gave me her hand to kiss ; and to be short, her Majestie wished me to resort oftener to her Court, and by some of her Privy Chamber to give her Majestie to wete (know) when I came there.'

Another visit took place on October 10, 1580 :— 'The Queenes Majestie to my great comfort (*horâ quintâ*) came with her train from the Court, and at my dore graciously calling me unto her, on horseback exhorted me briefly to take my mother's death patiently ; and withal told me, that the Lord Treasurer had greatly commended my doings for her title royall, which he had to examine. The which title in two rolls of velome parchment his Honour had some houres before brought home, and delivered to Mr. Hudson for me to receive at my coming from my mother's buriall at church. Her Majestie re· membered also then, how at my wives buriall it was her fortune likewise to call upon me at my house, as before is noted.'

Dee's library—as libraries went then—was not unworthy of royal inspection. Its proud possessor computed it to be worth £2,000, which, at the present value of money, would be equal, I suppose, to £10,000. It consisted of about 4,000 volumes, bound and unbound, a fourth part being MSS. He speaks of four ' written books '—one in Greek, two in French, and one in High Dutch—as having cost him £533, and inquires triumphantly what must have been the value of some hundred of the best of all the other written books, some of which were the *autographia* of excellent and seldom-heard-of authors ? He adds that he spent upwards of forty years in collecting this library from divers places beyond the seas, and with much research and labour in England.

Of the ' precious books ' thus collected, Dee does not mention the titles ; but he has recorded the rare and exquisitely made ' instruments mathematical ' which belonged to him : An excellent, strong, and fair quadrant, first made by that famous Richard Chancellor who boldly carried his discovery-ships past the Icy Cape, and anchored them in the White Sea. There was also an excellent *radius astro-nomicus*, of ten feet in length, the staff and cross very curiously divided into equal parts, after Richard Chancellor's quadrant manner. Item, two globes of Mercator's best making : on the celestial sphere Dee, with his own hand, had set down divers comets, their places and motions, according to his individual observation. Item, divers other instruments, as the theorie of the eighth sphere, the ninth and tenth, with an horizon and meridian of copper, made by Mercator specially for Dr. Dee. Item, sea-compasses of different kinds. Item, a magnet-stone, commonly called a loadstone, of great virtue. Also an excellent watch-clock, made by one Dibbley, ' a notable workman, long since dead,' by which the time might sensibly be measured in the seconds of an hour—that is, not to fail the 360th part of an hour. We need not dwell upon his store of documents relating to Irish and Welsh estates, and of ancient seals of arms; but my curiosity, I confess, is somewhat stirred by his reference to 'a great bladder,' with about four pounds weight of 'a very sweetish thing,' like a brownish gum, in it, artificially prepared by thirty times purifying, which the doctor valued at upwards of a hundred crowns.

While engaged in learned studies and correspondence with learned men, Dee found time to indulge in those wild semi-mystical, transcendental visions which engaged the imagination of so many mediæval students. The secret of 'the philosopher's stone' led him into fascinating regions of speculation, and the ecstasies of Rosicrucianism dazzled him with the idea of holding communication with the inhabitants of the other world. How far he was sincere in these pursuits, how far he imparted into them a spirit of charlatanry, I think it is impossible to determine. Perhaps one may venture to say that, if to some small extent an impostor, he was, to a much larger extent, a dupe; that if he deceived others, he also deceived himself; nor is he, as biography teaches, the only striking example of the credulous enthusiast who mingles with his enthusiasm, more or less unconsciously, a leaven of hypocrisy. As early as 1571 he complains, in the preface to his 'English Euclid,' that he is jeered at by the populace as a conjurer. By degrees, it is evident, he begins to feel a pride in his magical attainments. He records with the utmost gravity his remarkable dreams, and endeavours to read the future by them. He insists, moreover, on strange noises which he hears in his chamber. In those days a favourite method of summoning the spirits was to bring them into a glass or stone which had been prepared for the purpose; and in his diary, under the date of May 25, 1581, he records—for the first time—that he had held intercourse in this way with supra-mundane beings.

Combining with his hermetico-magical speculations religious exercises of great fervour, he was thus engaged, one day in November, 1582, when suddenly upon his startled vision rose the angel Uriel ' at the west window of his laboratory,' and presented him with a translucent stone, or crystal, of convex shape, possessing the wonderful property of introducing its owner to the closest possible communication with the world of spirits. It was necessary at times that this so-called mirror should be turned in different positions before the observer could secure the right focus; and then the spirits appeared on its surface, or in different parts of the room by reason of its action. Further, only one person, whom Dee calls the *skryer*, or seer, could discover the spirits, or hear and interpret their voices, just as there can be but one medium, I believe, at a spiritualistic séance of the present day. But, of course, it was requisite that, while the medium was absorbed in his all-important task, some person should be at hand to describe what he saw, or professed to see, and commit to paper what he heard, or professed to hear; and a seer with a lively imagination and a fluent tongue could go very far in both directions. This humbler, secondary position Dee reserved for himself. Probably his invention was not sufficiently fertile for the part of a medium, or else he was too much in earnest to practise an intentional deception. As the crystal showed him nothing, he himself said so, and looked about for someone more sympathetic, or less conscientious. His choice fell at first on a man named Barnabas Saul, and he records in his diary how, on October 9, 1581, this man ' was strangely troubled by a spiritual creature about midnight.' In a MS. preserved in the British Museum, he relates some practices which took place on December 2, beginning his account with this statement: ' I willed the skryer, named Saul, to looke into my great crystalline globe, if God had sent his holy angel Azrael, or no.' But Saul was a fellow of small account, with a very limited inventive faculty, and on March 6, 1582, he was obliged to confess 'that he neither heard nor saw any spiritual creature any more.' Dee and his inefficient, unintelligent skryer then quarrelled, and the latter was dismissed, leaving behind him an unsavoury reputation.

EDWARD KELLY.

Soon afterwards our magician made the acquaintance of a certain Edward Kelly (or Talbot), who was in every way fitted for the mediumistic *rôle*. He was clever, plausible, impudent, unscrupulous, and a most accomplished liar. A native of Worcester, where he was born in 1555, he was bred up, according to one account, as a druggist, according to another as a lawyer; but all accounts agree that he became an adept in every kind of knavery. He was pilloried, and lost his ears (or at least was condemned to lose them) at Lancaster, for the offence of coining, or for forgery; afterwards retired to Wales, assumed the name of Kelly, and practised as a conjurer and alchemist. A story is told of him which illustrates the man's unhesitating audacity, or, at all events, the notoriety of his character: that he carried with him one night into the park of Walton-le-Dale, near Preston, a man who thirsted after a knowledge of the future, and, when certain incantations had been completed, caused his servants to dig up a corpse, interred only the day before, that he might compel it to answer his questions.

How he got introduced to Dr. Dee I do not profess to know; but I am certainly disinclined to accept the wonderful narrative which Mr. Waite renders in so agreeable a style—that Kelly, during his Welsh sojourn, was shown an old manuscript which his landlord, an innkeeper, had obtained under peculiar circumstances. ' It had been discovered in the tomb of a bishop who had been buried in a neighbouring church, and whose tomb had been sacrilegiously up-torn by some fanatics,' in the hope of securing the treasures reported to be concealed within it. They found nothing, however, but the aforesaid manuscript, and two small ivory bottles, respectively containing a ponderous white and red powder. ' These pearls

beyond price were rejected by the pigs of apostasy:
one of them was shattered on the spot, and its
ruddy, celestine contents for the most part lost.   The
remnant, together with the remaining bottle and the
unintelligible manuscript, were speedily disposed of
to the innkeeper in exchange for a skinful of wine.'
The innkeeper, in his turn, parted with them for one
pound sterling to Master Edward Kelly, who, believing he had obtained a hermetic treasure, hastened
to London to submit it to Dr. Dee.

This accomplished and daring knave was engaged
by the credulous doctor as his skryer, at a salary of
£50 per annum, with 'board and lodging,' and all expenses paid.   These were liberal terms; but it must be
admitted that Kelly earned them.   Now, indeed, the
crystal began to justify its reputation!   Spirits
came as thick as blackberries, and voices as numerous
as those of rumour!   Kelly's amazing fertility of
fancy never failed his employer, upon whose confidence he established an extraordinary hold, by judici-
ously hinting doubts as to the propriety of the work
he had undertaken.   How could a man be other than
trustworthy, when he frankly expressed his suspicions of the *mala fides* of the spirits who responded
to the summons of the crystal?   It was impossible—
so the doctor argued—that so candid a medium
could be an impostor, and while resenting the imputations cast upon the ' spiritual creatures,' he came to
believe all the more strongly in the man who
slandered them.   The difference of opinion gave rise,
of course, to an occasional quarrel.   On one occasion

(in April, 1582) Kelly specially provoked his employer by roundly asserting that the spirits were
demons sent to lure them to their destruction; and
by complaining that he was confined in Dee's house
as in a prison, and that it would be better for him to
be near Cotsall Plain, where he might walk abroad
without danger.

Some time in 1583 a certain 'Lord Lasky,' that is,
Albert Laski or Alasco, prince or waiwode of Siradia
in Poland, and a guest at Elizabeth's Court, made
frequent visits to Dee's house, and was admitted to
the spirit exhibitions of the crystal.   It has been suggested that Kelly had conceived some ambitious pro-
jects, which he hoped to realize through the agency
of this Polish noble, and that he made use of the
crystal to work upon his imagination.   Thenceforward the spirits were continually hinting at great
European revolutions, and uttering vague predictions
of some extraordinary good fortune which was in preparation for Alasco.   On May 28 Dee and Kelly
were sitting in the doctor's study, discussing the
prince's affairs, when suddenly appeared—perhaps it
was an optical trick of the ingenious Kelly—' a
spiritual creature, like a pretty girl of seven or nine
years of age, attired on her head, with her hair rowled
up before, and hanging down very long behind, with
a gown of soy, changeable green and red, and with a
train; she seemed to play up and down, and seemed
to go in and out behind my books, lying in heaps;
and as she should ever go between them, the books
seemed to give place sufficiently, dividing one heap

from the other while she passed between them.
And so I considered, and heard the diverse reports
which E. K. made unto this pretty maid, and I said,
" Whose maiden are you ?" ' Here follows the conversation—inane and purposeless enough, and yet
deemed worthy of preservation by the credulous
doctor :

DOCTOR DEE'S CONVERSATION WITH THE SPIRITUAL CREATURE.

SHE. Whose man are you ?

DEE. I am the servant of God, both by my bound duty, and
also (I hope) by His adoption.

A VOICE. You shall be beaten if you tell.

SHE. Am not I a fine maiden ? give me leave to play in your
house ; my mother told me she would come and dwell here.

> (*She went up and down with most lively gestures of a young
> girl playing by herself, and divers times another spake
> to her from the corner of my study by a great perspective
> glasse, but none was seen beside herself.*)

SHE. Shall I ? I will. (*Now she seemed to answer me in the
foresaid corner of my study.*) I pray you let me tarry a little ?
(*Speaking to me in the foresaid corner.*)

DEE. Tell me what you are.

SHE. I pray you let me play with you a little, and I will tell
you who I am.

DEE. In the name of Jesus then, tell me.

SHE. I rejoice in the name of Jesus, and I am a poor little
maiden ; I am the last but one of my mother's children ; I have
little baby children at home.

DEE. Where is your home ?

SHE. I dare not tell you where I dwell, I shall be beaten.

DEE. You shall not be beaten for telling the truth to them that
love the truth ; to the Eternal Truth all creatures must be
obedient.

SHE. I warrant you I will be obedient; my sisters say they
must all come and dwell with you.

DEE. I desire that they who love God should dwell with me,
and I with them.

SHE. I love you now you talk of God.

DEE. Your eldest sister—her name is Esimĕli.

SHE. My sister is not so short as you make her.

DEE. O, I cry you mercy ! she is to be pronounced Esimīli !

KELLY. She smileth ; one calls her, saying, Come away, maiden.

SHE. I will read over my gentlewomen first ; my master Dee will teach me if I say amiss.

DEE. Read over your gentlewomen, as it pleaseth you.

SHE. I have gentlemen and gentlewomen ; look you here.

KELLY. She bringeth a little book out of her pocket. She pointeth to a picture in the book.

SHE. Is not this a pretty man ?

DEE. What is his name ?

SHE. My (mother) saith his name is Edward : look you, he hath a crown upon his head ; my mother saith that this man was Duke of York.

And so on.

The question here suggests itself, Was this passage of nonsense Dr. Dee's own invention ? And has he compiled it for the deception of posterity ? I do not believe it. It is my firm conviction that he recorded in perfect good faith—though I own my opinion is not very complimentary to his intelligence—the extravagant rigmarole dictated to him by the archknave Kelly, who, very possibly, added to his many ingenuities some skill in the practices of the ventriloquist. No great amount of artifice can have been necessary for successfully deceiving so admirable a subject for deception as the credulous Dee. It is probable that Dee may sometimes have suspected he was being imposed upon ; but we may be sure he was very unwilling to admit it, and that he did his best to banish from his mind so unwelcome a suspicion. As for Kelly, it seems clear that he had conceived some widely ambitious and daring scheme, which, as I have said, he hoped to carry out through the instrumentality of Alasco, whose interest he endeavoured to stimulate by flattering his vanity, and representing the spiritual creature as in possession of a pedigree which traced his descent from the old Norman family of the Lacys.

With an easy invention which would have done credit to the most prolific of romancists, he daily developed the characters of his pretended visions.* Consulting the crystal on June 2, he professed to see a spirit in the garb of a husbandman, and this spirit rhodomontaded in mystical language about the great work Alasco was predestined to accomplish in the conversion and regeneration of the world. Before this invisible fictionist retired into his former obscurity, Dee petitioned him to use his influence on behalf of a woman who had committed suicide, and of another who had dreamed of a treasure hidden in a cellar. Other interviews succeeded, in the course of which much more was said about the coming purification of humanity, and it was announced that a new code of laws, moral and religious, would be entrusted

---

* 'Adeo viro præ credulo errore jam factus sui impos et mente captus, et Dæmones, quo arctius horrendis hisce Sacris adhærescent illius ambitioni vanæ summæ potestatis in Patria adipiscendæ spe et expectatione lene euntis illum non solius Poloniæ sed alterius quoque regni, id est primo Poloniæ, deinde alterius, viz. Moldaviæ Regem fore, et sub quo magnæ universi mundi mutationes incepturas esse, Judæos convertendos, et ab illo Saræmos et Ethnicos vexillo crucis superandos, facili ludificarentur.'—Dr. Thomas Smith, 'Vitæ Eruditissimorum ac Illustrium Virorum,' London, 1707. 'Vita Joannis Dee,' p. 25.

to Dee and his companions. What a pity that this code was never forthcoming ! A third spirit, a maiden named Galerah, made her appearance, all whose revelations bore upon Alasco, and the greatness for which he was reserved : 'I say unto thee, his name is in the Book of Life. The sun shall not passe his course before he be a king. His counsel shall breed alteration of his State, yea, of the whole world. What wouldst thou know of him ?'

'If his kingdom shall be of Poland,' answered Dee, 'in what land else ?'

'Of two kingdoms,' answered Galerah.

'Which ? I beseech you.'

'The one thou hast repeated, and the other he seeketh as his right.'

'God grant him,' exclaimed the pious doctor, 'sufficient direction to do all things so as may please the highest of his calling.'

'He shall want no direction,' replied Galerah, 'in anything he desireth.'

Whether Kelly's invention began to fail him, or whether it was a desire to increase his influence over his dupe, I will not decide ; but at this time he revived his pretended conscientious scruples against dealing with spirits, whom he calumniously declared to be ministers of Satan, and intimated his intention of departing from the unhallowed precincts of Mortlake. But the doctor could not bear with equanimity the loss of a skryer who rendered such valuable service, and watched his movements with the vigilance of alarm. It was towards the end of June, the month

made memorable by such important revelations, that
Kelly announced, one day, his design of riding from
Mortlake to Islington, on some private business.
The doctor's fears were at once awakened, and he fell
into a condition of nervous excitement, which, no
doubt, was exactly what Kelly had hoped to pro-
voke. 'I asked him,' says Dee, 'why he so hasted to
ride thither, and I said if it were to ride to Mr.
Henry Lee, I would go thither also, to be acquainted
with him, seeing now I had so good leisure, being
eased of the book writing. Then he said, that one
told him, the other day, that the Duke (Alasco) did
but flatter him, and told him other things, both
against the Duke and me. I answered for the Duke
and myself, and also said that if the forty pounds'
annuity which Mr. Lee did offer him was the chief
cause of his minde setting that way (contrary to
many of his former promises to me), that then I
would assure him of fifty pounds yearly, and would
do my best, by following of my suit, to bring it to
pass as soon as I possibly could, and thereupon did
make him promise upon the Bible. Then Edward
Kelly again upon the same Bible did sweare unto me
constant friendship, and never to forsake me ;' and,
moreover, said that unless this had so fallen out, he
would have gone beyond the seas, taking ship at
Newcastle within eight days next. And so we plight
our faith each to other, taking each other by the
hand upon these points of brotherly and friendly
fidelity during life, which covenant I beseech God
to turn to His honour, glory, and service, and the

comfort of our brethren (His children) here on earth.'

This concordat, however, was of brief duration. Kelly, who seems to have been in fear of arrest,* still threatened to quit Dee's service ; and by adroit pressure of this kind, and by unlimited promises to Alasco, succeeded in persuading his two confederates to leave England clandestinely, and seek an asylum on Alasco's Polish estates. Dee took with him his second wife, Jane Fromond, to whom he had been married in February, 1578, his son Arthur (then about four years old), and his children by his first wife. Kelly was also accompanied by his wife and family.

On the night of September 21, 1583, in a storm of rain and wind, they left Mortlake by water, and dropped down the river to a point four or five miles below Gravesend, where they embarked on board a Danish ship, which they had hired to take them to Holland. But the violence of the gale was such that they were glad to transfer themselves, after a narrow escape from shipwreck, to some fishing-smacks, which landed them at Queenborough, in the Isle of Sheppey, in safety. There they remained until the gale abated, and then crossed the Channel to Brill on the 30th. Proceeding through Holland and Friesland to Embden and Bremen, they thence made their way to Stettin, in Pomerania, arriving on Christmas Day, and remaining until the middle of January.

* He was suspected of coining false money, but Dr. Dee declares he was innocent. (June, 1583.)

Meanwhile, Kelly was careful not to intermit those revelations from the crystal which kept alive the flame of credulous hope in the bosom of his two dupes, and he was especially careful to stimulate the ambition of Alasco, whose impoverished finances could ill bear the burden imposed upon them of supporting so considerable a company. They reached Siradia on February 3, 1584, and there the spirits suddenly changed the tone of their communications; for Kelly, having unexpectedly discovered that Alasco's resources were on the brink of exhaustion, was accordingly prepared to fling him aside without remorse. The first spiritual communication was to the effect that, on account of his sins, he would no longer be charged with the regeneration of the world, but he was promised possession of the Kingdom of Moldavia. The next was an order to Dee and his companions to leave Siradia, and repair to Cracow, where Kelly hoped, no doubt, to get rid of the Polish prince more easily. Then the spirits began to speak at shorter intervals, their messages varying greatly in tone and purport, according, I suppose, as Alasco's pecuniary supplies increased or diminished; but eventually, when all had suffered severely from want of money, for it would seem that their tinctures and powders never yielded them as much as an ounce of gold, the spirits summarily dismissed the unfortunate Alasco, ordered Dee and Kelly to repair to Prague, and entrusted Dee with a Divine communication to Rudolph II., the Emperor of Germany.

Quarrels often occurred between the two adepts during the Cracow period. In these Kelly was invariably the prime mover, and his object was always the same : to confirm his influence over the man he had so egregiously duped. At Prague, Dee was received by the Imperial Court with the distinction due to his well-known scholarship; but no credence was given to his mission from the spirits, and his pretensions as a magician were politely ignored. Nor was he assisted with any pecuniary benevolences; and the man who through his crystal and his skryer had apparently unlimited control over the inhabitants of the spiritual world could not count with any degree of certainty upon his daily bread. He failed, moreover, to obtain a second interview with the Emperor. On attending at the palace, he was informed that the Emperor had gone to his country seat, or else that he had just ridden forth to enjoy the pleasures of the chase, or that his imperfect acquaintance with the Latin tongue prevented him from conferring with Dee personally ; and eventually, at the instigation of the Papal nuncio, Dee was ordered to depart from the Imperial territories (May, 1586).

The discredited magician then betook himself to Erfurt, and afterwards to Cassel. He would fain have visited Italy, where he anticipated a cordial welcome at those Courts which patronized letters and the arts, but he was privately warned that at Rome an accusation of heresy and magic had been preferred against him, and he had no desire to fall into the fangs of the Inquisition. In the autumn

6

of 1586, the Imperial prohibition having apparently
been withdrawn, he followed Kelly into Bohemia;
and in the following year we find both of them
installed as guests of a wealthy nobleman, named
Rosenberg, at his castle of Trebona.   Here they
renewed their intercourse with the spirit world, and
their operations in the transmutation of metals.
Dee records how, on December 9, he reached the
point of projection!   Cutting a piece out of a brass
warming-pan, he converted it—by merely heating it
in the fire, and pouring on it a few drops of the
magical elixir—a kind of red oil, according to some
authorities—into solid, shining silver.   And there
goes an idle story that he sent both the pan and the
piece of silver to Queen Elizabeth, so that, with her
own eyes, she might see how exactly they tallied,
and that the piece had really been cut out of the
pan!   About the same time, it is said, the two
magicians launched into a profuse expenditure,—
Kelly, on one of his maid-servants getting married,
giving away gold rings to the value of £4,000.   Yet,
meanwhile, Dee and Kelly were engaged in sharp
contentions, because the spirits fulfilled none of the
promises made by the latter, who, his invention
(I suppose) being exhausted, resolved, in April,
1587, to resign his office of 'skryer,' and young
Arthur Dee then made an attempt to act in his
stead.

   The conclusion I have arrived at, after studying
the careers and characters of our two worthies, is
that they were wholly unfitted for each other's

society ; a barrier of ' incompatibility ' rose straitly between them. Dee was in earnest ; Kelly was practising a sham. Dee pursued a shadow which he believed to be a substance ; Kelly knew that the shadow was nothing more than a shadow. Dee was a man of rare scholarship and considerable intellectual power, though of a credulous and superstitious temper ; Kelly was superficial and ignorant, but clever, astute, and ingenious, and by no means prone to fall into delusions. The last experiment which he made on Dee's simple-mindedness stamps the man as the rogue and knave he was ; while it illustrates the truth of the preacher's complaint that there is nothing new under the sun. The doctrine of free marriage propounded by American enthusiasts was a *remanet* from the ethical system of Mr. Edward Kelly.

Kelly had long been on bad terms with his wife, and had conceived a passionate attachment towards Mrs. Dee, who was young and charming, graceful in person, and attractive in manner. To gratify his desires, he resorted to his old machinery of the crystal and the spirits, and soon obtained a revelation that it was the Divine pleasure he and Dr. Dee should exchange partners. Demoralized and abased as Dee had become through his intercourse with Kelly, he shrank at first from a proposal so contrary to the teaching and tenor of the religion he professed, and suggested that the revelation could mean nothing more than that they ought to live on a footing of cordial friendship. But the spirits insisted on a literal interpretation of their command. Dee yielded, comparing himself with much unction to Abraham, who, in obedience to the Divine will, consented to the sacrifice of Isaac. The parallel, however, did not hold good, for Abraham saved his son, whereas Dr. Dee lost his wife!

It was then Kelly's turn to affect a superior morality, and he earnestly protested that the spirits could not be messengers from heaven, but were servants of Satan. Whereupon they then declared that he was no longer worthy to act as their interpreter. But why dwell longer on this unpleasant farce? By various means of cajolery and trickery, Kelly contrived to accomplish his design.

This communistic arrangement, however, did not long work satisfactorily—at least, so far as the ladies were concerned; and one can easily understand that Mrs. Dee would object to the inferior position she occupied as Kelly's paramour. However this may be, Dee and Kelly parted company in January, 1589; the former, according to his own account, delivering up to the latter the mysterious elixir and other substances which they had made use of in the transmutation of metals. Dee had begun to turn his eyes wistfully towards his native country, and welcomed with unfeigned delight a gracious message from Queen Elizabeth, assuring him of a friendly reception. In the spring he took his departure from Trebona; and it is said that he travelled with a pomp and circumstance worthy of an ambassador, though it is difficult

to reconcile this statement with his constant complaints of poverty. Perhaps, after all, his three
coaches, with four horses to each coach, his two or
three waggons loaded with baggage and stores,
and his hired escort of six to twenty-four soldiers,
whose business it was to protect him from the
enemies he supposed to be lying in wait for him,
existed only, like the philosopher's stone, in the
imagination! He landed at Gravesend on December 2, was kindly received by the Queen at Richmond
a day or two afterwards, and before the year had run
out was once more quietly settled in his house 'near
the riverside' at Mortlake.

Kelly, whom the Emperor Maximilian II. had
knighted and created Marshal of Bohemia, so strong
a conviction of his hermetic abilities had he impressed
on the Imperial mind, remained in Germany. But
the ingenious, plausible rogue was kept under such
rigid restraint, in order that he might prepare an
adequate quantity of the transmuting stone or
powder, that he wearied of it, and one night endeavoured to escape. Tearing up the sheets of his
bed, he twisted them into a rope, with which to
lower himself from the tower where he was confined.
But he was a man of some bulk ; the rope gave way
beneath his weight, and falling to the ground, he
received such severe injuries that in a few days he
expired (1593).

Dee's later life was, as Godwin remarks, 'bound
in shallows and miseries.' He had forfeited the

respect of serious-minded men by his unworthy con-
federacy with an unscrupulous adventurer. The
Queen still treated him with some degree of consideration, though she had lost all faith in his
magical powers, and occasionally sent him assistance.
The unfortunate man never ceased to weary her with
the repetition of his trials and troubles, and strongly
complained that he had been deprived of the income
of his two small benefices during his six years'
residence on the Continent. He related the sad tale
of the destruction of his library and apparatus by
an ignorant mob, which had broken into his house
immediately after his departure from England, excited by the rumours of his strange magical practices.
He enumerated the expenses of his homeward
journey, arguing that, as it had been undertaken by
the Queen's command, she ought to reimburse him.
At last (in 1592) the Queen appointed two members
of her Privy Council to inquire into the particulars
of his allegations. These particulars he accordingly
put together in a curious narrative, which bore the
long-winded title of :

'The Compendious Rehearsall of John Dee, his dutiful Declara-
cion and Proof of the Course and Race of his Studious Lyfe, for
the Space of Halfe an Hundred Yeares, now (by God's Favour and
Helpe) fully spent, and of the very great Injuries, Damages, and
Indignities, which for those last nyne Years he hath in England
sustained (contrary to Her Majesties very gracious Will and
express Commandment), made unto the Two Honourable Commissioners, by Her Most Excellent Majesty thereto assigned,
according to the intent of the most humble Supplication of the
said John, exhibited to Her Most Gracious Majestie at Hampton
Court, Anno 1592, November 9.'

It has been remarked that in this ' Compendious Rehearsal ' he alludes neither to his magic crystal, with its spiritualistic properties, nor to the wonderful powder or elixir of transmutation.   He founds his claim to the Queen's patronage solely upon his intellectual eminence and acknowledged scholarship. Nor does he allude to his Continental experiences, except so far as relates to his homeward journey. But he is careful to recapitulate all his services, and the encomiastic notices they had drawn from various quarters, while he details his losses with the most elaborate minuteness.   The quaintest part of his lamentable and most fervent petition is, however, its conclusion.   Having shown that he has tried and exhausted every means of raising money for the support of his family, he concludes :

' Therefore, seeing the blinded lady, Fortune, doth not governe in this commonwealth, but *justitia* and *prudentia*, and that in better order than in Tullie's "Republica," or bookes of offices, they are laied forth to be followed and performed, most reverently and earnestly (yea, in manner with bloody teares of heart), I and my wife, our seaven children, and our servants (seaventeene of us in all) do this day make our petition unto your Honors, that upon all godly, charitable, and just respects had of all that, which this day you have seene, heard, and perceived, you will make such report unto her Most Excellent Majestie (with humble request for speedy reliefes) that we be not constrained to do or suffer otherwise than becometh Christians, and true, and faithfull, and obedient subjects to doe or suffer ; and all for want of due mainteynance.'

The main object Dee had in view was the mastership of St. Cross's Hospital, which Elizabeth had formerly promised him.   This he never received ; but in December, 1594, he was appointed to the

Chancellorship of St. Paul's Cathedral, which in the
following year he exchanged for the wardenship of
the College at Manchester. He still continued his
researches into supernatural mysteries, employing
several persons in succession as 'skryers'; but he
found no one so fertile in invention as Kelly, and the
crystal uttered nothing more oracular than answers
to questions about lovers' quarrels, hidden treasures,
and petty thefts—the common stock-in-trade of the
conjurer. In 1602 or 1604, he retired from his
Manchester appointment, and sought the quiet and
seclusion of his favourite Mortlake. His renown as
'a magician' had greatly increased—not a little, it
would seem, to his annoyance; for on June 5, 1604,
we find that he presented a petition to James I. at
Greenwich, soliciting his royal protection against the
wrong done to him by enemies who mocked him as
'a conjurer, or caller, or invocator of devils,' and
solemnly asserting that 'of all the great number of
the very strange and frivolous fables or histories
reported and told of him (as to have been of his
doing) none were true.' It is said that the treatment Dee experienced at this time was the primary
cause of the Act passed against personal slander
(1604)—a proof of legislative wisdom which drew
from Dee a versified expression of gratitude—in
which, let us hope, the sincerity of the gratitude is
not to be measured by the quality of the verse. It is
addressed to 'the Honorable Members of the
Commons in the Present Parliament,' and here is a
specimen of it, which will show that, though Dee's

crystal might summon the spirits, it had no control over the Muses:

> ' The honour, due unto you all,
>   And reverence, to you each one
>   I do first yield most spe-ci-all ;
>   Grant me this time to heare my mone.
>
> ' Now (if you will) full well you may
>   Fowle sclaundrous tongues for ever tame ;
>   And helpe the truth to beare some sway
>   In just defence of a good name.'

Thenceforward Dee sinks into almost total obscurity. His last years were probably spent in great tribulation ; and the man who had dreamed of converting, Midas-like, all he touched into gold, seems frequently to have wanted bread. It was a melancholy ending to a career which might have been both useful and brilliant, if his various scholarship and mental energy had not been expended upon a delusion. Unfortunately for himself, Dee, with all his excellent gifts, wanted that greatest gift of all, a sound judgment. His excitable fancy and credulous temper made him the dupe of his own wishes, and eventually the tool of a knave far inferior to himself in intellectual power, but surpassing him in strength of will, in force of character, in audacity and inventiveness. Both knave and dupe made but sorry work of their lives. Kelly, as we have seen, broke his neck in attempting to escape from a German prison, and Dee expired in want and dishonour, without a friend to receive his last sigh.

He died at Mortlake in 1608, and was buried in

the chancel of Mortlake Church, where, long afterwards, Aubrey, the gossiping antiquary, was shown
an old marble slab as belonging to his tomb.

His son Arthur, after acting as physician to the
Czar of Russia and to our own Charles I., established
himself in practice at Norwich, where he died.
Anthony Wood solemnly records that this Arthur, in
his boyhood, had frequently played with quoits of
gold, which his father had cast at Prague by means
of his 'stone philosophical.' How often Dee must
have longed for some of those 'quoits' in his last sad
days at Mortlake, when he sold his books, one by
one, to keep himself from starvation!

After Dee's death, his fame as a magician underwent an extraordinary revival; and in 1659, when
the country was looking forward to the immediate
restoration of its Stuart line of kings, the learned
Dr. Meric Casaubon thought proper to publish, in
a formidable folio volume, the doctor's elaborate report of his—or rather Kelly's—supposed conferences
with the spirits—a notable book, as being the initial
product of spiritualism in English literature. In
his preface Casaubon remarks that, though Dee's
'carriage in certain respects seemed to lay in works of
darkness, yet all was tendered by him to kings and
princes, and by all (England alone excepted) was
listened to for a good while with good respect, and by
some for a long time embraced and entertained.'
And he adds that 'the fame of it made the Pope
bestir himself, and filled all, both learned and unlearned, with great wonder and astonishment. . . .

As a whole, it is undoubtedly not to be paralleled in its kind in any age or country.'

NOTE.

In the curious 'Apologia' published by Dee, in 1595, in the form of a letter to the Archbishop of Canterbury, 'containing a most briefe Discourse Apologeticall, with a plaine Demonstration and formal Protestation, for the lawfull, sincere, very faithfull and Christian course of the Philosophicall studies and exercises of a certaine studious Gentleman, an ancient Servant to her most excellent Maiesty Royall,' he furnishes a list of 'sundry Bookes and Treatises' of which he was the author. The best known of his printed works is the 'Monas Hieroglyphica, Mathematicè, Anagogicè que explicata' (1564), dedicated to the Emperor Maximilian. Then there are 'Propæ deumata Aphoristica;' 'The British Monarchy,' otherwise called the 'Petty Navy Royall: for the politique security, abundant wealth, and the triumphant state of this kingdom (with God's favour) procuring' (1576); and 'Paralaticæ Commentationis, Praxcosque Nucleus quidam' (1573). His unpublished manuscripts range over a wide field of astronomical, philosophical, and logical inquiry. The most important seem to be 'The first great volume of famous and rich Discoveries,' containing a good deal of speculation about Solomon and his Ophirian voyage; 'Prester John, and the first great Cham;' 'The Brytish Complement of the perfect Art of Navigation;' 'The Art of Logicke, in English;' and 'De Hominis Corpore, Spiritu, et Anima: sive Microcosmicum totius Philo sophiæ Naturalis Compendium.'

The character drawn of Dr. Dee by his learned biographer, Dr. Thomas Smith, by no means confirms the traditional notion of him as a crafty and credulous practiser in the Black Art. It is, on the contrary, the portrait of a just and upright man, grave in his demeanour, modest in his manners, abstemious in his habits; a man of studious disposition and benevolent temper; a man held in such high esteem by his neighbours that he was called upon to arbitrate when any differences arose between them; a fervent Christian, attentive to all the offices of the Church, and zealous in the defence of her faith.

Here is the original: 'Si mores exterioremque vitæ cultum contemplemur, non quicquam ipsi in probrum et ignominium verti

possit ; ut pote sobrius, probus, affectibus sedatis, compositisque
moribus, ab omni luxu et gulâ liber, justi et æqui studiosis-
simus, erga pauperes beneficus, vicinis facilis et benignus,
quorum lites, atrisque partibus contendentium ad illum tanquam
ad sapientum arbitrum appellantibus, moderari et desidere solebat :
in publicis sacris cœtibus et in orationibus frequens, articulorum
Christianæ fidei, in quibus omnes Orthodoxi conveniunt, strenuus
assertor, zelo in hæreses, à primitiva Ecclesia damnatas, flagrans,
inqui Peccōrum, qui virginitatem B. Mariæ ante partum Christi
in dubium vocavit, accerimè invectus : licet de controversiis inter
Romanenses et Reformatos circa reliqua doctrinæ capita non adeo
semperosè solicitus, quin sibi in Polonia et Bohemia, ubi religio
ista dominatur, Missæ interesse et communicare licere putaverit,
in Anglia, uti antea, post redditum, omnibus Ecclesiæ Anglicanæ
ritibus conformis.'   It must be admitted that Dr. Smith's Latin is
not exactly ' conformed ' to the Ciceronian model.

CHAPTER III.

DR. DEE'S DIARY.

I AM not prepared to say, with its modern editor, that Dr. Dee's Diary* sets the scholar magician's character in its true light more clearly than anything that has yet been printed; but I concede that it reveals in a very striking and interesting manner the peculiar features of his character—his superstitious credulity, and his combination of shrewdness and simplicity—as well as his interesting habits. I shall therefore extract a few passages to assist the reader in forming his opinion of a man who was certainly in many respects remarkable.

(i.) I begin with the entries for 1577:

'1577, January 16th.—The Erle of Leicester, Mr. Philip Sidney, Mr. Dyer,† etc., came to my house (at Mortlake).

'1577, January 22nd.—The Erle of Bedford came to my house.

'1577, March 11th.—My fall uppon my right nuckel bone, *hora* 9 *fere mane*, wyth oyle of Hypericon (*Hypericum*, or St. John's Wort) in twenty-four howers eased above all hope : God be thanked for such His goodness of (to ?) His creatures.

---

* 'The Private Diary of Dr. John Dee,' edited by J. O. Halliwell (Phillipps) for the Camden Society, 1842.

† This was Sir Edward Dyer, the friend of Spenser and Sidney, remembered by his poem ' My Mind to me a Kingdom is.'

'1577, March 24th.—Alexander Simon, the Ninevite, came to me, and promised me his service into Persia.

'1577, May 1st.—I received from Mr. William Harbut of St. Gillian his notes uppon my "Monas."*

'1577, May 2nd.—I understode of one Vincent Murfryn his abbominable misusing me behinde my back ; Mr. Thomas Besbich told me his father is one of the cokes of the Court.

'1577, May 20th.—I hyred the barber of Cheswik, Walter Hooper, to kepe my hedges and knots in as good order as he saw them then, and that to be done with twice cutting in the yere at the least, and he to have yerely five shillings, meat and drink.

'1577, June 26th.—Elen Lyne gave me a quarter's warning.

'1577, August 19.—The "Hexameron Brytanicum" put to printing. (Published in 1577 with the title of "General and Rare Memorials pertayning to the perfect Art of Navigation.")

'1577, November 3rd.—William Rogers of Mortlak about 7 of the clok in the morning, cut his own throte, *by the fiende his instigator.*

'1577, November 6th.—Sir Umfrey Gilbert† cam to me to Mortlak.

'1577, November 22nd.—I rod to Windsor to the Q. Majestie.

'1577, November 25th.—I spake with the Quene *hora quinta;* I spoke with Mr. Secretary Walsingham.‡ I declared to the Quene her title to Greenland, Estotiland, and Friesland.

'1577, December 1st.—I spoke with Sir Christopher Hatton ; he was made Knight that day.

'1577, December –th.—I went from the Courte at Wyndsore.

'1577, December 30th.—Inexplissima illa calumnia de R. Edwardo, iniquissima aliqua ex parte in me denunciebatur : ante aliquos elapsos diro, sed . . . sua sapientia me innocentem.'

I cannot ascertain of what calumny against Edward VI. Dee had been accused; but it is to be hoped that his wish was fulfilled, and that he was acquitted of it before many days had elapsed.

I have omitted some items relating to moneys

---

* The 'Monas Hieroglyphica.'

† The celebrated navigator, whose heroic death is one of our worthiest traditions.

‡ A warm and steady friend to Dr. Dee.

borrowed. It is sufficiently plain, however, that Dee never intended his Diary for the curious eyes of the public, and that it mainly consists of such memoranda as a man jots down for his private and personal use. Assuredly, many of these would never have been recorded if Dee had known or conjectured that an inquisitive antiquarian, some three centuries later, would exhume the confidential pages, print them in imperishable type, and expose them to the world's cold gaze. It seems rather hard upon Dr. Dee that his private affairs should thus have become everybody's property! Perhaps, after all, the best thing a man can do who keeps a diary is to commit it to the flames before he shuffles off his mortal coil, lest some laborious editor should eventually lay hands upon it, and publish it to the housetops with all its sins upon it! But as in Dr. Dee's case the offence has been committed, I will not debar my readers from profiting by it.

(ii.) 1578-1581.

'1578, June 30th.—I told Mr. Daniel Rogers, Mr. Hackluyt of the Middle Temple being by, that Kyng Arthur and King Maty, both of them, did conquer Gelindia, lately called Friseland, which he so noted presently in his written copy of Mon . . . thensis (?), for he had no printed boke thereof.'

What a pity Dr. Dee has not recorded his authority for King Arthur's Northern conquests! The Mr. Hackluyt here mentioned is the industrious compiler of the well-known collection of early voyages.

Occasionally Dee relates his dreams, as on September 10, 1579: 'My dream of being naked, and my skyn all overwrought with work, like some kinde of tuft mockado, with crosses blue and red; and on

my left arme, about the arme, in a wreath, this word
I red—*sine me nihil potestis facere.*'

Sometimes he resorts to Greek characters while
using English words:

'1579, December 9th.—Θις νιγτ μι υυιφ δρεμιδ θατ ονε καμ το 'ερ
ανδ τουχεδ 'ερ, σαινγ, "Μιστρές Δεε, γου αρ κονκεινεδ οφ χιλδ, υος ναμε
μυστ βε Ζαχαριας ; βε οφ γοδ χερε, ε σαλ. δο υυελ ας θις δοθ !"

'1579, December 28th.—I reveled to Roger Coke the gret
secret of the elixir of the salt οφ ακετελς, ονε υππον α υνδρεδ.'

Other entries refer to this Mr. Roger Coke, or
Cooke, who seems to have been Dee's pupil or appren-
tice, and at one time to have enjoyed his confidence.
They quarrelled seriously in 1581.

'1581, September 5th.—Roger Cook, who had byn with me
from his 14 years of age till 28, of a melancholik nature, pycking
and devising occasions of just cause to depart on the suddayn,
about 4 of the clok in the afternone requested of me lycense to
depart, wheruppon rose whott words between us ; and he, imagining with himself that he had, the 12 of July, deserved my great
displeasure, and finding himself barred from view of my philosophicall dealing with Mr. Henrik, thought that he was utterly
recast from intended goodness toward him. Notwithstanding
Roger Cook his unseamely dealing, I promised him, if he used
himself toward me now in his absens, one hundred pounds as
sone as of my own clene hability I myght spare so much ; and
moreover, if he used himself well in life toward God and the
world, I promised him some pretty alchimicall experiments,
whereuppon he might honestly live.'

'1581, September 7th.—Roger Cook went for altogether from
me.'

In February, 1601, however, this quarrel was
made up.

(iii.) Of the learned doctor's colossal credulity the
Diary supplies some curious proofs:

'1581, March 8th.—It was the 8 day, being Wensday, hora
noctis 10-11, the strange noyse in my chamber of knocking ; and

the voyce, ten times repeted, somewhat like the shriek of an owle, but more longly drawn, and more softly, as it were in my chamber.

'1581, August 3rd.—All the night very strange knocking and rapping in my chamber. August 4th, and this night likewise.

'1581, October 9th.—Barnabas Saul, lying in the . . . hall, was strangely trubled by a spirituall creature about mydnight.

'1582, May 20th.—Robertus Gardinerus Salopiensis lactum mihi attulit minimum de materia lapidis, divinitus sibi revelatus de qua.

'1582, May 23rd.—Robert Gardiner declared unto me hora 4½ a certeyn great philosophicall secret, as he had termed it, of a spirituall creature, and was this day willed to come to me and declare it, which was solemnly done, and with common prayer.

'1590, August 22nd.—Ann, my nurse, had long been tempted by a wycked spirit : but this day it was evident how she was possessed of him. God is, hath byn, and shall be her protector and deliverer ! Amen.

'1590, August 25th.—Anne Frank was sorowful, well comforted, and stayed in God's mercyes acknowledging.

'1590, August 26th.—At night I anoynted (in the name of Jesus) her brest with the holy oyle.

'1590, August 30th.—In the morning she required to be anoynted, and I did very devoutly prepare myself, and pray for virtue and powr, and Christ his blessing of the oyle to the expulsion of the wycked, and then twyce anoynted, the wycked one did rest a while.'

The holy oil, however, proved of no effect. The poor creature was insane. On September 8 she made an attempt to drown herself, but was prevented. On the 29th she eluded the dexterity of her keeper, and cut her throat.

(iv.) Occasionally we meet with references to historic events and names, but, unfortunately, they are few :

'1581, February 23rd.—I made acquayntance with Joannes Bodonius, in the Chamber of Presence at Westminster, the ambassador being by from Monsieur.'

7

Bodonius, or Bodin, was the well-known writer upon witchcraft.

'1581, March 23rd.—At Mortlak came to me Hugh Smyth, who had returned from Magellan strayghts and Vaygatz.

'1581, July 12th.—The Erle of Leicester fell fowly out with the Erle of Sussex, Lord Chamberlayn, calling each other trayter, whereuppon both were commanded to kepe theyr chamber at Greenwich, wher the court was.'

This was the historic quarrel, of which Sir Walter Scott has made such effective use in his 'Kenilworth.'

'1583, January 13th.—On Sonday, the stage at Paris Garden fell down all at once, being full of people beholding the bear-bayting. Many being killed thereby, more hurt, and all amased. The godly expownd it as a due plage of God for the wickedness ther used, and the Sabath day so profanely spent.'

This popular Sabbatarian argument, which occasionally crops up even in our own days, had been humorously anticipated, half a century before, by Sir Thomas More, in his 'Dyalogue' (1529): 'At Beverley late, much of the people being at a bear-baiting, the church fell suddenly down at evening-time, and overwhelmed some that were in it. A good fellow that after heard the tale told—" So," quoth he, " now you may see what it is to be at evening prayers when you should be at the bear-baiting!" '

The Paris Garden Theatre at Bankside had been erected expressly for exhibitions of bear-baiting. The charge for admission was a penny at the gate, a penny at the entry of the scaffold or platform, and a penny for 'quiet standing.' During the Commonwealth this cruel sport was prohibited; but it was revived at the Restoration, and not finally suppressed until 1835.

'1583, January 23rd.—The Ryght Honorable Mr. Secretary Walsingham came to my howse, where by good luk he found Mr. Adrian Gilbert (of the famous Devonshire family of seamen), and so talk was begonne of North West Straights discovery.

'1583, February 11th.—The Quene lying at Richmond went to Mr. Secretary Walsingham to dinner; she coming by my dore, graciously called me to her, and so I went by her horse side, as far as where Mr. Hudson dwelt. Ερ μαιεστι αξεδ με οβυσχυρελι οφ μουνσιευρις στατε : διξε βισθανατος εριτ.

'1583, March 6th.—I, and Mr. Adrian Gilbert and John Davis (the Arctic discoverer), did mete with Mr. Alderman Barnes, Mr. Tounson, Mr. Young and Mr. Hudson, about the N. W. voyage.

'1583, April 18th.—The Quene went from Richmond toward Greenwich, and at her going on horsbak, being new up, she called for me by Mr. Rawly (Sir Walter Raleigh) his putting her in mynde, and she sayd, " quod defertur non aufertur," and gave me her right hand to kiss.

'1590, May 18th.—The two gentlemen, the unckle Mr. Richard Candish (Cavendish), and his nephew, the most famous Mr. Thomas Candish, who had sayled round about the world, did visit me at Mortlake.

'1590, December 4th.—The Quene's Majestie called for me at my dore, circa 3½ a meridie as she passed by, and I met her at Est Shene gate, where she graciously, putting down her mask, did say with mery chere, "I thank thee, Dee; there wus never promisse made, but it was broken or kept." I understode her Majesty to mean of the hundred angels she promised to have sent me this day, as she yesternight told Mr. Richard Candish.

'1595, October 9th.—I dyned with Sir Walter Rawlegh at Durham House.'

(v.) Some of the entries which refer to Dee's connection with Lasco and Kelly are interesting:

'1583, March 18th.—Mr. North from Poland, after he had byn with the Quene he came to me. I received salutation from Alaski, Palatine in Poland.

'1583, May 13th.—I became acquaynted with Albertus Laski

at 7½ at night, in the Erle of Leicester his chamber, in the court at Greenwich.

'1583, May 18th.—The Prince Albertus Laski came to me at Mortlake, with onely two men. He came at afternone, and tarryed supper, and after sone set.

'1583, June 15th.—About 5 of the clok cum the Polonian prince, Lord Albert Lasky, down from Bisham, where he had lodged the night before, being returned from Oxford, whither he had gon of purpose to see the universityes, wher he was very honorably used and enterteyned. He had in his company Lord Russell, Sir Philip Sydney, and other gentlemen : he was rowed by the Quene's men, he had the barge covered with the Quene's cloth, the Quene's trumpeters, etc. He came of purpose to do me honour, for which God be praysed !

'1583, September 21st.—We went from Mortlake, and so the Lord Albert Lasky, I, Mr. E. Kelly, our wives, my children and familie, we went toward our two ships attending for us, seven or eight myle below Gravesende.

'1586, September 14th.—Trebonam venimus.

'1586, October 18th.—E. K. recessit a Trebona versus Pragam curru delatus ; mansit hic per tres hebdomadas.

'1586, December 19th.—Ad gratificandam Domino Edouardo Garlando, et Francisco suo fratri, qui Edouardus nuncius mihi missus erat ab Imperatore Moschoriæ ut ad illum venirem, E. K. fecit proleolem (?) lapidis in proportione unius . . . gravi arenæ super quod vulgaris oz. et ⅓ et producta est optimè auri oz. fere : quod aurum post distribuimus a crucibolo una dedimus Edouardo.

'1587, January 18th.—Rediit E. K. a Praga. E. K. brought with him from the Lord Rosenberg to my wyfe a chayne and juell estemed at 300 duckettes ; 200 the juell stones, and 100 the gold.

'1587, September 28th.—I delivered to Mr. Ed. Kelley (earnestly requiring it as his part) the half of all the animall which was made. It is to weigh 20 oz. ; he wayed it himself in my chamber : he bowght his waights purposely for it. My lord had spoken to me before for some, but Mr. Kelly had not spoken.

'1587, October 28th and 29th.—John Carp did begyn to make furnaces over the gate, and he used of my rownd bricks, and for the yron pot was contented now to use the lesser bricks, 60 to make a furnace.

'1587, November 8th.—E. K. terribilis expostulatio, accusatio, etc., hora tertia a meridie.

'1587, December 12th.—Afternone somewhat, Mr. Ed. Kelly [did] his lamp overthrow, the spirit of wyne long spent to nere, and the glas being not stayed with buks about it, as it was wont to be ; and the same glass so flitting on one side, the spirit was spilled out, and burnt all that was on the table where it stode, lynnen and written bokes, —as the bok of Zacharias, with the "Alkanor" that I translated out of French, for some by [boy ?] spirituall could not ; "Rowlaschy," his third boke of waters philosophicall ; the boke called "Angelicum Opus ;" all in pictures of the work from the beginning to the end ; the copy of the man of Badwise "Conclusions for the Transmution of Metalls ;" and 40 leaves in 4to., entitled "Extractiones Dunstat," which he himself extracted and noted out of Dunstan his boke, and the very boke of Dunstan was but cast on the bed hard by from the table.'

This so-called 'Book of St. Dunstan' was one which Kelly professed to have bought from a Welsh innkeeper, who, it was alleged, had found it among the ruins of Glastonbury.

'1588, February 8th.—Mr. E. K., at nine of the clok, afternone, sent for me to his laboratory over the gate to see how he distilled sericon, according as in tyme past and of late he heard of me out of Ripley.   God lend his heart to all charity and virtue !

'1588, August 24th.—Vidi divinam aquam demonstratione magnifici domini et amici mei incomparabilis D[omini] Ed. Kelii ante meridiem tertia hora.

'1588, December 7th.—γρεατ φρενδχιπ προμισιδ φορ μανι, ανδ τυυο ουυχες φορ θε θινγ.'*

---

* This Diary, written in a very small and illegible hand on the margins of old almanacs, was discovered by Mr. W. H. Black in the Ashmolean Library at Oxford.

CHAPTER IV.

MAGIC AND IMPOSTURE—A COUPLE OF KNAVES.

THE secrecy, the mystery, and the supernatural pretensions associated with the so-called occult sciences necessarily recommended them to the knave and the cheat as instruments of imposition. If some of the earlier professors of Hermeticism, the first seekers after the philosophical stone, were sincere in their convictions, and actuated by pure and lofty motives, it is certain that their successors were mostly dishonest adventurers, bent upon turning to their personal advantage the credulous weakness of their fellow-creatures. With some of these the chief object was money ; others may have craved distinction and influence ; others may have sought the gratification of passions more degrading even than avarice or ambition. At all events, alchemy became a synonym for fraud : a magician was accepted as, by right of his vocation, an impostor ; and the poet and the dramatist pursued him with the whips of satire, invective, and ridicule, while the law prepared for him the penalties usually inflicted upon criminals. These penalties, it is true, he very frequently con-

trived to elude ; in many instances, by the exercise of
craft and cunning ; in others, by the protection of
powerful personages, to whom he had rendered ques-
tionable services ; and again in others, because the
agent of the law did not care to hunt him down so
long as he forbore to bring upon himself the glare of
publicity.   Thus it came to pass that generation after
generation saw the alchemist still practising his unwholesome trade, and probably he retained a good deal
of his old notoriety down to as late a date as the
beginning of the eighteenth century.   It must be
admitted, however, that his alchemical pursuits
gradually sank into obscurity, and that it was more
in the character of an astrologer, and as a manufac-
turer of love-potions and philtres, of charms and
waxen images—not to say as a pimp and a bawd—
that he looked for clients.   In the *Spectator*, for instance, that admirable mirror of English social life in
the early part of the eighteenth century, you will find
no reference to alchemy or the alchemist ; but in the
Guardian Addison's light humour plays readily enough
round the delusions or deceptions of the astrologer.
The reader will remember the letter which Addison
pretends to have received with great satisfaction from
an astrologer in Moorfields.   And in contemporary
literature generally, it will be found that the august
inquirer into the secrets of nature, who aimed at the
transmutation of metals and the possession of immortal youth, had by this time been succeeded by an
obscure and vulgar cheat, who beguiled the ignorant
and weak by his jargon about planetary bodies, and

his cheap stock-in-trade of a wig and a gown, a wand, a horoscope or two, and a few coloured vials. This 'modern magician' is, indeed, a common character in eighteenth-century fiction.

But a century earlier the magician retained some little of the 'pomp and circumstance' of the old magic, and was still the confidant of princes and nobles, and not seldom the depository of State secrets involving the reputation and the honour of men and women of the highest position. So much as this may be truly asserted of Simon Forman, who flourished in the dark and criminal period of the reign of James I., when the foul practices of mediæval Italy were transferred for the first and last time to an English Court. Forman was born at Quidham, a village near Wilton, in Wilts, in 1552. Little is known of his early years ; but he seems to have received a good education at the Sarum Grammar School, and afterwards to have been apprenticed to a druggist in that ancient city. Endowed with considerable natural gifts and an ambitious temper, he made his way to Oxford, and was entered at Magdalene College, but owing to lack of means was unable to remain as a student for more than two years. To improve his knowledge of astrology, astronomy, and medicine, he visited Portugal, the Low Countries, and the East.

On his return he began to practise as a physician in Philpot Lane, London ; but, as he held no diploma, was four times imprisoned and fined as a quack. Eventually he found himself compelled to

take the degree of M.D. at Cambridge (June 27,
1603) ; after which he settled in Lambeth, and carried
on the twofold profession of physician and astrologer.
In his comedy of 'The Silent Woman,' Ben Jonson
makes one of his characters say : 'I would say thou
hadst the best philtre in the world, and could do
more than Madam Medea or Doctor Forman,' whence
we may infer that the medicines he compounded were
not of the orthodox kind or approved by the faculty.
Lovers resorted to him for potions which should
soften obdurate hearts ; beauties for powders and
washes which might preserve their waning charms ;
married women for drugs to relieve them of the
reproach of sterility ; rakes who desired to corrupt
virtue, and impatient heirs who longed for immediate
possession of their fortunes, for compounds which
should enfeeble, or even kill. Such was the character
of Doctor Forman's sinister ' practice.' Among those
who sought his unscrupulous assistance was the infamous Countess of Essex, though Forman died
before her nefarious schemes reached the stage of
fruition.

His death, which took place on the 12th of September, 1611, was attended (it is said) by remarkable circumstances. The Sunday night previous, ' his
wife and he being at supper in their garden-house,
she being pleasant, told him she had been informed
he could resolve whether man or wife should die
first. " Whether shall I," quoth she, "bury you or
no ?" " Oh, Truais," for so he called her, " thou shalt
bury me, but thou wilt much repent it." " Yea, but

how long first ?"   "I shall die," said he, "on Thursday night."   Monday came ; all was well.   Tuesday
came, he not sick.   Wednesday came, and still he
was well, with which his impertinent wife did much
twit him in his teeth.   Thursday came, and dinner
was ended, he very well ; he went down to the water-
side, and took a pair of oars to go to some buildings
he was in hand with in Puddle Dock.   Being in the
middle of the Thames, he presently fell down, only
saying, "An impost, an impost," and so died.   A
most sad storm of wind immediately following.'

It seems as if these men could never die without
bringing down upon the earth a grievous storm or
tempest !   The preceding story, however, partakes
too much of the marvellous to be very easily accepted.

According to Anthony Wood, this renowned
magician was 'a person that in horary questions,
especially theft, was very judicious and fortunate'
(in other words, he was well served by his spies and
instruments) ; 'so, also, in sickness, which was
indeed his masterpiece ; and had good success in
resolving questions about marriage, and in other
questions very intricate.   He professed to his wife
that there would be much trouble about Sir Robert
Carr, Earl of Somerset, and the Lady Frances, his
wife, who frequently resorted to him, and from whose
company he would sometimes lock himself in his
study one whole day.   He had compounded things
upon the desire of Mrs. Anne Turner, to make the
said Sir Robert Carr calid *quo ad hanc*, and Robert,
Earl of Essex frigid *quo ad hanc ;* that his, to his wife

the Lady Frances, who had a mind to get rid of him
and be wedded to the said Sir Robert.   He had also
certain pictures in wax, representing Sir Robert and
the said Lady, to cause a love between each other,
with other such like things.'

A CAUSE CÉLÈBRE.

Lady Frances Howard, second daughter of the
Earl of Suffolk, was married, at the age of thirteen,
to Robert, Earl of Essex, who was only a year older.
The alliance was dictated by political considerations,
and had been recommended by the King, who did
not fail to attend the gorgeous festivities that celebrated the occasion (January 5th, 1606).   As it was
desirable that the boy-bridegroom should be separated
for awhile from his child-wife, the young Earl was sent
to travel on the Continent, and he did not return to
claim his rights as a husband until shortly after
Christmas, 1609, when he had just passed his
eighteenth birthday.   In the interval his wife had
developed into one of the most beautiful, and, unfortunately, one of the most dissolute, women in
England.   Naturally impetuous, self-willed, and unscrupulous, she had received neither firm guidance nor
wise advice at the hands of a coarse and avaricious
mother.   Nor was James's Court a place for the cultivation of the virtues of modesty and self-restraint.
The young Countess, therefore, placed no control upon
her passions, and had already become notorious for her
disregard of those obligations which her sex usually
esteem as sacred.   At one time she intrigued with

Prince Henry, but he dismissed her in angry disgust at her numerous infidelities. Finally, she crossed the path of the King's handsome favourite, Sir Robert Carr, and a guilty passion sprang up between them. It is painful to record that it was encouraged by her great-uncle, Lord Northampton, who hoped through Carr's influence to better his position at Court ; and it was probably at his mansion in the Strand that the plot was framed of which I am about to tell the issue. But the meetings between the two lovers sometimes took place at the house of one of Carr's agents, a man named Coppinger.

At first, when Essex returned, the Countess refused to live with him ; but her parents ultimately compelled her to treat him as her husband, and even to accompany him to his country seat at Chartley. There she remained for three years, wretched with an inconceivable wretchedness, and animated with wild dreams of escape from the husband she hated to the paramour she loved.

For this purpose she sought the assistance of Mrs. Anne Turner, the widow of a respectable physician, and a woman of considerable personal charms, who had become the mistress of Sir Arthur Mainwaring.* Mrs. Turner introduced her to Dr. Simon Forman, and an agreement was made that Forman should

---

* This woman has a place in the records of fashion as introducer of the novelty of yellow-starching the extensive ruffs which were then generally worn. When Lord Chief Justice Coke sentenced her to death (as we shall hereafter see) for her share in the murder of Overbury, he ordered that 'as she was the person who had brought yellow-starched ruffs into vogue, she

exercise his magical powers to fix young Carr's affections irrevocably upon the Countess. The intercourse
between the astrologer and the ladies became very
frequent, and the former exercised all his skill to
carry out their desires. At a later period, Mrs.
Forman deposed in court 'that Mrs. Turner and her
husband would sometimes be locked up in his study
for three or four hours together,' and the Countess
learned to speak of him as her 'sweet father.'

The Countess next conceived the most flagitious
designs against her husband's health; and, to carry
them out, again sought the assistance of her unscrupulous quack, who accordingly set to work,
made waxen images, invented new charms, supplied
drugs to be administered in the Earl's drinks, and
washes in which his linen was to be steeped. These
measures, however, did not prove effectual, and
letters addressed by the Countess at this time to
Mrs. Turner and Dr. Forman complain that 'my lord
is very well as ever he was,' while reiterating the sad
story of her hatred towards him, and her design to
be rid of him at all hazards. In the midst of the
intrigue came the sudden death of Dr. Forman, who
seems to have felt no little anxiety as to his share in
it, and, on one occasion, as we have seen, professed
to his wife 'that there would be much trouble about
Carr and the Countess of Essex, who frequently
resorted unto him, and from whose company he would

---

should be hanged in that dress, that the same might end in shame
and detestation.' As the hangman was also adorned with yellow
ruffs, it is no wonder that Coke's prediction was amply fulfilled.

sometimes lock himself in his study a whole day.'
Mrs. Forman, when, at a later date, examined in
court, deposed 'that Mrs. Turner came to her house
immediately after her husband's death, and did demand certain pictures which were in her husband's
study, namely, one picture in wax, very mysteriously
apparelled in silk and satin ; as also another made in
the form of a naked woman, spreading and laying
forth her hair in a glass, which Mrs. Turner did confidently affirm to be in a box, and she knew in what
part of the room in the study they were.'   We also
learn that Forman, in reply to the Countess's reproaches, averred that the devil, as he was informed,
had no power over the person of the Earl of Essex.
The Countess, however, was not to be diverted from
her object, and, after Forman's death, employed two
or three other conjurers—one Gresham, and a Doctor
Lavoire, or Savory, being specially mentioned.

What followed has left a dark and shameful stain
on the record of the reign of James I.   The King
personally interfered on behalf of his favourite, and
resolved that Essex should be compelled to surrender
his wife.   For this purpose the Countess was instructed to bring against him a charge of conjugal
incapacity ; and a Commission of right reverend pre-
lates and learned lawyers, under the presidency—one
blushes to write it—of Abbot, Archbishop of Canterbury, was appointed to investigate the loathsome
details.   A jury of matrons was empanelled to determine the virginity of Lady Essex, and, as a pure
young girl was substituted in her place, their verdict

was, of course, in the affirmative! As for the Commission, it decided, after long debates, by a majority of seven to five, that the Lady Frances was entitled to a divorce—the majority being obtained, however, only by the King's active exercise of his personal influence (September, 1613). The lady having thus been set free from her vows by a most shameless intrigue, James hurried on a marriage between her and his favourite, and on St. Stephen's Day it was celebrated with great splendour. In the interval Carr had been raised to the rank and title of Earl of Somerset, and his wife had previously been made Viscountess Rochester.

A strenuous opponent of these unhallowed nuptials had been found in the person of Sir Thomas Overbury, a young man of brilliant parts, who stood towards Somerset in much the same relation that Somerset stood towards the King. At the outset he had looked with no disfavour on his patron's intrigue with Lady Frances, but had actually composed the love-letters which went to her in the Earl's name; but, for reasons not clearly understood, he assumed a hostile attitude when the marriage was proposed. As he had acquired a knowledge of secrets which would have made him a dangerous witness before the Divorce Commission, the intriguers felt the necessity of getting him out of the way. Accordingly, the King pressed upon him a diplomatic appointment on the Continent, and when this was refused committed him to the Tower. There he lingered for some months in failing health until a dose of poison terminated his sufferings on September 13, 1613, rather more than three months before the completion of the marriage he˚ had striven ineffectually to prevent.   This poison was unquestionably administered at the instigation of Lady Essex, though under what circumstances it is not easy to determine.   The most probable supposition seems to be that an assistant of Lobell, a French apothecary who attended Overbury, was bribed to administer the fatal drug.

For two years the murder thus foully committed remained unknown, but in the summer of 1615, when James's affection for Somerset was rapidly declining, and a new and more splendid favourite had risen in the person of George Villiers, some information of the crime was conveyed to the King by his secretary, Winwood.   How Winwood obtained this information is still a mystery; but we may, perhaps, conjecture that he received it from the apothecary's boy, who, being taken ill at Flushing, may have sought to relieve his conscience by confession.   A few weeks afterwards, Helwys, the Lieutenant of the Tower, under an impression that the whole matter had been discovered, acknowledged that frequent attempts had been made to poison Overbury in his food, but that he had succeeded in defeating them until the apothecary's boy eluded his vigilance.   Who sent the poison he did not know.   The only person whose name he had heard in connection with it was Mrs. Turner, and the agent employed to convey it was, he said, a certain Richard Weston, a former servant of Mrs. Turner, who had been admitted into the Tower as a keeper, and entrusted with the immediate charge of Overbury.

On being examined, Weston at first denied all knowledge of the affair; but eventually he confessed that, having been rebuked by Helwys, he had thrown away the medicaments with which he had been entrusted; and next he accused Lady Somerset of instigating him to administer to Overbury a poison, which would be forwarded to him for that purpose. Then one Rawlins, a servant of the Earl, gave information that he had been similarly employed. As soon as Somerset heard that he was implicated, he wrote to the King protesting his innocence, and declaring that a conspiracy had been hatched against him. But many suspicious particulars being discovered, he was committed to the custody of Sir Oliver St. John; while Weston, on October 23, was put on his trial for the murder of Overbury, and found guilty, though no evidence was adduced against him which would have satisfied a modern jury.

On November 7 Mrs. Turner was brought before the Court. Her trial excited the most profound curiosity, and Westminster Hall was crowded by an eager multitude, who shuddered with superstitious emotion when the instruments employed by Forman in his magical rites were exposed to view.* It would

---

* Arthur Wilson, in his 'Memoirs,' furnishes a strange account of the practices in which Lady Essex, Mrs. Turner, and the conjurer took part. 'The Countess of Essex,' he says, 'to strengthen her designs, finds out one of her own stamp, Mrs. Turner, a doctor of physic's widow, a woman whom prodigality and looseness had brought low; yet her pride would make her fly any pitch, rather

seem that Mrs. Turner, when arrested, immediately
sent her maid to Forman's widow, to urge her to

than fall into the jaws of Want. These two counsel together how
they might stop the current of the Earl's affection towards his
wife, and make a clear passage for the Viscount in his place. To
effect which, one Dr. Forman, a reputed conjurer (living at
Lambeth) is found out; the women declare to him their grievances;
he promises sudden help, and, to amuse them, frames many little
pictures of brass and wax—some like the Viscount and Countess,
whom he must unite and strengthen, others like the Earl of Essex,
whom he must debilitate and weaken; and then with philtrous
powders, and such drugs, he works upon their persons. And to
practise what effects his arts would produce, Mrs. Turner, that
loved Sir Arthur Manwaring (a gentleman then attending the
Prince), and willing to keep him to her, gave him some of the
powder, which wrought so violently with him, that through a
storm of rain and thunder he rode fifteen miles one dark night
to her house, scarce knowing where he was till he was there.
Such is the devilish and mad rage of lust, heightened with art
and fancy.

'These things, matured and ripened by this juggler Forman,
gave them assurance of happy hopes. Her courtly incitements,
that drew the Viscount to observe her, she imputed to the
operation of those drugs he had tasted; and that harshness and
stubborn comportment she expressed to her husband, making
him (weary of such entertainments) to absent himself, she thought
proceeded from the effects of those unknown potions and powders
that were administered to him. So apt is the imagination to take
impressions of those things we are willing to believe.

' The good Earl, finding his wife nurseled in the Court, and seeing
no possibility to reduce her to reason till she were estranged from the
relish and taste of the delights she sucked in there, made his condition again known to her father. The old man, being troubled with
his daughter's disobedience, embittered her, being near him, with
wearisome and continued chidings, to wean her from the sweets
she doted upon, and with much ado forced her into the country.
But how harsh was the parting, being sent away from the place
where she grew and flourished ! Yet she left all her engines and
imps behind her : the old doctor and his confederate, Mrs. Turner,
must be her two supporters. She blazons all her miseries to them

burn—before the Privy Council sent to search her house—any of her husband's papers that might contain dangerous secrets. She acted on the advice, but overlooked a few documents of great importance, including a couple of letters written by Lady Essex to Mrs. Turner and Forman. The various articles seized in Forman's house referred, however, not to the murder of Overbury, but to the conjurations employed against the Earls of Somerset and Essex. 'There was shewed in Court,' says a contemporary report, 'certaine pictures of a man and a woman made in lead, and also a moulde of brasse wherein they were cast, a blacke scarfe alsoe full of white crosses, which Mrs. Turner had in her custody,' besides 'inchanted paps and other pictures.' There was also a parcel of Forman's written charms and incantations. 'In some of those parchments the devill had particular names, who were conjured to torment the lord Somersett and Sir Arthur Mannering, if theire loves

at her depart, and moistens the way with her tears. Chartley was an hundred miles from her happiness; and a little time thus lost is her eternity. When she came thither, though in the pleasantest part of the summer, she shut herself up in her chamber, not suffering a beam of light to peep upon her dark thoughts. If she stirred out of her chamber, it was in the dead of the night, when sleep had taken possession of all others but those about her. In this implacable, sad, and discontented humour, she continued some months, always murmuring against, but never giving the least civil respect to, her husband, which the good man suffered patiently, being loth to be the divulger of his own misery; yet, having a manly courage, he would sometimes break into a little passion to see himself slighted and neglected; but having never found better from her, it was the easier to bear with her.'

should not contynue, the one to the Countesse, the
other to Mrs. Turner.' Visions of a dingy room
haunted by demons, who had been summoned from
the infernal depths by Forman's potent spells, stimulated the imagination of the excited crowd until they
came to believe that the fiends were actually there in
the Court, listening in wrath to the exposure of their
agents; and, behold! in the very heat and flush of
this extravagant credulity, a sudden crack was heard
in one of the platforms or scaffolds, causing 'a great
fear, tumult, and commotion amongst the spectators
and through the hall, every one fearing hurt, as if the
devil had been present and grown angry to have his
workmanship known by such as were not his own
scholars.' The narrator adds that there was also a
note showed in Court, made by Dr. Forman, and
written on parchment, signifying what ladies loved
what lords; but the Lord Chief Justice would not
suffer it to be read openly. This 'note,' or book, was a
diary of the doctor's dealings with the persons named;
and a scandalous tradition affirms that the Lord Chief
Justice would not have it read because his wife's name
was the first which caught his eye when he glanced
at the contents.

Mrs. Turner's conviction followed as a matter of
course upon Weston's. There was no difficulty in
proving that she had been concerned in his proceedings, and that if he had committed a crime she
was *particeps criminis.* Both she and Weston died
with an acknowledgment on their lips that they
were justly punished. Her end, according to all

accounts, was sufficiently edifying. Bishop Goodman quotes the narrative of an eye-witness, one
Mr. John Castle, in which we read that, 'if detestation of painted pride, lust, malice, powdered hair,
yellow bands, and the rest of the wardrobe of Court
vanities ; if deep sighs, tears, confessions, ejacula-
tions of the soul, admonitions of all sorts of
people to make God and an unspotted conscience
always our friends ; if the protestation of faith and
hope to be washed by the same Saviour and the like
mercies that Magdalene was, be signs and demon-
strations of a blessed penitent, then I will tell you
that this poor broken woman went *a cruce ad
gloriam*, and now enjoys the presence of her and our
Redeemer. Her body being taken down by her
brother, one Norton, servant to the Prince, was in a
coach conveyed to St. Martin's-in-the-Fields, where,
in the evening of the same day, she had an honest
and a decent burial.' Her sad fate seems to have
appealed strongly to public sympathy, and to have
drawn a veil of oblivion over the sins and follies
of her misspent life. A contemporary versifier
speaks of her in language worthy of a Lucretia :

> 'O how the cruel cord did misbecome
> Her comely neck ! and yet by Law's just doom
> Had been her death. Those locks, like golden thread,
> That used in youth to enshrine her globe-like head,
> Hung careless down ; and that delightful limb,
> Her snow-white nimble hand, that used to trim
> Those tresses up, now spitefully did tear
> And rend the same ; nor did she now forbear
> To beat that breast of more than lily-white,
> Which sometime was the bed of sweet delight.

From those two springs where joy did whilom dwell,
Grief's pearly drops upon her pale cheek fell.'

The next to suffer was an apothecary named
Franklin, from whom the poison had been procured.
' Before he was executed, he threw out wild hints of
the existence of a plot far exceeding in villainy that
which was in course of investigation. He tried to
induce all who would listen to him to believe that
he knew of a conspiracy in which many great lords
were concerned ; and that not only the late Prince
[Henry] had been removed by unfair means, but that
a plan had been made to get rid of the Electress
Palatine and her husband. As, however, all this
was evidently only dictated by a hope of escaping the
gallows, he was allowed to share with the others a
fate which he richly deserved.'

After the execution of these smaller culprits, some
months elapsed before Bacon, as Attorney-General,
was directed to proceed against the greater. It was
not until May 24, 1616, that the Countess of
Somerset was put upon her trial before the High
Steward's Court in Westminster Hall. Contemporary testimony differs strangely as to her behaviour.
One authority says that, whilst the indictment was
being read, she turned pale and trembled, and when
Weston's name was mentioned hid her face behind
her fan. Another remarks : ' She won pity by her
sober demeanour, which, in my opinion,' he adds,
' was more curious and confident than was fit for a
lady in such distress, yet she shed, or made show of

some tears, divers times.' The evidence against her was too strong to be confuted, and she pleaded guilty. When the judge asked her if she had anything to say in arrest of judgment, she replied, in low, almost inaudible tones, that she could not extenuate her fault. She implored mercy, and begged that the lords would intercede with the King on her behalf. Sentence was then pronounced, and the prisoner sent back to the Tower, to await the King's decision.

On the following day the Earl was tried. Bacon again acted as prosecutor, and in his opening speech he said that the evidence to be brought forward by the Government would prove four points : 1. That Somerset bore malice against Overbury before the latter's imprisonment ; 2. That he devised the plan by which that imprisonment was effected ; 3. That he actually sent poisons to the Tower ; 4. That he had made strenuous efforts to conceal the proofs of his guilt. He added that he himself would undertake the management of the case on the first two points, leaving his subordinates, Montague and Crew, to deal with the third and fourth.

Bacon had chosen for himself a comparatively easy task. The ill-feeling that had existed between Overbury and his patron was beyond doubt ; while it was conclusively shown, and, indeed, hardly disputed, that Somerset had had a hand in Overbury's imprisonment, and in the appointment of Helwys and Weston as his custodians. Passages from Lord Northampton's letters to the Earl proved the existence of a plot in which both were mixed up, and that Helwys had expressed an opinion that Overbury's death would be a satisfactory termination of the imbroglio. But he might probably have based this opinion on the fact that Overbury was seriously ill, and his recovery more than doubtful.

When Bacon had concluded his part of the case, Ellesmere, who presided, urged Somerset to confess his guilt. ' No, my lord,' said the Earl calmly, ' I came hither with a resolution to defend myself.'

Montague then endeavoured to demonstrate that the poison of which Overbury died had been administered with Somerset's knowledge. But he could get no further than this : that Somerset had been in the habit of sending powders, as well as tarts and jellies, to Overbury ; but he did not, and could not prove that the powders were poisonous. Nor was Serjeant Crew able to advance the case beyond the point reached by Bacon ; he could argue only on the assumption of Somerset's guilt, which his colleagues had failed to establish.

In our own day it would be held that the case for the prosecution had completely broken down ; and I must add my conviction that Somerset was in no way privy to Overbury's murder. He had assented to his imprisonment, because he was weary of his importunity ; but he still retained a kindly feeling towards him, and was evidently grieved at the serious nature of his illness. As a matter of fact, it was not proved even that Overbury died of poison, though I admit that this is put beyond doubt by collateral circumstances. Somerset's position, however, before judges who were more or less hostilely disposed, with the agents of the Crown bent on obtaining his conviction, and he himself without legal advisers, was both difficult and dangerous. He was embarrassed by the necessity of keeping back part of his case. He was unable to tell the whole truth about Overbury's imprisonment. He could not make known all that had passed between Lady Essex and himself before marriage, or that Overbury had been committed to the Tower to prevent him from giving evidence which would have certainly quashed Lady Essex's proceedings for a divorce. And, in truth, if he mustered up courage to tell this tale of shame, he could not hope that the peers, most of whom were his enemies, would give credence to it, or that, if they believed it, they would refrain from delivering an adverse verdict.

Yet he bore himself with courage and ability, when, by the flickering light of torches, for the day had gone down, he rose to make his defence. Acknowledging that he had consented to Overbury's imprisonment in order that he might throw no obstacles in the way of his marriage with Lady Essex, he firmly denied that he had known anything of attempts to poison him. The tarts he had sent were wholesome, and of a kind to which Overbury was partial; if any had been tampered with, he was unaware of it. The powders he had received from Sir Robert Killigrew, and simply sent them on ; and Overbury had admitted, in a letter which was before the Court, that they had done him no mischief. Here Crew interrupted : The three powders from Killigrew had been duly accounted for ; but there was a fourth powder, which had not been accounted for, and had (it was assumed) contained poison. Now, it was improbable that the Earl could remember the exact history of every powder sent to Overbury two years before, and, besides, it was a mere assumption on the part of the prosecution that this fourth powder was poison. But Somerset's inability to meet this point was made the most of, and gave the peers a sufficient pretext for declaring him guilty. The Earl received his sentence with the composure he had exhibited throughout the arduous day, which had shown how a nature enervated by luxury and indulgence can be braced up by the chill air of adversity, and contented himself with expressing a hope that the Court would intercede with the King for mercy.

I have dwelt at some length on the details of this celebrated trial because it is the last (in English jurisprudence) in which men and women of rank have been mixed up with the secret practices of the magician ; though, for other reasons, it is one of very unusual interest. In briefly concluding the recital, I may state that James was greatly relieved when the trial was over, and he found that nothing damaging to himself had been disclosed. It is certain that Somerset was in possession of some dark secret, the revelation of which was much dreaded by the King ; so that precautions had even been taken, or at all events meditated, to remove him from the Court if he entered upon the dangerous topic, and to continue the trial in his absence. He would probably have been silenced by force. The Earl, however, refrained from hazardous disclosures, and James could breathe in peace.

On July 13, the King pardoned Lady Somerset, who was certainly the guiltiest of all concerned. The Earl was left in prison, with sentence of death suspended over him for several years, in order, no doubt, to terrify him into silence. A few months before his death, James appears to have satisfied himself that he had nothing to fear, and ordered the Earl's release (January, 1622). Had he lived, he would probably have restored him to his former influence and favour.*

DR. LAMBE.

A worthy successor to Simon Forman appeared in Dr. Lambe, or Lamb, who, in the first two Stuart reigns, attained a wide celebrity as an astrologer and a quack doctor. A curious story respecting his pretended magical powers is related by Richard Baxter in his 'Certainty of the World of Spirits' (1691). Meeting two acquaintances in the street, who evidently desired some experience of his skill in the occult art, he invited them home with him, and

---

* See 'The State Trials;' 'The Carew Letters;' Spedding, 'Life and Letters of Lord Bacon;' Amos, 'The Grand Oyer of Poisoning;' and S. R. Gardiner, 'History of England,' vol. iv., 1607-1616.

ushered them into an inner chamber.   There, to their amazement, a tree sprang up before their eyes in the middle of the floor.   Before they had ceased to wonder at this sight surprising, three diminutive men entered, with tiny axes in their hands, and, nimbly setting to work, soon felled the tree.   The doctor then dismissed his guests, who went away with a conviction that he was as potent a necromancer as Roger Bacon or Cornelius Agrippa.

That same night a tremendous gale arose, so that the house of one of Lambe's visitors rocked to and fro, threatening to topple over with a crash, and bury the man and his wife in the ruins.   In great terror his wife inquired, 'Were you not at Dr. Lambe's to-day?'   The husband acknowledged that it was so. 'And did you bring anything away from his house?' Yes: when the dwarfs felled the tree, he had been foolish enough to pick up some of the chips, and put them in his pocket.   Here was the cause of the hurricane!   With all speed he got rid of the chips; the storm immediately subsided, and the remainder of the night was spent in undisturbed repose.

Lambe was notorious for the lewdness of his life and his evil habits.   But his supposed skill and success as a soothsayer led to his being frequently consulted by George Villiers, Duke of Buckingham, with the result that each helped to swell the volume of the other's unpopularity.   The Puritans were angered at the Duke's resort to a man of Lambe's character and calling ; the populace hated Lambe as the tool and instrument of the Duke.   In 1628 the

brilliant favourite of Charles I. was the best-hated
man in England, and every slander was hurled at
him that the resources of political animosity could
supply. The ballads of the time—an indisputably
satisfactory barometer of public opinion—inveighed
bitterly and even furiously against his luxuriousness,
his love of dress, his vanity, his immorality, and his
proved incompetence as soldier and statesman. He
was accused of having poisoned Lords Hamilton,
Lennox, Southampton, Oxford, even James I. himself. He had sat in his boat, out of the reach of
danger, while his soldiers perished under the guns of
Ré. He had corrupted the chastest women in England
by means of the love-philtre which Dr. Lambe concocted for him. In a word, the air was full of the
darkest and dreadest accusations.

Lambe's connection with the Duke brought on a
catastrophe which his magical art failed to foresee or
prevent. He was returning, one summer evening—it
was June 13—from the play at the Fortune Theatre,
when he was recognised by a company of London
prentices. With a fine scent for the game, they
crowded round the unfortunate magician, and hooted
at him as the Duke's devil, hustling him to and fro,
and treating him with cruel roughness. To save
himself from further violence, he hired some sailors
to escort him to a tavern in Moorgate Street, where
he supped. On going forth again, he found that
many of his persecutors lingered about the door; and,
bursting into a violent rage, he threatened them with
his vengeance, and told them 'he would make them

dance naked.' Still guarded by his sailors, he hurried homeward, with the mob close at his heels, shouting and gesticulating, and increasing every minute both in numbers and fury. In the Old Jewry he turned to face them with his protectors; but this movement of defence, construed into one of defiance, stimulated the passions of the populace to an ungovernable pitch; they made a rush at him, from which he took refuge in the Windmill tavern. A volley of stones smashed against pane and door; and with shouts, screams, and yells, they demanded that he should be given up. But the landlord, a man of courage and humanity, would not throw the poor wretch to his pursuers as the huntsman throws the captured fox to the fangs of his hounds. He detained him for some time, and then he provided him with a disguise before he would suffer him to leave. The precaution was useless, for hate is keen of vision: the man was recognised; the pursuit was resumed, and he was hunted through the streets, pale and trembling with terror, his dress disordered and soiled, until he again sought an asylum. The master of this house, however, fell into a paroxysm of alarm, and dismissed him hastily, with four constables as a body-guard. But what could these avail against hundreds? They were swept aside—the doctor, bleeding and exhausted, was flung to the ground, and sticks and stones rained blows upon him until he was no longer able to ask for mercy. One of his eyes was beaten out of its socket; and when he was rescued at length by a posse of constables and soldiers, and conveyed to the Compter prison, it was a dying man who was borne unconscious across its threshold.

Such was the miserable ending of Dr. Lambe. Charles I. was much affected when he heard of it; for he saw that it was a terrible indication of the popular hostility against Lambe's patron. The murderers had not scrupled to say that if the Duke had been there they would have handled him worse; they would have minced his flesh, so that every one of them might have had a piece. Summoning to his presence the Lord Mayor and Aldermen, the King bade them discover the offenders; and when they failed in what was an impossible task, he imposed a heavy fine upon the City.

The ballad-writers of the day found in the magician's fate an occasion for attacking Buckingham: one of them, commenting on his supposed contempt for Parliament, puts the following arrogant defiance into his mouth:

> ' Meddle with common matters, common wrongs,
> To th' House of Commons common things belong. . .
> Leave him the oar that best knows how to row
> And State to him that the best State doth know. . .
> Though Lambe be dead, *I'll* stand, and you shall see
> I'll smile at them that can but bark at me.'

CHAPTER V.

THE LAST OF THE ENGLISH MAGICIANS: WILLIAM LILLY.

'Lilly was a prominent, and, in the opinion of many of his contemporaries, a very important personage in the most eventful period of English history. He was a principal actor in the farcical scenes which diversified the bloody tragedy of civil war; and while the King and the Parliament were striving for mastery in the field, he was deciding their destinies in the closet. The weak and the credulous of both parties who sought to be instructed in "destiny's dark counsels," flocked to consult the "wily Archimagus," who, with exemplary impartiality, meted out victory and good fortune to his clients, according to the extent of their faith and the weight of their purses. A few profane Cavaliers might make his name the burthen of their malignant rhymes—a few of the more scrupulous among the saints might keep aloof in sanctified abhorrence of the "Stygian sophister"— but the great majority of the people lent a willing and reverential ear to his prophecies and prognostications. Nothing was too high or too low, too mighty or too insignificant, for the grasp of his genius. The stars, his informants, were as communicative on the most trivial as on the most important subjects. If a scheme was set on foot to rescue the King, or to retrieve a stray trinket; to restore the royal authority, or to make a frail damsel an honest woman; to cure the nation of anarchy, or a lap-dog of a surfeit —William Lilly was the oracle to be consulted. His almanacks were spelled over in the tavern, and quoted in the Senate; they nerved the arm of the soldier, and rounded the period of the orator. The fashionable beauty, dashing along in her calash from

St. James's or the Mall, and the prim starched dame from Watling Street or Bucklersbury, with a staid foot-boy, in a plush jerkin, plodding behind her—the reigning toast among "the men of wit about town," and the leading groaner in a tabernacle concert— glided alternately into the study of the trusty wizard, and poured into his attentive ear strange tales of love, or trade, or treason. The Roundhead stalked in at one door, whilst the Cavalier was hurried out at the other.

'The confessions of a man so variously consulted and trusted, if written with the candour of a Cardan or a Rousseau, would indeed be invaluable. The "Memoirs of William Lilly, though deficient in this particular, yet contain a variety of curious and interesting anecdotes of himself and his contemporaries, which, when the vanity of the writer or the truth of his art is not con- cerned, may be received with implicit credence.

'The simplicity and apparent candour of his narrative might induce a hasty reader of this book to believe him a well-meaning but somewhat silly personage, the dupe of his own speculations— the deceiver of himself as well as of others. But an attentive examination of the events of his life, even as recorded by himself, will not warrant so favourable an interpretation. His systematic and successful attention to his own interest, his dexterity in keeping on "the windy side of the law," his perfect political pliability, and his presence of mind and fertility of resources when entangled in difficulties, indicate an accomplished impostor, not a crazy enthusiast. It is very possible and probable that, at the outset of his career, he was a real believer in the truth and lawfulness of his art, and that he afterwards felt no inclination to part with so pleasant and so profitable a delusion. . . Of his success in deception, the present narrative exhibits abundant proofs. The number of his dupes was not confined to the vulgar and illiter- ate, but included individuals of real worth and learning, of hostile parties and sects, who courted his acquaintance and respected his predictions. His proceedings were deemed of sufficient import- ance to be twice made the subject of a Parliamentary inquiry; and even after the Restoration—when a little more scepticism, if not more wisdom, might have been expected—we find him examined by a Committee of the House of Commons respecting his foreknowledge of the Great Fire of London. We know not whether it "should more move our anger or our mirth" to see our assemblage of British Senators—the contemporaries of

Hampden and Falkland, of Milton and Clarendon, in an age which moved into action so many and such mighty energies—gravely engaged in ascertaining the cause of a great national calamity from the prescience of a knavish fortune-teller, and puzzling their wisdoms to interpret the symbolical flames which blazed in the misshapen woodcuts of his oracular publications.

'As a set-off against these honours may be mentioned the virulent and unceasing attacks of almost all the party scribblers of the day; but their abuse he shared in common with men whose talents and virtues have outlived the malice of their contemporaries.'—*Retrospective Review.*

WILLIAM LILLY was born at Diseworth, in Leicestershire, on May 1, 1602. He came of an old and reputable family of the yeoman class, and his father was at one time a man of substance, though, from causes unexplained, he fell into a state of great impoverishment. William from the first was intended to be a scholar, and at the age of eleven was sent to the grammar-school at Ashby-de-la-Zouch, where he made a fair progress in his classical studies. In his sixteenth year he began to be much troubled in his dreams regarding his chances of future salvation, and felt a large concern for the spiritual welfare of his parents. He frequently spent the night in weeping and praying, and in an agony of fear lest his sins should offend God. That in this exhibition of early piety he was already preparing for his career of self-hypocrisy and deception, I will not be censorious enough to assert; but in after-life his conscience was certainly much less sensitive, and he ceased to trouble himself about the souls of any of his kith and kin.

He was about eighteen when the collapse of his father's circumstances compelled him to leave school.

He had used his time and opportunities so well that he had gained the highest form, and the highest place on that form. He spoke Latin as readily as his native tongue; could improvise verses upon any theme—all kinds of verses, hexameter, pentameter, phalenciac, iambic, sapphic—so that if any ingenious youth came from remote schools to hold public disputations, Lilly was always selected as the Ashby-de-la-Zouch champion, and in that capacity invariably won distinction. 'If any minister came to examine us,' he said, 'I was brought forth against him, nor would I argue with him unless in the Latin tongue, which I found few could well speak without breaking Priscian's head; which, if once they did, I would complain to my master, *Non bene intelliget linguare Latinam, nec prorsus loquitur.* In the derivation of words, I found most of them defective; nor, indeed, were any of them good grammarians. All and every of those scholars who were of my form and standing went to Cambridge, and proved excellent divines; only I, poor William Lilly, was not so happy; fortune then frowning upon my father's present condition, he not in any capacity to maintain me at the University.'

The *res angustæ domi* pressing heavily upon the quick-witted, ingenious, and active young fellow, he set forth—as so many Dick Whittingtons have done before and since—to make his fortune in London City. His purse held only 20s., with which he purchased a new suit—hose, doublets, trunk, and the like—and with a donation from his friends of 10s., he took leave of his father ('then in Leicester gaol for debt') on April 4th, and tramping his way to London, in company with 'Bradshaw the carrier,' arrived there on the 9th. When he had gratified the carrier and his servants, his capital was reduced to 7s. 6d. in money, a suit of clothes on his back, two shirts, three bands, one pair of shoes, and as many stockings. The master to whom he had been recommended— Leicestershire born, like himself—a certain Gilbert Wright, received him kindly, purchasing for him a new cloak—a welcome addition to Lilly's scanty wardrobe; and Lilly then settled down, contentedly enough, to his laborious duties, though they were hardly of a kind to gratify the tastes of an earnest scholar. 'My work,' he says, 'was to go before my master to church; to attend my master when he went abroad; to make clean his shoes; sweep the street; help to drive bucks when he washed; fetch water in a tub from the Thames (I have helped to carry eighteen tubs of water in one morning); weed the garden ; all manner of drudgeries I willingly performed; scrape trenchers,' etc.

In 1624 his mistress (he says) died of cancer in the breast, and he came into possession—by way of legacy, I suppose—of a small scarlet bag belonging to her, which contained some rare and curious things. Among others, several sigils, amulets, or charms: some of Jupiter in trine, others of the nature of Venus; some of iron, and one of gold—pure angel gold, of the bigness of a thirty-shilling piece of King

James's coinage. In the circumference, on one side, was engraven, *Vicit Leo de tribu Judæ Tetragrammaton*, and within the middle a holy lamb. In the circumference on the obverse side were Amraphel and three $^+_+{}^+$, and in the centre, *Sanctus Petrus Alpha et Omega.*

According to Lilly, this sigil was framed under the following circumstances :

'His mistress's former husband travelling into Sussex, happened to lodge in an inn, and to lie in a chamber thereof, wherein, not many months before, a country grazier had lain, and in the night cut his own throat. After this night's lodging he was perpetually, and for many years, followed by a spirit, which vocally and articulately provoked him to cut his throat. He was used frequently to say, "I defy thee, I defy thee," and to spit at the spirit. This spirit followed him many years, he not making anybody acquainted with it; at last he grew melancholy and discontented, which being carefully observed by his wife, she many times hearing him pronounce, "I defy thee," desired him to acquaint her with the cause of his distemper, which he then did. Away she went to Dr. Simon Forman, who lived then in Lambeth, and acquaints him with it; who having framed this sigil, and hanged it about his neck, he wearing it continually until he died, was never more molested by the spirit. I sold the sigil for thirty-two shillings, but transcribed the words *verbatim* as I have related.'

Lilly continued some time longer in the service of Master Gilbert Wright. When the plague broke out in London in 1625, he, with a fellow-servant, was left in charge of his employer's house. He seems to have taken things easily enough, notwithstanding the sorrow and suffering that surrounded him on every side. Purchasing a bass-viol, he hired a master to instruct him in playing it ; the intervals he spent in bowling in Lincoln's Inn Fields, with Wat the

Cobbler, Dick the Blacksmith, and such-like companions. 'We have sometimes been at our work at six in the morning, and so continued till three or four in the afternoon, many times without bread or drink all that while. Sometimes I went to church and heard funeral sermons, of which there was then great plenty. At other times I went early to St. Antholin's, in London, where there was every morning a sermon. The most able people of the whole city and suburbs were out of town ; if any remained, it were such as were engaged by parish officers to remain ; no habit of a gentleman or woman continued; the woeful calamity of that year was grievous, people dying in the open fields and in open streets. At last, in August, the bills of mortality so increased, that very few people had thoughts of surviving the contagion. The Sunday before the great bill came forth, which was of five thousand and odd hundreds, there was appointed a sacrament at Clement Danes'; during the distributing whereof I do very well remember we sang thirteen parts of the 119th Psalm. One Jacob, our minister (for we had three that day, the communion was so great), fell sick as he was giving the sacrament, went home, and was buried of the plague the Thursday following.'

Having been led by various circumstances to apply himself to the study of astrology, he sought a guide and teacher in the person of one Master Evans, whom he describes as poor, ignorant, boastful, drunken, and knavish ; he had a character, or reputation, however, for erecting a figure (or horoscope) predicting future events, discovering secrets, restoring stolen goods, and even for raising spirits, when it so pleased him. Of this crafty cheat he relates an extraordinary story. Some time before Lilly became acquainted with him, Lord Bothwell and Sir Kenelm Digby visited him at his lodgings in the Minories, in order that they might enjoy what is nowadays called a spiritualistic séance.' The magician drew the mysterious circle, and placed himself and his visitors within it. He began his invocations ; but suddenly Evans was caught up from the others, and transferred, he knew not how, to Battersea Fields, near the Thames. Next morning a countryman discovered him there, fast asleep, and, having roused him, informed him, in answer to his inquiries, where he was. Evans in the afternoon sent a messenger to his wife, to acquaint her with his safety, and dispel the apprehensions she might reasonably entertain. Just as the messenger arrived, Sir Kenelm Digby also arrived, not un-naturally curious to learn the issue of the preceding day's adventure. This monstrous story Evans told to Lilly, who, I suppose, affected to believe it, and asked him how such an issue chanced to attend on his experiment. Because, the knave replied, in per-forming the invocation rites, he had carelessly omitted the necessary suffumigation, and at this omission the spirit had taken offence. It is evident that the spirits insist on being treated with due regard to etiquette.

Lilly, by the way, records some quaint biographical particulars respecting the astrologers of his time ;

they are not of a nature, however, to elevate our ideas of the profession. One would almost suppose that free intercourse with the inhabitants of the unseen world had an exceptionally bad effect on the morals and manners of the mortals who enjoyed it ; or else the spirits must have had a penchant for low society. Lilly speaks of one William Poole, who was a nibbler at astrological science, and, in addition, a gardener, an apparitor, a drawer of lime, a plasterer, a bricklayer ; in fact, he bragged of knowing no fewer than seventeen trades—such was the versatility of his genius ! It is pleasant to know that this wonderfully clever fellow could condescend to ' drolling,' and even to writing poetry (heaven save the mark!), of which Lilly, in his desire to astonish posterity, has preserved a specimen. Master Poole's rhymes, however, are much too offensively coarse to be transferred to these pages.

This man of many callings died about 1651 or 1652, at St. Mary Overy's, in Southwark, and Lilly quotes a portion of his last will and testament :

'*Item.* I give to Dr. Arder all my books, and one manuscript of my own, worth one hundred of Lilly's Introduction.

'*Item.* If Dr. Arder gives my wife anything that is mine, I wish the D—l may fetch him body and soul.'

Terrified at this uncompromising malediction, the doctor handed over all the deceased conjurer's books and goods to Lilly, who in his turn handed them over to the widow ; and in this way Poole's curse was eluded, and his widow got her rights.

The true name of this Dr. Arder, it seems, was

Richard Delahay. He had originally practised as an attorney ; but falling into poverty, and being driven from his Derbyshire home by the Countess of Shrewsbury, he turned to astrology and physic, and looked round about him for patients, though with no very great success. He had at one time known a Charles Sledd, a friend of Dr. Dee, ' who used the crystal, and had a very perfect sight '—in modern parlance, was a good medium.

Dr. Arder often declared to Lilly that an angel had on one occasion offered him a lease of life for a thousand years, but for some unexplained reasons he declined the valuable freehold. However, he outlived the Psalmist's span, dying at the ripe old age of eighty.

A much more famous magician was John Booker, who, in 1632 and 1633, gained a great notoriety by his prediction of a solar eclipse in the nineteenth degree of Aries, 1633, taken out of ' Leuitius de Magnis Conjunctionibus,' namely, ' O Reges et Principes,' etc., both the King of Bohemia and Gustavus, King of Sweden, dying during ' the effects of that eclipse.'

John Booker was born at Manchester, of good parentage, in 1601. In his youth he attained a very considerable proficiency in the Latin tongue. From his early years we may take it that he was destined to become an astrologer—he showed so great a fancy (otherwise inexplicable !) for poring over old almanacks. In his teens he was despatched to London to serve his apprenticeship to a haberdasher

in Lawrence Lane.   But whether he contracted a
distaste for the trade, or lacked the capital to start
on his own account, he abandoned it on reaching
manhood, and started as a writing-master at Hadley,
in Middlesex.   It is said that he wrote singularly
well, 'both Secretary and Roman.'   Later in life he
officiated as clerk to Sir Christopher Clithero, Alderman of London, and Justice of the Peace, and also to
Sir Hugh Hammersley, Alderman, and in these
responsible positions became well known to many
citizens who, like Cowper's John Gilpin, were 'of
credit and renown.'

In star-craft this John Booker was a past master !
His verses upon the months, framed according to their
different astrological significations, 'being blessed
with success, according to his predictions,' made him
known all over England.   He was a man of 'great
honesty,' abhorring any deceit in the art he loved and
studied.   So says Lilly ; but it is certain that if an
astrologer be in earnest, he must deceive himself, if
he do not deceive others.   This Booker had much
good fortune in detecting thefts, and was not less an
adept in resolving love-questions.   His knowledge of
astronomy was by no means limited ; he understood
a good deal of physic ; was a great advocate of the
antimonial cup, whose properties were first discovered by Basil Valentine ; not unskilled in chemistry, though he did not practise it.   He died in the
sweet odour of a good reputation in 1667, leaving
behind him a tolerable library (which was purchased
by Elias Ashmole, the antiquary), a widow, four

children, and the MSS. of his annual prognostications. During the Long Parliament period he published his 'Bellum Hibernicale,' which is described as 'a very sober and judicious book,' and, not long before his death, a small treatise on Easter Day, wherein he displayed a laudable erudition.

Lilly has also something to say about a Master Nicholas Fiske, licentiate in physic, who came of a good old family, and was born near Framlingham, in Suffolk. He was educated for the University, but preferred staying at home, and studying astrology and medicine, which he afterwards practised at Colchester, and at several places in London.

'He was a person very studious, laborious, of good apprehension, and had by his own industry obtained both in astrology, physic, arithmetic, astronomy, geometry, and algebra, singular judgment: he would in astrology resolve horary questions very soundly, but was ever diffident of his own abilities. He was exquisitely skilful in the art of directions upon nativities, and had a good genius in performing judgment thereupon; but very unhappy he was that he had no genius in teaching his scholars, for he never perfected any. His own son Matthew hath often told me that when his father did teach any scholars in his time, they would principally learn of him. *He had Scorpio ascending* (!), and was secretly envious to those he thought had more parts than himself. However, I must be ingenuous, and do affirm that by frequent conversation with him I came to know which were the best authors, and much to enlarge my judgment, especially in the art of directions: he visited me most days once after I became acquainted with him, and would communicate his most doubtful questions unto me, and accept of my judgment therein rather than his own.'

Resuming his own life-story, Lilly records an important purchase which he made in 1634—the

great astrological treatise, the 'Ars Notaria,' a large
parchment volume, enriched with the names and
pictures of those angels which are thought and believed by wise men to teach and instruct in all the
several liberal sciences—as if heaven were a scientific
academy, with the angels giving lectures as professors
of astrology, medicine, mathematics, and the like !
Next he describes how he sought to extend his fame
as a magician by attempting the discovery of a
quantity of treasure alleged to have been concealed
in the cloister of Westminster Abbey ; and having
obtained permission from the authorities, he repaired
thither, one winter night, accompanied by several
gentlemen, and by one John Scott, a supposed expert
in the use of the Mosaical or divining rods.   The
hazel rods were duly played round about the cloister,
and on the west side turned one over the other, a
proof that the treasure lay there.   The labourers,
after digging to a depth of six feet, came upon a
coffin ; but as it was not heavy, Lilly refrained from
opening it, an omission which he afterwards regretted.
From the cloister they proceeded to the Abbey
Church, where, upon a sudden, so fierce, so high, so
blustering and loud a wind burst forth, that they
feared the west end of the church would fall upon
them.   Their rods would not move at all ; the
candles and torches, all but one, were extinguished,
or burned very dimly.   John Scott, Lilly's partner,
was amazed, turned pale, and knew not what to think
or do, until Lilly gave command to dismiss the
demons.   This being done, all was quiet again, and the

party returned home about midnight. 'I could never since be induced,' says Master Lilly, with sublime impertinence, 'to join with any in such-like actions. The true miscarriage of the business,' he adds, 'was by reason of so many people being present at the operation ; for there were about thirty, some laughing, others deriding, *so that if we had not dismissed the demons, I believe most part of the Abbey Church had been blown down !* Secrecy and intelligent operators,' he adds, 'with a strong confidence and knowledge of what they are doing, are best for this work.' They are, at all events, for conspiracy and collusion.

In reading a narrative like this, one finds it not easy to satisfy one's self how far it has been written in good faith, or how far it is compounded of credulity or of conscious deception—how far the writer has unwittingly imposed upon himself, or is knowingly imposing upon the reader. That Lilly should gravely transmit to posterity such a record, if aware that it was an audacious invention, seems hardly credible ; and yet it is still less credible that a man so shrewd and keen-witted should believe in the operations of demons, and in their directing a blast of wind against the Abbey Church because they resented his search for a hidden treasure, to which they at least could have no claim ! As great wit to madness nearly is allied, so is there a dangerous proximity between credulity and imposture, and the man who begins by being a dupe often ends by becoming a knave. Perhaps there are times when the axiom should be reversed.

Lilly's astrological pursuits appear to have affected

his health : he grew lean and haggard, and suffered
much from hypochondria ; so that, at length, he
resolved to try the curative effects of country air,
and removed, in the spring of 1636, to Hersham, a
quiet and picturesque hamlet, near Walton-on-the-
Thames.   He did not give up his London house,
however, until thirty years later (1665), when he
finally settled at Hersham as a country gentleman,
and a person of no small consideration.

Having recovered his health in his rural quarters,
our great magician returned to London, and practised
openly his favourite art.   But a secret intelligence
apprising him that he was not sufficiently an adept,
he again withdrew into the country, where he
remained for a couple of years, immersed, I suppose,
in occult studies.   We may take it that he really
entered on a professional career in 1644, when a
'happy thought' inspired him to bring out the first
yearly issue of his prophetical almanac, or 'Merlinus
Anglicus Junior.'   In his usual abrupt and dis-
jointed style he gives the following account of
his publication : 'I had given, one day, the copy
thereof unto the then Mr. [afterwards Sir Bul-
strode] Whitlocke, who by accident was reading
thereof in the House of Commons.   Ere the Speaker
took the chair, one looked upon it, and so did many,
and got copies thereof ; which, when I heard, I
applied myself to John Booker to license it, for then
he was licenser of all mathematical books. . . . He
wondered at the book, make many impertinent obli-
terations, formed many objections, swore it was not

possible to distinguish betwixt King and Parliament [O shrewd John Booker !]; at last licensed it according to his own fancy. I delivered it unto the printer, who being an arch Presbyterian, had five of the ministry to inspect it, *who could make nothing of it*, but said that it might be printed, for in that I meddled not with their Dagon. The first impression was sold in less than one week. When I presented some [copies] to the members of Parliament, I complained of John Booker, the licenser, who had defaced my book ; they gave me order forthwith to reprint it as I would, and let me know if any durst resist me in the reprinting or adding what I thought fit : so the second time it came forth as I would have it.'

In June, 1644, Lilly published his 'Supernatural Sight,' and also 'The White King's Prophecy,' of which, in three days, eighteen hundred copies were sold. He issued the second volume of his 'Prophetical Merlin,' in which he made use of the King's nativity, and discovering that *his ascendant was approaching to the quadrature of Mars about June,* 1645, delivered himself of this oracular utterance, as ambiguous as any that every fell from the lips of the Pythian priestess :

'If now we fight, a victory stealeth upon us—'

which he afterwards boasted to be a clear prediction of the defeat of Charles I. at Naseby, and, of course, would equally well have served to have explained a royal victory. Whitlocke, in his 'Memorials of Affairs in his own Times,' states that he met the astrologer in the spring of 1645, and jestingly asking him what events were likely to take place, Lilly repeated this prophecy of a victory. He remarks that in 1648 some of Lilly's prognostications 'fell out very strangely, particularly as to the King's fall from his horse about this time.' But it would have been strange if a man so well informed of public affairs, and so shrewd, as William Lilly, had never been right in his forecasts. And a lucky coincidence will set an astrologer up in credit for a long time, his numerous failures being forgotten.

In this same memorable and eventful year he published his 'Starry Messenger,' with an interpretation of three mock suns, or *parhelia*, which had been seen in London on the 29th of May, 1644, King Charles II.'s birthday. Complaint was immediately made to the Parliamentary Committee of Examination that it contained treasonable and scandalous matter. Lilly was summoned before the Committee, but several of his friends were upon it, and voted the charges against him frivolous—as, indeed, they were— so that he met with his usual good fortune, and came off with flying colours.

All the English astrologers of the old school seem to have been startled and confounded by the innovations of this dashing young magician, with his yearly almanacks and political predictions and self-advertisement, especially a certain Mr. William Hodges, who lived near Wolverhampton, and candidly confessed that Lilly did more by astrology than he himself could do by the crystal, though he understood its use as well as any man in England. Though a strong royalist, he could never strike out any good fortune for the King's party—the stars in their courses fought against Charles Stuart. The angels whom he interviewed by means of the crystal were Raphael, Gabriel, and Ariel; but his life was wanting in the purity and holiness which ought to have been conspicuous in a man who was favoured by communications from such high celestial sources.

A proof of his skill is related by Lilly on the authority of Lilly's partner, John Scott.

Scott had some knowledge of surgery and physic; so had Will Hodges, who had at one time been a schoolmaster. Having some business at Wolverhampton, Scott stayed for a few weeks with Hodges, and assisted him in dressing wounds, letting blood, and other chirurgical matters. When on the point of returning to London, he asked Hodges to show him the face and figure of the woman he should marry. Hodges carried him into a field near his house, pulled out his crystal, bade Scott set his foot against his, and, after a pause, desired him to look into the crystal, and describe what he saw there.

'I see,' saith Scott, 'a ruddy-complexioned wench, in a red waistcoat, drawing a can of beer.'

'She will be your wife,' cried Hodges.

'You are mistaken, sir,' rejoined Scott. 'So soon as I come to London, I am engaged to marry a tall gentlewoman in the Old Bailey.'

'You will marry the red gentlewoman,' replied Hodges, with an air of imperturbable assurance.

10

On returning to London, Scott, to his great astonishment, found that his tall gentlewoman had jilted him, and taken to herself another husband. Two years afterwards, in the course of a Kentish journey, he refreshed himself at an inn in Canterbury ; fell in love with its ruddy-complexioned barmaid ; and, when he married her, remembered her red waistcoat, her avocation, and Mr. Hodges 'his crystal.'

An amusing story is told of this man Hodges.

A neighbour of his, who had lost his horse, recovered the animal by acting upon the astrologer's advice. Some years afterwards he unluckily conceived the idea of playing upon the wise man a practical joke, and obtained the co-operation of one of his friends. He had certainly recovered his horse, he said, in the way Hodges had shown him, but it was purely a chance, and would not happen again. ' So come, let us play him a trick. I will leave some boy or other at the town's end with my horse, and we will then call on Hodges and put him to the test.'

This was done, and Hodges said it was true the horse was lost, and would never be recovered.

' I thought what fine skill you had,' laughed the gentleman ; my horse is walking in a lane at the town's end.'

Whereupon Hodges, with an oath, as was his evil habit, asserted that the horse was gone, and that his owner would never see him again. Ridiculing the wise man without mercy, the gentleman departed, and hastened to the town's end, and there, at the appointed place, the boy lay stretched upon the ground, fast asleep, with the bridle round his arm, but the horse was gone !

Back to Hodges hurried the chap-fallen squire, ashamed of his incredulity, and eagerly seeking assistance. But no ; the conjurer swore freely—' Be gone—be gone about your business ; go and look for your horse.' He went and he looked, east and west, and north and south, but his horse saw never more.

Let us next hear what Lilly has to tell us of Dr. Napper, the parson of Great Lindford, in Buckinghamshire, the advowson of which parish belonged to him. He sprang from a good old stock, according to the witness of King James himself. For when his brother, Robert Napper, an opulent Turkey merchant, was to be made a baronet in James's reign, some dispute arose whether he could prove himself a gentleman for three or more descents. 'By my soul,' exclaimed the King, 'I will certify for Napper, that he is of above three hundred years' standing in his family ; all of them, by my soul, gentlemen !' The parson was legitimately and truly master of arts ; his claim to the title of doctor, however, seems to have been dubious. Miscarrying one day in the pulpit, he never after ventured into it, but all his lifetime kept in his house some excellent scholar to officiate for him, allowing him a good salary. Lilly speaks highly of his sanctity of life and knowledge of medicine, and avers that he cured the falling sickness by constellated rings, and other diseases by amulets.

The parents of a maid who suffered severely from the falling sickness applied to him, on one occasion, for a cure. He fashioned for her a constellated ring, upon wearing of which she completely recovered. Her parents chanced to make known the cure to some scrupulous divines, who immediately protested that it was done by enchantment. 'Cast away the ring,' they said ; 'it's diabolical ! God cannot bless you, if you do not cast it away.' The ring was thrown into a well, and the maid was again afflicted with her epilepsy, enduring the old pain and misery for a weary time. At last the parents caused the well to be emptied, and regained the ring, which the maid again made use of, and recovered from her fits. Thus things went on for a year or two, until the Puritan divines, hearing that she had resumed the ring, insisted with her parents until they threw the ring away altogether ; whereupon the fits returned with such violence that they betook themselves to the doctor, told their story, acknowledged their fault, and once more besought his assistance. But he could not be persuaded to render it, observing that those who despised God's mercies were not capable or not worthy of enjoying them.

We do not dismiss this story as entirely apocryphal, knowing that, in the cure or mitigation of nervous diseases, the imagination exercises a wonderful influence. There are well-authenticated instances of 'faith healing' not a whit less extraordinary than this case described by Lilly of the maiden and the ring. It would be trivial, perhaps, to hint that a good many maidens have been cured of some, at least, of their ailments by *a ring*.

In 1646 Lilly printed a collection of prophecies, with the explanation and verification of 'Aquila ; or, The White King's Prophecy,' as also the nativities of Archbishop Laud and the Earl of Strafford, and a learned speech, which the latter intended to have spoken on the scaffold. In the following year he completed his 'Introduction unto Astrology,' or 'Christian Astrology,' and was summoned, along with John Booker, to the head-quarters of Fairfax, at Windsor. They were conveyed thither in great pomp and circumstance, with a coach and four horses, welcomed in hearty fashion, and feasted in a garden where General Fairfax lodged. In the course of their interview with the general he said to them :

'That God had blessed the army with many signal victories, and yet their work was not finished. He hoped God would go along with them until His work was done. They sought not themselves, but the welfare and tranquillity of the good people and whole nation ; and, for that end, were resolved to sacrifice both their lives and their own fortunes. As for the art that Lilly and Booker studied, he hoped it was lawful and agreeable to God's Word : he himself understood it not, but doubted not they both feared God, and therefore had a good opinion of them both.'

Lilly replied :

'My lord, I am glad to see you here at this time. Certainly, both the people of God, and all others of this nation, are very sensible of God's mercy, love, and favour unto them, in directing the Parliament to nominate and elect you General of their armies, a person so religious, so valiant.

'The several unexpected victories obtained under your Excellency's conduct will eternize the same unto all posterity.

'We are confident of God's going along with you and your army until the great work, for which He ordained you both, is fully perfected, which we hope will be the conquering and subversion of your and the Parliament's enemies; and then a quiet settlement and firm peace over all the nation unto God's glory, and full satisfaction of tender consciences.

'Sir, as for ourselves, we trust in God; and, as Christians, we believe in Him. We do not study any art but what is lawful and consonant to the Scriptures, Fathers, and antiquity, which we humbly desire you to believe.'

They afterwards paid a visit to Hugh Peters, the famous Puritan ecclesiastic, who had lodgings in the Castle. They found him reading 'an idle pamphlet,' which he had received from London that morning. 'Lilly, thou art herein,' he exclaimed. 'Are not you there also?' 'Yes, that I am,' he answered.

The stanza relating to Lilly ran as follows :

> 'From th' oracles of the Sibyls so silly,
> The curst predictions of William Lilly,
> And Dr. Sibbald's Shoe-Lane Philly,
> Good Lord, deliver me.'

After much conference with Hugh Peters, and some private discourse betwixt the two 'not to be divulged,' they parted, and Master Lilly returned to London.

In 1647 he published 'The World's Catastrophe,' 'The Prophecies of Ambrose Merlin' (both or which were translated by Elias Ashmole), and 'Trithemius of the Government of the World, by the Presiding Angels'—all three tracts in one volume.

Notwithstanding his services to the Parliamentary cause, Lilly secretly retained a strong attachment towards Charles I., and he was consulted by Mrs. Whorwood, a lady who enjoyed the royal confidence, as to the best place for the concealment of the King, when he escaped from Hampton Court. After the usual sham of 'erecting a figure' had been gone through, Lilly advised that a safe asylum might be found in Essex, about twenty miles from London. 'She liked my judgment very well,' he says, and being herself of sharp judgment, remembered a place in Essex about that distance, where was an excellent house, and all conveniences for his reception. But, either guided by an irresistible destiny, or misled by Ashburnham, whose good faith has been sometimes doubted, he went away in the night-time westward, and surrendered himself to Colonel Hammond, in the Isle of Wight.

With another unfortunate episode in the King's later career, Lilly was also connected. During the King's confinement at Carisbrooke the Kentishmen, in considerable numbers, rose in arms, and joined with Lord Goring ; at the same time many of the best ships revolted, and a movement on behalf of the King was begun among the citizens of London. 'His Majesty then laid his design to escape out of prison by sawing the iron bar of his chamber window ; a small ship was provided, and anchored not far from the Castle, to bring him into Sussex ; horses were provided ready to carry him through Sussex into Kent, so that he might be at the head of the army in Kent, and from thence to march immediately to London, where thousands then would have armed for him.' Lilly was brought acquainted with the plot, and employed a locksmith in Bow Lane to make a saw for cutting asunder the iron bar, and also procured a supply of aqua fortis. But, as everybody knows, the King was unable to force his body through the narrow casement, even after the removal of the bar, and the plot failed.

When the Parliament sent Commissioners into the Island to negotiate with Charles the terms of a concordat, of whom Lord Saye was one, Lady Whorwood again sought Lilly's assistance and advice. After perusing his 'figure,' he told her the Commissioners would arrive in the Island on such a date; elected a day and hour when the King would receive the Commissioners and their propositions; and as soon as these were read, advised the King to sign them, and in all haste to accompany the Commissioners to London. The army being then far removed from the capital, and the citizens stoutly enraged against the Parliamentary leaders, Charles promised he would do so. But, unfortunately, he allowed Lord Saye to dissuade him from signing the propositions, on the assurance that he had a powerful party both in the House of Lords and the House of Commons, who would see that he obtained more favourable conditions. Thus was lost almost his last chance of retaining his crown, and baffling the designs of his enemies.

Whilst the King, in his last days, was at Windsor Castle, on one occasion, when he was taking the air upon the leads, he looked through Captain Wharton's

'Almanack.' 'My book,' saith he, 'speaks well as to the weather.' A Master William Allen, who was standing by, inquired, 'What saith his antagonist, Mr. Lilly?' 'I do not care for Lilly,' remarked his Majesty, 'he has always been against me,' infusing some bitterness into his expressions. 'Sir,' observed Allen, 'the man is an honest man, and writes but what his art informs him.' 'I believe it,' said his Majesty, 'and that Lilly understands astrology as well as any man in Europe.'

In 1648 the Council of State acknowledged Lilly's services with a grant of £50, and a pension of £100 a year, which, however, he received for two years only.

In the following January, while the King lay at St. James's House, Lilly began his observations, he tells us, in the following oracular fashion:

'I am serious, I beg and expect justice; either fear or shame begins to question offenders.

'The lofty cedars begin to divine a thundering hurricane is at hand; God elevates man contemptible.

'Our demigods are sensible, we begin to dislike their actions very much in London; more in the country.

'Blessed be God, who encourages His servants, makes them valiant, and of undaunted spirit to go on with His decrees: upon a sudden, great expectations arise, and men generally believe a quiet and calm time draws nigh.'

Our garrulous and egotistical conjurer, who seems really to have believed that he exercised a considerable influence upon the course of events, though his position was no more important than that of the fly upon the wheel, evidently wished to connect these commonplaces with the execution of Charles I. :

'In Christmas holidays,' he writes, 'the Lord Gray of Groby, and Hugh Peters, sent for me to Somerset House, with directions to bring them two of my almanacks. I did so. Peters and he read January's observations. "If we are not fools and knaves," saith he, "we shall do justice." Then they whispered. *I understood not their meaning until his Majesty* was beheaded. They applied what I wrote of justice to be understood of his Majesty, *which was contrary to my intention;* for Jupiter, the first day of January, became direct; and Libra is a sign signifying justice. I implored for justice generally upon such as had cheated in their places, being treasurers and such-like officers. I had not then heard the least intimation of bringing the King unto trial, and yet the first day thereof I was casually there, it being upon a Saturday. For going to Westminster every Saturday in the afternoon, in these times, at Whitehall I casually met Peters. "Come, Lilly, wilt thou go hear the King tried?" "When?" said I. "Now—just now; go with me." I did so, and was permitted by the guard of soldiers to pass up to the King's Bench. Within one quarter of an hour came the judges; presently his Majesty, who spoke excellently well, and majestically, without impediment in the least when he spoke. I saw the silver top of his staff unexpectedly fall to the ground, which was took up by Mr. Rushworth ; and then I heard Bradshaw, the judge, say to his Majesty : " Sir, instead of answering the Court, you interrogate their power, which becomes not one in your condition." These words pierced my heart and soul, to hear a subject thus audaciously to reprehend his Sovereign, who ever and anon replied with great magnanimity and prudence.'

Lilly tells us that during the siege of Colchester he and his fellow-astrologer, Booker, were sent for, to encourage the soldiers by their vaticinations, and in this they succeeded, as they assured them the town would soon be surrendered—which was actually the case. Our prophet, however, if he could have obtained leave to enter the town, would have carried all his sympathies, and all his knowledge of the condition of affairs in the Parliament's army, to Sir Charles Lucas, the Royalist Governor. He had a narrow escape with his life during his sojourn in the camp of the besiegers. A couple of guns had been placed so as to command St. Mary's Church, and had done great injury to it. One afternoon he was standing in the redoubt and talking with the cannoneer, when the latter cried out for everybody to look to himself, as he could see through his glass that there was a piece in the Castle loaded and directed against his work, and ready to be discharged. Lilly ran in hot haste under an old ash-tree, and immediately the cannon-shot came hissing over their heads. 'No danger now,' said the gunner, 'but begone, for there

are five more loading !' And so it was. Two
hours later those cannon were fired, and unluckily
killed the cannoneer who had given Lilly a timely
warning.

The practice of astrology must have been exceedingly lucrative, for Lilly is known to have acquired a
considerable fortune. In 1651 he expended £1,030 in
the purchase of fee-farm rents, equal in value to £120
per annum. And in the following year he bought
his house at Hersham, with some lands and buildings,
for £950. In the same year he published his ' Annus
Tenebrosus,' a title which he chose *not* ' because of the
great obscurity of the solar eclipse,' but in allusion to
' those underhand and clandestine counsels held in
England by the soldiery, of which he would never,
except *in generals*, give information to any Parliament
man.' Unfortunately, Lilly's knowledge was always
embodied ' in generals,' and the misty vagueness of
his vaticinations renders it impossible for the reader
to pin them down to any definite meaning. You
may apply them to all events—or to none. Their
elastic indications of things good and evil may be
made to suit the events of the nineteenth century
almost as well as those of the seventeenth.

Many characters Mr. William Lilly must be owned
to have represented with great success. But that all-
essential one—if we desire to secure the confidence of
our contemporaries, and the respect of posterity—of
an honest man, I fear he was never able to personate
successfully. Of the craft and cunning he could at
times display he records a striking illustration—

evidently with entire satisfaction to himself, and apparently never suspecting that it might not be so favourably regarded by others, and especially by those plain, commonplace people who make no pretensions to hermetic learning or occult knowledge, but have certain unsophisticated ideas as to the laws of morality and fair dealing.

In his 1651 ' Almanack ' he asserted that the Parliament stood upon tottering foundations, and that the soldiery and commonalty would combine against it—a conclusion at which every intelligent onlooker must by that time have arrived, without ' erecting a figure ' or consulting the starry heavens.

This previous attempt at forecasting the future ' lay for a whole week,' says its author, ' in the Parliament House, much criticised by the Presbyterians; one disliking this sentence, another that, and others disliking the whole. In the end a motion was made that it should be examined by a Committee of the House, with instructions to report concerning its errors.

' A messenger attached me by a warrant from that Committee. I had private notice ere the messenger came, and hasted unto Mr. Speaker Lenthall, ever my friend. He was exceeding glad to see me, told me what was done, called for " Anglicus," marked the passages which tormented the Presbyterians so highly. I presently sent for Mr. Warren, the printer, an assured cavalier, obliterated what was most offensive, put in other more significant words, and desired only to have six amended against next morning, which

very honestly he brought me. I told him my design
was to deny the book found fault with, to own only
the six books. I told him I doubted he would be
examined. "Hang them!" said he; "they are all
rogues. I'll swear myself to the devil ere they shall
have an advantage against you, by my oath."

'The day after, I appeared before the Committee.
At first they showed me the true "Anglicus," and
asked if I wrote and printed it.'

Lilly, after pretending to inspect it, denied all
knowledge of it, asserting that it must have been
written with a view to do him injury by some
malicious Presbyterian, at the same time producing
the six amended copies, to the great surprise and per-
plexity of the Committee. The majority, however,
were inclined to send him to prison, and some had
proposed Newgate, others the Gate House, when one
Brown, of Sussex, who had been influenced to favour
Lilly, remarked that neither to Newgate nor the Gate
House were the Parliament accustomed to send their
prisoners, and suggested that the most convenient
and legitimate course would be for the Sergeant-at-
Arms to take this Mr. Lilly into custody.

'Mr. Strickland, who had for many years been the
Parliament's ambassador or agent in Holland, when
he saw how they inclined, spoke thus:

'"I came purposely into the Committee this day
to see the man who is so famous in those parts where
I have so long continued. I assure you his name is
famous over all Europe. I come to do him justice.
A book is produced by us, and said to be his; he

denies it; we have not proved it, yet will commit him. Truly this is great injustice. It is likely he will write next year, and acquaint the whole world with our injustice, and so well he may. It is my opinion, first to prove the book to be his ere he be committed."

' Another old friend of mine spoke thus:

' " You do not know the many services this man hath done for the Parliament these many years, or how many times, in our greatest distresses, on applying unto him, he hath refreshed our languishing expectations; he never failed us of comfort in our most unhappy distresses. I assure you his writings have kept up the spirits both of the soldiery, the honest people of this nation, and many of us Parliament men; and at last, for a slip of his pen (if it were his), to be thus violent against him, I must tell you, I fear the consequence urged out of the book will prove effectually true. It is my counsel to admonish him hereafter to be more wary, and for the present to dismiss him."

' Notwithstanding anything that was spoken on my behalf, I was ordered to stand committed to the Sergeant-at-Arms. The messenger attached my person said I was his prisoner. As he was carrying me away, he was called to bring me again. Oliver Cromwell, Lieutenant-General of the army, having never seen me, caused me to be produced again, when he steadfastly beheld me for a good space, and then I went with the messenger; but instantly a young clerk of that Committee asks the messenger what he

did with me. Where is the warrant? Until that is
signed you cannot seize Mr. Lilly, or shall [not].
Will you have an action of false imprisonment against
you? So I escaped that night, but next day stayed
the warrant. That night Oliver Cromwell went to
Mr. R——, my friend, and said: " What, never a man
to take Lilly's cause in hand but yourself'? None to
take his part but you? He shall not be long there."
Hugh Peters spoke much in my behalf to the Committee, but they were resolved to lodge me in the
Sergeant's custody. One Millington, a drunken
member, was much my enemy, and so was Cawley
and Chichester, a deformed fellow, unto whom I had
done several courtesies.

' First thirteen days I was a prisoner, and though
every day of the Committee's sitting I had a petition
to deliver, yet so many churlish Presbyterians still
appeared I could not get it accepted. The last day
of the thirteen, Mr. Joseph Ash was made chairman,
unto whom my cause being related, he took my petition, and said I should be bailed in despite of them
all, but desired I would procure as many friends as I
could to be there. Sir Arthur Haselrig and Major
Galloway, a person of excellent parts, appeared for me,
and many more of my old friends came in. After two
whole hours' arguing of my cause by Sir Arthur and
Major Galloway, and other friends, the matter came
to this point: I should be bailed, and a Committee
nominated to examine the printer. The order of the
Committee being brought afterwards to him who
should be Chairman, he sent me word, do what I

would, he would see all the knaves hanged, or he would examine the printer. This is the truth of the story.'

Lilly's biographer, however anxious he may be to imitate biographers generally, and whitewash his hero, feels that in this episode of his life the great seer fell miserably below the heroic standard, and was guilty of pusillanimous as well as unveracious and dishonourable conduct. Yet Lilly is evidently unaware of the unfavourable light in which he has shown himself, and ambles along in an easy and well-satisfied mood, as if to the sound of universal applause.

On February 26, 1654, Lilly lost his second wife, and I regret to say he seems to have borne the loss with astonishing equanimity. On April 20 Cromwell expelled from the House our astrologer's great enemies, the Parliament men, and thereby won his most cordial applause. He breaks out, indeed, into a burst of devotional praise—Gloria Patri—as if for some special and never-to-be-forgotten mercy. A German physician, then resident in London, sent to him the following epigram:

Strophe Alcaica: Generoso Domino Gulielmo Lillio Astrologo, de dissoluto super Parliamento:

' Quod calculasti Sydere prævio,
Miles peregit numine conscio;
Gentis videmus nunc Senatum
Marti togaque gravi leviatum.'

His widower's weeds, if he ever wore them, he soon discarded, marrying his third wife in October,

11

eight months after the decease of his second. This, his latest partner and helpmate, was signified in his nativity, he says, by *Jupiter in Libra*, which seems to have been a great comfort to him, and perhaps to his wife also. 'Jupiter in Libra' sounds as well, indeed, as 'that blessed word, Mesopotamia.'

In reference to the restoration of Charles II., in 1660, Lilly unearths an old prophecy attributed to Ambrose Merlin, and written, he says, 990 years before.

'He calls King James the Lion of Righteousness, and saith, when he died, or was dead, there would reign a noble White King; this was Charles I. The prophet discovers all his troubles, his flying up and down, his imprisonment, his death, and calls him Aquila. What concerns Charles II. is,' says Lilly, 'the subject of our discourse ; in the Latin copy it is thus :

'*Deinde ab Austro veniet cum Sole super ligneos equos, et super spumantem inundationem maris, Pullus Aquilæ navigans in Britanniam.*

'*Et applicans statim tunc altam domum Aquilæ sitiens, et cito aliam sitiet.*

'*Deinde Pullus Aquilæ nidificabit in summa rupe totius Britanniæ : nec juvenis occidet, nec ad senem vivet.*'

This, in an old copy, is Englished thus :

'After then shall come through the south with the sun, on horse of tree, and upon all waves of the sea, the Chicken of the Eagle, sailing into Britain, and arriving anon to the house of the Eagle, he shall show fellowship to these beasts.

'After, the Chicken of the Eagle shall nestle in the highest rock of all Britain : nay, he shall nought be slain young ; nay, he nought come old.'

Master William Lilly then supplies an explanation, or, as he calls it, a verification, of these venerable predictions. We shall give it in his own words :

'His Majesty being in the Low Countries when the Lord-General had restored the secluded members, the Parliament sent part of the royal navy to bring him for England, which they did in May, 1660. Holland is east from England, so he came with the sun ; but he landed at Dover, a port in the south part of England. Wooden horses are the English ships.

'*Tunc nidificabit in summo rupium.*

'The Lord-General, and most of the gentry in England, met him in Kent, and brought him unto London, then to White-hall.

'Here, by the highest Rooch (some write Rock) is intended London, being the metropolis of all England.

'Since which time, unto this very day, I write this story, he hath reigned in England, and long may he do hereafter.' (Written on December 20, 1667.)

Lilly quotes a prophecy, printed in 1588, in Greek characters, which exactly deciphered, he says, the long troubles the English nation endured from 1641 to 1660, but he omits to tell us where he saw it, or who was its author. It ended in the following mysterious fashion :

'And after that shall come a dreadful dead man, and with him a royal G' (it is gamma, Γ, in the Greek, intending C in the Latin, being the third letter in the alphabet), 'of the best blood in the world, and he shall have the crown, and shall set England in the right way, and put out all heresies.'

To a man who could read the secrets of the stars, and divine the events of the future, there was, of course, nothing mysterious or obscure in these lines, and their meaning he had no difficulty in determining. Monkery having been extinguished above eighty or ninety years, and the Lord-General's name being *Monk*, what more clear than that he must be the 'dead man'? And as for the royal Γ, or C, who came of the best blood of the world, it was evident that he could be no other than Charles II.? The unlearned reader, who has neither the stars nor the crystal to assist him, will, nevertheless, arrive at the conclusion that if prophecies can be interpreted in this liberal fashion, there is nothing to prevent even him from assuming the *rôle* of an interpreter !

But let it be noted that, according to our brilliant magicians, 'these two prophecies were not given vocally by the angels, but by inspection of the crystal in types and figures, or by apparition, the circular way, where, at some distance, the angels appear, representing by forms, shapes, and motions, what is demanded. It is very rare, yea, even in our days, for any operator or master to have the angels speak articulately ; *when they do speak, it is like the Irish, much in the throat.*'

In June, 1660, Lilly was summoned before a Committee of the House of Commons to answer to an inquiry concerning the executioner employed to behead Charles I. Here is his account of the examination :

' God's providence appeared very much for me that day, for walking in Westminster Hall, Mr. Richard Pennington, son to my old friend, Mr. William Pennington, met me, and inquiring the cause of my being there, said no more, but walked up and down the Hall, and related my kindness to his father unto very many Parliament men of Cheshire and Lancashire, Yorkshire, Cumberland, and those northern counties, who numerously came up into the Speaker's chamber, and bade me be of good comfort ; at last he meets Mr. Weston, one of the three [the two others were Mr. Prinn and Colonel King] unto whom my matter was referred for examination, who told Mr. Pennington that he came purposely to punish me, and would be bitter against me ; but hearing it related, namely, my singular kindness and preservation of old Mr. Pennington's estate, to the value of £6,000 or £7,000, "I will do him all the good I can," says he. "I thought he had never done any good ; let me see him, and let him stand behind me where I sit." I did so. At my first appearance, many of the young members affronted me highly, and demanded several scurrilous questions. Mr. Weston held a paper before his mouth ; bade me answer nobody but Mr. Prinn ; I obeyed his command, and saved myself much trouble thereby ; and when Mr. Prinn put any difficult or doubtful query unto me, Mr. Weston prompted me with a fit answer. At last, after almost one hour's tugging, I desired to be fully heard what I could say as to the person who cut Charles I.'s head off. Liberty being given me to speak, I related what follows, viz. :

'That the next Sunday but one after Charles I. was beheaded, Robert Spavin, Secretary unto Lieutenant-General Cromwell at that time, invited himself to dine with me, and brought Anthony Peirson and several others along with him to dinner: that their principal discourse all dinner-time was only who it was that beheaded the King. One said it was the common hangman; another, Hugh Peters; others also were nominated, but none concluded. Robert Spavin, so soon as dinner was done, took me by the hand, and carried me to the south window: saith he, " These are all mistaken, they have not named the man that did the fact: it was Lieutenant-Colonel Joyce. I was in the room when he fitted himself for the work, stood behind him when he did it; when done, went in again with him. There is no man knows this but my master, namely, Cromwell, Commissary Ireton, and myself." " Doth not Mr. Rushworth know it?" said I. " No, he doth not know it," saith Spavin. The same thing Spavin since had often related unto me when we were alone. Mr. Prinn did, with much civility, make a report hereof in the House; yet Norfolk, the Serjeant, after my discharge, kept me two days longer in arrest, purposely to get money of me. He had six pounds, and his messenger forty shillings; and yet I was attached but upon Sunday, examined on Tuesday, and then discharged, though the covetous Serjeant detained me until Thursday. By means of a friend, I cried quittance with Norfolk, which friend was to pay him his salary at that time, and abated Norfolk three pounds, which he spent every penny at one dinner, without inviting the wretched Serjeant; but in the latter end of the year, when the King's Judges were arraigned at the Old Bailey, Norfolk warned me to attend, believing I could give information concerning Hugh Peters. At the Sessions I attended during its continuance, but was never called or examined. There I heard Harrison, Scott, Clement, Peters, Harker, Scroop, and others of the King's Judges, and Cook the Solicitor, who excellently defended himself; I say, I did hear what they could say for themselves, and after heard the sentence of condemnation pronounced against them by the incomparably modest and learned Judge Bridgman, now Lord Keeper of the Great Seal of England.'

In spite of Spavin's circumstantial statement, as recorded by Lilly, it is now conclusively established that the executioner of Charles I. was Richard Brandon, the common executioner, who had previously beheaded the Earl of Strafford. It is said that he was afterwards seized with poignant remorse for the act, and died in great mental suffering. His body was carried to the grave amid the execrations of an excited and angry populace.

Though our astrologer, as we have seen, was at

heart a Royalist, his services towards the Parliamentary cause were sufficiently conspicuous to expose him after the Restoration to a good deal of persecution ; and he found it advisable to sue out his pardon under the Great Seal, which cost him, as he takes care to tell us, £13 6s. 8d.

He claimed to have foreseen the Restoration, and all the good things which flowed—or were expected to have flowed—from that 'auspicious event.' In page 111 of his 'Prophetical Merlin,' published in 1644, dwelling upon three sextile aspects of Saturn and Jupiter made in 1659 and 1660, he says: 'This, their friendly salutation, comforts us in England: every man now possesses his own vineyard; our young youth grow up unto man's estate, and our old men live their full years; our nobles and gentlemen rest again ; our yeomanry, many years disconsolated, now take pleasure in their husbandry. The merchant sends out ships, and hath prosperous returns ; the mechanic hath quick trading ; here is almost a new world ; new laws, new lords. Now any county of England shall shed no more tears, but rejoice with and in the many blessings God gives or affords her annually.'

He also wrote, he says, to Sir Edward Walker, Garter King-at-Arms in 1659, when, by the way, the restoration of Charles II. was an event that loomed in the near future, and was anticipated by every man of ordinary political sagacity : 'Tu, Dominusque vester videbitis Angliam, infra duos annis ' (You and your Lord shall see England within two years). 'For

in 1662,' adds the arch impostor, in his strange
astrological jargon, ' his moon came by direction to
the body of the sun.'

' *But he came in upon the ascendant directed unto the
trine of Sol and antiscion of Jupiter.*'

No doubt he did. Who would presume to contradict our English Merlin?

In 1663 and 1664 he served as churchwarden—
surely the first and last astrologer who filled that respectable office—of Walton-upon-Thames, settling as
well as he could the affairs of that ' distracted parish'
upon his own charges.

An absurdly frivolous accusation was brought
against him in the year 1666. He was once more summoned before a Committee of the House of Commons,
because in his book, ' Monarchy or No Monarchy,'
published in 1651, he had introduced sixteen plates,
of which the eighth represented persons digging
graves, with coffins and other emblems of mortality,
and the thirteenth a city in flames. Hence it was
inferred that he must have had something to do with
the Great Fire which had destroyed so large a part of
London, if not with the Plague, which had almost
depopulated it. The chairman, Sir Robert Burke,
on his coming into the Committee's presence, addressed him thus:

' Mr. Lilly, this Committee thought fit to summon
you to appear before them this day, to know if you
can say anything as to the cause of the late Fire, or
whether there might be any design therein. You
are called the rather hither, because in a book of

yours, long since printed, you hinted some such thing by one of your hieroglyphics.'

Whereto Mr. Lilly replied, with a firm assumption of superior wisdom and oracular knowledge :

'May it please your Honours,—After the beheading of the late King, considering that in the three subsequent years the Parliament acted nothing which concerned the settlement of the nation in peace; and seeing the generality of people dissatisfied, the citizens of London discontented, the soldiery prone to mutiny, I was desirous, according to the best knowledge God had given me, to make inquiry by the art I studied, what might from that time happen unto the Parliament and nation in general. At last, having satisfied myself as well as I could, and perfected my judgment therein, I thought it most convenient to signify my intentions and conceptions thereof in Forms, Shapes, Types, Hieroglyphics, etc., without any commentary, that so my judgment might be concealed from the vulgar, and made manifest only unto the wise. I herein imitating the examples of many wise philosophers who had done the like.'

'Sir Robert,' saith one, 'Lilly is yet *sub vestibulo.*'

'Having found, sir,' continued Lilly, 'that the city of London should be sadly afflicted with a great plague, and not long after with an exorbitant Fire, I framed those two hieroglyphics as represented in the book, which in effect have proved very true.'

'Did you foresee the year ?' inquired a member of the Committee.

'I did not,' said Lilly, 'nor was desirous; of that

I made no scrutiny. Now, sir,' he proceeded, 'whether there was any design of burning the city, or any employed to that purpose, I must deal ingenuously with you, that since the Fire, I have taken much pains in the search thereof, but cannot or could not give myself any the least satisfaction therein. I conclude, that it was the only finger of God; but what instruments he used thereunto, I am ignorant.'

In 1665 Lilly finally left London, and settling down at Hersham, applied himself to the study of medicine, in which he arrived at so competent a degree of knowledge, assisted by diligent observation and experiment, that, in October, 1670, on a testimonial from two physicians of the College in London, he obtained from the Archbishop of Canterbury a license to practise. In his new profession this clever, plausible fellow was, of course, successful. Every Saturday he rode to Kingston, whither the poorer sort flocked to him from all the countryside, and he dispensed his advice and prescriptions freely and without charge. From those in a better social position he now and then took a shilling, and sometimes half a crown, if it were offered to him; but he never demanded a fee. And, indeed, his charity towards the poor seems to have been real and unaffected. He displayed the greatest care in considering and weighing their particular cases, and in applying proper remedies for their infirmities—a line of conduct which gained him deserved popularity.

Gifted with a robust constitution, he enjoyed good health far on into old age. He seems to have had no serious illness until he was past his seventy-second birthday, and from this attack he recovered completely. In November, 1675, he was less fortunate, a severe attack of fever reducing him to a condition of great physical weakness, and so affecting his eyesight that thenceforward he was compelled to employ the services of an amanuensis in drawing up his annual astrological budget. After an attack of dysentery, in the spring of 1681, he became totally blind ; a few weeks later he was seized with paralysis ; and on June 9 he passed away, 'without any show of trouble or pangs.'

He was buried, on the following evening, in the chancel of Walton Church, where Elias Ashmole, a month later, placed a slab of fair black marble ('which cost him six pounds four shillings and sixpence '), with the following epitaph, in honour of his departed friend: 'Ne Oblivione conteretur Urna GULIELMI LILLII, Astrologi Peritissimi Qui Fatis cessit, Quinto Idus Junii, Anno Christi Juliano, MDCLXXXI, Hoc illi posuit amoris Monumentum ELIAS ASHMOLE, Armiger.' There is a pagan flavour about the phrases ' Qui Fatis cessit,' and ' Quinto Idus Junii,' and they read oddly enough within the walls of a Christian church.

There are two sides to every shield. As regards our astrologer, the last of the English magicians who held a position of influence, let us first take the silver side, as presented in the eulogistic verse of Master

George Smalridge, scholar at Westminster. Thus it is that he describes his hero's capacity and potentiality. 'Our prophet's gone,' he exclaims in lugubrious tones—

> 'No longer may our ears
> Be charmed with musick of th' harmonious spheres:
> Let sun and moon withdraw, leave gloomy night
> To show their Nuncio's fate, who gave more light
> To th' erring world, than all the feeble rays
> Of sun or moon; taught us to know those days
> Bright Titan makes; followed the hasty sun
> Through all his circuits; knew the unconstant moon,
> And more constant ebbings of the flood;
> And what is most uncertain, th' factious brood,
> Flowing in civil broils: by the heavens could date
> The flux and reflux of our dubious state.
> He saw the eclipse of sun, and change of moon
> He saw; but seeing would not shun his own:
> Eclipsed he was, that he might shine more bright,
> And only changed to give a fuller light.
> He having viewed the sky, and glorious train
> Of gilded stars, scorned longer to remain
> In earthly prisons: could he a village love
> Whom the twelve houses waited for above?'

The other side of the shield is turned towards us by Butler, who, in his 'Hudibras,' paints Lilly with all the dark enduring colours which a keen wit could place at the disposal of political prejudice. When Hudibras is unable to solve 'the problems of his fate,' Ralpho, his squire, advises him to apply to the famous thaumaturgist. He says:

> 'Not far from hence doth dwell
> A cunning man, hight Sidrophel,
> That deals in Destiny's dark counsels,
> And sage opinions of the Moon sells;
> To whom all people, far and near,
> On deep importances repair:

When brass and pewter hap to stray,
And linen slinks out o' the way;
When geese and pullen are seduced,
And sows of sucking pigs are choused;
When cattle feel indisposition,
And need th' opinion of physician;
When murrain reigns in hogs or sheep,
And chickens languish of the pip;
When yeast and outward means do fail,
And have no pow'r to work on ale;
When butter does refuse to come,
And love proves cross and humoursome;
To him with questions, and with urine,
They for discov'ry flock, or curing.'

After this humorous *reductio ad absurdum* of Lilly's pretensions as an astrologer, the satirist proceeds to allude to his dealings with the Puritan party:

'Do not our great Reformers use
This Sidrophel to forebode news;
To write of victories next year,
And castles taken, yet i' th' air?
Of battles fought at sea, and ships
Sunk, two years hence, the last eclipse?'

The satirist then devotes himself to a minute exposure of Lilly's pretensions:

'He had been long t'wards mathematics,
Optics, philosophy, and statics;
Magic, horoscopy, astrology,
And was old dog at physiology;
But as a dog that turns the spit
Bestirs himself, and plies his feet
To climb the wheel, but all in vain,
His own weight brings him down again,
And still he's in the self-same place
Where at his setting out he was;
So in the circle of the arts
Did he advance his nat'ral parts . . .

> Whate'er he laboured to appear,
> His understanding still was clear ;
> Yet none a deeper knowledge boasted,
> Since old Hodge Bacon and Bob Grosted.'

(Robert Grostête, Bishop of Lincoln [*temp.*
Henry III.], whose learning procured him among
the ignorant the reputation of being a conjurer.)

> ' He had read Dee's prefaces before
> The Dev'l and Euclid o'er and o'er ;
> And all th' intrigues 'twixt him and Kelly,
> Lascus, and th' Emperor, would tell ye ;
> But with the moon was more familiar
> Than e'er was almanack well-willer ;
> Her secrets understood so clear,
> That some believed he had been there ;
> Knew when she was in fittest mood
> For cutting corns or letting blood . . .'

Continuing his enumeration of the conjurer's
various and versatile achievements, the poet says
he can—

> ' Cure warts and corns with application
> Of med'cines to th' imagination ;
> Fright agues into dogs, and scare
> With rhymes the toothache and catarrh ;
> Chase evil spirits away by dint
> Of sickle, horse-shoe, hollow flint ;
> Spit fire out of a walnut-shell,
> Which made the Roman slaves rebel ;
> And fire a mine in China here
> With sympathetic gunpowder.
> He knew whats'ever's to be known,
> But much more than he knew would own . . .
> How many diff'rent specieses
> Of maggots breed in rotten cheese ;
> And which are next of kin to those
> Engendered in a chandler's nose ;
> Or those not seen, but understood,
> That live in vinegar and wood.'

In the course of the long dialogue that takes place
between Hudibras and the astrologer, Butler con-
trives to introduce a clever and trenchant exposure
of the follies and absurdities, the impositions and
assumptions, of the art of magic. With reference to
the pretensions of astrologers, he observes that—

> 'There's but the twinkling of a star
> Between a man of peace and war,
> A thief and justice, fool and knave,
> A huffing officer and a slave,
> A crafty lawyer and pick-pocket,
> A great philosopher and a blockhead,
> A formal preacher and a player,
> A learn'd physician and man-slayer;
> As if men from the stars did suck
> Old age, diseases, and ill-luck,
> Wit, folly, honour, virtue, vice,
> Trade, travel, women, claps, and dice;
> And draw, with the first air they breathe,
> Battle and murder, sudden death.
> Are not these fine commodities
> To be imported from the skies,
> And vended here among the rabble,
> For staple goods and warrantable?
> Like money by the Druids borrowed
> In th' other world to be restored.'

The character of Lilly is to some extent a problem,
and I confess it is not one of easy or direct solution.
As I have already hinted, it is always difficult to draw
the line between conscious and unconscious imposture
—to determine when a man who has imposed upon
himself begins to impose upon others. But was
Lilly self-deceived? Or was he openly and knowingly
a fraud and a cheat? For myself I cannot answer
either question in the affirmative. I do not think he

was entirely innocent of deception, but I also believe that he was not wholly a rogue. I think he had a lingering confidence in the reality of his horoscopes, his figures, his stellar prophecies; though at the same time he did not scruple to trade on the credulity of his contemporaries by assuming to himself a power and a capacity which he did not possess, and knew that he did not possess. Despite his vocation, he seems to have lived decently, and in good repute. The activity of his enemies failed to bring against him any serious charges, and we know that he enjoyed the support of men of light and leading, who would have stood aloof from a common charlatan or a vulgar knave. He was, it is certain, a very shrewd and quick observer, with a keen eye for the signs of the times, and a wide knowledge of human nature; and his success in his peculiar craft was largely due to this alertness of vision, this practical knowledge, and to the ingenuity and readiness with which he made use of all the resources at his command.

NOTE.—DR. DEE'S MAGIC CRYSTAL.

Horace Walpole gives an amusing account of Kelly's famous crystal, and of the useful part it played in a burglary committed at his house in Arlington Street in the spring of 1771. At the time, he was taking his ease at his Strawberry Hill villa, near Teddington, when a courier brought him news of what had occurred. Writing to his friend, Sir Horace Mann, March 22, he says:

'I was a good quarter of an hour before I recollected that it was very becoming to have philosophy enough not to care about what one does care for; if you don't care, there is no philosophy in bearing it. I despatched my upper servant, breakfasted, fed the bantams as usual, and made no more hurry to town than Cincinnatus would if he had lost a basket of turnips. I left in my drawers £270 of bank bills and three hundred guineas, not to mention all my gold and silver coins, some inestimable miniatures, a little plate, and a good deal of furniture, under no guard but that of two maidens. . . .

'When I arrived, my surprise was by no means diminished. I found in three different chambers three cabinets, a large chest, and a glass case of china wide open, the locks not picked, but forced, and the doors of them broken to pieces. You will wonder that this should surprise me, when I had been prepared for it. Oh, the miracle was that I did not find, nor to this time have found, the least thing missing! In the cabinet of modern medals there were, and so there are still, a series of English coins, with downright John Trot guineas, half-guineas, shillings, sixpences, and every kind of current money. Not a single piece was removed. Just so in the Roman and Greek cabinet, though in the latter were some drawers of papers, which they had tumbled and scattered about the floor. A great exchequer desk, that belonged to my father, was in the same room. Not being able to force the lock, the philosophers (for thieves that steal nothing deserve the title much more than Cincinnatus or I) had wrenched a great flapper of brass with such violence as to break it into seven pieces. The trunk contained a new set of chairs of French tapestry, two screens, rolls of prints, and a suit of silver stuff that I had made for the King's wedding. All was turned topsy-turvy, and nothing stolen. The glass case and cabinet of shells had been handled as roughly by these impotent gallants. Another little table with drawers, in which, by the way, the key was left, had been opened too, and a metal standish, that they ought to have taken for silver, and a silver hand-candlestick that stood upon it, were untouched. Some plate in the pantry, and all my linen just come from the wash, had no more charms for them than gold or silver. In short, I could not help laughing, especially as the only two movables neglected were another little table with drawers and the money, and a writing-box with the bank-notes, both in the same room where they made the first havoc. In short, they had broken out a panel in the door of the area, and unbarred and unbolted it, and gone out at the street-door, which they left wide open at five o'clock in the morning. A passenger had found it so, and alarmed the maids, one of whom ran naked into the street, and by her cries waked my Lord Romney, who lives opposite. The poor creature was in fits for two days, but at first, finding my coachmaker's apprentice in the street, had sent him to Mr. Conway, who immediately despatched him to me before he knew how little damage I had received, the whole of which consists in repairing the doors and locks of my cabinets and coffers.

'All London is reasoning on this marvellous adventure, and not one argument presents itself that some other does not contradict. I insist that I have a talisman. You must know that last winter, being asked by Lord Vere to assist in settling Lady Betty Germaine's auction, I found in an old catalogue of her collection this article, " *The Black Stone into which Dr. Dee used to call his spirits.*" Dr. Dee, you must know, was a great conjurer in the days of Queen Elizabeth, and has written a folio of the dialogues he held with his imps. I asked eagerly for this stone; Lord Vere said he knew of no such thing, but if found, it should certainly be at my service. Alas, the stone was gone ! This winter I was again employed by Lord Frederick Campbell, for I am an absolute auctioneer, to do him the same service about his father's (the Duke of Argyll's) collection. Among other odd things, he produced a round piece of shining black marble in a leathern case as big as the crown of a hat, and asked me what that possibly could be ? I screamed out, "Oh, Lord ! I am the only man in England that can tell you ! . . . It is Dr. Dee's ' Black Stone.' " It certainly is; Lady Betty had formerly given away or sold, time out of mind, for she was a thousand years old, that part of the Peterborough collection which contained natural philosophy. So, or since, the Black Stone had wandered into an auction, for the lotted paper was still on it. The Duke of Argyll, who bought everything, bought it. Lord Frederick [Campbell] gave it to me; and if it was not this magical stone, which is only of high-polished coal, that preserved my chattels, in truth I cannot guess what did.'*

At the great Strawberry Hill sale, in 1842, which dispersed the Walpole Collection, it was described in the catalogue as 'a singularly interesting and curious relic of the superstition of our ancestors —the celebrated *Speculum of Kennel Coal*, highly polished, in a leathern case. It is remarkable for having been used to deceive the mob (!) by the celebrated Dr. Dee, the conjurer, in the reign of Queen Elizabeth,' etc.

---

* Horace Walpole (Earl of Orford), ' Letters,' v. 290, *et seq.*

The authorities of the British Museum purchased this 'relic of the superstition of our ancestors' for the sum of twelve guineas. It is neither more nor less than what it has been described, a polished piece of cannel-coal, and thus explains the allusion in Butler's 'Hudibras':

> ' Kelly did all his feats upon
> The devil's looking-glass—a stone.'

CHAPTER VI.

ENGLISH ROSICRUCIANS.

It is not very easy to trace the origin of the Rosicrucian Brotherhood. It is not easy, indeed, to get at the true derivation of the name 'Rosicrucian.' Some authorities refer it to that of the ostensible founder of the society, the mysterious Christian Rosenkreuse, but who can prove that such an individual ever existed? Others borrow it from the Latin word *ros*, dew, and *crux*, a cross, and explain it thus : 'Dew,' of all natural bodies, was esteemed the most powerful solvent of gold ; and 'the cross,' in the old chemical language, signified *light*, because the figure of a cross exhibits at the same time the three letters which form the word *lux*. 'Now, lux is called the seed, or menstruum, of the red dragon; or, in other words, that gross and corporeal light, which, when properly digested and modified, produces gold.' So that, according to this derivation, a Rosicrucian is one who by the intervention and assistance of the 'dew' seeks for 'light'—that is, the philosopher's stone. But such an etymology is evidently too fanciful, and assumes too much to be readily accepted, and we try a third

derivation, namely, from *rosa* and *crux ;* in support
of which may be adduced the oldest official documents of the brotherhood, which style it the ' Broe-
derschafft des Roosen Creutzes,' or Rose-Crucians, or
' Fratres Rosatæ Crucis ;' while the symbol of the
order is ' a red rose on a cross.' Both the rose and
the cross possess a copious emblematic history, and
their choice by a secret society, which clothed its
beliefs and fancies in allegorical language, is by no
means difficult to understand. ' The rose,' says
Eliphas Levi, in his ' Histoire de la Magie,' ' which
from time immemorial has been the symbol of beauty
and life, of love and pleasure, expressed in a mystical
manner all the protestations of the Renaissance. It
was the flesh revolting against the oppression of the
spirit; it was Nature declaring herself to be, like
Grace, the daughter of God ; it was Love refusing to
be stifled by celibacy ; it was Life desiring to be no
longer barren ; it was Humanity aspiring to a natural
religion, full of love and reason, founded on the revelation of the harmonies of existence of which the rose
was for initiates the living and blooming symbol. . . .
The reunion of the rose and the cross—such was the
problem proposed by supreme initiation, and, in effect,
occult philosophy, being the universal synthesis,
should take into account all the phenomena of Being.
It may be doubted, however, whether this ingenious
symbolism has anything at all to do with Rosicrucianism ; but it is not the less a fact that the rose
and the cross were chosen because they were recognised emblems. And probably because the rose typi-

fied secrecy, while the cross was a protest against the tyranny and superstition of the Papacy.

We hear nothing of Rosicrucianism until the beginning of the seventeenth century. The earlier alchemists knew nothing of its theosophic doctrines; and the earlier Rosicrucians did not dabble in alchemy. The connection between the two was established at a later date; when the quest of the 'elixir of life' and the 'philosopher's stone' was grafted upon the mysticism which had taken up the ancient teaching of the Alexandrian Platonists, combining with it much of the allegorical jargon of Paracelsus, and something of the theology of Luther and the German Reformers. The antiquity claimed for the brotherhood in the 'Fama Fraternitatis' is purely a myth. For my own part, I must regard as its virtual founder— though he may not have been its actual initiator— the celebrated Johann Valentine Andreas, who with wide and profound learning united a lively imagina- tion, and was, moreover, a man of pure and lofty purpose. The regeneration of humanity, the extirpa- tion of the vices and follies which had sprung up in the dark shadow of the mediæval Church, was the dream of his life; and it is beyond doubt that he hoped to realize it by secret societies bound together for the purpose of reforming the morals of the age and inspiring men with a love of wisdom. This is proved by three of his acknowledged works, namely, 'Reipublicæ Christianapolitanæ Descriptio,' 'Turris Babel, sive Judiciorum de Fraternitate Rosaceæ Crucis Chaos,' and 'Christianæ Societatis Idea'; and

I venture to think, though Mr. Waite will not have
it so, that the author of these works was also the
author of the 'Fama,' as well as of the 'Confessio
Fraternitatis' and the 'Nuptæ Chymicæ,' in which he
gathered up all the floating dreams and traditions
bearing on his subject, and gave to them a certain
form and order, infusing into them a fascinating
poetical colouring, and inspiring them with his own
idealistic speculations.

'Akin to the school of the ancient Fire-Believers,'
says Ennemoser, 'and of the magnetists of a later
period, of the same cast as those speculators and
searchers into the mysteries of Nature, drawing from
the same well, are the theosophists of the sixteenth
and seventeenth centuries. These practised chemistry,
by which they asserted they could explore the pro-
foundest secrets of Nature. As they strove, above all
earthly knowledge, after the Divine, and sought the
Divine light and fire, through which all men can
acquire the true wisdom, they were called the Fire-
Philosophers (*philosophi per ignem*).' They were
identical with the Rosicrucians, and in the books of
the later Rosicrucians we meet with the same mysticism and transcendental philosophy as in theirs.

Whether we agree in accepting Andreas as the
founder of the order, or as simply its hierophant, we
must admit that the rise of Rosicrucianism dates from
the publication of the 'Fama' and the 'Confessio
Fraternitatis.' They produced an immense sensation,
passed through several editions, and were devoured
by multitudes of eager readers. 'In the library at

Gottingen,' says De Quincey (adapting from Professor Buhle), 'there is a body of letters addressed to the imaginary order of Father Rosy Cross, from 1614 to 1617, by persons offering themselves as members. . . . As certificates of their qualifications, most of the candidates have enclosed specimens of their skill in alchemy and cabalism. . . . Many other literary persons there were at that day who forbore to write letters to the society, but threw out small pamphlets containing their opinions of the order, and of its place of residence.'

It is not my business, however, to write a history of Rosicrucianism. I have desired simply to say so much about its origin as will serve as a preface to my account of the principal English members of the brotherhood. The reader who would know more about its origin and extension, its pretensions and professors, may consult Heckethorn's ' Secret Societies of all Ages and Countries,' Ennemoser's ' History of Magic,' Thomas de Quincey's essay on ' Rosicrucians and Freemasons,' and Arthur Edward Waite's ' Real History of the Rosicrucians.' *

The greatest English Rosicrucian, and most distinguished of the disciples of Paracelsus, was Robert Fludd (or Flood, or De Fluctibus), a man of singular erudition, of great though misdirected capacity, and of a vivid and fertile imagination.

The second son of Sir Thomas Flood, Treasurer of War to Queen Elizabeth, he was born at Milgate

---

* See also Louis Figuier's ' L'Alchimie et les Alchimistes,' a popular and agreeable survey ; and the more erudite work of Professor Buhle.

House, in the parish of Bersted, Kent, in the year
1574. At the age of seventeen he was entered of
St. John's College, Oxford. His father had originally
intended him for a military life, but finding that his
inclinations led him into the peaceful paths of scholarship, he forbore to oppose them, and the youth entered
upon a particular study of medicine, which drew him,
no doubt, into a pursuit of alchemy and chemistry.
Having graduated both in the arts and sciences, he
went abroad, and for six years travelled over France,
Germany, Italy, and Spain, making the acquaintance
of the principal Continental scholars, as well as of the
enthusiasts who belonged to the theosophic school of
the divine Paracelsus, and the adepts who dabbled in
the secrets of the Cabala. Returning to England in
1605, he became a member of the College of Physicians,
and settled down to practise in Coleman Street, London,
where, about 1616, he was visited by the celebrated
German alchemist, Michael Maier.

His active imagination stimulated by his knowledge of the Rosicrucian doctrines, he resolved on
revealing to his countrymen the true light of science
and wisdom. He had already, as a believer in the
theory of magnetism, introduced into England the
celebrated ' weapon salve ' of Paracelsus, which healed
the severest wound by sympathy—not being applied
to the wound itself, but to the weapon or instrument
that had caused it. The recipe, as formulated by
Paracelsus, would hardly be approved by modern
practitioners: ' Take of moss growing on the head of
a thief who has been hanged and left in the air, of

real mummy, of human blood still warm, one ounce each ; of human suet, two ounces ; of linseed-oil, turpentine, and Armenian bole, of each two drachms. Mix together thoroughly in a mortar, and keep the salve in a narrow oblong urn.' This, or, I presume, some similar compound, Fludd tried with success in several cases, and no wonder ; for while the sword was anointed and put away, the wound was well washed and carefully bandaged—a process which has been known to succeed in our own day without the intervention of any salve whatever! Fludd contended that every disease might be cured by the magnet if it were properly applied ; but that as every man had, like the earth, a north pole and a south, magnetism could be produced only when his body occupied a boreal position. The salve, at all events, grew into instant favour. Among other believers in its virtues was Sir Kenelm Digby, who, however, converted the salve into a powder, which he named ' the powder of sympathy.' But it had its incredulous opponents, of whom the most strenuous was a certain Pastor Foster, who published an invective entitled ' Hyplocrisma Spongus ; or, A Sponge to Wipe Away the Weapon Salve,' and affirmed that it was as bad as witchcraft to use or recommend such an unguent, that its inventor, the devil, would at the Last Day claim every person who had meddled with it. ' The devil,' he said, ' gave it to Paracelsus, Paracelsus to the Emperor, the Emperor to a courtier, the courtier to Baptista Porta, and Baptista Porta to Doctor Fludd, a doctor of physic, yet living and practising in the

famous city of London, who now stands tooth and
nail for it.' Tooth and nail Dr. Fludd met his adversary, and the public were infinitely amused by the
vehemence of his style in his pamphlet, ' The Spung-
ing of Parson Foster's Spunge ; wherein the Spunge-
carrier's immodest Carriage and Behaviour towards
his Brethren is detected ; the bitter Flames of his
Slanderous Reports are, by the sharp Vinegar of
Truth, corrected and quite extinguished ; and, lastly,
the Virtuous Validity of his Spunge in wiping away
the Weapon Salve, is crushed out and clean abolished.'

In all the dreams of the mediæval philosophy—in
the philosopher's stone and the stone philosophic, in
the universal alkahest, in the magical ' elixir vitæ '—
Dr. Fludd was a serious believer. It was a favourite
hypothesis of his that all things depended on two
principles—*condensation*, or the boreal principle, and
rarefaction, the southern or austral. The human
body, he averred, was governed by a number of
demons, whom he distributed over a rhomboidal
figure. Further, he taught that every disease had
its own particular demon, the evil influence of which
could be neutralized only by the assistance of the
demon placed opposite to it in the rhomboid. The
doctrines of the Rosicrucian brotherhood he defended
with a charming enthusiasm, and when they had
been attacked by Libavius and others, he set them
forth in what he conceived to be their true light in his
' Apologia Compendiaria Fraternitatem de Rosca-
Cruce suspicionis et infamiæ Maculis Aspersam,' etc.
(published at Leyden in 1616)—a work which entitles

him to be regarded as the high-priest of their mysteries. It was severely criticised, however, by contemporary men of science, as by Kepler, Gassendus (in his 'Epistolica Exercitatio'), and Mersenne, whose searching analysis of the pretensions of the fraternity provoked from Fludd an elaborate reply, entitled 'Summum Bonum, quod est Magiæ, Cabalæ, Alchemiæ, Fratrum Roseæ-Crucis verorum, et adversus Mersenium Calumniatorem.'*

In addition to the foregoing works, Fludd gave to the world:

1. 'Utriusque Cosmi, Majoris et Minoris, Technica Historia,' 2 vols., folio, Oppenheim, 1616; 2. 'Tractatus Apologeticus Integritatem Societatis de Rosea-Cruce Defendens,' Leyden, 1617; 3. 'Monochordon Mundi Symphoniacum, seu Replicatio ad Apologiam Johannis Kepleri,' Frankfort, 1620; 4. 'Anatomiæ Amphitheatrum effigie triplici Designatum,' Frankfort, 1623; 5. 'Philosophia Sacra et vere Christiana, seu Meteorologica Cosmica,' Frankfort, 1626; 6. 'Medicina Catholica, seu Mysterium Artis Medicandi Sacrarium,' Frankfort, 1631; 7. 'Integrum Morborum Mysterium,' Frankfort, 1631; 8. 'Clavis Philosophiæ et Alchymiæ,' Frankfort, 1633; 9. 'Philosophia Mosaica,' Goudac. 1638; and 10. 'Pathologia Dæmoniaca,' Goudac, 1640.

The last two treatises were posthumous publications.

---

* This is sometimes ascribed to Joachim Fritz, but no one can doubt that virtually it is Fludd's, who accompanied it with a defence of his general philosophical teaching, entitled 'Sophiæ cum Moriâ Certamen.' But whose was 'the Wisdom,' and whose 'the Folly'?

Fludd died in London in 1637, and was buried in Bersted Church, where an imposing monument perpetuates his memory.   It represents him seated, with his hand on a book, from the perusal of which his head has just been lifted.   Just below are two volumes (there were eight originally) in marble, inscribed respectively, 'Mysterium Cabalisticum' and 'Philosophia Sacra.'   The epitaph runs as follows: 'viii. Die Mensis vii. A° Dⁿⁱ, M.D.C.XXXVII.   Odoribvs vana vaporat crypta tegit cineres nec speciosa tros qvod mortale minvs tibi.   Te committimvs vnvm ingenii vivent hic monvmenti tvi nam tibi qvi similis scribit moritvrqve sepvlchrvm pro tota eternvm posteritate facit.   Hoc monvmentvm Thomas Flood Gore Courti in-coram apud Cantianos armiger infœlicissimum in charissimi patrvi svi memoriam erexit die Mensis Avgvsti, M.D.C.XXXVII.'

I shall not weary the reader with an analysis of any of Fludd's elaborately mystical productions. They are as dead as anything can be, and no power that I know of could breathe into them the breath of life.   But I may quote a few specimen or sample sentences, so to speak, which will afford an idea of their style and tone :

'Particulars are frequently fallible, but universal never.   Occult philosophy lays bare Nature in her complete nakedness, and alone contemplates the wisdom of universals by the eyes of intelligence.   Accustomed to partake of the rivers which flow from the Fountain of Life, it is unacquainted with grossness and with clouded waters.'

In reference to Music, which he says stands in the same relation to arithmetic as medicine to natural philosophy, he revives the Pythagorean idea of the harmony of the universe : ' What is this music (of men) compared with that deep and true music of the wise, whereby the proportions of natural things are investigated, the harmonical concord and the qualities of the whole world are revealed, by which also con- nected things are bound together, peace established between conflicting elements, and whereby each star is perpetually suspended in its appointed place by its weight and strength, and by the harmony of its herent spirit.'

Light.—' Nothing in this world can be accom- plished without the mediation or divine act of light.'

Magic.—' That most occult and secret department of physics, by which the mystical properties of natural substances are extracted, we term Natural Magic. The wise kings who (led by the new star from the east) sought the infant Christ, are called Magi, because they had attained a perfect knowledge of natural things, whether celestial or sublunar. This branch of the Magi also includes Solomon, since he was versed in the arcane virtues and properties of all substances, and is said to have understood the nature of every plant, from the cedar to the hyssop. Magicians who are proficient in the mathematical division construct marvellous machines by means of their geometrical knowledge ; such were the flying dove of Archytas, and the brazen heads of Roger Bacon and Albertus Magnus, which are said to have spoken. Venefic magic is familiar with potions, philtres, and with the various preparations of poisons; it is, in a measure, included in the natural division, because a knowledge of the properties of natural things is requisite to produce its results. Necromantic magic is divided into Goëtic, maleficent, and theurgic. The first consists in diabolical commerce with unclean spirits, in rites of criminal curiosity, in illicit songs and invocations, and in the invocation of the souls of the dead. The second is the adjuration of the devils by the virtue of Divine names. The third pretends to be governed by good angels and the Divine will, but its wonders are most frequently performed by evil spirits, who assume the names of God and of the angels. This department of necromancy can, however, be performed by natural powers, definite rites and ceremonies, whereby celestial and Divine virtues are reconciled and drawn to us ; the ancient Magi formulated in their secret books many rules of this doctrine. The last species of magic is the thaumaturgic, begetting illusory phenomena ; by this art the Magi produced their phantasms and other marvels.'

The Creation.—' According to Fludd's philosophy,' says Mr. Waite, ' the whole universe was fashioned after the pattern of an archetypal world which existed in the Divine ideality, and was framed out of unity in a threefold manner. The Eternal Monad or Unity, without any regression from His own central profundity, compasses complicitly the three cosmical dimensions, namely, root, square, and cube. If we multiply unity as a root, in itself, it will produce only unity for its square, which being again multiplied in itself, brings forth a cube, which is one with root and square. Thus we have three branches differing in formal progression, yet one unity in which all things remain potentially, and that after a most abstruse manner. The archetypal world was made by the egression of one out of one, and by the regression of that one, so emitted into itself by emanation. According to this ideal image, or archetypal world, our universe was subsequently fashioned as a true type and exemplar of the Divine Pattern ; for out of unity in His abstract existence, viz., as it was hidden in the dark chaos, or potential mass, the bright flame of all formal being did shine forth, and the spirit of wisdom, proceeding from them both, conjoined the formal emanation with the potential matter, so that by the union of the divine emanation of light, and the substantial darkness, which was water, the heavens were made of old, and the whole world.'*

THOMAS VAUGHAN.

Another English Rosicrucian to whom allusion must briefly be made is Thomas Vaughan, who in his writings assumes the more classical appellation of Eugenius Philalethes ('truth-lover'), and in his travels was known as Carnobius in Holland, and Doctor Zheil in America. He was born about 1612 ; was educated at Oxford ; wandered afterwards

* Waite, 'History of the Rosicrucians,' p. 385.

through many countries; embraced the delusions of alchemy and the Rosy Cross; accreted round his personality a number of wild and extravagant stories; and finally disappeared into such complete oblivion that the time and place of his death are alike unknown.

The writings attributed to him are: 1. 'Anthroposophia Magica; or, A Discourse of the Nature of Man and his State after Death;' and 'Anima Magica Abscondita; or, A Discourse of the Universall Spirit of Nature,' London, 1650. 2. 'Magia Adamica; or, The Antiquities of Magic,' same place and date. 3. 'The Man-Mouse taken in a Trap;' a reply to Henry More, who had criticised his 'Anthroposophia Magica.' 4. 'Lumen de Lumine; or, A New Magicall Light discovered and communicated to the World,' London, 1651. 5. 'The Second Wash; or, The Moor Scoured Once More, being a charitable Cure for the Distractions of Abazonomastix' [Henry More], London, 1651. 6. 'The Fame and Confession of the Fraternity of R. C., with a Preface annexed thereto, and a short declaration of their physicall work,' London, 1652. 7. 'Euphrates; or, The Waters of the East, being a Short Discourse of that Great Fountain whose water flows from Fire, and carries in it the beams of the Sun and Moon,' London, 1656. 8. 'A Brief Natural History,' London, 1669. And 9. 'Introitus Apertus ad Occlusum Regis Palatium. Philalethæ Tractatus Tres: i. Metallorum Metamorphosis; ii. Brevis Manductio ad Rubrium Cœlestem; iii. Fons Chymicæ Veritatis,' London, 1678.

Vaughan seems to have led a wandering life, and to have fallen 'often into great perplexities and dangers from the mere suspicion that he possessed extraordinary secrets.' The suspicion, I should say, was abundantly justified, since he made gold at will, and knew the composition of the wonderful elixir ! On one occasion, he tells us, he went to a goldsmith, desiring to sell him twelve hundred marks' worth of gold ; but the goldsmith at first sight pronounced that it had never come out of any mine, but was the production of art, seeing that it was not of the standard of any known kingdom. Vaughan adds that he was so confounded at this statement—though, surely, he must have expected it—that he at once departed, *leaving the gold behind him.* But the strangest part of his history is, that a writer in 1749 speaks of him as living *then*, at the respectable old age of 137. 'A person of great credit at Nuremberg, in Germany, affirms that he conversed with him but a year or two ago. Nay, it is further asserted that this very individual is the president of the Illuminated in Europe, and that he sits as such in all their annual meetings.' Mayhap he is sitting at them still ! Only if he have discovered, not only the secret of the transmutation of metals, but that of the indefinite prolongation of life, is it not cruelly selfish of him to withhold it—we will not say from the world at large, which deserves to be punished for its scepticism and incredulity, but from the members of his own fraternity ?

JOHN HEYDON.

The English Rosicrucians are few in number—*rari gurgite in vasto nantes*—and when I have added John Heydon to Vaughan and Fludd, I shall have named the most distinguished. Heydon was the author of ' The Wise Man's Crown; or, The Glory of the Rosie Cross' (1664); 'The Holy Guide, leading the Way to Unite Art and Nature, with the Rosie Cross Uncovered' (1662); and ' A New Method of Rosicrucian Physic; by John Heydon, the Servant of God and the Secretary of Nature' (1658). In the last-named he describes himself as an attorney—who will not pity his clients, if he had any?—practising at Westminster Hall all term times as long as he lived, and in the vacations devoting himself to alchemical and Rosicrucian speculation. His introduction ('An Apologue for an Epilogue') is full of such outrageous nonsense as to suggest suspicion of his sanity. He speaks of Moses, Elias, and Ezekiel as the prophets and founders of Rosicrucianism. Its present believers, he says, may be few in number, but their position is incomparably glorious. They are the eyes and ears of the great King of the universe, seeing all things and hearing all things; they are seraphically illuminated; they belong to the holy company of embodied souls and immortal angels; they can assume any shape at will, and possess the power of working miracles. They can walk in the air, banish epidemics from stricken cities, pacify the most violent storms, heal every disease, and turn all metals into gold.

He had known, he says, two illustrious brethren, named Williams and Walford, and had seen them per-form miracles—a statement which brands him either as a knave or a dupe. 'I desired one of them to tell me,' he says, 'whether my complexion were capable of the society of my good genius. "When I see you again," said he (which was when he pleased to come to me, for I knew not where to go to him), "I will tell you." When I saw him afterwards, he said: "You should pray to God: for a good and holy man can offer no greater or more acceptable service to God than the oblation of himself—his soul." He said also, that the good genii were the benign eyes of God, running to and fro in the world, and with love and pity beholding the innocent endeavours of harmless and single-hearted men, ever ready to do them good and to help them.'

Heydon advocated, without enforcing his precepts by example, the Rosicrucian dogma, that men could live without eating and drinking, affirming that all of us could exist in the same manner as the singular people dwelling near the source of the Ganges, described by his namesake, Sir Christopher Heydon* (but certainly by no other traveller), who had no mouths, and therefore could not eat, but lived by the breath of their nostrils—except when they went on a far journey, and then, to recuperate their strength, they inhaled the scent of flowers. He dilated on the 'fine foreign fatness' which characterized really pure air—the

* Author of 'A Defence of Judiciall Astrologie,' printed at Cambridge in 1603.

air being impregnated with it by the sunbeams—and affirmed that it should suffice for the nourishment of the majority of mankind. He was not unwilling, however, that people with gross appetites should eat animal food, but declared it to be unnecessary for them, and that a much more efficacious mode would be to use the meat, nicely cooked, as a plaster on the pit of the stomach. By adopting this external treatment, they would incur no risk of introducing diseases, as they did by the broad and open gate of the mouth, as anyone might see by the example of drink; for so long as a man sat in water, he knew no thirst. He had been acquainted—so he declared —with many Rosicrucians who, by using wine as a bath, had fasted from solid food for several years. And, as a matter of fact, one might fast all one's life, though prolonged for 300 years, if one ate no meat, and so avoided all risk of infection by disease.

Growing confidential in reference to his imaginary fraternity, he states that its chiefs always carried about with them their symbol, the R.C., an ebony cross, flourished and decked with roses of gold; the cross typifying Christ's suffering for the sins of mankind, and the golden roses the glory and beauty of His Resurrection. This symbol was carried in succession to Mecca, Mount Calvary, Mount Sinai, Haran, and three other places, which I cannot pretend to identify —Casele, Apamia, and Chaulateau Viciosa Caunuch : these were the meeting-places of the brotherhood.

'The Rosie Crucian Physick or Medicines,' says this bravely-mendacious gentleman, 'I happily and unexpectedly light upon in Arabia, which will prove a restoration of health to all that are afflicted with sickness which we ordinarily call natural, and all other diseases. These men have no small insight into the body : Walford, Williams, and others of the Fraternity now living, may bear up in the same likely equipage with those noble Divine Spirits their Predecessors; though the unskilfulness in men commonly acknowledges more of supernatural assistance in hot, unsettled fancies, and perplexed melancholy, than in the calm and distinct use of reason; yet, for mine own part, I look upon these Rosic Crucians above all men truly inspired, and more than any that professed themselves so this sixteen hundred years, and I am ravished with admiration of their miracles and transcendant mechanical inventions, for the solving the Phænomenon of the world. I may, without offence, therefore, compare them with Bezaliel, Aholiab, those skilful workers of the Tabernacle, who, as Moses testifies, were filled with the Spirit of God, and therefore were of an excellent understanding to find out all manner of curious work.'

The plain fact is that Heydon's books are *fictions*— purely imaginative work, based on some rough and ready knowledge of the old alchemy and the new magic; partly allegorical and mystical, such as a quick invention might readily conceive under the influence of theosophic study, and partly borrowed from Henry More, and other writers of the same stamp. The island inhabited by Rosicrucians, which he describes in the introduction to ' The Holy Guide,' was evidently suggested by Sir Thomas More's 'Utopia,' and Bacon's 'New Atlantis.' It would be easy to point out his obligations elsewhere.

I may add, in bringing this chapter to a close, that Dr. Edmund Dickenson, one of Charles II.'s physicians, professed to be a member of the brotherhood, and wrote a book upon one of their supposed doctrines, entitled 'De Quinta Essentia Philosophorum,' which was printed at Oxford in 1686.

Whatever may be our opinion of Rosicrucianism, which, I believe, still finds some believers and adepts in this country, we must acknowledge that the literature of poetry and fiction is indebted to it considerably. The machinery of Pope's exquisite poem, 'The Rape of the Lock,' was borrowed from Paracelsus and Jacob Böhmen—not directly, it is true, but through the medium of the Abbé de Villars' sparkling romance, 'Le Comte de Gabalis.' 'According to those gentlemen,' says Pope, 'the four elements are inhabited by spirits, which they call sylphs, gnomes, nymphs, and salamanders.'

The Rosicrucian water-nymph supplied La Motte Fouqué with the idea of that graceful and lovely creation, 'Undine,' and Sir Walter Scott has invested his 'White Lady of Avenel' with some of her attributes.

William Godwin's romance of 'St. Leon' turns on the Rosicrucian fancy of immortal life; while Lord Lytton's 'Zanoni' is practically a Rosicrucian fiction. The influence of the Rosicrucian writers is also apparent in the same author's 'A Strange Story.'

BOOK II.

WITCHES AND WITCHCRAFT.

CHAPTER I.

EARLY HISTORY OF WITCHCRAFT IN ENGLAND.

To various conspicuous and easily intelligible causes
the witch and the warlock, like the necromancer and
the astrologer, owed their power with the multitude.
First, there was the eager desire which humanity not
unnaturally feels to tear aside the veil of Isis, and
obtain some knowledge of that Other World which is
hidden so completely from it. Next must be taken
into account man's greed for temporal advantages,
his anxiety to direct the course of events to his
personal benefit; and, lastly, his malice against his
fellows. Thus we see that the influence enjoyed by
the sorcerer and the magician had its origin in the
unlawful passions of humanity, in whose history the
pages that treat of witches and witchcraft are painful
and humiliating reading.

To define the limit between the special functions of
the magician and the witch is somewhat difficult,
more especially as the position of the witch gradually
decreased in reputation and importance. There is a
great gulf between the witch of Endor, or the witch
of classical antiquity, or the witch of the Norse Sagas,

or the witch of the Saxons, and the English or
Scottish witch of the sixteenth and seventeenth centuries.   The former were surrounded with an atmosphere of dread and mystery; the latter was the
creature of vulgar and commonplace traditions.   In
the early age of witchcraft, the witch, like the magician, summoned spirits from the vasty deep, discovered the hiding-places of concealed treasures,
struck down men or beasts by her spells, or covered
the heavens with clouds and let loose the winds of
destruction and desolation.   Both could blight the
promise of the harvest, baffle the plans of their
enemies, or wither the health of their victims.   But
while the magician was frequently a man of ability
and learning, and belonged to the cultured classes,
the witch was almost always a woman of the lower
orders, ignorant and uneducated, though occasionally
ladies of high rank, and even ecclesiastics, have been
accused of practising withcraft.

While witchcraft was a power in the land, the
witch, or warlock, was popularly supposed to be the
direct instrument, and, indeed, the bond-slave, of the
Evil One, fulfilling his behests in virtue of a compact, written in letters of blood, by which the witch
made over her soul to the Infernal Power in return
for the enjoyment of supernatural prerogatives for a
fixed period.   This treaty having been concluded,
the witch received a mark on some part of the body,
which was thenceforward insensible of pain—the
stigma or devil's mark, by which he might know his
own again.   A familiar imp or spirit was assigned to

her, generally in the form of an animal, and more particularly in that of a black cat or dog. Round this general idea were gathered a number of horrible and unclean conceptions, on which, happily, it will not be necessary to enlarge. The devil, it was said, resorted to carnal communication with his servants, being denominated *succubus* when the favourite was a female, and *incubus* when a male was chosen. It was alleged, too, that on certain occasions the devil, with his familiars, and the great company of witches and warlocks whose souls he had bought, assembled in the dead of night in some remote and savage wilderness, to hold that frightful carnival of the Witches' Sabbat which Goethe has depicted so powerfully in the second part of 'Faust.' The human imagination has not invented, I think, any scene more horrible, more degrading, or more bestial. We may suppose, however, that it was not conceived by any single mind, or even people, or in any single generation, but that it gradually took up additional details from different nations, at different times, until it was developed into the terrible whole presented by the mediæval writers.

This wild and awful revel was called the Sabbat because it took place after midnight on Friday; that is, on the Jewish Sabbath—a curious illustration of the popular antipathy against the Jews.

The spot where it was held never bloomed again with flower or herb; the burning feet of the demons blighted it for ever.

Witch or warlock who failed to obey the summons

of the master was lashed by devils with rods made of scorpions or serpents, in chastisement of his or her contumacy.

The guests repaired thither, according to the belief entertained in France and England, upon broom-sticks; but in Spain and Italy it was thought that the devil himself, in the shape of a goat, conveyed them on his back, which he contracted or elongated according to the number he carried. The witch, when starting on her aerial journey, would not quit her house by door or window; but astride on her broomstick made her exit by the chimney. During her absence, to prevent the suspicions of her neighbours from being aroused, an inferior demon assumed the semblance of her person, and lay in her bed, pre-tending to be ill or asleep.

A curious story may here be introduced. In April, 1611, a Provençal curé, named Gaurifidi, was accused of sorcery before the Parliament of Aix. In the course of trial much was said in proof of the power of the demons. Several witnesses asserted that Gaurifidi, after rubbing himself with a magic oil, repaired to the Sabbat, and afterwards returned to his chamber down the chimney. One day, when this sort of thing was exciting the imagination of the judges, an extraordinary noise was heard in the chimney of the hall, terminating suddenly in the apparition of a tall black man, who shook his head vigorously. The judges, thinking the devil had come in person to the rescue of his servant, took to their heels, with the exception of one Thorm, the reporter, who was so hemmed in by his desk that he was unable to move. Terror-stricken at the sight before him, with his body all of a tremble, and his eyes starting from his head, he made repeated signs of the cross, until the supposed fiend was equally alarmed, since he could not understand the cause of the reporter's evident perturbation. On recovering from his embarrassment he made himself known — he was a sweep, who had been operating on a chimney on the roof above, but, when ready to return, had mistaken the entrance, and thus unwillingly intruded himself into the chamber of the Parliament.

The unclean ceremonies of the Witches' Sabbat were 'inaugurated' by Satan, who, in his favourite assumption of a huge he-goat (a suggestion, no doubt, from Biblical imagery), with one face in front, and another between his haunches, took his place upon his throne. After all present had done homage by kissing him on the posterior face, he appointed a master of the ceremonies, and, attended by him, made a personal examination of any guest to ascertain if he or she bore the stigma, which indicated his right of ownership. Any who were found without it received the mark at once from the master of the ceremonies, while the devil bestowed on them a nickname. Thereafter all began to dance and sing with wild extravagance—

> ' There is no rest to-night for anyone :
> When one dance ends another is begun '—

until some neophyte arrived, and sought admission into the circle of the initiated. Silence prevailed

while the newcomer went through the usual form of
denying her salvation, spitting upon the Bible, kissing
the devil, and swearing obedience to him in all things.
The dancing then renewed its fury, and a hoarse chorus
went up of—

> ' Alegremos, alegremos,
> Que gente va tenemos !'

When spent with the violent exercise, they sat
down, and, like the witches in ' Macbeth,' related
the evil things each had done since the last Sabbat,
those who had not been sufficiently active being
chastised by Satan himself until they were drenched
in blood.   A dance of toads was the next entertainment.   They sprang up out of the earth by thousands,
and danced on their hind-legs while Satan played on
the bagpipes or the trumpet, after which they solicited
the witches to reward them for their exertions by
feeding them *with the flesh of unbaptized babes.*   Was
there ever a more curious mixture of the grotesque
and the horrible?   At a stamp from the devil's foot
they returned to the earth whence they came, and a
banquet was served up, the nature of which the reader
may be left to imagine!   Dancing was afterwards
resumed, while those who had no partiality for the
pastime found amusement in burlesquing the sacrament of baptism, the toads being again summoned
and sprinkled with holy water, while the devil made
the sign of the cross, and the witches cried out in
chorus: 'In nomine Patricâ, Aragueaco Patrica,
agora, agora! Valentia, jurando gome guito goustia !'
that is, 'In the name of Patrick, Patrick of Aragon
now, now, all our ills are over !'

Sometimes the devil would cause the witches to strip themselves, and dance before him in their nakedness, each with a cat tied round her neck, and another suspended from her body like a tail. At cockcrow the whole phantasmagoria vanished.

One cannot help wondering who first conceived the idea of these horrid saturnalia. Did it spring from the diseased imagination of some half-mad monk, brooding in the solitude of his silent cell, who gathered up all these unclean and grim images and worked them into so ghastly a picture? They are partly heathen, partly Christian; partly classical, partly Teutonic—a strange and unwholesome compound, as 'thick and slab' as the hell-broth mixed by the hags on 'the blasted heath'!

In these pages I am concerned only with our own 'tight little island,' into which the superstition was most certainly introduced by the northern invaders. It would derive strength and consistency from the teaching of the Old Testament, which distinctly recognises the existence of witchcraft. 'Let not a witch live!' is the command given in Exodus (chapter xxii.); and similar threats against witches, wizards and the like frequently occur in the books of Leviticus and Deuteronomy. Says Sir William Blackstone: 'To deny the possibility, nay, the actual existence of witchcraft and sorcery, is at once flatly to contradict the revealed Word of God in various passages of the Old and New Testaments, and the thing itself is a truth to which every nation in the world hath, in its turn, borne testimony, either by

example seemingly well attested, or by prohibitory
laws, which at least suppose the possibility of a
commerce with evil spirits.' The Church at a very
early period admitted its existence, and fulminated
against all who practised it. The fourth canon of the
Council of Auxerre, in 525, stringently prohibited all
resort to sorcerers, diviners, augurs, and the like. A
canon of the Council held at Berkhampstead in 696
condemned to corporal punishment, or mulcted in a
fine, every person who made sacrifices to the evil
spirits. Under the name of *sortilegium*, the offence
was treated eventually as a kind of heresy, for which,
on the first occasion, the offender, if penitent, was
punished by the Ecclesiastical Courts; but if there
were no abjuration, or a relapse after abjuration, she
was handed over to the secular power to be executed
by authority of the writ *de heretico comburendo*. At a
later date, statutes against witchcraft were enacted
by Parliament, and the offence was both tried and
punished by the civil power. Such statutes were
passed in the reigns of Henry VIII., Elizabeth, and
James I. Legislation derives its chief support from
public opinion; and these statutes are a proof that
the existence of witchcraft was generally believed in.
'For centuries in this country,' says Mr. Inderwick,
'strange as it may now appear, a denial of the existence of such demoniacal agency was deemed equal to
a confession of atheism, and to a disbelief in the
Holy Scriptures themselves. Not only did Lord
Chancellors, Lord Keepers, benches of Bishops, and
Parliament after Parliament attest the truth and the

existence of witchcraft, but Addison, writing as late
as 1711, in the pages of the *Spectator*, after describing
himself as hardly pressed by the arguments on both
sides of this question, expresses his own belief that
there is, and has been, witchcraft in the land.' At
the same time, it is pleasant to remember that there
have almost always been a few minds, bolder and more
enlightened than the rest, to protest against a credulity
which led to acts of the greatest inhumanity, and
fostered a grotesque and dangerous superstition.

It is in the twelfth century that we first obtain, in
England, any distinct indications of the nature of
this superstition, and it is then we first meet with
the written compact between the devil and his victim.
The story of the old woman of Berkeley, with which
Southey's ballad has made everybody familiar, is
related by William of Malmesbury, on the authority
of a friend who professed to have been an eye-witness
of the facts. When the devil, we read, announced to
the witch that the term of her compact had nearly
expired, she summoned to her presence the monks of
the neighbouring monastery and her children, confessed her sins, acknowledged her criminal compact,
and displayed a curious anxiety lest Satan should
secure her body as well as her soul. ' Sew me in a
stag's hide,' she said, ' and, placing me in a stone
coffin, shut me in with lead and iron. Load this
with a heavy stone, and fasten down the whole with
three iron chains. Let fifty psalms be sung by night,
and fifty masses be said by day, to baffle the power
of the demons, and if you can thus protect my body

14—2

for three nights, on the fourth day you may safely bury it in the ground.' These precautions, though religiously observed, proved ineffectual. On the first night the monks bravely resisted the efforts of the fiends, who, however, on the second night, renewed the attack with increased vehemence, burst open the gates of the monastery, and rent asunder two of the chains which held down the coffin. On the third night, so terrible was the hurly-burly, that the monastery shook to its foundations, and the terror-stricken priests paused, aghast, in the midst of their ministrations. Then the doors flew apart, and into the sacred place stalked a demon, who rose head and shoulders above his fellows. Stopping at the coffin, he, in a terrible voice, commanded the dead to rise. The woman answered that she was bound by the third chain: whereupon the demon put his foot on the coffin, the chain snapped like a thread, the coffin-lid fell off, the witch arose, and was hurried to the church-door, where the demon, mounting a huge black horse, swung his victim on to the crupper, and galloped away into the darkness with the swiftness of an arrow, while her shrieks resounded through the air.

There are many allusions in the old monastic chronicles which illustrate the development of public opinion in reference to witches and their craft. Thus, John of Salisbury describes the nocturnal assemblies of the witches, the presence of Satan, the banquet, and the punishment or reward of the guests according to the failure or abundance of their zeal. William of Malmesbury tells us that on the highroad to Rome

dwelt a couple of beldams, of ill repute, who enticed
the weary traveller into their wretched hovel, and by
their incantations transformed him into a horse, a
dog, or some other animal—similar to the transforma-
tions we read of in Oriental tales—and that this
animal they sold to the first comer, in this way
picking up a tolerable livelihood.   One day, a
jongleur, or mountebank, asked for a night's lodging,
and when he disclosed his vocation to the two hags,
they informed him that they had an ass of remarkable
capacity, which, indeed, could do everything but speak,
and that they were willing to sell it.   The sum asked
was large, but the ass displayed such wonderful intelligence that the jongleur gladly paid it, and departed, taking with him the ass and a piece of advice
from the old women—not to let the ass go near running water.   For some time all went well, the ass
became an immense attraction, and the jongleur was
growing passing rich, when, in one of his drunken
fits, he allowed the animal to escape.   Running directly
to the nearest stream, it plunged in, and immediately
resumed its original shape as a handsome young man,
who explained that he had been transformed by the
spells of the two crones.

   The first trial for witchcraft in England occurred
in the tenth year of King John, when, as recorded in
the ' Abbreviatio Placitorum,' Agnes, wife of Ado the
merchant, accused one Gideon of the crime ; but he
proved his innocence by the ordeal of red-hot iron.
The first trial which has been reported with any
degree of particularity belongs to the year 1324.

Some citizens of Coventry, it would appear, had suffered severely at the hands of the prior, who had been supported in his exactions by the two Despensers, Edward II.'s unworthy favourites. In revenge, they plotted the death of the prior, the favourites, and the King. For this purpose they sought the assistance of a famous magician of Coventry, named Master John of Nottingham, and his man, Robert Marshall of Leicester. The conspiracy was revealed by the said Robert Marshall, probably because his pecuniary reward was unsatisfactory, and he averred that John of Nottingham and himself, having agreed to carry out the desire of the citizens, the latter, on Sunday, March 13, brought an instalment of the stipulated fee, together with seven pounds of wax and two yards of canvas ; that with this wax he and his master made seven images, representing respectively the King (with his crown), the two Despensers, the prior, his caterer, and his steward, and one Richard de Lowe—the last named being introduced merely as a lay-figure on which to test the efficacy of the charm.

The two wizards retired to an old ruined house at Shorteley Park, about half a league from Coventry, where they remained at work for several days, and about midnight on the Friday following Holy Cross Day, the said Master John gave to the said Robert a sharp-pointed leaden branch, and commanded him to insert it about two inches deep in the forehead of the image representing Richard de Lowe, this being intended as an experiment. It was done, and next morning Master John sent his servant to Lowe's house to inquire after his condition, who found him screaming and crying 'Harrow!' He had lost his memory, and knew no one, and in this state he continued until dawn on the Sunday before Ascension, when Master John withdrew the branch from the forehead of the image and thrust it into the heart. There it remained until the following Wednesday, when the unfortunate man expired. Such was Robert Marshall's fable, as told before the judges; but apparently it met with little credence, and the trial, after several adjournments, fell to the ground.

Wonderful stories are told by the later chroniclers of a certain Eudo de Stella, who had acquired great notoriety as a sorcerer. William of Newbury says that his 'diabolical charms' collected a large company of disciples, whom he carried with him from place to place, adding to their number wherever he stopped. At times he encamped in the heart of a wood, where sumptuous tables were suddenly spread with all kinds of dainty dishes and fragrant wines, and every wish breathed by the meanest guest was immediately fulfilled. Some of Eudo's followers, however, confided to our authority that there was a strange want of solidity in these magically-supplied viands, and that though they ate of them continually, they were never satisfied. But it appears that whoever once tasted of the sorcerer's meats, or received from him a gift, thereby became enrolled among his followers. And the chronicler supplies this irrefutable proof: A knight of his acquaintance paid a visit to the wizard,

and endeavoured to turn him from his evil practices.
When he departed, Eudo presented his squire with
a handsome hawk, which the knight, observing,
advised him to cast away. Not so the squire: he
rejoiced in his high-mettled bird; but they had
scarcely got out of sight of the wizard's camp before
the hawk's talons gripped him more and more
closely, and at last it flew away with him, and he was
never more heard of.

The trial of Dame Alicia Kyteler, or Le Poer,
takes us across the seas, but it furnishes too many
interesting particulars to be entirely ignored.
Hutchinson informs us that, in 1324, Bishop de
Ledrede, of Ossory, in the course of a visitation of
his diocese, came to learn that, in the city of Kilkenny, there had long resided certain persons
addicted to various kinds of witchcraft; and that the
chief offender among them was a Dame Alicia
Kyteler. As she was a woman of considerable
wealth, which might prove of great benefit to the
Church, the episcopal zeal blazed up strongly, and
she and her accomplices were ordered to be put upon
their trial.

The accusation against them was divided into
seven distinct heads:

First: That, in order to give effect to their sorcery,
they were wont altogether to deny the faith of Christ
and of the Church for a year or month, according as
the object to be attained was greater or less, so that
during this longer or shorter period they believed in
nothing that the Church believed, and abstained from

worshipping Christ's body, from entering a church, from hearing Mass, and from participating in the Sacrament. Second: That they propitiated the demons with sacrifices of living animals, which they tore limb from limb, and offered, by scattering them in cross-roads, to a certain demon, Robert Artisson (*filius Artis*), who was 'one of the poorer class of hell.' Third: That by their sorceries they sought responses and oracles from demons. Fourth: That they used the ceremonies of the Church in their nocturnal meetings, pronouncing, with lighted candles of wax, sentence of excommunication even against the persons of their own husbands, naming expressly every member, from the sole of the foot to the top of the head, and at length extinguishing the candles with the exclamation, 'Fi! fi! fi! Amen!' Fifth: That with the intestines and other inner parts of cocks sacrificed to the demons, with 'certain horrible worms,' various herbs, the nails of dead men, the hair, brains, and clothes of children who had died unbaptized, and other things too disgusting to mention, boiled in the skull of a certain robber who had been beheaded, on a fire made of oak-sticks, they had invented powders and ointments, and also candles of fat boiled in the said skull, with certain charms, which things were to be instrumental in exciting love or hatred, and in killing or torturing the bodies of faithful Christians, and for various other unlawful purposes. Sixth: That the sons and daughters of the four husbands of the same Dame Alice had made their complaint to the Bishop, that

she, by such sorcery, had procured the death of her
husbands, and had so beguiled and infatuated them,
that they had given all their property to her and her
son [by her first husband, William Outlawe], to the
perpetual impoverishment of their own sons and heirs :
insomuch that her present [and fourth] husband, Sir
John Le Poer, was reduced to a most miserable condition of body by her ointments, powders, and other
magical preparations; but, being warned by her
maidservant, he had forcibly taken from his wife the
keys of her house, in which he found a bag filled
with the ' detestable ' articles above mentioned, which
he had sent to the Bishop. Seventh: That there
existed an unholy connection between the said Lady
Alice and the demon called Robert Artisson, who
sometimes appeared to her in the form of a cat,
sometimes in that of a black shaggy dog, and at
others in the form of a black man, with two tall
companions as black as himself, each carrying in his
hand a rod of iron. Some of the old chroniclers
embroider upon this charge the fanciful details that
her offering to the demon was nine red cocks' and
nine peacocks' eyes, which were paid on a certain
stone bridge at a cross-road; that she had a magical
ointment,* which she rubbed upon a coulter or

---

* So in Duclerq's ' Memoires ' (' Collect. du Panthéon '), p. 141,
we read of a case at Arras, in which the sorcerers were accused of
using such an ointment : 'D'ung oignement que le diable leur
avoit baillé, ils oindoient une vergue de bois bien petite, et leurs
palmes et leurs mains, puis mectoient celle virguelte entre leurs
jambes, et tantost ils s'en volvient où ils voullvient estre, pur-
desseures bonnes villes, bois et cams ; et les portoit le diable
au lieu où ils debvoient faire leur assemblée.'

plough handle, in order that the said coulter might
carry her and her companions whithersoever they
wished to go; that in her house was found a consecrated wafer, with the devil's name written upon it;
and that, sweeping the streets of Kilkenny between
complin and twilight, she raked up all the ordure
towards the doors of her son, William Outlawe,
saying to herself:

'To the house of William my son,
  Hie all the wealth of Kilkenny town.'

The lady, rejoicing in powerful friends and
advisers, defied the Bishop and all his works.   She
was excommunicated, and her son summoned to
appear before the Bishop for the offence of harbouring
and concealing her; but Dame Alice's friends re-
taliated by throwing the Bishop into prison for
several days.   He revenged himself by placing the
whole diocese under an interdict, and again summoning William Outlawe to appear on a certain day; but
before the day arrived, he in his turn was cited before
the Lord Justice, to answer for having imposed an
interdict on his diocese, and to defend himself against
accusations submitted by the seneschal.   The Bishop
pleaded that it was unsafe for him to travel; but the
plea was not allowed, and, to save himself from further
molestation, he recalled the interdict.

The quarrel was not yet fought out.   On the
Monday following the octave of Easter, the seneschal,
Arnold de la Poer, held his judicial court in the
Assize Hall at Kilkenny.   Thither repaired the
Bishop, and, though refused admission, he forced his

way in, robed in full pontificals, carrying in his hand
the Host in pyx of gold, and attended by a numerous
train of friars and clergy. But he was received with
a storm of insults and reproaches, which compelled
him to retire. Upon his repeated protests, however,
and at the intercession of some influential personages,
his return was permitted. Being ordered to take
his stand at the criminal's bar, he exclaimed that
Christ had never been treated so before, since He
stood at the bar before Pontius Pilate ; and he loudly
called upon the seneschal to order the arrest of the
persons accused of sorcery, and their deliverance into
his hands. When the seneschal abruptly refused,
he opened the book of the decretals, and saith, ' You,
Sir Arnold, are a knight, and instructed in letters,
and that you may not have the excuse of ignorance,
we are prepared to prove by these decretals that you
and your officials are bound to obey our order in this
matter, under heavy penalties.'

'Go to the church with your decretals,' replied the
seneschal, ' and preach there, for none of us here will
listen to you.'

In the Bishop's character there must have been a
fine strain of perseverance, for all these rebuffs failed
to baffle him, and he actually succeeded, after a succession of disappointments and a constant renewal of
difficulties, in obtaining permission to bring the
alleged offenders to trial. Most of them suffered
imprisonment ; but Dame Alice escaped him, being
secretly conveyed to England. Of all concerned in
the affair, only one was punished Petronella of

Meath, who was selected as a scapegoat, probably because she had neither friends nor means of defence.

By order of the Bishop she was six times flogged, after which the poor tortured victim made a confession, in which she declared not only her own guilt, but that of everybody against whom the Bishop had proceeded.   She affirmed that in all Britain, nay, indeed, in the whole world, was no one more skilled in magical practices than Dame Alice Kyteler.   She was brought to admit the truth—though in her heart she must have known its absolute falsehood*—of the episcopal indictment, and pretended that she had been present at the sacrifices to the Evil One—that she had assisted in making the unguents with the unsavoury materials already mentioned, and that with these unguents different effects were produced upon different persons—the faces of certain ladies, for instance, being made to appear horned like goats ; that she had been present at the nocturnal revelries, and, with her mistress's assistance, had frequently pronounced sentence of excommunication against her own husband, with all due magical rites ; that she had attended Dame Alice in her assignations with the demon, Robert Artisson, and had seen acts of an immorality so foul that I dare not allude to it pass

---

* That is, of sacrificing to the Evil One, of meeting the demon Robert Artisson, and so on ; though it is quite possible that strange unguents were made and administered to different persons, and that Dame Alice and her companions played at being sorcerers. Some of the so-called witches, as we shall see, encouraged the deception on account of the influence it gave them.

between them. Having been coerced and tortured
into this amazingly wild and fictitious confession,
the poor woman was declared guilty, sentenced, and
burned alive, the first victim of the witchcraft delusion in Ireland.

It is worthy of observation that the mind of the
public was roused to a much stronger feeling of
hostility against witchcraft than against magic.
Alchemists, astrologers, fortune-tellers, diviners, and
the like, might incur suspicion, and sometimes punishment ; but, on the whole, they were treated with
tolerance, and even with distinction. For this
inequality of treatment two or three reasons suggest
themselves. In the crime of witchcraft the central
feature was the compact with the demon, and it was
natural that men should resent an act which entailed
the eternal loss of the soul. Again, witchcraft, much
more frequently than magic, was the instrument of
personal ill-feeling, and was more generally directed
against the lower classes. The magician seldom used
his power except when liberally paid by an employer ;
the witch, it was thought, exercised her skill for the
gratification of her own malice. However this may
be, an imputation of witchcraft became, in the fifteenth
century, a formidable affair, ensuring the death or
ruin of the unfortunate individual against whom it
was made. There was no little difficulty in defend-
ing one's self; and in truth, once made, it clung to
its victim like a Nessus's shirt, and with a result as
deadly.

Its value as a political 'move' was shown in the persecution of the Knights Templars, and, in our own history, in Cardinal Beaufort's intrigue against Humphrey, Duke of Gloucester, who governed England as Protector during the minority of Henry VI.

The Cardinal struck at the Duke through his beautiful wife, Eleanor Cobham. In July, 1441, two ecclesiastics, Roger Bolingbroke, and Thomas Southwell, a canon of St. Stephen's Chapel, were arrested on a charge of high treason ; 'for it was said that the said Master Roger should labour to consume the King's person by way of necromancy ; and that the said Master Thomas should say masses upon certain instruments with the which the said Master Roger should use his said craft of necromancy.' Bolingbroke was a scholar, an adept in natural science, and an ardent student of astronomy : William of Worcester describes him as one of the most famous clerks of the world. One Sunday, after having undergone rigorous examination, he was conveyed to St. Paul's Cross, where he was mounted 'on a high stage above all men's heads in Paul's Churchyard, whiles the sermon endured, holding a sword in his right hand and a sceptre in his left, arrayed in a marvellous array, wherein he was wont to sit when he wrought his necromancy.'

The Duchess of Gloucester, meanwhile, perceiving that her ruin was intended, fled to sanctuary at Westminster. Before the King's Council Bolingbroke was brought to confess that he had plied his magical trade at the Duchess's instigation, 'to know what should fall of her, and to what estate she should come.' In other words, he had cast her horoscope, a proceeding common enough in those days, and one which had no treasonable complexion. The Cardinal's party, however, seized upon Bolingbroke's confession, and made such use of it that the unfortunate lady was cited to appear before an ecclesiastical tribunal composed of Chichcley, Archbishop of Canterbury, Cardinal Beaufort, Bishop of Winchester, Cardinal Kemp, Archbishop of York, and Ayscough, Bishop of Salisbury, on July 2, 'to answer to divers articles of necromancy, of witchcraft or sorcery, of heresy, and of treason.' Bolingbroke was brought forward as a witness, and repeated that the Duchess 'first stirred him to labour in his necromancy.'

After this, he and Southwell were indicted as principals of treason, and the Duchess as accessory, though, if his story were true, their positions should have been reversed. At the same time, a woman named Margery Goodman, and known as the 'Witch of Eye,' was burned at Smithfield because in former days she had given potions and philtres to Eleanor Cobham, to enable her to secure the Duke of Gloucester's affections. Roger Bolingbroke was hung, drawn, and quartered, according to the barbarous custom of the age; Southwell escaped a similar fate by dying in the Tower before the day appointed for his trial. The charge of high treason brought against them rested entirely on the allegation that, at the Duchess's request, they had made a waxen image to resemble the King, and had placed it before a fire, that, as it gradually melted, so might the King gradually languish away and die. As for the Duchess, she was sentenced to do penance, which she fulfilled 'right meekly, so that the more part of the people had her in great compassion,' on Monday, November 13, 1441, walking barefoot, with a lighted taper in her hand, from Temple Bar to St. Paul's, where she offered the taper at the high altar. She repeated the penance on the Wednesday and Friday following, walking to St. Paul's by different routes, and on each occasion was accompanied by the Lord Mayor, the sheriffs, and the various guilds, and by a multitude of people, whom the repute of her beauty and her sorrows had attracted, so that what was intended for a humiliation became really a triumph. She was afterwards imprisoned in Chester Castle, and thence transferred to the Isle of Man.

The charge of sorcery which Richard III. brought against Lord Hastings, accusing him of having wasted his left arm, though from his birth it had been fleshless, dry, and withered, is made the basis of an effective scene in Shakespeare's 'Richard III.' His brother's widow, Queen Elizabeth Woodville, was included in the charge, and Jane Shore was named as her accomplice. This frail beauty was brought before the Council, and accused of having 'endeavoured the ruin and destruction of the Protector in several ways,' and particularly 'by witchcraft had decayed his body, and with the Lord Hastings had contrived to assassinate him.' The indictment, however, was not sus-

15

tained, and her offence was reduced to that of lewd living. Whereupon she was handed over to the Bishop of London to do public penance for her sin on Sunday morning in St. Paul's Cathedral church. Clothed in a white sheet, with a wax taper in her hand, and a cross borne before her, she was led in procession from the episcopal palace to the cathedral, where she made open confession of her fault. The moral effect of this exhibition seems to have been considerably marred by the beauty of the penitent, which produced upon the multitude an impression similar to that which the bared bosom of Phryne produced upon her judges in the days of old.

In 1480 Pope Innocent VIII. issued a Bull enjoining the detection, trial, and punishment (by burning) of witches. This was the first formal recognition of witchcraft by the head of the Church. In England the first Act of Parliament levelled at it was passed in 1541. Ten years later two more statutes were enacted, one relating to false prophecies, and the other to conjuration, witchcraft and sorcery. But in no one of these was witchcraft condemned *qua* witchcraft; they were directed against those who, by means of spells, incantations, or compacts with the devil, threatened the lives and properties of their neighbours. When, in 1561, Sir Edward Waldegrave, one of Mary Stuart's councillors, was arrested by order of Secretary Cecil as 'a mass-monger,' the Bishop of London, to whom he was remitted, felt no disposition to inflict a heavy penalty for hearing or saying of mass; but, on inquiry, he discovered that the officiating priest had been concerned in concocting 'a love-philtre,' and he then decided that sorcery would afford a safer ground for process. He applied, therefore, to Chief Justice Catlin, to learn what might be the law in such cases, and was astonished when he was told that no legal provision had been made for them. Previously they came before the Church Courts; but these had been deprived of their powers by the Reformation, and the only precedent he could find for moving in the matter belonged to the reign of Edward III., and was thus entered on the roll:

'Ung homme fut prinse en Southwark avec ung teste et ung visaige dung homme morte avec ung lyvre de sorcerie en son male et fut amesné en banke du Roy devant Knyvet Justice, mais nulle indictment fut vers lui, por qui les clerkes luy fierement jurement que jamais ne feroit sorcerie en après, et fut delyvon del prison, et le teste et les lyvres furent arses a Totehyll a les costages du prisonnier.' (That is: A man was taken in Southwark, with a dead man's skull and a book of sorcery in his wallet, and was brought up at the King's Bench before Knyvet Justice; but no indictment was laid against him, for that the clerks made him swear he would meddle no more with sorcery, and the head and the books were burnt at Tothill Fields at the prisoner's charge.)

But in the following year Parliament passed an Act which defined witchcraft as a capital crime, whether it was or was not exerted to the injury of the lives, limbs, and possessions of the lieges. Thenceforward the persecution of witches took its place among English institutions. During the latter years of Elizabeth's reign several instances occurred. Thus, on July 25, 1589, three witches were burnt at Chelmsford. The popular mind was gradually familiarized with the idea of witchcraft, and led to concentrate its attention on the individual marks, or characteristics, which were supposed to indicate its professors. Even among the higher classes a belief in its existence became very general, and it is startling to find a man like the learned and pious Bishop Jewell, in a sermon before Queen Elizabeth, saying: 'It may please your Grace to understand that witches and sorcerers within these last four years are marvellously increased within this your Grace's realm. Your Grace's subjects pine away even unto the death ; their colour fadeth ; their flesh rotteth ; their speech is benumbed ; their senses are bereft ! I pray God they may never practise further than upon the subject !' (1598).

The witches in 'Macbeth'—those weird sisters who met at midnight upon the blasted heath, and in their caldron brewed so deadly a 'hell-broth'—partake of the dignity of the poet's genius, and belong to the vast ideal world of his imagination. No such midnight hags crossed the paths of ordinary mortals. The Elizabethan witch, who scared her neighbours in town and village, and flourished on their combined ignorance and superstition, appears, however, in 'The Merry Wives of Windsor,' where Master Ford describes 'the fat woman of Brentford' as 'a witch, a quean, an old cozening quean!' He adds: 'Have I not forbid her my house? She comes of errands, does she? We are simple men; we do not know what's brought to pass under the profession of fortune-telling. She works by charms, by spells, by the figure; and such daubery as this is beyond our

element.' Most of Master Ford's contemporaries, I
fear, were, in this matter, 'simple men.' Even persons of rank and learning, of position and refinement,
were as credulous as their poorer, more ignorant, and
more vulgar neighbours ; were just as ready to believe
that an untaught village crone had made a compact
with the devil, and bartered her soul for the right of
straddling across a broom or changing herself into a
black cat !

Near Warboise, in Huntingdonshire, in 1593, lived
two gentlemen of good estate—Mr. Throgmorton and
Sir Samuel Cromwell. The former had five daughters,
of whom the eldest, Joan, was possessed with a lively
imagination, which busied itself constantly with ghosts
and witches. On one occasion, when she passed the
cottage of an old and infirm woman, known as Mother
Samuel, the good dame, with a black cap on her head,
was sitting at her door knitting. Mistress Joan exclaimed that she was a witch, hurried home, went into
convulsions, and declared that Mother Samuel had
bewitched her. In due course, her sisters followed
her example, and they too laid the blame of their fits
on Mother Samuel. The parents, not less infatuated
than the children, lent ready ears to their wild tales,
and carried them to Lady Cromwell, who, as a friend
of Mrs. Throgmorton, took the matter up right
earnestly, and resolved that the supposed witch
should be put to the ordeal. Sir Samuel was by
no means unwilling ; and the children, encouraged
by this prompt credulity, let loose their fertile inven-

tions. They declared that Mother Samuel sent a
legion of evil spirits to torment them incessantly.
Strange to say, these spirits had made known their
names, which, though grotesque, had nothing of a
demoniac character about them — 'First Smack,'
'Second Smack,' 'Third Smack,' 'Blue,' 'Catch,'
'Hardname,' and ' Pluck '—names invented, of course,
by the young people themselves.

At length the aggrieved Throgmorton, summoning
all his courage, repaired to Mother Samuel's humble
residence, seized upon the unhappy old crone, and
dragged her into his own grounds, where Lady Cromwell and Mrs. Throgmorton and her children thrust
long pins into her body to see if they could draw
blood. With unmeasured violence, Lady Cromwell
tore the old woman's cap from her head, and plucked
out a handful of her gray hair, which she gave to
Mrs. Throgmorton to burn, as a charm that would
protect her from all further evil practices. Smarting
under these injuries, the poor old woman, in a moment
of passion, invoked a curse upon her torturers—a
curse afterwards remembered against her, though at
the time she was allowed to depart. For more than
a year her life was made miserable by the incessant
persecution inflicted upon her by the two hostile
families, who, on their part, declared that her demons
brought upon them all kinds of physical ills, prevented their ewes and cows from bearing, and turned
the milk sour in the dairy-pans. It so happened
that Lady Cromwell was seized with a sudden illness,
of which she died, and though some fifteen months

had elapsed since the utterance of the curse, on poor Mother Samuel was placed the responsibility. Sir Samuel Cromwell, therefore, felt called upon to punish her for her ill-doing.

By this time the old woman, partly through listening to the incessant repetition of the charges against her, and partly, perhaps, from a weak delight in the notoriety she had attained, had come to believe, or to think she believed, that she was really the witch everybody declared her to be—just as a young versifier is sometimes deluded into a conviction of his poetic genius through unwisely crediting the eulogies of an admiring circle of friends and relatives. On one occasion, she was forcibly conveyed into Mrs. Throgmorton's house when Joan was in one of her frequently-recurring fits, and ordered to exorcise the demon that was troubling the maid, with the formula: ' As I am a witch, and the causer of Lady Cromwell's death, I charge thee, fiend, to come out of her !' The poor creature did as she was told, and confessed, besides, that her husband and her daughter were her associates in witchcraft, and that all three had sold their souls to the devil. On this confession the whole family were arrested, and sent to Huntingdon Gaol. Soon afterwards they were tried before Mr. Justice Fenner, and put to the torture.

In her agony the old woman confessed anything that was required of her—she was a witch, she had bewitched the Throgmortons, she had caused the death of Lady Cromwell. Her husband and her daughter, stronger-minded, resolutely asserted their innocence. Ignorance, however, would not be denied its victims ; all three were sentenced to be hanged, and to have their bodies burned. The daughter, who was young and comely, was regarded compassionately by many persons, and advised to gain at least a respite by pleading pregnancy. She indignantly refused to sacrifice her good name. They might falsely call her a witch, she exclaimed, but they should not be able to say that she had acknowledged herself to be a harlot. Her old mother, however, caught at the idea, and openly asserted that she was with child, the court breaking out into loud laughter, in which she fatuously joined. The three victims suffered on April 7, 1595.

Out of the confiscated property of the Samuels, Sir Samuel Cromwell, as lord of the manor, received a sum of £40, which he converted into an annual rent-charge of 40s. for the endowment of an annual sermon or lecture on the iniquity of witchcraft, to be delivered by a D.D. or B.D. of Queen's College, Cambridge. This strange memorial of a shameful and ignorant superstition was discontinued early in the eighteenth century.

In 1594, Ferdinando, Earl of Derby, died in and from the firm conviction that he was mortally bewitched, though he had no knowledge of the person who had so bewitched him.

About the same time there lived in an obscure part of Lancashire, not far from Pendle, two families of the names of Dundike and Chattox respectively, who both pretended to enjoy supernatural privileges, and were therefore as bitterly antagonistic as if they had belonged to different political factions.   Their neighbours, however, seem to have believed in the superior claims of the head of the Dundike family, Mother Dundike, who pretended that she had enjoyed her unhallowed powers for half a century.   The year in which occurred the incidents I am about to describe was, so to speak, her jubilee.

Mother Dundike must have been a woman of lively imagination, if we may form conclusions from her graphic account of the circumstances attending her initiation into the great army of ' the devil's own.'   One day, when returning from a begging expedition, she was accosted by a boy, dressed in a parti-coloured garment of black and white, who proved to be a demon, or evil spirit, and promised her that, in return for the gift of her soul, she should have anything and everything she desired.   On inquiring his name, she was told it was Tib; and here I may note that the ' princes and potentates ' of the nether world seem to have had a great predilection for monosyllabic names, and names of a vulgar and commonplace character. The upshot of the conversation between Tib and the woman was the surrender of her soul on the liberal conditions promised, and for the next five or six years the said devil frequently appeared unto her ' about daylight-gate ' (near evening), and asked what she would have or do.   With wonderful unselfishness she replied, ' Nothing.'   Towards the end of the sixth year, on a quiet Sabbath morning, while she lay asleep, Tib came in the shape of a brown dog, forced himself to her knee, and, as she wore no other garment than a smock, succeeded in drawing blood. Awaking suddenly, she exclaimed, 'Jesu, save my child!' but had not the power to say, 'Jesu, save *me!*' Whereupon the brown dog vanished, and for a space of eight weeks she was 'almost stark mad.'

The matter-of-fact style which distinguishes Mother Dundike's confession may also be traced in the statements of her children and grandchildren, who all speak as if witchcraft were an everyday reality, and as if evil spirits in various common disguises went to and fro in the land with edifying regularity. Let us turn to the evidence, if such it may be called, of Alison Device, a girl of about thirteen or fourteen years of age. Incriminating her grandmother without scruple, she declared that when they were on the tramp, the old woman frequently persuaded her to allow a devil or 'familiar' to suck at some part of her body, after which she might have and do what she would—though, strange to say, neither she nor anyone else ever availed themselves of their powers to improve their material condition, but lingered on in poverty and privation. James Device, one of Mother Dundike's grandsons, said that on Shrove Tuesday she bade him go to church to receive the sacrament—not, however, to eat the consecrated bread, but to bring it away, and deliver it to 'such a Thing' as should meet him on his way homeward. But he disobeyed the injunction, and ate the sacred bread. On his way home, when about fifty yards from the church, he was met by a 'Thing in the shape of a hare,' which asked him whether he had brought the bread according to his grandmother's directions. He answered that he had not; and therefore the Thing threatened to rend him in pieces, but he got rid of it by calling upon God.

Some few days later, hard by the new church in Pendle, a Thing appeared to him like to a brown dog, asked him for his soul, and promised in return that he should be avenged on his enemies. The virtuous youth replied, somewhat equivocatingly, that his soul was not his to give, but belonged to his Saviour Jesus Christ; as much as was his to give, however, he was contented to dispose of. Two or three days later James Device had occasion to go to Cave Hall, where a Mrs. Towneley angrily accused him of having stolen some of her turf, and drove him from her door with violence. When the devil next appeared—this time like a *black* dog—he found James Device in the right temper for a deed of wickedness. He was instructed to make an image of clay like Mrs. Towneley; which he did, and dried it the same night by the fire, and daily for a week crumbled away the said image, and two days after it was all gone Mrs. Towneley died! In the following Lent, one John Duckworth, of the Launde, promised him an old shirt; but when young Device went to his house for the gift, he was denied, and sent away with contumely. The spirit 'Dandy' then appeared to him, and exclaimed: 'Thou didst touch the man Duckworth,' which he, James Device, denied; but the spirit persisted: 'Yes; thou *didst* touch him, and therefore he is in my power.' Device then agreed with the demon that the said Duckworth should meet with the same fate as Mrs. Towneley, and in the following week he died.

It is a curious fact that the old woman Chattox, the head of the rival faction of practitioners in witchcraft, accused Mother Dundike of having inveigled her into the ranks of the devil's servants.   This was about 1597 or 1598.   To Mrs. Chattox the Evil One appeared—as he has appeared to too many of her sex—in the shape of a man.   Time, midnight; place, Elizabeth Dundike's tumble-down cottage.   He asked, as usual, for her soul, which she at first refused, but afterwards, at Mother Dundike's advice and solicitation, agreed to part with.   'Whereupon the said wicked spirit then said unto her, that he must have one part of her body for him to suck upon; the which she denied then to grant unto him; and withal asked him, what part of her body he would have for that use; who said, he would have a place of her right side, near to her ribs, for him to suck upon; whereunto she assented.   And she further said that, at the same time, there was a Thing in the likeness of a spotted bitch, that came with the said spirit unto the said Dundike, which did then speak unto her in Anne Chattox's hearing, and said, that she should have gold, silver, and worldly wealth at her will; and at the same time she saith there was victuals, viz., flesh, butter, cheese, bread, and drink, and bid them eat enough.   And after their eating, the devil called Fancy, and the other spirit

calling himself Tib carried the remnant away. And
she saith, that although they did eat, they were never
the fuller nor better for the same; and that at their
said banquet the said spirits gave them light to see
what they did, although they had neither fire nor
candle-light; and that there be both she-spirits and
(he-)devils.'

In a later chapter I shall have occasion to refer
to the confessions of the various persons implicated in this 'Great Oyer' of witchcraft. What
comes out very strongly in them is the hostility
which existed between the Chattoxes and the Dundikes, and their respective adherents. In Pendle
Forest there were evidently two distinct parties, one
of which sought the favour and sustained the pretensions of Mother Dundike, the other being not less
steadfast in allegiance to Mother Chattox. As to
these two beldams, it is clear enough that they
encouraged the popular credulity, resorted to many
ingenious expedients for the purpose of supporting
their influence, and unscrupulously employed that
influence in furtherance of their personal aims. They
knowingly played at a sham game of commerce with
the devil, and enjoyed the fear and awe with which
their neighbours looked up to them. It flattered
their vanity; and perhaps they played the game so
long as to deceive themselves. 'Human passions are
always to a certain degree infectious. Perceiving
the hatred of their neighbours, they began to think
that they were worthy objects of detestation and
terror, that their imprecations had a real effect, and

their curses killed.   The brown horrors of the forest
were favourable to visions, and they sometimes almost
believed that they met the foe of mankind in the
night.'   To the delusions of the imagination, especially when suggested by pride and vanity, there are no
means of putting a limit ; and it is quite possible that
in time these women gave credence to their own absurd
inventions, and saw a demon or familiar spirit in
every hare or black or brown dog that accidentally
crossed their path.

For awhile the witches created a reign of terror in
the forest.   But the interlacing animosities which
gradually sprang up between its inhabitants were the
fertile source of so much disorder that, at length, a
county magistrate of more than ordinary energy,
Roger Nowell, Esq., described as a very honest and
religious gentleman, conceived the idea that, by suppressing them, he should do the State good service.
Accordingly he ordered the arrest of Dundike and
Chattox, Alison Device, and Anne Redfern, and each,
in the hope of saving her life, having made a full
confession, he committed them to Lancaster Castle,
on April 2, 1612, to take their trials at the next
assizes.

No attempt was made, however, to search Malkin
Tower.   This lonely ruin was regarded with superstitious dread by the peasantry, who durst never
approach it, on account of the strange unearthly
noises and the weird creatures that haunted its wild
recesses.   James Device, when examined afterwards
by Nowell, deposed that about a month before his

arrest, as he was going towards his mother's house in the twilight, he met a brown dog coming from it, and, of course, a brown dog was the disguise of an evil spirit. About two or three nights after, he heard a great number of children shrieking and crying pitifully in the same uncanny neighbourhood; and at a later date his ears were shocked by a loud yelling, 'like unto a great number of cats.' We have heard the same sounds ourselves, at night, in places which did not profess to be haunted ! It is very possible that Dame Dundike, who was obviously a crafty old woman, with much knowledge of human nature, had something to do with these noises and appearances, for it was to her interest to maintain the eerie reputation of the Tower, and prevent the intrusion of inquisitive visitors. With all her little secrets, it was natural enough she should say, ' *Procul este, profani,*' while she would necessarily seize every opportunity of extending and strengthening her authority.

It was the general belief that the Malkin Tower was the place where the witches annually kept their Sabbath on Good Friday, and in 1612, after Dame Dundike's arrest, they met there as usual, in exceptionally large numbers, and, after the usual feasting, conferred together on ' the situation '—to use a slang phrase of the present day. Elizabeth Device presided, and asked their advice as to the best method of obtaining her mother's release. There must have been some daring spirits among those old women; for it was proposed—so runs the record—to kill

Lovel, the gaoler of Lancaster Castle, and another man of the name of Lister, accomplish an informal 'gaol-delivery,' and blow up the prison ! Even with the help of their familiars, they would have found this a difficult and dangerous enterprise, and we do not wonder that the proposal met with general disfavour.

Seldom, if ever, do conspirators meet without a traitor in their midst ; and on this occasion there was a traitor in Malkin Tower in the person of Janet Device, the youngest daughter of Alison Device, and grand-daughter of the unfortunate old woman who was lying ill and weak in Lancaster Gaol. A girl of only nine years of age, she was an experienced liar and thoroughly unscrupulous ; and having been bribed by Justice Nowell, she informed against the persons present at this meeting, and secured their arrest. The number of prisoners at Lancaster was increased to twelve, among whom were Elizabeth Device, her son James, and Alice Nutter, of Rough Lea, a lady of good family and fair estate. There is good reason to believe that the last-named was in no way implicated in the doings of the so-called witches, but that she was introduced by Janet Device to gratify the greed of some of her relatives— who, in the event of her death, would inherit her property—and the ill-feeling of Justice Nowell, whom she had worsted in a dispute about the boundary of their respective lands. The charges against her were trivial, and amounted to no more than that she had been present at the Malkin Tower convention, and had joined with Mother Dundike and

Elizabeth Device in bewitching to death an old man named Mitton. The only witnesses against her were Janet and Elizabeth Device, neither of whom was worthy of credence.

Blind old Mother Dundike escaped the terrible penalty of an unrighteous law by dying in prison before the day of trial. But justice must have been well satisfied with its tale of victims. Foremost among them was Mother Chattox, the head of the anti-Dundike faction—'a very old, withered, spent, and decrepit creature,' whose sight was almost gone, and whose lips chattered with the meaningless babble of senility. When judgment was pronounced upon her, she uttered a wild, incoherent prayer for Divine mercy, and besought the judge to have pity upon Anne Redfern, her daughter. The next person for trial was Elizabeth Device, who is described as having been branded 'with a preposterous mark in nature, even from her birth, which was her left eye standing lower than the other; the one looking down, the other looking up; so strangely deformed that the best that were present in that honourable assembly and great audience did affirm they had not often seen the like.' When this woman discovered that the principal witness against her was her own child, she broke out into such a storm of curses and reproaches that the proceedings came to a sudden stop, and she had to be removed from the court before her daughter could summon up courage to repeat the fictions she had learned or concocted. The woman was, of course, found guilty, as were

16

also James and Alison Device, Alice Nutter, Anne Redfern, Katherine Hewit, John and Jane Balcock, all of Pendle, and Isabel Roby, of Windle, most of whom strenuously asserted their innocence to the last. On August 13, the day after their trial, they were burnt 'at the common place of execution, near to Lancaster'—the unhappy victims of the ignorance, superstition, and barbarity of the age.

Janet Device, as King's evidence, obtained a pardon, though she acknowledged to have taken part in the practices of her parents, and confessed to having learned from her mother two prayers, one to cure the bewitched, and the other to get drink. The former, which is obviously a *pasticcio* of the old Roman Catholic hymns and traditional rhymes, runs as follows :

> 'Upon Good Friday, I will fast while I may
> Untill I heare them knell
> Our Lord's owne bell.
> Lord in His messe
> With His twelve Apostles good,
> What hath He in His hand ?
> Ligh in leath wand :
> What hath He in His other hand ?
> Heaven's door key.
> Open, open, Heaven's door keys !
> Stark, stark, hell door.
> Let Criznen child
> Goe to its mother mild ;
> What is yonder that crests a light so farrndly ?
> Thine owne deare Sonne that's nailed to the Tree.
> He is naild sore by the heart and hand,
> And holy harne panne.
> Well is that man
> That Fryday spell can,
> His child to learne ;

> A crosse of blew and another of red,
> As good Lord was to the Roode.
> Gabriel laid him downe to sleepe
> Upon the ground of holy weepe;
> Good Lord came walking by.
> Sleep'st thou, wak'st thou, Gabriel ?
> No, Lord, I am sted with sticks and stake
> That I can neither sleepe nor wake :
> Rise up, Gabriel, and goe with me,
> The stick nor the stake shall never dure thee.
> Sweet Jesus, our Lord.   Amen !

The other prayer consisted only of the Latin phrase: 'Crucifixus hoc signum vitam æternam. Amen.'*

* Thomas Pott's 'Wonderful Discoverie of Witches in the Countie of Lancashire' (1615), reprinted by the Chetham Society, 1845.

CHAPTER II.

WITCHCRAFT IN ENGLAND IN THE 17TH CENTURY.

THE accession of James I., a professed demonologist,
and an expert in all matters relating to witchcraft,
gave a great impulse to the persecution of witches in
England. 'Poor old women and girls of tender age
were walked, swum, shaved, and tortured; the
gallows creaked and the fires blazed.' In accordance
with the well-known economic law, that the demand
creates the supply, it was found that, in proportion
as trials and tortures increased, so did the number
of witches, until half the old hags in England supposed themselves, or were supposed by others, to
have made compacts with the devil. Legislation
then augmented its severity, and Parliament, in compliance with the wishes of the new King, passed an
Act by which sorcery and witchcraft were made
felony, without benefit of clergy. For some years
the country was witch-ridden, and it is appalling to
think of the hundreds of hapless, ignorant, and
innocent creatures who were cruelly done to death
under the influence of this extraordinary mania.

A remarkable case tried at King's Lynn in 1606 is reported in Howell's ' State Trials.' I avail myself of the summary furnished by Mr. Inderwick.

Marie, wife of Henry Smith, grocer, confessed, under examination, that, being indignant with some of her neighbours because they prospered in their trade more than she did, she oftentimes cursed them ; and that once, while she was thus engaged, the devil appeared in the form of a black man, and willed that she should continue in her malice, envy, and hatred, banning and cursing, and then he would see that she was revenged upon all to whom she wished evil. There was, of course, a compact insisted upon : that she should renounce God, and embrace the devil and all his works. After this he appeared frequently— once as a mist, once as a ball of fire, and twice he visited her in prison with a pair of horns, advising her to make no confession, but to rely upon him.

The evidence of the acts of witchcraft was as follows :

John Oakton, a sailor, having struck her boy, she cursed him roundly, and hoped his fingers would rot off, which took place, it was said, two years after-wards.

She quarrelled with Elizabeth Hancock about a hen, alleging that Elizabeth had stolen it. When the said Elizabeth denied the theft, she bade her go in-doors, for she would repent it; and that same night Elizabeth had pains all over her body, and her bed jumped up and down for the space of an hour or more. Elizabeth then consulted her father, and was taken by him to a wizard named Drake, who taught her how to concoct a witch-cake with all the nastiest ingredients imaginable, and to apply it, with certain words and conjurations, to the afflicted parts. For the time Elizabeth was cured; but some time afterwards, when she had been married to one James Scott, a great cat began to go about her house, and having done some harm, Scott thrust it twice through with his sword. As it still ran to and fro, he smote it with all his might upon its head, but could not kill it, for it leaped upwards almost a yard, and then crept down. Even when put into a bag, and dragged to the muck-hill, it moved and stirred, and the next morning was nowhere to be found. And this same cat, it was afterwards sworn, sat on the chest of Cicely Balye, and nearly suffocated her, because she had quarrelled with the witch about her manner of sweeping before her door; and the said witch called the said Cicely 'a fat-tailed sow,' and said her fatness would shortly be abated, as, indeed, it was.

Edmund Newton swore that he had been afflicted with various sicknesses, and had been banged in the face with dirty cloths, because he had undersold Marie Smith in Dutch cheeses. She also sent to him a person clothed in russet, with a little bush beard and a cloven foot, together with her imps, a toad, and a crab. One of his servants took the toad and put it into the fire, when it made a groaning noise for a quarter of an hour before it was consumed, 'during which time Marie Smith, who sent it, did endure (as was reported) torturing pains, testifying the grief she felt by the outcries she then made.'

Upon this evidence—such as it was—and upon her own confession, Marie Smith was convicted and sentenced to death. On the scaffold she humbly acknowledged her sins, prayed earnestly that God might forgive her the wrongs she had done her neighbours, and asked that a hymn of her own choosing—' Lord, turn not away Thy face '—might be sung. Then she died calmly. It is, no doubt, a curious fact—if, indeed, it *be* a fact, but the evidence is by no means satisfactory—that she confessed to various acts of witchcraft, and to having made a compact with the devil; but even this alleged confession cannot receive our credence when we reflect on the inherent absurdity and impossibility of the whole affair.

In 1619, Joan Flower and her two daughters, Margaretta and Philippa, formerly servants at Belvoir Castle, were tried before Judges Hobart and Bromley, on a charge of having bewitched to death two sons of the sixth Earl of Rutland, and found guilty. The mother died in prison; the two daughters were executed at Lincoln.

THE LANCASHIRE WITCHES.

My chronological survey next brings me to the famous case of the Lancashire witches.

I have already told the story of the Dundikes and the Chattoxes, and their exploits in Pendle Forest. In the same locality, two-and-twenty years later, lived a man of the name of Robinson, to whom it occurred that the prevalent belief in witchcraft might be turned to account against his neighbours. In this design he made his son—a lad about eleven years old—his instrument. After he had been properly trained, he was instructed by his father, on February 10, 1633, to go before two justices of the peace, and make the following declaration :

That, on All Saints' Day, while gathering wild plums in Wheatley Lane, he saw a black greyhound and a brown scamper across the fields. They came up to him familiarly, and he then discovered that each wore a collar shining like gold. As no one accompanied them, he concluded that they had broken loose from their kennels; and as at that moment a hare started up only a few paces from him, he thought he would set them to hunt it, but his efforts were all in vain ; and in his wrath he took the strings that hung from their collars, tied both to a little bush, and then whipped them. Whereupon, in the place of the black greyhound, started up the wife of a man named Dickinson, and in that of the brown a little boy. In his amazement, young Robinson (so he said) would have run away, but he was stayed by Mistress Dickinson, who pulled out of her pocket ' a piece of silver much like unto a fine shilling,' and offered it to him, if he promised to be silent. But he refused, exclaiming: ' Nay, thou art a witch !' Whereupon, she again put her hand in her pocket, and drew forth a string like a jingling bridle, which she put over the head of the small boy, and, behold, he was turned into a white horse, with a change as quick as that of a scene in a pantomime. Upon this white horse the woman placed, by force, young Robinson, and rode with him as far as the Hoar-Stones—a house at which the witches congregated together — where divers persons stood about the door, while others were riding towards it on horses of different colours. These dismounted, and, having tied up their horses, all went into the house, accompanied by their friends, to the number of threescore. At a blazing fire some meat was roasting, and a young woman gave Robinson flesh and bread upon a trencher, and drink in a glass, which, after the first taste, he refused, and would have no more, saying it was nought. Presently, observing that certain of the company repaired to an adjoining barn, he followed, and saw six of them on their knees, pulling at six several ropes which were fastened to the top of the house, with the result that joints of meat smoking hot, lumps of butter, and milk 'syleing,' or straining from the said ropes, fell into basins placed underneath them. When these six were weary, came other six, and pulled right lustily; and all the time they were pulling they made such foul faces that they frightened the peeping lad, so that he was glad to steal out and run home.

No sooner was his escape discovered than a party of the witches, including Dickinson's wife, the wife of a man named Loynds, and Janet Device, took up the pursuit, and over field and scaur hurried headlong, nearly overtaking him at a spot called Boggard Hole,

when the opportune appearance of a couple of horse-
men induced them to abandon their quarry. But
young Robinson was not yet ' out of the wood.' In
the evening he was despatched by his father to bring
home the cattle, and on the way, in a field called the
Ollers, he fell in with a boy who picked a quarrel
with him, and they fought together until the blood
flowed from his ears, when, happening to look down,
he saw that his antagonist had cloven feet, and, much
affrighted, set off at full speed to execute his commission. Perceiving a light like that of a lantern, he
hastened towards it, in the belief it was carried by a
neighbour; but on arriving at the place of its shining
he found there a woman whom he recognised as the
wife of Loynds, and immediately turned back. Falling
in again with the cloven-footed boy, he thought it
prudent to take to his heels, but not before he had
received a blow on the back which pained him sorely.

In support of this extraordinary story, the elder
Robinson deposed that he had certainly sent his son
to bring in the kine ; that, thinking he was away too
long, he had gone in search of him, and discovered
him in such a distracted condition that he knew
neither his father nor where he was, and so continued
for very nearly a quarter of an hour before he came
to himself.

The persons implicated by the boy Robinson were
immediately arrested, and confined in Lancaster
Castle. Some of them—for he told various stories,
and in each introduced new characters—he did not
know by name, but he protested that on seeing them

he should recognise them, and for this purpose he was carried about to the churches in the surrounding district to examine the congregations. The method adopted is thus described by Webster: 'It came to pass that this said boy was brought into the church of Kildwick, a large parish church, where I (being then curate there) was preaching in the afternoon, and was set upon a stall (he being but about ten or eleven years old) to look about him, which moved some little disturbance in the congregation for awhile. And, after prayers, I inquiring what the matter was, the people told me it was the boy that discovered witches, upon which I went to the house where he was to stay all night, where I found him and two very unlikely persons that did conduct him and manage his business. I desired to have some discourse with the boy in private, but they utterly refused. Then, in the presence of a great many people, I took the boy near me and said: "Good boy, tell me truly, and in earnest, didst thou see and hear such strange things of the meeting of witches as is reported by many that thou dost relate, or did not some person teach thee to say such things of thyself?" But the two men, not giving the boy leave to answer, did pluck him from me, and said he had been examined by two able justices of the peace, and they did never ask him such a question; to whom I replied, the persons accused therefore had the more wrong.'

In all, some eighteen women, married and single— the charge was generally made against women, as probably less capable of self-defence, and more impressionable than men—were brought to trial at Lancaster Assizes. There was really no evidence against them but the boy Robinson's, and to sustain it his unfortunate victims were examined for the *stigmata*, or devil-marks, which, of course, were found in ample quantity. Against seventeen a verdict of guilty was returned, one or two being convicted on their own confessions—the most perplexing incident in the whole case, for as these confessions were unquestionably false, they who made them were really *lying away their own lives*. By what impulse of morbid vanity, or diseased craving for notoriety, or strange mental delusion, were they inspired? And whence came the wild and even foul ideas which formed the staple of their delirious narratives? How did these quiet, stolid, unlettered Lancashire peasant-women become possessed of inventions worthy of the grimmest of German tales of *diablerie*? It is easier to ask these questions than to answer them ; but when the witch mania was once kindled in a neighbourhood it seems, like a pestilential atmosphere, to have stricken with disease every mind that was predisposed to the reception of unwholesome impressions.

The confession of Margaret Johnson, made on March 9, 1613, has been printed before, but it has so strong a psychological interest that I cannot omit it here. It may be taken as a type of the confessions made by the victims of credulity under similar circumstances :

‘ Betweene seven or eight yeares since, shee being in her house at Marsden in greate passion and anger, and discontented, and withall oppressed with some want, there appeared unto her a spirit or devill in the similitude and proportion of a man, apparelled in a suite of black, tied about with silke pointes, whoe offered her, yff shee would give him her soule, hee would supply all her wantes, and bring to her whatsoever shee wanted or needed, and at her appointment would helpe her to kill and revenge her either of men or beastes, or what she desired ; and, after a sollicitation or two, shee contracted and condicioned with the said devill or spiritt for her soule. And the said devill had her call him by the name of Memillion, and when shee called hee would bee ready to doe her will. And she saith that in all her talke and conference shee called the said Memillion her god.

'And shee further saith that shee was not at the greate meetinge of the witches at Hare-stones in the forest of Pendle on All Saintes Day last past, but saith shee was at a second meetinge the Sunday after All Saintes Day at the place aforesaid, where there was at that time betweene thirty and forty witches, which did all ride to the same meetinge. And thead of the said meetinge was to consult for the killing and hunting of men and beastes ; and that there was one devill or spiritt that was more greate and grand devill than the rest, and yff anie witch desired to have such an one, they might have such an one to kill or hurt anie body. And she further saith, that *such witches as have sharpe bounes are generally for the devill to prick them with which have no papps nor duggs, but raiseth blood from the place pricked with the boune, which witches are more greate and grand witches than they which have papps or dugs (!)*. And shee being further asked what persons were at their last meetinge, she named one Carpnell and his wife, Rason and his wife, Pickhamer and his wife, Duffy and his wife, and one Jane Carbonell, whereof Pickhamer's wife is the most greate, grand, and anorcyent witch; and that one witch alone can kill a beast, and yf they bid their spiritt or devill to goe and pricke or hurt anie man in anie particular place, hee presently will doe it. And that their spiritts have usually knowledge of their bodies. And shee further saith the men witches have women spiritts, and women witches have men spiritts ; that Good Friday is one of their constant daies of their generall meetinge, and that on Good Friday last they had a meetinge neere Pendle water-side ; and saith that their spirit doeth tell them where their meetinge must bee, and in what place ; and saith that if a witch desire to be in anie place upon a soddaine, that, on a dogg, or a tod, or a catt, their spiritt will presently convey them thither, or into anie room in anie man's house.

'But shee saith it is not the substance of their bodies that doeth goe into anie such roomes, but their spiritts that assume such shape and forme. And shee further saith that the devill, after hee begins to sucke, will make a papp or a dug in a short time, and the matter hee sucketh is blood. And further saith that the devill can raise foule wether and stormes, and soe hee did at their meetinges. And shee further saith that when the devill came to suck her pappe, he came to her in the likeness of a catt, sometimes of one collour, and sometimes of another. And since this trouble befell her, her spirit hath left her, and shee never saw him since.'

Happily, the judge who presided at the trial of these deluded and persecuted unfortunates was dissatisfied with the evidence, and reprieved them until he had time to communicate with the Privy Council, by whose orders Bridgman, Bishop of Chester, proceeded to examine into the principal cases. Three of the supposed criminals, however, had died of anxiety and suffering before the work of investigation began, and a fourth was sick beyond recovery. The cases into which the Bishop inquired were those of Margaret Johnson, Frances Dicconson, or Dickinson, Mary Spencer, and Mrs. Hargrave. Margaret Johnson the good Bishop describes as a widow of sixty, who was deeply penitent. 'I will not add,' she said, 'sin to sin. I have already done enough, yea, too much, and will not increase it. I pray God I may repent.' This victim of hallucination had confessed herself to be a witch, as we have seen, and was characterized by the Bishop as 'more often faulting in the particulars of her actions.' Frances Dicconson, however, and Mary Spencer, absolutely denied the truth of the accusations brought against them. Frances, according to the boy Robinson, had changed herself into a dog ; but it transpired that she had had a quarrel with the elder Robinson. Mary Spencer, a young woman of twenty, said that Robinson cherished much ill-feeling against her parents, who had been convicted of witch-craft at the last assizes, and had since died. She repeated the Lord's Prayer and the Apostles' Creed, and declared that she defied the devil and all his works. A story had been set afloat that she used to call her pail to follow her as she ran. The truth was that she often trundled it down-hill, and called to it in jest to come after her if she outstripped it. She could have explained every circumstance in court, ' but the wind was so loud and the throng so great, *that she could not hear the evidence against her.'*

This last touch, as Mr. S. R. Gardiner remarks, completes the tragedy of the situation. ' History,' as he says, ' occupies itself perforce mainly with the sorrows of the educated classes, whose own peers have left the records of their wrongs. Into the sufferings of the mass of the people, except when they have been lashed by long-continued injustice into frenzy, it is hard to gain a glimpse. For once the veil is lifted, and we see, as by a lightning flash, the forlorn and unfriended girl, to whom the inhuman laws of her country denied the services of an advocate, baffled by the noisy babble around her in her efforts to speak a word on behalf of her innocence. The very Bishop who examined her was under the influ-ence of the legal superstition that every accused person was the enemy of the King. He had heard, he said, that the father of the boy Robinson had offered, for forty shillings, to withdraw his charge against Frances Dicconson, "but such evidence being, as the lawyers speak, against the King," he "thought it not meet without further authority to examine."'

The Bishop, however, like the judge, was dissatisfied with the evidence; and the accused persons were eventually sent up to London, where they were examined by the King's physicians, the Bishops, the Privy Council, and by King Charles himself. Some medical men and midwives reported that Margaret Johnson was deceived in her idea that she bore on her body a sign or mark that her blood had been sucked. Doubts as to the truth of the boy Robinson's story being freely entertained, he was separated from his father, and he then revealed the whole invention to the King's coachman. He had heard stories told of witches and their doings, and out of these had concocted his ghastly fiction to save himself a whipping for having neglected to bring home his mother's cows. His father, perceiving at once how much might be made out of the tale, took it up and expanded it; manipulated it so as to serve his feelings of revenge or avarice, and then taught the boy how to repeat the enlarged and improved version. It was all a lie—from beginning to end. The day on which he pretended to have been carried to the Witches' Sabbath at the Hoar-Stones, he was a mile distant, gathering plums in a farmer's orchard. The accused were then admitted to the King's presence, and assured that their lives were safe. Further than this Charles seems to have been unable to go; for as late as 1636 these innocent and ill-treated persons were still lying in Lancaster Castle. It is satisfactory to state, however, that both the boy Robinson and his father were thrown into prison.

Fresh cases of witchcraft sprang up in the Pendle district, and early in 1636 four more women were condemned to death at the Lancaster Assizes. Bishop Bridgman, who was again directed to make inquiries, found that two of them had died in gaol, and that of the two others, one had been convicted on a madman's evidence, and that of a woman of ill fame; while the only proof alleged against the other was that a fleshy excrescence of the size of a hazel-nut grew on her right ear, and the end of it, being bloody, was supposed to have been sucked by a familiar spirit. The two women seem to have been pardoned; but, as in the former case, public opinion set too strongly against them to admit of their being released.

THE WITCHES OF SALMESBURY.

The singular circumstances connected with the supposed outbreak of witchcraft in Pendle Forest have, to a great extent, obscured the strange case of the witches of Salmesbury, though it presents several features worthy of consideration.

Three persons were accused—Jennet Bierley, Ellen Bierley, and Jane Southworth—and their supposed victim was one Grace Sowerbutts. In the language

17

of Mr. Thomas Potts, they were led into error by
'a subtle practice and conspiracy of a seminary priest,
or Jesuit, whereof this county of Lancaster hath good
store, who by reason of the general entertainment
they find, and great maintenance they have, resort
hither, being far from the eye of Justice, and, therefore, *procul a fulmine.*' At their trial, which took
place before Mr. Justice Bromley at Lancaster, on
Wednesday, August 19, the evidence of Grace Sowerbutts was to the following effect:

That for the space of *some years past* (at the time
of the trial she was only fourteen) she had been
haunted and vexed by four women, namely, Jennet
Bierley, her grandmother, Ellen Bierley, wife to
Henry Bierley, Jane Southworth, and a certain Old
Dorwife.   Lately, these four women drew her by the
hair of her head, and laid her on the top of a hay-
mow in the said Henry Bierley's barn.   Not long
after, Jennet Bierley met her near her house, first
appearing in her own likeness, and after that as a
black dog, and when she, Grace Sowerbutts, went
over a stile, she picked her off.   However, she was
not hurt, and, springing to her feet, she continued
her way to her aunt's at Osbaldeston.   That evening
she told her father what had occurred.   On Saturday,
April 4, going towards Salmesbury Butt to meet her
mother, she fell in, at a place called the Two Briggs,
with Jennet Bierley, first in her own shape, and afterwards in the likeness of a two-legged black dog; and
this dog kept close by her side until they came to a
pool of water, when it spake, and endeavoured to

persuade her to drown herself therein, saying it
was a fair and an easy death. Whereupon, she
thought there came to her one in a white sheet, and
carried her away from the pool, and in a short space
of time both the white thing and the black dog departed; but after Grace had crossed two or three
fields, the black dog re-appeared, and conveyed her
into Hugh Walshman's barn close at hand, laid her
upon the floor, covered her with straw on her body
and hay on her head, and lay down on the top of the
straw—for how long a time Grace was unable to
determine; because, she said, her speech and senses
were taken from her. When she recovered her con-
sciousness, she was lying on a bed in Walshman's
house, having been removed thither by some friends
who had found her in the barn within a few hours of
her having been taken there. As it was Monday
night when she came to her senses, she had been in
her trance or swoon, according to her marvellous
story, for about forty-eight hours.

On the following day, Tuesday, her parents fetched
her home; but at the Two Briggs Jennet and Ellen
Bierley appeared in their own shapes, and she fell
down in another trance, remaining unable to speak or
walk until the following Friday.

All this was remarkable enough, but Grace Sowerbutts—or the person who had tutored her—felt it was
not sufficiently grim or gruesome to make much
impression on a Lancashire jury, accustomed in witch
trials to much more harrowing details. She proceeded, therefore, to recall an incident of a more

attractive character. A good while, she said, before the trance business occurred, she accompanied her aunt, Ellen Bierley, and her grandmother, Jennet Bierley, to the house of one Thomas Walshman. It was night, and all the household were asleep, but the doors flew open, and the unexpected visitors entered. Grace and Ellen Bierley remained below, while Jennet made her way to the sleeping-room of Thomas Walshman and his wife, and thence brought a little child, which, as Grace supposed, must have been in bed with its father and mother. Having thrust a nail into its navel, she afterwards inserted a quill, and sucked for a good while (!); then replaced the child with its parents, who, of course, had never roused from their sleep. The child did not cry when it was thus abused, but thenceforth languished, and soon afterwards died. And on the night after its burial, the said Jennet and Ellen Bierley, taking Grace Sowerbutts with them, went to Salmesbury churchyard, took up the body, and carried it to Jennet's house, where a portion of it was boiled in a pot, and a portion broiled on the coals. Of both portions Jennet and Ellen partook, and would have had Grace join them in the ghoul-like repast, but she refused. Afterwards Jennet and Ellen seethed the bones in a pot, and with the fat that came from them said they would anoint their bodies, so that they might sometimes change themselves into other shapes.

The next story told by this abandoned girl is too foul and coarse for these pages, and we pass on to the conclusion of her evidence. On a certain occasion, she said, Jane Southworth, a widow, met her at the door of her father's house, carried her to the loft, and laid her upon the floor, where she was found by her father unconscious, and unconscious she remained till the next day. The widow Southworth then visited her again, took her out of bed, and placed her upon the top of a hayrick, three or four yards from the ground. She was discovered in this position by a neighbour's wife, and laid in her bed again, but remained speechless and senseless as before for two or three days. A week or so after her recovery, Jane Southworth paid her a third visit, took her away from her home, and laid her in a ditch near the house, with her face downwards. The usual process followed: she was discovered and put to bed, but continued unconscious—this time, however, only for a day and a night. And, further, on the Tuesday before the trial, the said Jane Southworth came again to her father's house, took her and carried her into the barn, and thrust her head amongst 'a company of boards' which were standing there, where she was soon afterwards found, and, being again placed in a bed, remained in her old fit until the Thursday night following.

After Grace Sowerbutts had finished her evidence, Thomas Walshman was called, who proved that his child died when about a year old, but of what disease he knew not; and that Grace Sowerbutts had been found in his father's barn, and afterwards carried into his house, where she lay till the Monday night 'as if she had been dead.' Then one John Singleton's deposition was taken: That he had often heard his old master, Sir John Southworth, say, touching the widow Southworth, that she was, as he thought, an evil woman and a witch, and that he was sorry for her husband, who was his kinsman, for he believed she would kill him. And that the said Sir John, in coming or going between Preston and his own house at Salmesbury, mostly avoided passing the old wife's residence, though it was the nearest way, entirely *out of fear of the said wife.* (Brave Sir John!)

This evidence, it is clear, failed to prove against the prisoners a single direct act of witchcraft; but so credulous were judge and jury in matters of this kind, that, notwithstanding the vague and suspicious character of the testimony brought forward, it would have gone hard with the accused, but for an accidental question which disclosed the fact that the girl, Grace Sowerbutts, had been prompted in her incoherent narrative, and taught to sham her fits of unconsciousness, by a Roman priest or Jesuit, named Thompson or Southworth, who was actuated by motives of fanaticism.

'How well this project,' exclaims the indignant Potts, 'to take away the lives of these innocent poor creatures by practice and villainy, to induce a young scholar to commit perjury, to accuse her own grandmother, aunt, etc., agrees either with the title of a Jesuit or the duty of a religious Priest, who should rather profess sincerity and innocency than practise treachery. But this was lawful, for they are heretics accursed, to leave the company of priests, to frequent churches, hear the word of God preached, and profess religion sincerely.' The horrors which he taught his promising pupil, Thompson probably gathered from the pages of Bodin and Delrio, or some of the other demonologists. Potts continues:

'Who did not condemn these women upon this evidence, and hold them guilty of this so foul and horrible murder? But Almighty God, who in His providence had provided means for their deliverance, although the priest, by the help of the Devil, had provided false witnesses to accuse them; yet God had prepared and placed in the seat of justice an upright judge to sit in judgment upon their lives, who after he had heard all the evidence at large against the prisoners for the King's Majesty, demanded of them what answer they could make. They humbly upon their knees, with weeping tears, desired him for God's cause to examine Grace Sowerbutts, who set her on, or by whose means this accusation came against them.'

The countenance of Grace Sowerbutts immediately underwent a great change, and the witnesses began to quarrel and accuse one another. The judge put some questions to the girl, who, for the life of her, could make no direct or intelligible answer, saying, with obvious hesitation, that she was put to a master to learn, but he had told her nothing of this.

'But here,' continues Potts, 'as his lordship's care and pains was great to discover the practices of those odious witches of the Forest of Pendle, and other

places, now upon their tribunal before him; so was
he desirous to discover this damnable practice to
accuse these poor women and bring their lives in
danger, and thereby to deliver the innocent.

'And as he openly delivered it upon the bench, in
the hearing of a great audience: That if a Priest or
Jesuit had a hand in one end of it, there would
appear to be knavery and practice in the other end
of it. And that it might better appear to the whole
world, examined Thomas Sowerbutts what [the]
Master taught his daughter: in general terms, he
denied all.

'The wench had nothing to say, but her Master
told her nothing of this. In the end, some that were
present told his lordship the truth, and the prisoners
informed him how she went to learn with one
Thompson, a Seminary Priest, who had instructed
and taught her this accusation against them, because
they were once obstinate Papists, and now came to
Church. Here is the discovery of this Priest, and of
his whole practice. Still this fire increased more and
more, and one witness accusing another, all things
were laid open at large.

'In the end his lordship took away the girl from
her father, and committed her to Mr. Leigh, a very
religious preacher, and Mr. Chisnal, two Justices of
the Peace, to be carefully examined.'

The examination was as follows:

'Being demanded whether the accusation she laid
upon her grandmother, Jennet Bierley, Ellen Bierley,
and Jane Southworth, of witchcraft, namely, of the

killing of the child of Thomas Walshman with a nail in the navel, the boiling, eating, and oiling, thereby to transform themselves into divers shapes, was true; she doth utterly deny the same; or that ever she saw any such practices done by them.

'She further saith, that one Master Thompson, which she taketh to be Master Christopher Southworth, to whom she was sent to learn her prayers, did persuade, counsel, and advise her, to deal as formerly hath been said against her said Grandmother, Aunt, and Southworth's wife.

'And further she confesseth and saith, that she never did know, or saw any Devils, nor any other Visions, as formerly by her hath been alleged and informed.

'Also she confesseth and saith, that she was not thrown or cast upon the hen-ruff and hay-mow in the barn, but that she went up upon the Mow herself by the wall-side.

'Being further demanded whether she ever was at the Church, she saith, she was not, but promised hereafter to go to the Church, and that very willingly.'

The three accused were also examined, and declared their belief that Grace Sowerbutts had been trained by the priest to accuse them of witchcraft, because they 'would not be dissuaded from the Church.'

'These examinations being taken, they were brought into the Court, and there openly in the presence of this great audience published and declared to the jury of life and death; and thereupon the gentlemen of their jury required to consider of them. For

although they stood upon their Trial, for matter of
fact of witchcraft, murther, and much more of the
like nature: yet in respect all their accusations did
appear to be practice, they were now to consider of
them and to acquit them. Thus were these poor
innocent creatures, by the great care and pains of this
honourable Judge, delivered from the danger of this
conspiracy; this bloody practice of the Priest laid
open: of whose fact I may lawfully say, *Etiam si ego
tacuero clamabunt lapides.*

' These are but ordinary with Priests and Jesuits:
no respect of blood, kindred, or friendship can move
them to forbear their conspiracies; for when he had
laboured treacherously to seduce and convert them,
and yet could do no good, then devised he this
means.

' God of His great mercy deliver us all from them
and their damnable conspiracies: and when any of his
Majesty's subjects, so free and innocent as these, shall
come in question, grant them as honourable a trial,
as reverend and worthy a judge to sit in judgment
upon them, and in the end as speedy a deliverance.

' And for that which I have heard of them, seen with
my eyes, and taken pains to read of them, my humble
prayer shall be to God Almighty, *Vt convertantur
ne pereant. Aut confundantur ne noccant.*'*

I pass on to a remarkable trial for witchcraft which
took place at Taunton Assizes in August, 1626, one

* Potts, ' Wonderful Discoverie of Witches in the Countie of
Lancaster ' (1613).

Edward Ball and Joan Greedie being charged with having practised upon a certain Edward Dinham.

It seems that the complainant, when under the witch-spell, possessed no fewer than three voices— namely, his own natural voice, and two artificial voices, of which one was shrill and pleasant, the other deadly and hollow. These two voices belonged respectively to the good and evil spirits which alternately prevailed over him. As it is said that they spoke without any movement of the lips or tongue, it is probable the man was a natural ventrilo-quist, and made use of his gift to imperil the lives of Ball and Greedie, against whom he may have enter-tained a hostile feeling. He gave the following specimen of the conversation which took place between him and his spirits:

GOOD SPIRIT. How comes this man to be thus tormented ?
BAD SPIRIT. He is bewitched.
GOOD. Who hath done it ?
BAD. That I may not tell.
GOOD. Aske him agayne.
DINHAM. Come, come, prithee, tell me who hath bewitched me
BAD. A woman in greene cloathes and a black hatt, with a large poll ; and a man in a gray suite, with blue stockings.
GOOD. But where are they ?
BAD. She is at her house, and hee is at a taverne in Ycohall [Youghal] in Ireland.
GOOD. But what are their names ?
BAD. Nay, that I will not tell.
GOOD. Then tell half of their names.
BAD. The one is Johan, and the other Edward.
GOOD. Nowe tell me the other half.
BAD. That I may not.
GOOD. Aske him agayne.
DINHAM. Come, come, prithee, tell me the other half.
BAD. The one is Greedie, and the other Ball.

This information having been obtained, a messenger is sent to a certain house, where the unfortunate Joan is straightway arrested. The conversation, if this absurd rigmarole can be so called, was afterwards resumed, the man conveniently going into one of his 'fits' for the purpose:

GOOD. But are these witches?
BAD. Yes; that they are.
GOOD. Howe came they to bee soe?
BAD. By discent.
GOOD. But howe by discent?
BAD. From the grandmother to the mother, and from the mother to the children.
GOOD. But howe aree they soe?
BAD. They aree bound to us, and wee to them.
GOOD. Lett mee see the bond.
BAD. Thou shalt not.
GOOD. Lett mee see it, and if I like I will seale alsoe.
BAD. Thou shalt, if thou wilt not reveale the contentes thereof.
GOOD. I will not.

As usual, the Good Spirit gets its way, and the bond is produced, drawing from the Good Spirit an exclamation of anguish: 'Alas! oh, pittifull, pittifull, pittifull! What? eight seales, bloody seales—four dead, and four alive? Ah, miserable!'

DINHAM. Come, come, prithee, tell me, Why did they bewitch me?
BAD. Because thou didst call Johane Greedie witche.
DINHAM. Why, is shee not a witche?
BAD. Yes; but thou shouldest not have said soe.
GOOD. But why did Ball bewitche him?
BAD. Because Greedie was not stronge enough.

A messenger is now sent after Ball; but on reaching his hiding-place, he finds that the poor man has just escaped, and he meets with people who had seen his flight. Dinham and his voices then join in a discourse, from which it appears that before they bewitched Dinham they had been guilty of various 'evil practices,' and had compassed the death of, at least, one of their victims. Six days afterwards Dinham has another 'fit,' and a second unsuccessful effort is made to track and arrest Ball. Disgusted with this failure, the Good Spirit strenuously opposes the Evil Spirit in his resolve to secure Dinham's soul:

BAD. I will have him, or else I will torment him eight tymes more.

GOOD. Thou shalt not have thy will in all thinges ; thou shalt torment him but four times more.

BAD. I will have thy soule.

GOOD. If thou wilt answer me three questions, I will seale and goe with thee.

BAD. I will.

GOOD. Who made the world ?

BAD. God.

GOOD. Who created mankynde ?

BAD. God.

GOOD. Wherefore was Christ Jesus His precious blood shed ?

BAD. I'le no more of that.

Here the patient was seized with the most violent convulsions, foaming at the mouth, and struggling with clenched hands and contorted limbs.

Another fit came off a few days afterwards, and in this Dinham was exposed to a double temptation:

BAD. If thou wilt give me thy soule, I will give thee gold enough.

GOOD. Thy gold will scald my fingers.

BAD. If thou wilt give me thy soule, I will give thee dice, and thou shalt winne infinite somes of treasure by play.

GOOD. If thou canst make every letter in this booke [a Prayer-book which Dinham held in his hand] a die, I will.

BAD. That I cannott.

GOOD. Laudes, laudes, laudes!

BAD. Thou shalt have *ladies* enough—ladies, ladies, ladies!...

GOOD. If thou canst make every letter in this book a ladie, I will.

Here the Bad Spirit made an attempt to cast away the book, but, after a violent struggle, was defeated; and then the Good Spirit celebrated his victory in 'the sweetest musicke that ever was heard.' Eventually Ball was captured, and Dinham then declared that his 'two voices' ceased to trouble him. Greedie and Ball were both committed for trial, but no record exists of their execution, and we may hope that they were acquitted of charges supported by such absurd and fallacious evidence.

Edward Fairfax, a man of ability and culture—the refined and melodious translator of Tasso's Christian epic—prosecuted six of his neighbours at York Assizes, in 1622, for practising witchcraft on his children. The grand jury found a true bill against them, and the accused were brought to trial. But the judge, who had been privately furnished with a certificate of their 'sober behaviour,' contrived so to influence the jury as to obtain a verdict of acquittal. The poet afterwards published an elaborate defence of his conduct. His folly may be excused, perhaps, since even such men as Raleigh and Bacon inclined towards a belief in witchcraft; and the judicious Evelyn makes it one of his principal com-

plaints against solitude that it created witches.
Hobbes, in his 'Leviathan,' takes, however, a more
enlightened view: 'As for witches,' he says, 'I
think not that their witchcraft is any real power; but
yet that they are justly punished for the false belief
they have that they can do such mischief, joined
with their purpose to do it if they can.'

Even the stir and tumult of the Civil War did not
suspend the persecuting activity of a degraded superstition. In 1644 eight witches of Manningtree, in
Essex, were accused of holding witches' meetings
every Friday night; were searched for teats and
devils' marks, convicted, and, with twenty-nine of
their fellows, hung. In the following year there
were more hangings in Essex; and in Norfolk a
score of witches suffered. In 1650 a woman was
hung at the Old Bailey as a witch. 'She was found
to have under her armpits those marks by which
witches are discovered to entertain their familiars.'
In April, 1652, Jean Peterson, the witch of Wapping,
was hung at Tyburn; and in July of the same year
six witches perished at Maidstone.

In 1653 Alice Bodenham, a domestic servant, was
tried at Salisbury before Chief Justice Wilde, and
convicted. It is not certain, however, that she was
executed.

In 1658 Jane Brooks was executed for practising
witchcraft on a boy of twelve, named Henry James,
at Chard, in Somersetshire; in 1663 Julian Cox, at
Taunton, for a similar offence.

THE WITCH-FINDER: MATTHEW HOPKINS.

The severe legislation against witchcraft had thus the effect—which invariably attends legislation when it becomes unduly repressive — of increasing the offence it had been designed to exterminate. It was attended, also, by another result, which is equally common—bringing to the front a number of informers who, at the cost of many innocent lives, turned it to their personal advantage. Of these witch-finders, the most notorious was Matthew Hopkins, of Manningtree, in Essex. When he first started his infamous trade, I cannot ascertain, but his success would seem to have been immediate. His earliest victims he found in his own neighbourhood. But, as his reputation grew, he extended his operations over the whole of Essex; and in a very short time, if any case of supposed witchcraft occurred, the neighbours sent for Matthew Hopkins as an acknowledged expert, whose skill would infalliby detect the guilty person.

His first appearance at the assizes was in the spring of 1645, when he accused an unfortunate old woman, named Elizabeth Clarke. To collect evidence against her, he watched her by night in a room in a Mr. Edwards's house, in which she was illegally detained. At her trial he had the audacity to affirm that, on the third night of his watching, after he had refused her the society of one of her imps, she confessed to him that, some six or seven years before, she had given herself over to the devil, who visited her in the form of 'a proper gentleman, with a hazel beard.'

Soon after this, he said, a little dog came in—fat, short-legged, and with sandy spots besprinkled on the white ground-colour of its tub-like body. When he prevented it from approaching the woman—who declared it was Jacmara, one of her imps—it straight-way vanished. Next came a greyhound, which she called Vinegar Tom; and next a polecat. Improving in fluent and fertile mendacity, Hopkins went on to assert that, on returning home that night, about ten of the clock, accompanied by his own greyhound, he saw his dog give a leap and a bound, and hark away as if hunting a hare; and on following him, he espied a little white animal, about the size of a kitten, and observed that his greyhound stood aloof from it in fright; and by-and-by this imp or kitten danced about the dog, and, as he supposed, bit a piece from its shoulder, for the greyhound came to him shrieking and crying, and bleeding from a great wound. Hopkins further stated that, going into his yard that same night, he saw a Black Thing, shaped like a cat, but thrice as big, sitting in a strawberry-bed, with its eyes fixed upon him. When he approached it, the Thing leaped over the pale towards him, as he thought, but, on the contrary, ran quite through the yard, with his greyhound after it, to a great gate, which was underset ' with a pair of tumbril strings,' threw it wide open, and then vanished, while his dog returned to him, shaking and trembling exceedingly.

In these unholy vigils of his, Hopkins was accompanied by one ' John Sterne, of Manningtree, gentle-man,' who, as a matter of course, confirmed all his

18

statements, and added the interesting detail that the third imp was called Sack-and-Sugar. The two wretches forced their way into the house of another woman, named Rebecca West, from whom they extracted a confession that the first time she saw the devil, he came to her at night, told her he must be her husband, and finally married her! The cruel tortures to which these and so many other unhappy females were exposed must undoubtedly have told on their nervous systems, producing a condition of hysteria, and filling their minds with hallucinations, which, perhaps, may partly have been suggested by the 'leading questions' of the witch-finders themselves. It is to be observed that their confessions wore a striking similarity, and that all the names mentioned of the so-called imps or familiars were of a ludicrous character, such as Prick - ear, Frog, Robin, and Sparrow. Then the excitement caused by these trials so wrought on the public mind that witnesses were easily found to testify—apparently in good faith—to the evil things done by the accused, and even to swear that they had seen their familiars. Thus one man declared that, passing at daybreak by the house of a certain Anne West, he was surprised to find her door open. Looking in, he descried three or four Things, like black rabbits, one of which ran after him. He seized and tried to kill him, but in his hands the Thing seemed a mere piece of wool, which extended lengthwise without any apparent injury. Full speed he made for a neighbouring spring, in which he tried to drown him, but as soon as he put the Thing in the

water, he vanished from his sight. Returning to the
house, he saw Anne West standing at the door 'in
her smock,' and asked her why she sent her imp
to trouble him, but received no answer.

His experiments having proved successful, Hopkins
took up witch-finding as a vocation, one which provided him with the means of a comfortable livelihood,
while it gratified his ambition by making him the
terror of many and the admiration of more, investing
him with just that kind of power which is delightful
to a narrow and commonplace mind. Assuming the
title of 'Witch-finder-General,' and taking with him
John Sterne, and a woman, whose business it was
to examine accused females for the devil's marks,
he travelled through the counties of Essex, Norfolk,
Huntingdon, and Sussex.

He was at Bury, in Suffolk, in August, 1645, and
there, on the 27th, no fewer than eighteen witches
were executed at once through his instrumentality.
A hundred and twenty more were to have been tried,
but the approach of the royal troops led to the
adjournment of the Assize. In one year this whole-
sale murderer caused the death of sixty poor creatures.
The 'test' he generally adopted was that of 'swimming,' which James I. recommends with much
unction in his 'Demonologie.' The hands and feet of
the accused were tied together crosswise, the thumb of
the right hand to the big toe of the left foot, and *vice
versâ*. She was then wrapped up in a large sheet or
blanket, and laid upon her back in a pond or river.
If she sank, she was innocent, but established her

innocence at the cost of her life; if she floated, which was generally the case, as her clothes afforded a temporary support, she was pronounced guilty, and hanged with all possible expedition.

Another 'test' was the repetition of the Lord's Prayer, which, it was believed, no witch could accomplish. Woe to the unfortunate creature who, in her nervousness, faltered over a syllable or stumbled at a word! Again she was forced into some awkward and painful attitude, bound with cords, and kept foodless and sleepless for four-and-twenty hours. Or she was walked continuously up and down a room, an attendant holding each arm, until she dropped with fatigue. Sometimes she was weighed against the church Bible, obtaining her deliverance if she proved to be heavier. But this last-named test was too lenient for the Witch-finder-General, who preferred the swimming ordeal.

One of his victims at Bury was a venerable clergyman, named Lowes, who had been Vicar of Brandeston, near Framlingham, for fifty years. 'After he was found with the marks,' says Sterne, 'in his confession'—when made, to whom, or under what circumstances, we are not informed—'he confessed that in pride of heart to be equal, or rather above God, the devil took advantage of him, and he covenanted with the devil, and sealed it with his blood, and had those familiars or spirits which sucked on the marks found on his body, and did much harm both by sea and land, especially by sea; for he confessed that he, being at Lungar Fort [Landguard Fort], in Suffolk, where he preached, as he walked upon the wall or works there, he saw a great sail of ships pass by, and that, as they were sailing by, one of his three imps, namely, his yellow one, forthwith appeared to him, and asked him what he should do, and he bade him go and sink such a ship, and showed his imp a new ship among the middle of the rest (as I remember), one that belonged to Ipswich ; so he confessed the imp went forthwith away, and he stood still and viewed the ships on the sea as they were a-sailing, and perceived that ship immediately to be in more trouble and danger than the rest ; for he said the water was more boisterous near that than the rest, tumbling up and down with waves, as if water had been boiled in a pot, and soon after (he said), in a short time, it sunk directly down into the sea as he stood and viewed it, when all the rest sailed down in safety ; then he confessed he made fourteen widows in one quarter of an hour.   Then Mr. Hopkins, as he told me (for he took his confession), asked him if it did not grieve him to see so many men cast away in a short time, and that he should be the cause of so many poor widows on a sudden ; but he swore by his Maker he was joyful to see what power his imps had : and so likewise confessed many other mischiefs, and had a charm to keep him out of the jail and hanging, as he paraphrased it himself; but therein the devil deceived him, for he was hanged that Michaelmas time, 1645, at Bury St. Edmunds.'   Poor old man !   This so-called confession has a very dubious air about it, and reads as if it had been invented by

Matthew Hopkins, who, as Sterne naïvely acknowledges, 'took the confessions,' apparently without
any witness or reporter being present.

The Witch-finder-General, when on his expedi-
tions of inquiry, assumed the style of a man of
fortune. He put up always at the best inns, and
lived in the most luxurious fashion, which he could
well afford to do, as, when invited to visit a town,
he insisted on payment of his expenses for board and
lodging, and a fee of twenty shillings. This sum he
claimed under any circumstances; but if he succeeded
in detecting any witches, he demanded another fee of
twenty shillings for each one brought to execution.
Generally his pretensions were admitted without
demur ; but occasionally he encountered a sturdy
opponent, like the Rev. Mr. Gaul, of Great Staughton,
in Huntingdonshire, who attacked him in a briskly-
written pamphlet as an intolerable nuisance. Hopkins
replied by an angry letter to one of the magistrates
of the town, in which he said : ' I am to come to
Kimbolton this week, and it shall be ten to one but I
will come to your town first; but I would certainly
know afore whether your town affords many sticklers
for such cattle [*i.e.* witches], or [is] willing to give
and afford us good welcome and entertainment, as
other where I have been, else I shall waive your
shire (not as yet beginning in any part of it myself),
and betake me to such places where I do and may
persist without control, but with thanks and recompense.'

Neither Mr. Gaul nor the magistrates of Great

Staughton showed any anxiety in regard to the witch-finder's threat. On the contrary, Mr. Gaul returned to the charge in a second pamphlet, entitled 'Select Cases of Conscience touching Witches and Witchcraft,' in which, while admitting the existence of witches—for he was not above the superstition of his age and country—he vigorously attacked Hopkins for accusing persons on insufficient evidence, and denounced the atrocious cruelties of which he and his associates were guilty. I have no doubt that this manly language helped to bring about a wholesome change of public opinion. In the eastern counties so bitter a feeling of resentment arose, that Hopkins found it advisable to seek fresh woods and pastures new. In the spring of 1647 he was at Worcester, where four unfortunates were condemned on the evidence of himself and his associates. But the indignation against him deepened and extended, and he hastily returned to his native town, trembling for his wretched life. There he printed a defence of his conduct, under the title of ' The Discovery of Witches, in answer to several queries lately delivered to the Judge of Assize for the county of Norfolk ; published by Matthew Hopkins, witch-finder, for the benefit of the whole kingdom.' His death occurred shortly afterwards. According to Sterne, he died the death of a righteous man, having ' no trouble of conscience for what he had done, as was falsely reported for him.' But the more generally accepted account is an instance of ' poetical justice '—of Nemesis satisfied—which I heartily hope is authentic. It is said that he was surrounded by a mob in a Suffolk village, and accused of being himself a wizard, and of having, by his tricks of sorcery, cheated the devil out of a memorandum-book, in which were entered the names of all the witches in England. 'Thus,' cried the populace, 'you find out witches, not by God's name, but by the devil's.' He denied the charge; but his accusers determined that he should be subjected to his favourite test. He was stripped; his thumbs and toes were tied together; he was wrapped in a blanket, and cast into a pond. Whether he was drowned, or whether he floated, was taken up, tried, sentenced, and executed, authorities do not agree; but they agree that he never more disturbed the peace of the realm as a witch-finder.

Butler has found a niche for this knave, among other knaves, in his 'Hudibras':

> 'Hath not this present Parliament
> A lieger to the Devil sent,
> Fully empowered to set about
> Finding revolted witches out?
> And has he not within a year
> Hanged threescore of them in one shire?
> Some only for not being drowned,
> And some for sitting above ground
> Whole days and nights upon their breeches,
> And, feeling pain, were hanged for witches. . .
> Who proved himself at length a witch,
> And made a rod for his own breech '—

the engineer hoist with his own petard—happily a by no means infrequent mode of retribution.

Sterne, the witch-finder's colleague, not unnaturally shared in the public disfavour, and in defence of himself and his deceased partner gave to the world a 'Confirmation and Discovery of Witchcraft,' in which he acknowledges to have been concerned in the detection and condemnation of some 200 witches in the counties of Essex, Suffolk, Northampton, Huntingdon, Bedford, Norfolk and Cambridge, and the Isle of Ely. He adds that 'in many places I never received penny as yet, nor any like, notwithstanding I have bonds for satisfaction, except I should sin; but many rather fall upon me for what hath been received, but I hope such suits will be disannulled, and that when I have been out of moneys for towns in charges and otherwise, such course will be taken that I may be satisfied and paid with reason.' One can hardly admire sufficiently the brazen effrontery of this appeal!

The number of persons imprisoned on suspicion of witchcraft grew so large as to excite the alarm of the Government, who issued stringent orders to the country magistrates to commit for trial persons brought before them on this charge, and forbade them to exercise summary jurisdiction. Eventually a commission was given to the Earl of Warwick, and others, to hold a gaol-delivery at Chelmsford. Lord Warwick, who had done good service to the State as Lord High Admiral, was sagacious and fair-minded. But with him went Dr. Edmund Calamy, the eminent Puritan divine, to see that no injustice was done to the parties accused. This proved an unfortunate choice; for Calamy, who, in his sermon before the judges, had enlarged on the enormity of the sin of witchcraft, sat on the bench with them, and unhappily influenced their deliberations in the direction of severity. As a result, sixteen persons were hanged at Yarmouth, fifteen at Chelmsford, besides some sixty at various places in Suffolk.

Whitlocke, in his 'Memorials,' speaks of many 'witches' as having been put upon their trial at Newcastle, through the agency of a man whom he calls 'the Witch-finder.' Another of the imitators of Hopkins, a Mr. Shaw, parson of Rusock, came to condign humiliation (1660). Having instigated some bucolic barbarians to put an old woman, named Joan Bibb, to the water-ordeal, she swam right vigorously in the pool, and struggled with her assailants so strenuously that she effected her escape. Afterwards she brought an action against the parson for instigating the outrage, and obtained £20 damages.

In 1664, Elizabeth Styles, of Bayford, Somersetshire, was convicted and sentenced to death, but died in prison before the day fixed for her execution. It is said that she made a voluntary confession— without inducement or torture—in the presence of the magistrates and several divines—another case (if it be true) of the morbid self-delusion which in times of popular excitement makes so many victims.

One feels the necessity of speaking with some degree of moderation respecting the credulity of the ignorant and uneducated classes, when one finds so

sound a lawyer and so admirable a Christian as Sir
Matthew Hale infected by the mania. No other blot,
I suppose, is to be found on his fame and character;
and that he should have incurred this indelible stain,
and fallen into so pitiable an error, is a problem by
no means easy of solution.

At the Lent Assize, in 1664, at Bury St. Edmunds,
two aged women, named Rose Cullender and Amy
Duny were brought before him on a charge of having
bewitched seven persons. The nature of the evidence
on which it was founded the reader will appreciate
from the following examples:

Samuel Pacey, of Lowestoft, a man of good repute
for sobriety and other homely virtues, having been
sworn, said: That on Thursday, October 10 last, his
younger daughter Deborah, about nine years old, fell
suddenly so lame that she could not stand on her
feet, and so continued till the 17th, when she asked
to be carried to a bank which overlooked the sea, and
while she was sitting there, Amy Duny came to the
witness's house to buy some herrings, but was denied.
Twice more she called, but being always denied, went
away grumbling and discontented. At this instant
of time the child was seized with terrible fits; complained of a pain in her stomach, as if she were being
pricked with pins, shrieking out 'with a voice like a
whelp,' and thus continuing until the 30th. This
witness added that Amy Duny, being known as a
witch, and his child having, in the intervals of her
fits, constantly exclaimed against her as the cause of
her sufferings, saying that the said Amy did appear

to her and frighten her, he began to suspect the said Amy, and accused her in plain terms of injuring his child, and got her 'set in the stocks.' Two days afterwards, his daughter Elizabeth was seized with similar fits; and both she and her sister complained that they were tormented by various persons in the town of bad character, but more particularly by Amy Duny, and by another reputed witch, Rose Cullender.

Another witness deposed that she had heard the two children cry out against these persons, who, they said, threatened to increase their torments tenfold if they told tales of them. 'At some times the children would see Things run up and down the house in the appearance of mice; and one of them suddenly snapped one with the tongs, and threw it in the fire, and it screeched out like a bat. At another time, the younger child, being out of her fits, went out of doors to take a little fresh air, and presently a little Thing like a bee flew upon her face, and would have gone into her mouth, whereupon the child ran in all haste to the door to get into the house again, shrieking out in a most terrible manner; whereupon this deponent made haste to come to her, but before she could reach her, the child fell into her swooning fit, and, at last, with much pain and straining, vomited up a twopenny nail with a broad head; and after that the child had raised up the nail she came to her understanding, and being demanded by this deponent how she came by this nail, she answered that the bee brought this nail and forced it into her mouth.'

Such evidence as this failing to satisfy Serjeant
Keeling, and several magistrates who were present,
of the guilt of the accused, it was resolved to resort
to demonstration by experiment. The persons bewitched were brought into court to touch the two
old women; and it was observed (says Hutchinson)
that when the former were in the midst of their fits,
and to all men's apprehension wholly deprived of all
sense and understanding, closing their fists in such a
manner as that the strongest man could not force
them open, yet, at the least touch of one of the
supposed witches—Rose Cullender, by name—they
would suddenly shriek out, opening their hands,
which accident would not happen at any other
person's touch. 'And lest they might privately see
when they were touched by the said Rose Cullender,
they were blinded with their own aprons, and the
touching took the same effect as before. There was
an ingenious person that objected there might be a
great fallacy in this experiment, and there ought not
to be any stress put upon this to convict the parties,
for the children might counterfeit this their distemper, and, perceiving what was done to them, they
might in such manner suddenly alter the erection
and gesture of their bodies, on purpose to induce
persons to believe that they were not natural, but
wrought strangely by the touch of the prisoners.
Wherefore, to avoid this scruple, it was privately
desired by the judge that the Lord Cornwallis, Sir
Edmund Bacon, and Mr. Serjeant Keeling, and some
other gentleman then in court, would attend one of

the distempered persons in the farthest part of the hall whilst she was in her fits, and then to send for one of the witches to try what would then happen, which they did accordingly; and Amy Duny was brought from the bar, and conveyed to the maid. They then put an apron before her eyes; and then one other person touched her hand, which produced the same effect as the touch of the witch did in the court. Whereupon the gentlemen returned, openly protesting that they did believe the whole transaction of the business was a mere imposture.' As, in truth, it was.

It is remarkable that Sir Matthew Hale was still unconvinced. He invited the opinion of Sir Thomas Browne, a man of great learning and ability—the author of the 'Religio Medici,' and other justly famous works—who admitted that the fits were natural, but thought them 'heightened by the devil co-operating with the malice of the witches, at whose instance he did the villanies.' Sir Matthew then charged the jury. There were, he said, two questions to be considered: First, whether or not these children were bewitched? And, second, whether the prisoners at the bar had been guilty of bewitching them? *That there were such creatures as witches, he did not doubt;* and he appealed to the Scriptures, which had affirmed so much, and also to the wisdom of all nations, which had enacted laws against such persons. Such, too, he said, had been the judgment of this kingdom, as appeared by that Act of Parliament which had provided punishment proportionable

to the quality of the offence. He desired them to
pay strict attention to the evidence, and implored the
great God of heaven to direct their hearts in so
weighty a matter; for to condemn the innocent, and
set free the guilty, was 'an abomination to the
Lord.'

After a charge of this description, the jury
naturally brought in a verdict of 'Guilty.' Sentence
of death was pronounced; and the two poor old
women, protesting to the last their innocence, suffered
on the gallows. Who will not regret the part played
by Sir Matthew Hale in this judicial murder? It is
no excuse to say that he did but share in the popular
belief. One expects of such a man that he will rise
superior to the errors of ordinary minds; that he
will be guided by broader and more enlightened
views—by more humane and generous sympathies.
Instead of attempting an apology which no act can
render satisfactory, it is better to admit, with Sir
Michael Foster, that 'this great and good man was
betrayed, notwithstanding the rectitude of his intentions, into a great mistake, under the strong bias of
early prejudices.'

Gradually, however, a disbelief in witchcraft grew
up in the public mind, as intellectual inquiry widened
its scope, and the relations of man to the Unseen
World came to be better understood. Among the
educated classes the old superstition expired much
more rapidly than among the poorer; and so we find
that though convictions became rarer, committals and
trials continued tolerably frequent until the closing

years of the eighteenth century. To the ghastly roll of victims, however, additions continued to be made. Thus in August, 1682, three women, named Temperance Lloyd, Susannah Edwards, and Mary Trembles, were tried at Exeter before Lord Chief Justice North and Mr. Justice Raymond, convicted of various acts of witchcraft, and sentenced to death. Before their trial they had confessed to frequent interviews with the devil, who appeared in the shape of a black man as long (or as short) as a man's arm ; and one of them acknowledged to have caused the death of four persons by witchcraft. Some portion of these monstrous fictions they recanted under the gallows; but even on the brink of the grave they persisted in claiming the character of witches, and in asserting that they had had personal intercourse with the devil.

In March, 1684, Alicia Welland was tried before Chief Baron Montague at Exeter, convicted, and executed.

To estimate the extent to which the belief in witchcraft, during the latter part of the seventeenth century, operated against the lives of the accused, Mr. Inderwick has searched the records of the Western Circuit, from 1670 to 1712 inclusive, and ascertained that out of fifty-two persons tried in that period on various charges of witchcraft, only seven were convicted, and one of these seven was reprieved. ' What occurred on the Western,' he remarks, ' probably went on at each of the several circuits into which the country was then divided ; and one cannot doubt that in Norfolk, Suffolk, Essex, Huntingdon, and Lancashire, where the witches mostly abounded, the charges and convictions were far more numerous than in the West.   The judges appear, however, not to have taken the line of Sir Matthew Hale, but, as far as possible, to have prevented convictions. Indeed, Lord Jeffreys—who, when not engaged on political business, was at least as good a judge as any of his contemporaries—and Chief Justice Herbert, tried and obtained acquittals of witches in 1685 and 1686 at the very time that they were engaged on the Bloody Assize in slaughtering the participators in Monmouth's rebellion.   It is also a remarkable fact that, from 1686 to 1712, when charges of witchcraft gradually ceased, charges and convictions of malicious injury to property in burning haystacks, barns, and houses, and malicious injuries to persons and to cattle, increased enormously, these being the sort of accusations freely made against the witches before this date.'

I think there can be little doubt that many evil-disposed persons availed themselves of the prevalent belief in witchcraft as a cover for their depredations on the property of their neighbours, diverting sus-picion from themselves to the poor wretches who, through accidental circumstances, had acquired notoriety as the devil's accomplices.   It would also seem probable that not a few of the reputed witches similarly turned to account their bad reputation.   It is not impossible, indeed, that there may be a certain degree of truth in the tales told of the witches' meetings, and that in some rural neighbourhoods the individuals suspected of being witches occasionally assembled at an appointed rendezvous to consult upon their position and their line of operations. The practices at these gatherings may not always have been kept within the limits of decency and decorum ; and in this way the loathsome details with which every account of the witches' meetings are embellished may have had a real foundation.

That the judges at length began persistently to discourage convictions for witchcraft is seen in the action of Lord Chief Justice Holt at the Bury St. Edmunds Assize in 1694. An old woman, known as Mother Munnings, of Harks, in Suffolk, was brought before him, and the witnesses against her retailed the village talk—how that her landlord, Thomas Purnel, who, to get her out of the house she had rented from him, had removed the street-door, was told that 'his nose should lie upward in the churchyard' before the following Saturday ; and how that he was taken ill on the Monday, died on the Tuesday, and was buried on the Thursday. How that she had a familiar in the shape of a polecat, and how that a neighbour, peeping in at her window one night, saw her take out of her basket a couple of imps—the one black, the other white. And how that a woman, named Sarah Wager, having quarrelled with her, was stricken dumb and lame. All this tittle-tattle was brushed aside in his charge by the strong common-sense of the judge; and the jury, under his direction, returned a verdict of 'Not guilty.' Dr. Hutchinson remarks : ' Upon particular inquiry of several in or near the town, I find most are satisfied that it is a very right judgment. She lived about two years after, without doing any known harm to anybody, and died declaring her innocence. Her landlord was a consumptive-spent man, and the words not exactly as they swore them, and the whole thing seventeen years before. . . . The white imp is believed to have been a lock of wool, taken out of her basket to spin; and its shadow, it is supposed, was the black one.'

In the same year (1694) a woman, named Margaret Elmore, was tried at Ipswich ; in 1695 one Mary Gay at Launceston; and in 1696 one Elizabeth Hume at Exeter ; but in each case, under the direction of Chief Justice Holt, a verdict of acquittal was declared. Thus the seventeenth century went its way in an unaccustomed atmosphere of justice and humanity.

CHAPTER III.

THE DECLINE OF WITCHCRAFT IN ENGLAND.

THE honour of discouraging prosecutions for witch-craft belongs in the first place to France, which abolished them as early as 1672, and for some years previously had refrained from sending any victims to the scaffold or the stake. In England, the same effect was partly due, perhaps, to the cynical humour of the Court of Charles II., where many, who before ventured only to doubt, no longer hesitated to treat the subject with ridicule. 'Although,' says Mr. Wright, 'works like those of Baxter and Glanvil had still their weight with many people, yet in the controversy which was now carried on through the instrumentality of the press, those who wrote against the popular creed had certainly the best of the argument. Still, it happened from their form and character that the books written to expose the absurdity of the belief in sorcery were restricted in their circulation to the more educated classes, while popular tracts in defence of witchcraft and collections of cases were printed in a cheaper form, and widely distributed among that class in society where the belief was most firmly rooted. The

effect of these popular publications has continued in
some districts down to the present day. Thus the
press, the natural tendency of which was to enlighten
mankind, was made to increase ignorance by pandering
to the credulity of the multitude.'

I have spoken of the seventeenth century as going
out in an atmosphere of justice and humanity. But
an ancient superstition dies hard, and the eighteenth
century, when it dawned upon the earth, found the
belief in witchcraft still widely extended in England.
Even men of education could not wholly surrender
their adhesion to it. We read with surprise Addison's opinion in *The Spectator*, 'that the arguments
press equally on both sides,' and see him balancing
himself between the two aspects of the subject in a
curious state of mental indecision. 'When I hear the
relations that are made from all parts of the world,' he
says, ' I cannot forbear thinking that there is such an
intercourse and commerce with evil spirits, as that
which we express by the name of witchcraft. But
when I consider,' he adds, 'that the ignorant and
credulous parts of the world abound most in these
relations, and that the persons among us who are
supposed to engage in such an infernal commerce are
people of a weak understanding and crazed imagination, and at the same time reflect upon the many
impostures and delusions of this nature that have
been detected in all ages, I endeavour to suspend my
belief till I hear more certain accounts than any which
have yet come to my knowledge.' And then he
comes to a halting and unsatisfactory conclusion,

which will seem almost grotesque to the reader of the preceding pages, with their details of *succubi* and *incubi*, imps and familiars, black cats, pole-cats, goats, and the like: ' In short, when I consider the question, whether there are such persons in the world as we call witches, my mind is divided between two opposite opinions, or, rather (to speak my thoughts freely), I believe in general that there is, and has been, such a thing as witchcraft, but, at the same time, can give no credit to any particular instance of it.'

Addison goes on to draw the picture of a witch of the period, ' Moll White,' who lived in the neighbourhood of Sir Roger de Coverley, ' a wrinkled hag, with age grown double.' This old woman had the reputation of a witch all over the country; her lips were observed to be always in motion, and there was not a switch about her house which her neighbours did not believe had carried her several hundreds of miles. ' If she chanced to stumble, they always found sticks or straws that lay in the figure of a cross before her. If she made any mistake at church, and cried Amen in a wrong place, they never failed to conclude that she was saying her prayers backwards. There was not a maid in the parish that would take a pin of her, though she should offer a bag of money with it. . . . If the dairy-maid does not make her butter to come so soon as she would have it, Moll White is at the bottom of the churn. If a horse sweats in the stable, Moll White has been upon his back. If a hare makes an unexpected escape from the hounds, the huntsman curses Moll White. . . .

'I have been the more particular in this account,' says Addison, 'because I know there is scarce a village in England that has not a Moll White in it. When an old woman begins to dote, and grow chargeable to a parish, she is generally turned into a witch, and fills the whole country with extravagant fancies, imaginary distempers, and terrifying dreams. In the meantime, the poor wretch that is the innocent occasion of so many evils begins to be frighted at herself, and sometimes confesses secret commerces and familiarities that her imagination forms in a delirious old age. This frequently cuts off charity from the greatest objects of compassion, and inspires people with a malevolence towards those poor decrepit parts of our species in whom human nature is defaced by infirmity and dotage.'

On March 2, 1703, one Richard Hathaway, apprentice to Thomas Wiling, a blacksmith in Southwark, was tried before Chief Justice Holt at the Surrey Assizes, as a cheat and an impostor, having pretended that he had been bewitched by Sarah Morduck, wife of a Thames waterman, so that he had been unable to eat or drink for the space of ten weeks together; had suffered various pains; had constantly vomited nails and crooked pins; had at times been deprived of speech and sight, and all through the wicked cunning of Sarah Morduck; further, that he was from time to time relieved of his ailments by scratching the said Sarah, and drawing blood from her. On these charges Sarah had been committed by the magistrates, and was tried as a witch at the Guildford Assizes in February, 1701. It was then proved in her defence that Dr. Martin, minister, of the parish of Southwark, hearing of Hathaway's troubles and method of obtaining relief, had resolved to put the matter to a fair test; and repairing to Hathaway's room, in one of his semi-conscious and wholly blind intervals, had, in the presence of many witnesses, pretended to give to the supposed sufferer the arm of Sarah Morduck, when it was really that of a woman whom he had called in from the street. Hathaway, in ignorance of the trick played upon him, scratched the wrong arm, and immediately professed to recover his sight and senses. On finding his deception discovered, Hathaway looked greatly ashamed, and attempted no defence or excuse, when Dr. Martin severely reproached him for his conduct.

The populace, however, remained unconvinced, and when Dr. Martin and his friends had departed, accompanied Hathaway to the house of Sarah Morduck, whom they savagely ill-treated. They then declared that the woman who had lent herself as a subject for experiment was also a witch, and loaded her with contumely, while her husband gave her a beating. It further appeared that, on one occasion, when Hathaway alleged he had been vomiting crooked pins and nails, he had been searched, and hundreds of packets of pins and nails found in his pockets, and on his hands being tied behind him, the vomiting immediately ceased. Eventually the jury acquitted Sarah Morduck, and branded Hathaway as a cheat and an impostor. The lower classes, however, received the verdict with contempt, mobbed Dr. Martin, and raised a collection for Hathaway as for a man of many virtues whom fortune had ill-treated. A magistrate, Sir Thomas Lane, who sided with the mob, summoned Sarah Morduck before him, and after she had been scratched by Hathaway in his presence, ordered her to be examined for devil-marks by two women and a doctor. Though none could be detected, his prejudice was so extreme that he committed her as a witch to the Wood Street Compter, refusing bail to the extent of £500. Dr. Martin, with other gentlemen, again came to her assistance, and ultimately she was released on reasonable surety.

The Government now thought it time to support the cause of justice, and, carrying out the verdict of the Guildford jury, indicted Hathaway as a cheat, and himself and his friends for assaulting Sarah Morduck. In addition to the evidence previously adduced, it was shown that, being in bad health, he had been placed in the custody of a Dr. Kenny, a surgeon, who, desiring to test the truth of his fasting, made holes in the partition wall of his compartment, and watched his proceedings for about a fortnight, during which period, while pretending to fast, he was observed to feed heartily on the food conveyed to him, and once, having received an extra allowance of whisky, he got tipsy, played a tune on the tongs, and danced before the fire. At the trial a Dr. Hamilton was called for the defence; but, Balaam-like, he banned rather than blessed, for having affirmed that the man's fasting was the chief evidence of witchcraft,

'Doctor,' said the Chief Justice, 'do you think it possible for a man to fast a fortnight?' 'I think not,' he replied. 'Can all the devils in hell help a man to fast so long?' 'No, my lord,' said the doctor; 'I think not.' These answers were conclusive; and without leaving the box, the jury found Hathaway guilty, and he was sentenced by Chief Justice Holt to pay a fine of one hundred marks, to stand in the pillory on the following Sunday for two hours at Southwark, the same on the Tuesday at the Royal Exchange, the same on the Wednesday at Temple Bar, the next day to be whipped at the House of Correction, and afterwards to be imprisoned with hard labour for six months.

Two reputed witches, Eleanor Shaw and Mary Phillips, were executed at Northampton on March 17, 1705; and on July 22, 1712, five Northamptonshire witches, Agnes Brown, Helen Jenkinson, A...... Bill, Joan Vaughan, and Mary Barber, suffered at the same place.

It is generally believed that the last time an English jury brought in a verdict of guilty in a case of witchcraft was in 1712, when a poor Hertfordshire peasant woman, named Jane Wenham, was tried before Mr. Justice Powell, sixteen witnesses, including three clergymen, supporting the accusation. The evidence was absurd and frivolous; but, in spite of its frivolousness and absurdity, and the poor woman's fervent protestations of innocence, and the judge's strong summing-up in her favour, a Hertfordshire jury convicted her. The judge was compelled by the law to pronounce sentence of death, but he lost no time in obtaining from the Queen a pardon for the unfortunate woman. But, on emerging from her prison, she was treated by the mob with savage ferocity; and, to save her from being lynched, Colonel Plumer, of Gilson, took her into his service, in which she continued for many years, earning and preserving the esteem of all who knew her.

But there is a record of an execution for witchcraft, that of Mary Hicks and her daughter, taking place in 1716 (July 28); and though it is not indubitably established, I do not think its authenticity can well be doubted.

In January, 1736, an old woman of Frome, reputed to be a witch, was dragged from her sick-bed, put astride on a saddle, and kept in a mill-pond for nearly an hour, in the presence of upwards of 200 people. The story goes that she swam like a cork, but on being taken out of the water expired immediately. A coroner's inquest was held on the body, and three persons were committed for trial for manslaughter; but it is probable that they escaped punishment, as nobody seems to have been willing to appear in the witness-box against them.

Among the vulgar, indeed, the superstition was hard to kill. In the middle of the last century, a poor man and his wife, of the name of Osborne, each about seventy years of age, lived at Tring, in Hertfordshire. On one occasion, Mother Osborne, as she was commonly called, went to a dairyman, appropriately named Butterfield, and asked for some buttermilk; but was harshly repulsed, and informed that he had scarcely enough for his hogs. The woman replied with asperity that the Pretender (it was in the '45 that this took place) would soon have him and his hogs. It was customary then to connect the Pretender and the devil in one's thoughts and aspirations; and the ignorant rustics soon afterwards, when Butterfield's calves sickened, declared that Mother Osborne had bewitched them, with the assistance of the devil. Later, when Butterfield, who had given up his farm and taken to an ale-house, suffered much from fits, Mother Osborne was again declared to be the cause (1751), and he was advised to send to Northampton-shire for an old woman, a white witch, to baffle her spells. The white witch came, confirmed, of course, the popular prejudice, and advised that six men, armed with staves and pitchforks, should watch Butterfield's house by day and night. The affair would here, per-haps, have ended; but some persons thought they could turn it to their pecuniary advantage, and, accordingly, made public notification that a witch would be ducked on April 22. On the appointed day hundreds flocked to the scene of entertainment. The parish officers had removed the two Osbornes for safety to the church; and the mob, in revenge, seized the governor of the workhouse, and, collecting a heap of straw, threatened to drown him, and set fire to the town, unless they were given up. In a panic of fear the parish officers gave way, and the two poor creatures were immediately stripped naked, their thumbs tied to their toes, and, each being wrapped in a coarse sheet, were dragged a couple of miles, and then flung into a muddy stream. Colley, a chimney-sweep, observing that the woman did not sink, stepped into the pool, and turned her over several times with a stick, until the sheet fell off, and her nakedness was exposed. In this miserable state—exhausted with fatigue and terror, sick with shame, half choked with mud—she was flung upon the bank ; and her persecutors—alas for the cruelty of ignorance!—kicked and beat her until she died. Her husband also sank under his barbarous maltreatment. It is satisfactory to know that Colley, as the worst offender, was brought to trial on a charge of wilful murder, found guilty, and most righteously hanged. The crowd, however, who witnessed his execution, lamented him as a martyr, unjustly punished for having delivered the world from one of Satan's servants, and overwhelmed with execrations the sheriff whose duty it was to see that the behests of the law were carried out.

In February, 1759, Susannah Hannaker, of Wingrove, Wilts, was put to the ordeal of weighing, but fortunately for herself outweighed the church Bible, against which she was tested. In June, 1760, at Leicester; in June, 1785, at Northampton; and in April, 1829, at Monmouth, persons were tried for ducking supposed witches. Similar cases have occurred in our own time. On September 4, 1863, a paralytic Frenchman died of an illness induced by his having been ducked as a wizard in a pond at Castle Hedingham, in Essex.

And an aged woman, named Anne Turner, reputed to be a witch, was killed by a man, partially insane, at the village of Long Compton, in Warwickshire, on September 17, 1875. But the reader needs no further illustrations of the longevity of human error, or the terrible vitality of prejudice, especially among the uneducated. The thaumaturgist or necromancer, with his wand, his magic circle, his alembics and crucibles, disappeared long ago, because, as I have already pointed out, his support depended upon a class of society whose intelligence was rapidly developed by the healthy influences of literature and science; but the sham astrologer and the pseudo-witch linger still in obscure corners, because they find their prey among the credulous and the ignorant. The more widely we extend the bounds of knowledge, the more certainly shall we prevent the recrudescence of such forms of imposture and aspects of delusion as in the preceding pages I have attempted to describe.

CHAPTER IV.

THE WITCHES OF SCOTLAND.

AMONG the people of Scotland, a more serious-minded
and imaginative race than the English, the superstition of witchcraft was deeply rooted at an early
period. Its development was encouraged not only
by the idiosyncrasies of the national character, but
also by the nature of the country and the climate in
which they lived. The lofty mountains, with their
misty summits and shadowy ravines—their deep
obscure glens—were the fitting homes of the wildest
fancies, the eëriest legends; and the storm crashing
through the forests, and the surf beating on the rocky
shore, suggested to the ear of the peasant or the
fisherman the voices of unseen creatures—of the
dread spirits of the waters and the air. To men who
believed in kelpie and wraith and the second sight,
a belief in witch and warlock was easy enough. And
it was not until the Calvinist reformers imported
into Scotland their austere and rigid creed, with its
literal interpretation of Biblical imagery, that witchcraft came to be regarded as a crime. It was not
until 1563 that the Parliament of Scotland passed a

statute constituting 'witchcraft and dealing with witches' a capital offence. It is true that persons accused of witchcraft had already suffered death—as the Earl of Mar, brother of James III., who was suspected of intriguing with witches and sorcerers in order to compass his brother's death, and Lady Glamis, in 1532, charged with a similar plot against James V.—but in both these cases it was the *treason* which was punished rather than the *sorcery*.

In the Scottish criminal records the first person who suffered death for the practice of witchcraft was a Janet Bowman, in 1572. No particulars of her offence are given; and against her name are written only the significant words, 'convict and byrnt.'

A remarkable case, that of Bessie Dunlop, belongs to 1576.* She was the wife of an Ayrshire peasant, Andrew Jack. According to her own statement, she was going one day from her house to the yard of Monkcastle, driving her cows to the pasture, and greeting over her troubles—for she had a milch-cow nigh sick to death, and her husband and child were lying ill, and she herself had but recently risen from childbed—when a strange man met her, and saluted her with the words, 'Gude day, Bessie!' She answered civilly, and, in reply to his questions, acquainted him with her anxieties; whereupon he informed her that her cow, her two sheep, and her child would die, but that her gude man would recover. She described this stranger in graphic language as 'an honest, wele-

---

* Pitcairn, 'Criminal Trials,' i. 49-58. This chapter is mainly founded on the reports in Pitcairn.

elderlie man, gray bairdit, and had ane gray coat
with Lumbart slevis of the auld fassoun; ane pair of
gray brekis and quhyte schankis, gartaurt above the
knee; ane black bonnet on his heid, cloise behind
and plane before, with silkin laissis drawin throw the
lippis thairof; and ane quhyte wand in his hand.'
He told Bessie that his name was *Thomas Reid*, and
that he had been killed at the Battle of Pinkie.
Extraordinary as was this information, it did not
seem improbable to her when she noted the manner
of his disappearance through the yard of Monkcastle:
'I thocht he gait in at ane narroware hoill of the
dyke [wall], nor ony erdlie man culd haif gaun
throw; and swa I was sumthing fleit [terrified].'

Thomas Reid's sinister predictions were duly fulfilled. Soon afterwards, he again met Bessie, and
boldly invited her to deny her religion, and the faith
in which she was christened, in return for certain
worldly advantages. But Bessie steadfastly refused.

This visitor of hers was under no fear of the
ordinance which is supposed to limit the mundane
excursions of 'spiritual creatures' to the hours
between sunset and cockcrow; for he generally made
his appearance at mid-day. It is not less singular
that he made no objection to the presence of humanity.
On one occasion he called at her house, where she sat
conversing with her husband *and three tailors*, and,
invisible to them, plucked her by the apron, and led
her to the door, and thence up the hill-end, where he
bade her stand, and be silent, whatever she might
hear or see. And suddenly she beheld twelve

20

persons, eight women and four men; the men clad in gentlemen's clothing, and the women with plaids round about them, very seemly to look at. Thomas was among them. They bade her sit down, and said: 'Welcome, Bessie; wilt thou go with us?' But she made no answer, and after some conversation among themselves, they disappeared in a hideous whirlwind.

When Thomas returned, he informed her that the persons she had seen were the 'good wights,' who dwell in the Court of Faëry, and he brought her an invitation to accompany them thither—an invitation which he repeated with much earnestness. She answered, with true Scotch caution: 'She saw no profit to gang that kind of gates, unless she knew wherefore.'

'Seest thou not me,' he rejoined, 'worth meat and worth clothes, and good enough like in person?'

The prospect, however, could not beguile her; and she continued firm in her simple resolve to dwell with her husband and bairns, whom she had no wish to abandon. Off went Thomas in a storm of anger; but before long he recovered his temper, and resumed his visits, showing himself willing to 'fetch and carry' at her request, and always treating her with the deference due to a wife and mother. The only benefit she derived from this friendship was, she said, the means of curing diseases and recovering stolen property, so that her witchcraft was of the simplest, innocentest kind. There was no compact with the devil, and it injured nobody—except doctors and thieves. Yet for yielding to this hallucination— the product of a vivid imagination, stimulated, we suspect, by much solitary reverie—Bessie Dunlop was 'convyct and byrnt.' Mayhap, as she was led to the death-fire, she may have dreamed that she had done better to have gone with Thomas Reid to the Court of Faëry!

The combination of the fairy folklore with the gloomier inventions of witchcraft occurs again in the case of Alison Pierson (1588). There was a certain William Simpson, a great scholar and physician, and a native of Stirling. While but a child, he was taken away from his parents ' by a man of Egypt, a giant,' who led him away to Egypt with him, ' where he remained by the space of twelve years before he came home again.' On his return, he made the acquaintance of Alison, who was a near relative, and cured her of certain ailments; but soon afterwards, less fortunate in treating himself, he died. Some months had passed when, one day as Alison was lying on her bed, sick and alone, she was suddenly addressed by a man in green clothes, who told her that, if she would be faithful, he would do her good. In her first alarm, she cried for help, but no one hearing, she called upon the Divine Name, when her visitor immediately disappeared. Before long, he came to her again, attended by many men and women; and compelling her to accompany them, they set off in a gay procession to Lothian, where they found puncheons of wine, with drinking-cups, and

enjoyed themselves right heartily.   Thenceforward
she was on the friendliest terms with the ' good neighbours,' even visiting the Fairy Queen at her court,
where, according to her own account, she was made
much of, was treated, indeed, as ' one of themselves,'
and allowed to see them compounding wonderful
healing-salves in miniature pans over tiny fires.

It would seem that this woman had acquired a considerable knowledge of ' herbs and simples,' and that
the medicines she made up effected remarkable cures.
No doubt it was for the purpose of enhancing the
value of her concoctions that she professed to have
obtained the secret of them from the fairies.   So great
was her repute for medicinal skill, that the Archbishop
of St. Andrews sought her advice in a dangerous
illness, and, by her directions, ate ' a sodden food,'
and at two draughts absorbed a quart of good claret
wine, which she had previously medicated, greatly
benefiting thereby.

Alison had a fertile fancy and a fluent tongue, and
told stories of the fairies and their doings which did
credit to her invention.   It does not appear that she
injured anybody, except, perhaps, by her drugs, but,
then, even the faculty sometimes do *that!*   But, like
Bessie Dunlop, she was convicted of witchcraft, and
burned.   The surprising thing about this and similar
cases is, that the poor woman should have assisted in
her own condemnation by devising such extraordinary
fictions.   What was the use of them ?   A prisoner on
a charge which, if proved against her, meant a terrible
death, what object did she expect to gain ?   Was it

all done for the sake of the temporary surprise and astonishment her tale created? that she might be the heroine of an hour?—Men have, we know, their strange ambitions, but if this were Alison Pierson's, it was one of the very strangest.

In the next case I shall bring forward, that of Dame Fowlis, we come upon the trail of actual crime. Dame Fowlis, second wife of the chief of the clan Munro, was by birth a Roise or Ross, of Balnagown. To effect the aggrandisement of her own family, she plotted the death of Robert, her husband's eldest son, in order to marry his wealthy widow to her brother, George Roise or Ross, laird of Balnagown ; but as he, too, was married, it was necessary to get rid of *his* wife also. For this ' double event,' she employed, with little attempt at concealment, three 'notorious witches' —Agnes Roy, Christian Roy, and Marjory Nayre MacAllister, alias Loskie Loncart—besides one William MacGillivordam, and several other persons of dubious reputation. About Midsummer, 1576, Agnes Roy was despatched to bring Loskie Loncart into Dame Fowlis' presence. The result of this interview was soon apparent. Clay images of the two doomed individuals were made, and exposed to the usual sorceries ; while MacGillivordam obtained a supply of poison from Aberdeen, which the cook was bribed to put into a dish intended for the lady of Balnagown's table. It did not prove mortal, as anticipated, but afflicted the unfortunate lady with a long and severe illness. Dame Fowlis, however, felt no remorse, but continued her plots, gradually widening their scope until she resolved to kill all her husband's children by his first wife, in order to secure the inheritance for her own. In May, 1577, she instructed Macgilli-vordam to procure a large quantity of poison. He refused, unless his brother was made privy to the transaction. I suppose this was done, as the poison was obtained, and proved to be so deadly in its nature that two persons—a woman and a boy—were killed by accidentally tasting of it.

Foiled in her scheme, Dame Fowlis resorted to the practices of witchcraft, and bought, in June, for five shillings, 'an elf arrow-head'—that is, a rude flint implement — belonging to the neolithic age. On July 2, she and her accomplices met together in secret conclave ; and having made an image of butter to resemble Robert Munro, they placed it against the wall; and then, with the elf arrow-head, Loskie Loncart shot at it for eight times, but each time without success, a proof that the familiars of the devil, like their master, could not always hit the mark. Meeting a second time for the same purpose, they made an image of clay, at which Loskie shot twelve times in succession, invariably missing, to the great disappointment of all concerned. The failure was ascribed to the elf arrow-head, and in August another was procured ; two figures of clay were also made, for Robert Munro and for Lady Balnagown, respectively ; at the latter Dame Fowlis shot twice, and at the former Loskie Loncart shot thrice ; but the shooting was no better than before, and the two images being

accidentally broken, the charm was destroyed.   It
was proposed to try poison again, but by this time
the authorities had gained information of what was
going on, and towards the end of November, Christian
Roy, who had been present at the third meeting, was
arrested.   Being put to the torture, she confessed
everything, and, together with some of her confederates, was convicted of witchcraft and burnt.
Dame Fowlis, who assuredly was not the least guilty
person, escaped to Caithness, but, after remaining in
concealment for nine months, was allowed to return to
her home.   In 1588, her husband died, and was
succeeded in his estates by Robert Munro, who
revived the charge of witchcraft against his step-
mother, and obtained a commission for her examination and that of her surviving accomplices.   Dame
Fowlis was put on her trial on July 22, 1590 ; but she
had money and friends, and contrived to obtain a verdict of acquittal.

It is one of the most remarkable features of this remarkable case that, as soon as her acquittal was pronounced, a new trial was opened, in which the defendant
was her other stepson, Hector Munro,* who had been,
only an hour before, the principal witness against her.
The allegations against him were: first, that, during the
sore sickness of his brother, in the summer of 1588, he
had consulted with ' three notorious and common
witches' respecting the best means of curing him, and
had sheltered them for several days, until compelled by
his father to send them about their business ; and,

* Pitcairn, *ut ante*, i. 192, 202, 285.

second, that falling ill himself, in January, 1559, he
had caused a certain Marion MacIngaruch, 'one of the
most notorious and rank witches in the whole realm,'
to be brought to him, and who, after administering
three draughts of water out of three stones which she
carried with her, declared that his sole chance of
recovery lay in the sacrifice of 'the principal man of
his blood.' After due consultation, they decided that
this vicarious sufferer must be George Munro, his
step - brother, the eldest son of Dame Fowlis.
Messengers were accordingly sent in search of him.
Apprehending no evil, he obeyed the call, and five
days afterwards arrived at the house of Hector
Munro. Following the directions of the witch,
Hector received his brother in silence, giving him his
left hand, and taking him by the right hand, and
uttering no word of greeting until he had spoken.
George, astounded by the chillness of his reception,
which he could not but contrast with the warmth of
the invitations, remained in his brother's sick-room an
hour without speaking. At last he asked Hector how
he felt. 'The better that you have come to visit
me,' replied Hector, and then was again silent, for so
the witch had ordained. An hour after midnight
appeared Marion MacIngaruch, with several assist-
ants; and, arming themselves with spades, they repaired to a nook of ground at the sea-side, situated
between the boundaries of the estates of the two
lairds, and there, removing the turf, they dug a grave
of the size of the invalid.

Marion returned to the house, and gave directions

to her confederates as to the parts they were to play in the startling scene which was yet to be enacted. It was represented to her that if George died suddenly suspicions would be aroused, with a result dangerous to all concerned; and she thereupon undertook that he should be spared until April 17 next thereafter. Hector was then wrapped up in a couple of blankets, and carried to the grave in silence. In silence he was deposited in it, and the turf lightly laid upon him, while Marion stationed herself by his side. His foster-mother, one Christiana Neill Dayzell, then took a young lad by the hand, and ran the breadth of nine ridges, afterwards inquiring of the witch 'who might be her choice,' and receiving for answer, 'That Hector was her choice to live, and his brother George to die for him.' This ceremony was thrice repeated, and the sick man was then taken from the grave, and carried home, the most absolute silence still being maintained.

Such an experience on a bitter January night might well have proved fatal to the subject of it; but, strange to say, Hector Munro recovered— probably from the effect on his imagination of rites so peculiar and impressive; whereas, in the month of April, George Munro was seized with a grievous illness, of which, in the following June, he died. Grateful for the cure she had effected, Hector received the witch Marion into high favour, installing her at his uncle's house of Kildrummadyis, entertaining her 'as if she had been his spouse, and giving her such pre-eminence in the county that none durst offend

her.' But it is the nature of such unhallowed con-
federacies to surrender, sooner or later, their dark,
dread secrets. Whispers spread abroad, gradually
shaping themselves into a connected story which
invited judicial investigation. A warrant was issued
for the arrest of Marion MacIngurach; but for some
time Hector Munro contrived to conceal her, until
Dame Fowlis discovered and made known that she
was lying in the house at Fowlis. She was arrested;
and, making a full confession of her actions, was
sentenced to death, and burnt. Hector Munro.
however, was more fortunate, and obtained his
acquittal.

JAMES I. AND THE WITCHES.

These, and other cases of witchcraft which, as the
mania extended, occurred in various parts of the
country, attracted the attention of King James, and
made a profound impression upon him. Taking up
the study of the subject with enthusiasm, he inquired
into the demonology of France and Germany, where
it had been matured into a science; and this so
thoroughly that he became, as already stated, an
expert, and was really entitled to pronounce authori-
tative decisions. His example, however, had a dis-
astrous effect, confirming and deepening the popular
credulity to such an extent that the common people,
for a time, might have been divided into two great
classes—witches and witch-finders. That in such
circumstances many acts of cruelty should be per-
petrated was inevitable. So complete was the de-

moralization, that the most trivial physical or mental peculiarity was held to be an indubitable witch-mark, and young and old were hurried to the stake like sheep to the slaughter.

In August, 1589, King James was married, by proxy, to Princess Anne of Denmark; and the impatient monarch was eagerly awaiting the arrival of his bride from Copenhagen, when the unwelcome intelligence reached him that the vessels conveying her and her suite had been overtaken by a storm, and, after a narrow escape from destruction, had put into the port of Upsal, in Norway, with the intention of remaining there until the following spring. The eager bridegroom, summoning up all his courage— he had no love for the sea—resolved to go in search of his queen, and, having found her, to conduct her to her new home. At Upsal the marriage was duly solemnized; and husband and wife then voyaged to Copenhagen, where they spent the winter. The homeward voyage was not undertaken until the following spring; and it was on May Day, 1590, that James and his Queen landed at Leith, after an experience of the sea which confirmed James's distaste for it.

The political disorder of the country, and the hold which the new superstition had obtained upon the minds of the people, encouraged the circulation of dark mysterious rumours in connection with the King's unfavourable passage; and a general belief soon came to be established that the tempestuous weather which had so seriously affected it was due to the intervention of supernatural powers, at the instigation of human treachery. Suspicion fixed at length upon the Earl of Bothwell, who was arrested and committed to prison; but in June, 1591, contrived to make his escape, and conceal himself in the remote recesses of the Highlands. Not long afterwards, some curious circumstances attending certain cures which a servant girl—Geillis, or Gillies, Duncan—had performed, led to her being suspected of witchcraft; and this suspicion opened up a series of investigations, which revealed the existence of an extraordinary conspiracy against the King's life.

Geillis Duncan was in the employment of David Seton, deputy-bailiff of the small town of Tranent, in Haddingtonshire. Unlike the witch of English rural life, she was young, comely, and fair-complexioned; and the only ground on which the idea of witchcraft was associated with her was the wonderful quickness with which she had cured some sick and diseased persons, the fact being that she was well acquainted with the healing properties of herbs. When her master severely interrogated her, she at once denied all knowledge of the mysteries of the black art. He then, without leave or license, put her to the torture; she still continued to protest her innocence. It was a popular conviction that no witch would confess so long as the devil-mark on her body remained undiscovered. She was subjected to an indecent examination—the stigma was found (said the examiners) on her throat; she was again subjected to the torture. The outraged girl's forti-

tude then gave way; she acknowledged whatever her
persecutors wished to learn. Yes, she *was* a *witch!*
She had made a compact with the devil; all her
cures had been effected by his assistance—quite a
new feature in the character of Satan, who has not
generally been suspected of any compassionate feeling
towards suffering humanity. That she had done
good instead of harm availed the unfortunate Geillis
nothing. She was committed to prison; and the
torture being a third time applied, made a fuller
confession, in which she named her accomplices or
confederates, some forty in number, residing in
different parts of Lothian. Their arrest and examination disclosed the particulars of one of the
strangest intrigues ever concocted.

The principal parties in it were Dr. Fian, or Frain,
a reputed wizard, also known as John Cunningham;
a grave matron, named Agnes Sampson; Euphemia
Macalzean, daughter of Lord Cliftonhall; and
Barbara Napier. Fian, or Cunningham, was a
schoolmaster of Tranent, and a man of ability and
education; but his life had been evil—he was a
vendor of poisons—and, though innocent of the preposterous crimes alleged against him, had dabbled in
the practices of the so-called sorcery. When a
twisted cord was bound round his bursting temples,
he would confess nothing; and, exasperated by his
fortitude, the authorities subjected him to the terrible
torture of 'the boots.' Even this he endured in
silence, until exhausted nature came to his relief
with an interval of unconsciousness. He was then

released; restoratives were applied; and, while he hovered on the border of sensibility, he was induced to sign 'a full confession.' Being remanded to his prison, he contrived, two days afterwards, to escape; but was recaptured, and brought before the High Court of Justiciary, King James himself being present. Fian strenuously repudiated the so-called confession which had been foisted upon him in his swoon, declaring that his signature had been obtained by a fraud. Whereupon King James, enraged at what he conceived to be the man's stubborn wilfulness, ordered him again to the torture. His fingernails were torn out with pincers, and long needles thrust into the quick; but the courageous man made no sign. He was then subjected once more to the barbarous 'boots,' in which he continued so long, and endured so many blows, that 'his legs were crushed and beaten together as small as might be, and the bones and flesh so bruised, that the blood and marrow spouted forth in great abundance, whereby they were made unserviceable for ever.'

As ultimately extorted from the unfortunate Fian, his confession shows a remarkable mixture of imposture and self-deception—a patchwork of the falsehoods he believed and those he invented. Singularly grotesque is his account of his introduction to the devil: He was lodging at Tranent, in the house of one Thomas Trumbill, who had offended him by neglecting to 'sparge' or whitewash his chamber, as he had promised; and, while lying in his bed, meditating how he might be revenged of the said Thomas, the devil, *clothed in white raiment,* suddenly appeared, and said: 'Will ye be my servant, and adore me and all my servants, and ye shall never want?' Never want! The bribe to a poor Scotch dominie was immense; Fian could not withstand it, and at once enlisted among 'the Devil's Own.' As his first act of service, he had the pleasure of burning down Master Trumbill's house. The next night Beelzebub paid him another visit, and put his mark upon him with a rod. Thereafter he was found lying in his chamber in a trance, during which, he said, he was carried in the spirit over many mountains, and accomplished an aërial circumnavigation of the globe. In the future he attended all the nightly conferences of witches and fiends held throughout Lothian, displaying so much energy and capacity that the devil appointed him to be his 'registrar and secretary.'

The first convention at which he was present assembled in the parish church of North Berwick, a breezy, picturesque seaport at the mouth of the Forth, about sixteen miles from Preston Pans. Satan occupied the pulpit, and delivered 'a sermon of doubtful speeches,' designed for their encouragement. His servants, he said, should never want, and should ail nothing, so long as their hairs were on, and they let no tears fall from their eyes. He bade them spare not to do evil, and advised them to eat, drink, and be merry: after which edifying discourse they did homage to him in the usual indecent manner. Fian, as I have said, was an evil-living man, and needed no exhortation from the devil to do wicked things.

In the course of his testimony he invented, as was so frequently the strange practice of persons accused of witchcraft, the most extravagant fictions—as, for instance: One night he supped at the miller's, a few miles from Tranent; and as it was late when the revel ended, one of the miller's men carried him home on horseback. To light them on their way through the dark of night, Fian raised up four candles on the horse's ears, and one on the staff which his guide carried; their great brightness made the midnight appear as noonday; but the miller's man was so terrified by the phenomenon that, on his return home, he fell dead.

Let us next turn to the confession of Agnes Sampson, 'the wise wife of Keith,' as she was popularly called. She was charged with having done grave injury to persons who had incurred her displeasure; but she seems, when all fictitious details are thrust aside, to have been simply a shrewd and sagacious old Scotchwoman, with much force of character, who made a decent living as a herb-doctor. Archbishop Spottiswoode describes her as matronly in appearance, and grave of demeanour, and adds that she was composed in her answers. Yet were those answers the wildest and most extraordinary utterances imaginable, and, if they be truly recorded, they convict her of unscrupulous audacity and un-failing ingenuity.

She affirmed that her service to the devil began after her husband's death, when he appeared to her in mortal likeness, and commanded her to renounce

Christ, and obey him as her master.   For the sake of
the riches he promised to herself and her children,
she consented; and thereafter he came in the guise of
a dog, of which she asked questions, always receiving
appropriate replies.   On one occasion, having been
summoned by the Lady Edmaston, who was lying
sick, she went out into the garden at night, and
called the devil by his terrestrial or mundane *alias*
of Elva.   He bounded over the stone wall in the
likeness of a dog, and approached her so close that
she was frightened, and charged him by 'the law he
believed in' to keep his distance.   She then asked
him if the lady would recover; he replied in the
negative.   In his turn he inquired where the gentlewomen, her daughters, were; and being informed
that they were to meet her in the garden, said that
one of them should be his leman.   'Not so,'
exclaimed the wise wife undauntedly; and the devil
then went away howling, like a whipped schoolboy,
and *hid himself in the well* until after supper.   The
young gentlewomen coming into the bloom and per-
fumes of the garden, he suddenly emerged, seized the
Lady Torsenye, and attempted to drag her into the
well; but Agnes gripped him firmly, and by her
superior strength delivered her from his clutches.
Then, with a terrible yell, he disappeared.

Yet another story: Agnes, with Geillis Duncan
and other witches, desiring to be revenged on the
deputy bailiff, met on the bridge at Fowlistruther,
and dropped a cord into the river, Agnes Sampson
crying, 'Hail!   Holloa!'   Immediately they felt the

end of the cord dragged down by a great weight; and on drawing it up, up came the devil along with it! He inquired if they had all been good servants, and gave them a charm to blight Seton and his property; but *it was accidentally diverted in its operation, and fell upon another person*—a touch of realism worthy of Defoe!

Euphemia Macalzean, a lady of high social position, daughter and heiress of Lord Cliftonhall (who was eminent as lawyer, statesman, and scholar), seems to have been involved in this welter of intrigue, conspiracy, and deception, through her adherence to Bothwell's faction, and her devotion to the Roman communion. Her confession was as grotesque and unveracious as that of any of her associates. She was made a witch (she said) through the agency of an Irishwoman 'with a fallen nose,' and, to perfect herself in the craft, had paid another witch, who resided in St. Ninian's Row, Edinburgh, for 'inaugurating' her with 'the girth of ane gret bikar,' revolving it 'oft round her head and neck, and ofttimes round her head.' She was accused of having administered poison to her husband, her father-in-law, and some other persons; and whatever may be thought of the allegations of sorcery and witchcraft, this heavier charge seems to have been well-founded. Euphemia said that her acquaintance with Agnes Sampson began with her first accouchement, when she applied to her to mitigate her pains, and she did so by transferring them to a dog. At her second accouchement, Agnes transferred them to a cat.

As a determined enemy of the Protestant religion,
Satan was inimical to King James's marriage with a
Protestant princess, and to break up an alliance which
would greatly limit his power for evil, he determined
to sink the ship that carried the newly-married couple
on their homeward voyage.   His first device was to
hang over the sea a very dense mist, in the hope that
the royal ship would miss her course, and strike on
some dangerous rock.   When this device failed,
Dr. Fian was ordered to summon all the witches to
meet their master at the haunted kirk of North
Berwick.   Accordingly, on All-Hallow-mass Eve,
they assembled there to the number of two hundred;
and each one embarking in 'a riddle,' or sieve,* they
sailed over the ocean 'very substantially,' carrying
with them flagons of wine, and making merry,
and drinking 'by the way.'   After sailing about for
some time, they met with their master, bearing in
his claws a cat, which had previously been drawn
nine times through the fire.   Handing it to one of
the warlocks, he bade him cast it into the sea, and
shout 'Hola!' whereupon the ocean became con-
vulsed, and the waters seethed, and the billows rose
like heaving mountains.   On through the storm
sailed this eerie company until they reached the
Scottish coast, where they landed, and, joining hands,
danced in procession to the kirk of North Berwick.
Geillis Duncan going before them, playing a reel
upon her Jew's-harp, or trump—formerly a favourite

* So the witch in 'Macbeth' (Act I., sc. 3) says:
'In a sieve I'll thither sail.'

musical instrument with the Scotch peasantry—and singing :

'Cummer, go ye before ; cummer, go ye ;
Gif ye will not go before, cummer, let me !'

Having arrived at their rendezvous, they danced round it 'withershins'—that is, in reverse of the apparent motion of the sun. Dr. Fian then blew into the keyhole of the door, which opened immediately, and all the witches and warlocks entered in. It was pitch-dark ; but Fian lighted the tapers by merely blowing on them, and their sudden blaze revealed the devil in the pulpit, attired in a black gown and hat. The description given of the fiend reveals the stern imagination of the North, and is characteristic of the 'weird sisters' of Scotland, who form, as Dr. Burton remarks, so grand a contrast to 'the vulgar grovelling parochial witches of England.' His body was hard as iron ; his face terrible, with a nose like an eagle's beak ; his eyes glared like fire ; his voice was gruff as the sound of the east wind ; his hands and legs were covered with hair, and his hands and feet were armed with long claws. On beholding him, witches and warlocks, with one accord, cried : 'All hail, master !' He then called over their names, and demanded of them severally whether they had been good and faithful servants, and what measure of success had attended their operations against the lives of King James and his bride—which surely he ought to have known ! Gray Malkin, a foolish old warlock, who officiated as beadle or janitor, heedlessly answered, That nothing ailed the King yet, God be thanked ! At which the devil, in a fury, leaped from the pulpit, and lustily smote him on the ears. He then resumed his position, and delivered his sermon, commanding them to act faithfully in their service, and do all the evil they could. Euphemia Macalzean and Agnes Sampson summoned up courage enough to ask him whether he had brought an image or picture of the King, that, by pricking it with pins, they might inflict upon its living pattern all kinds of pain and disease. The devil was fain to acknowledge that he had forgotten it, and was soundly rated by Euphemia for his carelessness, Agnes Sampson and several other women seizing the opportunity to load him with reproaches on their respective accounts.

On another occasion, according to Agnes Sampson, she, Dr. Fian, and a wizard of some energy, named Robert Grierson, with several others, left Grierson's house at Preston Pans in a boat, and went out to sea to 'a tryst.' Embarking on board a ship, they drank copiously of good wine and ale, after which they sank the ship and her crew, and returned home. And again, sailing from North Berwick in a boat like a chimney, they saw the devil—in shape and size resembling a huge hayrick—rolling over the great waves in front of them. They went on board a vessel called *The Grace of God*, where they enjoyed, as before, an abundance of wine and 'other good cheer.' On leaving it, the devil, who was underneath the ship, raised an evil wind, and it perished.

Some of these stories proved to be too highly

coloured even for the credulity of King James; and
he rightly enough exclaimed that the witches were,
like their master, 'extraordinary liars.' It is said,
however, that he changed his opinion after Agnes
Sampson, in a private conference which he accorded
to her, related the details of a conversation between
himself and the Queen that had taken place under
such circumstances as to ensure inviolable secrecy.
It is curious that a very similar story is told of
Jeanne Darc—whom our ancestors burned as a witch
—and King Charles VI. of France.

Despite the machinations of the devil and the
witches, King James and Queen Anne, as we know,
escaped every peril, and reached Leith in safety. The
devil sourly remarked that James was 'a man of
God,' and was evidently inclined to let him alone
severely; but the Preston Pans conspirators, instigated, perhaps, by some powerful personages who
kept prudently in the background, resolved on
another attempt against their sovereign's life. On
Lammas Eve (July 31, 1590), nine of the ring-
leaders, including Dr. Fian, Agnes Sampson,
Euphemia Macalzean, and Barbara Napier, with some
thirty confederates, assembled at the New Haven,
between Musselburgh and Preston Pans, at a spot
called the Fairy Holes, where they were met by the
devil in the shape of a black man, which was
'thought most meet to do the turn for the which
they were convened.' Agnes Sampson at once proposed that they should make a final effort for the
King's destruction. The devil took an unfavourable

view of the prospects of their schemes ; but he promised them a waxen image, and directed them to hang up and roast a toad, and to lay its drippings —mixed with strong wash, an adder's skin, and 'the thing on the forehead of a new-foaled foal'—in James's path, or to suspend it in such a position that it might drip upon his body. This precious injunction was duly obeyed, and the toad hung up where the dripping would fall upon the King, 'during his Majesty's being at the Brig of Dee, the day before the common bell rang, for fear the Earl Bothwell should have entered Edinburgh.' But the devil's foreboding was fulfilled, and the conspirators missed their aim, the King happening to take a different route to that by which he had been expected.

It is useless to repeat more of these wild and desperate stories, or to inquire too closely into their origin. Fact and fiction are so mixed up in them, and the embellishments are so many and so bold, that it is difficult to get at the nucleus of truth; but, setting aside the witch or supernatural element, we seem driven to the conclusion that these persons had combined together for some nefarious purpose. Whether they intended to compass the King's death by the superstitious practices which the credulity of the age supposed to be effective, or whether these practices were intended as a cover for surer means, cannot now be determined. Nor can we pretend to say whether all who were implicated in the plot by the confession of Geillis Duncan were really guilty.

Dr. Fian, at all events, protested his innocence to the last; and with regard to him and others, the evidence adduced was painfully inadequate. But they were all convicted and sentenced to death. In the case of Barbara Napier, the majority of the jury at first acquitted her on the principal charges; but the King was highly indignant, and threatened them with a trial for 'wilful error upon an assize.' To avoid the consequences, they threw themselves upon the King's mercy, and were benevolently 'pardoned.' Poor Barbara Napier was hanged. So was Dr. Fian, on Castle Hill, Edinburgh (in January, 1592), and burned afterwards. So were Agnes Sampson, Agnes Thomson, and their real or supposed confederates. The punishment of Euphemia Macalzean was exceptionally severe. Instead of the ordinary sentence, directing the criminal to be first strangled and then burnt, it was ordered that she should be 'bound to a stake, and burned in ashes, *quick* to the death.' This fate befell her on June 25, 1591.

It was an unhappy result of this remarkable trial that it confirmed King James in his belief that he possessed a rare faculty for the detection of witches and the discovery of witchcraft. Continuing his investigation of the subject with fanatical zeal, he published in Edinburgh, in 1597, the outcome of his researches in his 'Dæmonologie' — an elaborate treatise, written in the form of a dialogue, the spirit of which may be inferred from its author's prefatory observations : 'The fearful abounding,' he says, ' at this time and in this country, of these detestable slaves of the devil, the witches or enchanters, hath moved me (beloved reader) to despatch in post this following treatise of mine, not in any wise (as I protest) to serve for a show of mine own learning and ingene, but only (moved of conscience) to press thereby, so far as I can, to resolve the doubting hearts of many, both that such assaults of Satan are most certainly practised, and that the instrument thereof merits most severely to be punished, against the damnable opinions of two, principally in our age ; whereof the one called Scot, an Englishman, is not ashamed in public print to deny that there can be such thing as witchcraft, and so maintains the old error of the Sadducees in denying of spirits. The other, called Wierus, a German physician, sets out a public apology for all these crafts-folks, whereby procuring for them impunity, he plainly betrays himself to have been one of that profession.'

Not only is King James fully convinced of the existence of witchcraft, but he is determined to treat it as a capital crime. 'Witches,' he affirms, 'ought to be put to death, according to the laws of God, the civil and imperial law, and the municipal law of all Christian nations; yea, to spare the life, and not strike whom God bids strike, and so severely punish so odious a treason against God, is not only unlawful, but, doubtless, as great a sin in the magistrate as was Saul's sparing Agag.' Conscious that the evidence brought against the unfortunate victims was generally of the weakest possible character, he contends that because the crime is generally abominable, evidence in proof of it may be accepted which would be refused in other offences; as, for example, that of young children who are ignorant of the nature of an oath, and that of persons of notoriously ill-repute. And the sole chance of escape which he offers to the accused is that of the ordeal. ' Two good helps,' he says, ' may be used: the one is the finding of their marks, and the trying the insensibleness thereof; the other is their floating on the water, for, as in a secret murther, if the dead carcase be at any time thereafter handled by the murtherer, it will gush out of blood, as if the blood were raging to the Heaven, for revenge of the murtherer (God having appointed that secret supernatural sign for trial of that secret unnatural crime), so that it appears that God hath appointed (for a supernatural sign of the monstrous impiety of witches), that the water shall refuse to receive them in her bosom that have shaken off them the sacred water of baptism, and wilfully refused the benefit thereof ; no, not so much as their eyes are able to shed tears at every light occasion when they will ; yea, although it were dissembling like the crocodiles, God not permitting them to dissemble their obstinacy in so horrible a crime.'

Encouraged by the practice and teaching of their sovereign, the people of Scotland, whom the anthropomorphism of their religious creed naturally predisposed to believe in the personal appearances of the devil, undertook a regular campaign against those ill-fated individuals whom malice or ignorance, or their

own mental or physical peculiarities, or other causes,
branded as his bond-slaves and accomplices. Religious
animosity, moreover, was a powerful factor in stimu-
lating and sustaining the mania; and the Scotch
Calvinist enjoyed a double gratification when some
poor old woman was burned both as a witch and a
Roman Catholic. It has been calculated that, in the
period of thirty-nine years, between the enactment of
the Statute of Queen Mary and the accession of James
to the English throne, the average number of persons
executed for witchcraft was 200 annually, making an
aggregate of nearly 8,000. For the first nine years
about 30 or 40 suffered yearly; but latterly the annual
death-roll mounted up to 400 and 500. James at
last grew alarmed at the prevalence of witchcraft
in his kingdom, and seems to have devoted no small
portion of his time to attempts to detect and exterminate it.

In 1591 the Earl of Bothwell was imprisoned for
having conspired the King's death by sorcery, in
conjunction with a warlock named Richie Graham.
Graham was burned on March 8, 1592. Bothwell
was not brought to trial until August 10, 1593,
when several witches bore testimony against him,
but he obtained an acquittal.

In 1597, on November 12, four women were tried by
the High Court of Justiciary, in Edinburgh, on various
charges of witchcraft. Their names are recorded as
Christina Livingstone, Janet Stewart, Bessie Aikin,
and Christina Sadler. Their trials, however, present
no special features of interest.

Passing over half a century, we come to the recrudescence of the witch-mania, which followed on the
restoration of Charles II. Mr. R. Burns Begg has
recently edited for the Society of Antiquaries of
Scotland a report of various witch trials in Forfar
and Kincardineshire, in the opening years of that
monarch's reign, which supplies some further illustrations of the characteristics of Scottish witchcraft.
Here we meet with the strange word 'Covin' or
'Coven' (apparently connected with 'Covenant' or
'Convention') as applied to an organization or guild
of witches. In 1662 the Judge-General-Depute for
Scotland tried thirteen 'Coviners,' who had been
detected by the efforts of a committee consisting of
the ministers and schoolmasters of the district,
together with the 'Laird of Tullibole.' Of these
thirteen unfortunate victims only one was a man.
All were found guilty by the jury, and sentenced to
death. Eleven suffered at the stake ; one died before
the day of execution, and one was respited on account
of her pregnancy. The evidence was of the usual
extraordinary tenor, and the so-called 'confessions'
of the accused were not less puzzling than in other
cases. In Mr. Begg's opinion, which seems to me
well founded, there really *was* in and around the
Crook of Devon a local Covin, or regularly organized
band of so-called witches who acted under the direction of a person whom they believed to be Satan.
He suggests that at this period there would be many
wild and unscrupulous characters, disbanded soldiers,
and others, who found their profit in the 'blinded

allegiance' of the witches and warlocks. The difficulty is, what *was* this profit ? The witches do not seem to have paid anything in money or in kind. There are allusions which point to acts of immorality, and in several instances one can understand that personal enmities were gratified ; but on the whole the personators of Satan had scant reward for all their trouble. And how was it that they were never denounced by any of their victims ? How was it that the vigilance which detected the witches never tripped up their master ? How are we to explain the diversity of Satan's appearances ? At one time he was 'ane bonnie lad ;' at another, an 'unco-like man, in black-coloured clothes and ane blue bonnet ;' at another, a 'black iron-hard man ;' and yet again, 'ane little man in rough gray clothes.' Occasionally he brought with him a piper, and the witches danced together, and the ground under them was all fire-flaughts, and Andrew Watson had his usual staff in his hand, and although he is a blind man, yet danced he as nimbly as any of the company, and made also great merriment by singing his old ballads ; and Isabel Shyrrie did sing her song called ' Tinkletum, Tankletum.' Alas, that no obliging pen has transmitted ' Tinkletum, Tankletum' to posterity ! One could point to a good many songs which the world could have better spared. ' Tinkletum, Tankletum' —there is something amazingly suggestive in the words; possibilities of humour, perhaps of satire ; humour and satire which might have secured for Isabel Shyrrie a place among Scottish poetesses, whereas now she comes before us in no more attractive character than that of a Coviner—a deluded or self-deluding witch.

Let us next betake ourselves to the East Coast, and make the acquaintance of Isabel Gowdie, whose 'confessions' are among the most extraordinary documents to be met with even in the records o Scottish witchcraft. It is impossible, I think, to overrate their psychological interest. The first is, perhaps, the most curious; and as no summary or condensation would do justice to its details, I shall place it before the reader *in extenso*, with no other alteration than that of Englishing the spelling. It was made at Auldearn on April 13, 1662, in presence of the parish minister, the sheriff-depute of Nairn, and nine lairds and farmers of good position :

'As I was going betwixt the towns (*i.e.*, farmsteadings) of Drumdeevin and The Heads, I met with the Devil, and there covenanted in a manner with him; and I promised to meet him, in the night-time, in the Kirk of Auldearn,* which I did. And the first thing I did there that night, I denied my baptism, and did put the one of my hands to the crown of my head, and the other to the sole of my foot, and then renounced all betwixt my two hands over to the

---

* It is a singular circumstance, as Pitcairn remarks, that in almost all the confessions of witches, or at least of the Scottish witches, their initiation, and many of their meetings, are said to have taken place within churches, churchyards, and consecrated ground ; and a certain ritual, in imitation, or mockery, of the forms of the Church, is uniformly said to have been gone through.

Devil. He was in the Reader's desk, and a black book in his hand. Margaret Brodie, in Auldearn, held me up to the Devil to be baptized by him, and he marked me in the shoulder, and sucked out my blood at that mark, and spouted it in his hand, and, sprinkling it on my head, said, " I baptize thee, Janet, in my own name !" And within awhile we all removed. The next time that I met with him was in the New Wards of Inshoch. . . . He was a mickle, black, rough [hirsute] man, very cold ; and I found his nature all cold within me as spring-wall-water.* Sometimes he had boots, and sometimes shoes on his feet; but still his feet are forked and cloven. He would be sometimes with us like a deer or a roe. John Taylor and Janet Breadhead, his wife, in Belmakeith, . . . Douglas, and I myself, met in the kirkyard of Nairn, and we raised an unchristened child out of its grave ; and at the end of Bradley's cornfieldland, just opposite to the Mill of Nairn, we took the said child, with the nails of our fingers and toes, pickles of all sorts of grain, and blades of kail [colewort], and hacked them all very small, mixed together ; and did put a part thereof among the muck-heaps, and thereby took away the fruit of his corns, etc., and we parted it among two of our Covins. When we take corns at Lammas, we take but about two sheaves, when the corns are full ; or two stalks of kail, or thereby, and that gives us the fruit of the corn-land or kail-yard, where they grew. And it

* In the Forfarshire reports, alluded to on p. 332, the witches always speak of the devil's body and kiss as deadly cold.

may be, we will keep it until Yule or Pasche, and then divide it amongst us. There are thirteen persons [the usual number] in my Covin.

'The last time that our Covin met, we, and another Covin, were dancing at the Hill of Earlseat; and before that, betwixt Moynes and Bowgholl; and before that we were beyond the Mickle-burn; and the other Covin being at the Downie-hills, we went from beyond the Mickle-burn, and went beside them, to the houses at the Wood-End of Inshoch; and within a while went home to our houses. Before Candlemas we went be-east Kinloss, and there we yoked a plough of paddocks [frogs]. The Devil held the plough, and John Young, in Mebestown, our Officer, did drive the plough. Paddocks did draw the plough as oxen; *quickens wor sowmes* [dog-grass served for traces]; a riglon's [ram's] horn was a coulter, and a piece of a riglon's horn was a sock. We went two several times about; and all we of the Covin went still up and down with the plough, praying to the Devil for the fruit of that land, and that thistles and briars might grow there.

'When we go to any house, we take meat and drink; and we fill up the barrels with our own . . . . again; and we put besoms in our beds with our husbands, till we return again to them. We were in the Earl of Moray's house in Darnaway, and we got enough there, and did eat and drink of the best, and brought part with us. We went in at the windows. I had a little horse, and would say, "Horse and Hattock, in the Devil's name!" And then we would fly away, where we would, like as straws would fly upon a highway. We will fly like straws where we please; wild straws and corn-straws will be horses to us, and we put them betwixt our feet and say, "Horse and Hattock, in the Devil's name!" And when any see these straws in a whirlwind, and do not sanctify themselves, we may shoot them dead at our pleasure. Any that are shot by us, their souls will go to Heaven, but their bodies remain with us, and will fly as horses to us, as small as straws.*

'I was in the Downie Hills, and got meat there from the Queen of Fairy, more than I could eat. The Queen of Fairy is heavily clothed in white linen, and in white and lemon clothes, etc.; and the King of Fairy is a brave man, well favoured, and broad-faced, etc. There were elf-bulls, routing and skirling up and down there, and they affrighted me.

'When we take away any cow's milk, we pull the tail, and twine it and plait it the wrong way, in the Devil's name; and we draw the tedder (so made) in betwixt the cow's hinder-feet, and out betwixt the cow's fore-feet, in the Devil's name, and thereby take with us the cow's milk. We take sheep's milk even so [in the same manner]. The way to take or give back the milk again, is to cut that tedder. When we take away the strength of any person's ale, and give

---

* Pitcairn remarks, with justice, that the above details are, perhaps, in all respects the most extraordinary in the history of witchcraft of this or of any other country. Isabel Gowdie must have been a woman with a powerful and rank imagination, who, had she lived in the present day, might, perhaps, have produced a work of fiction of the school of Zola.

it to another, we take a little quantity out of each
barrel or stand of ale, and put it in a stoop in the
Devil's name, and in his name, with our own hands,
put it amongst another's ale, and give her the strength
and substance and "heall" of her neighbour's ale.
And to keep the ale from us, that we have no power
over it, is to sanctify it well.   We get all this power
from the Devil; and when we seek it from him, we
will him to be "our Lord."

'John Taylor, and Janet Breadhead, his wife, in
Belmakeith, Bessie Wilson in Aulderne, and Margaret
Wilson, spouse to Donald Callam in Aulderne, and I,
made a picture of clay, to destroy the Laird of Park's
male children.   John Taylor brought home the clay
in his plaid nook [the corner of his plaid]; his wife
broke it very small, like meal, and sifted it with a
sieve, and poured in water among it, in the Devil's
name, and wrought it very sure, like rye-bout [a stir-
about made of rye-flour]; and made of it a picture of
the laird's sons.   It had all the parts and marks of a
child, such as head, eyes, nose, hands, feet, mouth,
and little lips.   It wanted no mark of a child, and
the hands of it folded down by its sides.   It was like
a pow [lump of dough], or a flayed *egrya* [a sucking-
pig, which has been scalded and scraped].   We laid
the face of it to the fire, till it strakned [shrivelled],
and a clear fire round about it, till it was red like a
coal.   After that, we would roast it now and then;
each other day there would be a piece of it well
roasted.   The Laird of Park's whole male children
by it are to suffer, if it be not gotten and brokin, as

well as those that are born and dead already. It was
still put in and taken out of the fire in the Devil's
name. It was hung up upon a crock. It is yet in
John Taylor's house, and it has a cradle of clay about
it. Only John Taylor and his wife, Janet Breadhead, Bessie and Margaret Wilson in Aulderne, and
Margaret Brodie, these, and I, were only at the
making of it. All the multitude of our number of
witches, of all the Covins, kent [*kenned*, knew] all of
it, at our next meeting after it was made. And the
witches yet that are overtaken have their own powers,
and our powers which we had before we were taken,
both. But now I have no power at all.

'Margaret Kyllie, in . . . . is one of the other
Covin; Meslie Hirdall, spouse to Alexander Ross, in
Loanhead, is one of them; her skin is fiery. Isabel
Nicol, in Lochley, is one of my Covin. Alexander
Elder, in Earlseat, and Janet Finlay, his spouse, are
of my Covin. Margaret Haslum, in Moynes, is one;
Margaret Brodie, in Aulderne, Bessie and Margaret
Wilson there, and Jane Martin there, and Elspet
Nishie, spouse to John Mathew there, are of my
Covin. The said Jane Martin is the Maiden of our
Covin. John Young, in Mebestown, is Officer to
our Covin.

'Elspet Chisholm, and Isabel More, in Aulderne,
Maggie Brodie . . . . and I, went into Alexander
Cumling's litt-house [dye-house], in Aulderne. I
went in, in the likeness of a ken [jackdaw]; the said
Elspet Chisholm was in the shape of a cat. Isabel
More was a hare, and Maggie Brodie a cat, and . . . .

We took a thread of each colour of yarn that was on the said Alexander Cumling's litt-fatt [dyeing-vat], and did cast three knots on each thread, in the Devil's name, and did put the threads in the vat, *withersones* about in the vat in the Devil's name, and thereby took the whole strength of the vat away, that it could litt [dye] nothing but only black, according to the colour of the Devil, in whose name we took away the strength of the right colours that were in the vat.'

The second confession, made at Aulderne, on May 3, 1662, is not less remarkable than the foregoing :

'. . . . After that time there would meet but sometimes a Covin [*i.e.*, thirteen], sometimes more, sometimes less; but a Grand Meeting would be about the end of each Quarter. There is thirteen persons in each Covin; and each of us has one Sprite to wait upon us, when we please to call upon him. I remember not all the Sprites' names, but there is one called *Swin*, which waits upon the said Margaret Wilson in Aulderne; he is still [ever] clothed in grass-green; and the said Margaret Wilson has a nickname, called " Pickle nearest the wind." The next Sprite is called " Rosie," who waits upon Bessie Wilson, in Aulderne; he is still clothed in yellow; and her nickname is " Through the cornyard." . . . The third Sprite is called " The Roaring Lion," who waits upon Isabel Nicol, in Lochlors ; and [he is still clothed*] in sea-green ; her nickname is "Bessie Rule." The fourth Sprite is

* There are mutilations in the original manuscript, and the bracketed words are conjectural.

called "Mak Hector," who [waits upon Jane*] Martin, daughter to the said Margaret Wilson ; he is a young-like devil, clothed still in grass-green. [Jane Martin is*] Maiden to the Covin that I am of; and her nickname is "Over the dyke with it," because the Devil [always takes the*] Maiden in his hand nix time we damn "Gillatrypes ;" and when he would leap from . . .* he and she will say, "Over the dyke with it !" The name of the fifth Sprite is "Robert the [Rule," and he is still clothed in*] sad-dun, and seems to be a Commander of the rest of the Sprites ; and he waits upon Margaret Brodie, in Aulderne. [The name of the saxt Sprite] is called "Thief of Hell wait upon Herself ;" and he waits also on the said Bessie Wilson. The name of the seventh [Sprite is called] "The Read Reiver;" and he is my own Spirit, that waits on myself, and is still clothed in black. The eighth Spirit [is called] "Robert the Jackis," still clothed in dun, and seems to be aged. He is a glaiked, glowked Spirit ! The woman's [nickname] that he waits on is "Able and Stout !" [This was Bessie Hay.] The ninth Spirit is called "Laing," and the woman's nickname that he waits upon is "Bessie Bold" [Elspet Nishie]. The tenth Spirit is named "Thomas a Fiarie," etc. There will be many other Devils, waiting upon [our] Master Devil; but he is bigger and more awful than the rest of the Devils, and they all reverence him. I will ken

* There are mutilations in the original manuscript, and the bracketed words are conjectural.

them all, one by one, from others, when they appear like a man.

'When we raise the wind, we take a rag of cloth, and wet it in water; and we take a beetle and knock the rag on a stone, and we say thrice over:

'"I knock this rag upon this stane,
To raise the wind, in the Devil's name ;
It shall not lie until I please again !"

When we would lay the wind, we dry the rag, and say (thrice over) :

'"We lay the wind in the Devil's name,
[It shall not] rise while we [or I] like to raise it again !"

And if the wind will not lie instantly [after we say this], we call upon our Spirit, and say to him :

'"Thief ! Thief ! conjure the wind, and cause it to [lie ? . . .]"

We have no power of rain, but we will raise the wind when we please. He made us believe [. . .] that there was no God beside him.

'As for Elf arrow-heads, the Devil shapes them with his own hand [and afterwards delivers them ?] to Elf-boys, who " whyttis and dightis " [shapes and trims] them with a sharp thing like a packing-needle ; but [when I was in Elf-land ?] I saw them whytting and dighting them. When I was in the Elves' houses, they will have very . . . them whytting and dighting ; and the Devil gives them to us, each of us so many, when . . . Those that dightis them are little ones, hollow, and boss-backed [humped-backed]. They speak gowstie [roughly] like. When the Devil gives them to us, he says:

> " ' Shoot these in my name,
> And they shall not go heall hame !"

And when we shoot these arrows (we say) :

> " ' I shoot you man in the Devil's name,
> He shall nót win heall hame !
> And this shall be always true ;
> There shall not be one bit of him on lieiw " [on life, alive].

' We have no bow to shoot with, but spang [jerk] them from the nails of our thumbs. Sometimes we will miss ; but if they twitch [touch], be it beast, or man, or woman, it will kill, tho' they had a jack [a coat of armour] upon them. When we go in the shape of a hare, we say thrice over :

> ' " I shall go into a hare,
> With sorrow, and such, and mickle care ;
> And I shall go in the Devil's name,
> Ay, until I come home [again !]."

And instantly we start in a hare. And when we would be out of that shape, we will say :

> ' " Hare ! hare ! God send thee care !
> I am in a hare's likeness just now,
> But I shall be in a woman's likeness even [now]."

When we would go in the likeness of a cat, we say thrice over :

> ' " I shall go [intill ane cat],
> [With sorrow, and such, and a black] shot !
> And I shall go in the Devil's name,
> Ay, until I come home again !"

And if we [would go in a crow, then] we say thrice over :

> ' " I shall go intill a crow,
>   With sorrow, and such, and a black [thraw !
>   And I shall go in the Devil's name,]
>   Ay, until I come home again !"

And when we would be out of these shapes, we say:

> ' " Cat, cat [or crow, crow], God send thee a black shot [or black
>   thraw !]
>   I was a cat [or crow] just now,
>   But I shall be [in a woman's likeness even now].
>   Cat, cat " [as *supra*].

If we go in the shape of a cat, a crow, a hare, or any other likeness, etc., to any of our neighbours' houses, being witches, we will say:

> ' " [I (or we) conjure] thee go with us [or me] " !

And presently they become as we are, either cats, hares, crows, etc., and go [with us whither we would. When] we would ride, we take windle-straws, or been-stakes [bean-stalks], and put them betwixt our feet, and say thrice:

> ' " Horse and Hattock, horse and go,
>   Horse and pellatris, ho ! ho !"

And immediately we fly away wherever we would; and lest our husbands should miss us out of our beds, we put in a besom, or a three-legged stool, beside them, and say thrice over:

> ' " I lay down this besom [or stool] in the Devil's name,
>   Let it not stir till I come home again !"

And immediately it seems a woman, by the side of our husband.

'We cannot turn in[to] the likeness of [a lamb or a dove?] When my husband sold beef, I used to put a swallow's feather in the head of the beast, and [say thrice],

> '"[I] put out this beef in the Devil's name,
> That mickle silver and good price come hame!"

'I did even so [whenever I put] forth either horse, nolt [cattle], webs [of cloth], or any other thing to be sold, and still put in this feather, and said the [same words thrice] over, to cause the commodities sell well, and . . . . thrice over—

> '"Our Lord to hunting he [is gone]
> . . . . marble stone,
> He sent word to Saint Knitt . . ."

'When we would heal any sore or broken limb, we say thrice over . . . .

> '"He put the blood to the blood, till all up stood;
> The lith to the lith, Till all took nith;
> Our Lady charmed her dearly Son, With her tooth and her tongue,
> And her ten fingers—
> In the name of the Father, the Son, and the Holy Ghost!"

'And this we say thrice over, stroking the sore, and it becomes whole. 2ndlie. For the Bean-Shaw [bone-shaw, i.e., the sciatica], or pain in the haunch: "We are here three Maidens charming for the beanshaw; the man of the Midle-earth, blew beaver, landfever, maneris of stooris, the Lord fleigged (terrified) the Fiend with his holy candles and yard foot-stone! There she sits, and here she is gone! Let her never

come here again!"   3rdli. For the fevers, we say
thrice over, "I forbid the quaking-fevers, the sea-
fevers, the land-fevers, and all the fevers that God
ordained, out of the head, out of the heart, out of the
back, out of the sides, out of the knees, out of the
thighs, from the points of the fingers to the nibs of
the toes; net fall the fevers go, [some] to the hill,
some to the heep, some to the stone, some to the
stock.   In St. Peter's name, St. Paul's name, and all
the Saints of Heaven.   In the name of the Father,
the Son, and of the Holy Ghost!"   And when we
took the fruit of the fishes from the fishers, we went
to the shore before the boat would come to it; and
we would say, on the shore-side, three several times
over :

> ' "The fishers are gone to the sea,
>   And they will bring home fish to me ;
>   They will bring them home intill the boat,
>   But they shall get of them but the smaller sort !"

So we either steal a fish, or buy a fish, or get a fish
from them [for naught], one or more.   And with
that we have all the fruit of the whole fishes in the
boat, and the fishes that the fishermen themselves will
have will be but froth, etc.

' The first voyage that ever I went with the rest of
our Covins was [to] Ploughlands ; and there we shot
a man betwixt the plough-stilts, and he presently
fell to the ground, upon his nose and his mouth ; and
then the Devil gave me an arrow, and caused me
shoot a woman in that field; which I did, and she fell

down dead.*   In winter of 1660, when Mr. Harry
Forbes, Minister at Aulderne, was sick, we made a
bag of the galls, flesh, and guts of toads, pickles of
barley, parings of the nails of fingers and toes, the
liver of a hare, and bits of clouts.   We steeped all
this together, all night among water, all hacked (or
minced up) through other.   And when we did put it
among the water, Satan was with us, and learned us
the words following, to say thrice over.   They are
thus :

' 1st. " He is lying in his bed ; he is lying sick and sore ;
        Let him lie intill his bed two months and [three] days
        more !
' 2nd. " Let him lie intill his bed ; let him lie intill it sick and
        sore ;
        Let him lie intill his bed months two and three days
        more !
' 3rd. " He shall lie intill his bed, he shall lie in it sick and sore ;
        He shall lie intill his bed two months and three days
        more !"

' When we had learned all these words from the
Devil, as said is, we fell all down upon our knees,
with our hair down over our shoulders and eyes, and
our hands lifted up, and our eyes [upon] the Devil,
and said the foresaid words thrice over to the Devil,
strictly, against [the recovery of] Master Harry
Forbes [from his sickness].   In the night time we
came in to Mr. Harry Forbes's chamber, where he
lay, with our hands all smeared out of the bag, to
swing it upon Mr. Harry, when he was sick in his

* These, it is needless to say, were pure inventions, and by no
means amusing ones.

bed; and in the daytime [one of our] number, who
was most familiar and intimate with him, to wring or
swing the bag [upon the said Mr. Harry, as we
could] not prevail in the night time against him,
which was accordingly done. Any of . . . . comes in
to your houses, or are set to do you evil, they will look
uncouth - like, thrown . . . . hurly - like, and their
clothes standing out. The Maiden of our Covin,
Jane Martin, was [. . . . We] do no great matter
without our Maiden.

'And if a child be forespoken [bewitched], we take
the cradle . . . . through it thrice, and then a dog
through it; and then shake the belt above the fire
[. . . . and then cast it] down on the ground, till a
dog or cat go over it, that the sickness may come
[. . . . upon the dog or cat].'

With these extended quotations the reader will
probably be satisfied, and in concluding my account
of Isabel Gowdie, I must now adopt a process of
condensation.

Among other freaks and fancies of a disordered
imagination, Isabel declared that she merited to be
stretched upon a rack of iron, and that if torn to
pieces by wild horses, the punishment would not
exceed the measure of her iniquities. These iniquities
comprehended every act attributed by the superstition
of the time to the servants of the devil, which had
been carefully gathered up by this monomaniac from
contemporary witch-tradition. The cruellest thing
was, that she involved so large a number of innocent

persons in the peril into which she herself had reck-
lessly plunged, naming nearly fifty women, and I for-
get how many men, as her associates or accomplices.
She affirmed that they dug up from their graves the
bodies of unbaptized infants, and having dismembered
them, made use of the limbs in their incantations.
That when they wished to destroy an enemy's crops,
they yoked toads to his plough; and on the following
night the devil, with this strange team, drove furrows
into the land, and blasted it effectually. The devil,
it would seem, was so long and so incessantly occupied with high affairs in Scotland, that surely the
rest of the world must have escaped meanwhile the
evils of his interference! Witches, added Isabel, were
able to assume almost any shape, but their usual
choice was that of a hare, or perhaps a cat. There
was some risk in either assumption. Once it happened that Isabel, in her disguise of a hare, was hotly
pursued by a pack of hounds, and narrowly escaped
with her life. When she reached her cottage-door
she could feel the hot breath of her pursuers on her
haunches; but, contriving to slip behind a chest, she
found time to speak the magic words which alone
could restore her to her natural shape, namely:

> ' " Hare! hare! God send thee care!
> I am in a hare's likeness now;
> But I shall be a woman e'en now.
> Hare! hare! God send thee care!"

If witches, while wearing the shape of hare or cat,
were bitten by the dogs, they always retained the

marks on their human bodies. When the devil called a convention of his servants, each proceeded through the air—like the witches of Lapland and other countries — astride on a broomstick [or it might be on a corn or bean straw], repeating as they went the rhyme :

> ' Horse and paddock, horse and go,
> Horse and pellatris, ho ! ho !'

They · usually left behind them a broom, or three-legged stool, which, properly charmed and placed in bed, assumed a likeness to themselves until they returned, and prevented suspicion. This seems to have been the practice of witches everywhere. Witches specially favoured by their master were provided with a couple of imps as attendants, who boasted such very mundane names as ' The Roaring Lion,' ' Thief of Hell,' ' Ranting Roarer,' and 'Care for Nought '—a great improvement on the vulgar mono-syllables worn by the English imps—and were dressed, as already described, in distinguishing liveries : sea-green, pea-green, grass-green, sad-dun, and yellow. The witches were never allowed—at least, not in the infernal presence—to call themselves, or one another, by their baptismal names, but were required to use the appellations bestowed on the devil when he re-baptized them, such as 'Blue Kail,' 'Raise the Wind,' ' Batter-them-down Maggie,' and ' Able and Stout.' The reader will find in the reports of the trial much more of this grotesque nonsense—the vapourings of a distempered brain. The judges, however, took it seriously, and Isabel Gowdie, or Gilbert, and many of her presumed accomplices, were duly strangled and burned (in April, 1662).

CASE OF JANET WISHART.

The case of Janet Wishart, wife of John Leyis, carries us away to the North of Scotland. It presents some peculiar features, and therefore I shall put it before the reader, with no more abridgment than is absolutely needful. It is of much earlier date than the preceding.*

'i. In the month of April, or thereabout, in 1591, in the "gricking" of the day, [that is, in the dawn,] Janet Wishart, on her way back from the blockhouse and Fattie, where she had been holding conference with the devil, pursued Alexander Thomson, mariner, coming forth of Aberdeen to his ship, ran between him and Alexander Fidler, under the Castle Hill, as swift, it appeared to him, as an arrow could be shot forth of a bow, going betwixt him and the sun, and cast her "cantrips" in his way. Whereupon, the said Alexander Thomson took an immediate "fear and trembling," and was forced to hasten home, take to his bed, and lie there for the space of a month, so that none believed he would live;—one half of the day burning in his body, as if he had been roasting in an oven, with an extreme feverish thirst, "so that he could never be satisfied of drink," the other half of the day melting away his body with an extraordinarily cold sweat. And Thomson, knowing she

* From the 'Records of the Burgh of Aberdeen,' printed for the Spalding Club, 1841.

had cast this kind of witchcraft upon him, sent his
wife to threaten her, that, unless she at once relieved
him, he would see that she was burnt. And she,
fearing lest he should accuse her, sent him by the two
women a certain kind of beer and some other drugs
to drink, after which Thomson mended daily, and recovered his former health.'

It is to be noted that Janet flatly denied the
coming of Mrs. Thomson on any such errand.

'ii. Seven years before, on St. Bartholomew's Day,
when Andrew Ardes, webster [weaver], in his play,
took a linen towel, and put it about the said Janet's
neck, not fearing any evil from her, or that she would
be offended, Janet, "in a devilish fury and wodnes"
[madness], exclaimed, "Why teasest thou me?
Thou shalt die! I shall give bread to my bairns
this towmound [twelvemonth], but thou shalt not
bide a month with thine to give them bread." And
immediately after the said Andrew's departure from
her, he took to his bed for the space of eight days:
the one half of the day roasting in his whole body as
in a furnace, and the other half with a vehement
sweat melting away; so that, by her cruel murther
and witchcraft, the said Andrew Ardes died within
eight days. And the day after his departure, his
widow, "contracting a high displeasure," took to her
bed, and within a month deceased ; so that all their
bairns are now begging their meat.'

This was testified to be true by Elspeth Ewin,
spouse to James Mar, mariner, but was denied by
the accused.

' iii. Twenty-four years ago, in the month of May, when she dwelt on the School Hill, next to Adam Mair's, she was descried by Andrew Brabner the younger, John Leslie, of the Gallowgate, Robert Sanders, wright, Andrew Simson, tailor, and one Johnson, who were then schoolboys, stealing forth from the said Adam Mair's yard, at two in the morning, "greyn growand bear"; and instantly, being pointed out by the said scholars to the wife of the said Adam, she, in her fury, burst forth upon the scholars: "Well have ye schemed me, but I shall gar the best of you repent!" And she added that, ere four in the afternoon, she would make as many wonder at them as should see them. Upon the same day, between two and three in the afternoon, the said scholars passed to the Old Watergang in the Links to wash themselves; and after they had done so, and dried, the said John Leslie and Johnson took a race beside the Watergang, and desperately threw themselves into the midst of the Watergang, and were drowned, through the witchcraft which Janet had cast upon them. And thus, as she had promised, she did murder them.'

This was testified by Robert Sanders and Andrew Simson, but was denied by the accused.

'iv. Sixteen years since, or thereby, she [the accused] and Malcolm Carr's wife, having fallen at variance and discord, she openly vowed that the latter should be confined to her bed for a year and a day, and should not make for herself a single cake : immediately after which discord, the said Malcolm's wife

23

went to her own house, sought her bed, and lay half a year bed-stricken by the witchcraft Janet had cast upon her, according to her promise ; one half of the day burning up her whole body as in a fiery furnace, the other half melting away her body with an extraordinary sweat, with a *congealed coldness.*'

v. She was also accused of lending to Meryann Nasmith a pair of head-sheets in childbed, into which she put her witchcraft : which sheets, as soon as she knew they had taken heat about the woman's head, immediately she went and took them from her ; and before she [Janet] was well out of the house, Meryann went out of her mind, and was bound hand and foot for three days.

vi. Three years since, or thereby, James Ailhows, having been a long time in her service, Janet desired him to continue with her, and on his refusing, 'Gang where you please,' she said, 'I will see that you do not earn a single cake of bread for a year and a day.' And as soon as he quitted her service, he was seized with an extremely heavy sickness and (wodnes) delirium, with a continual burning heat and cold sweating, and lay bedfast half a year, according to her promise, through the devilish witchcraft she had cast upon him.   So that he was compelled to send to Benia for another witch to take the witchcraft from him : who came to this town and washed him in water *running south*, and put him through a girth, with some other ceremonies that she used.   And he paid her seventeen marks, and by her help recovered health again.

vii. For twenty years past she continually and nightly, after eleven o'clock, when her husband and servants had gone to their beds, put on a great fire, and kept it up all night, and sat before it using witchcraft, altogether contrary to the nature of well-living persons. And on those nights when she did not make up the fire, she went out of the house, and stayed away all night where she pleased.

viii. She caused . . . ., then in her service, and lately shepherd to Mr. Alexander Fraser, to take certain drugs of witchcraft made by her, such as old shoon, and cast them in the fire of John Club, stabler, her neighbour ; since which time, through her witchcraft, the said John Club has become completely impoverished.

ix. She and Janet Patton having fallen into variance and discord, Janet Patton called the witch 'Karling,' to whom she answered that she would give her to understand if she was a witch, and would try her skill upon her. And immediately afterwards, Janet Patton [like everybody else concerned in these mysterious doings] took to her bed, with a vehement, great, and extraordinary sickness, for one half the day, from her middle up, burning as in a fiery furnace, with an insatiable drought, which she could not slake; the other half-day, melting away with sweat, and from her middle down as cold as ice, so that through the witchcraft cast upon her she died within a month.

x. The particulars given of the case of James Lowe, stabler, are almost the same. He refused to lend his kill and barn, and on the same day he was

23—2

seized with this remarkable sickness—half a day burning hot, and half a day ice-cold. On his death-bed he accused Janet Wishart of being the cause of his misfortune, saying, "That if he had lent to her his kill and kilbarn, he wald haf bene ane lewand man." His wife and only son died of the same kind of disease, and his whole gear, amounting to more than £3,000, was altogether wracked and thrown away, so that there was left no memory of the said James, succession of his body, nor of their gear.

xi. John Pyet, stabler, is named as another victim.

xii. There is an air of novelty about the next case, that of John Allan, cutler, Janet Wishart's son-in-law. Quarrelling with his wife, he 'dang' her, 'where-upon Mistress Allan complained to her mother, who immediately betook herself to her son-in-law's house, 'bostit' him, and promised to gar him repent that ever he saw or kent her. Shortly afterwards, either she or the devil her master, in the likeness of a brown tyke, came nightly for five or six weeks to his window, forced it open, leaped upon the said John, dang and buffeted him, while always sparing his wife, who lay in bed with him, so that the said John became half-wod and furious. And this persecution continued, until he threatened to inform the ministry and kirk-session.

xiii. The next case must be given verbatim, it is so striking an example of ignorant prejudice:

'Four years since, or thereby, she came in to Walter Mealing's dwelling-house, in the Castlegate of Aber-deen, to buy wool, which they refused to sell. There-

after, she came to the said Walter's bairn, sitting on
her mother's knee, and the said Walter played with
her. And she said, " This is a comely child, a fine
child," without any further words, and would not
say " God save her !" And before she reached the
stair-foot, the bairn, by her witchcraft, in presence of
both her father and mother, " cast her gall," changed
her colour like dead, and became as weak as " ane
pair of glwffis," and melted continually away with an
extraordinary sweating and extreme drought, which
that same day eight days, at the same hour, she came
in first, and then the bairn departed. And for no
request nor command of the said Walter, nor others
whom he directed, she would not come in again to
the house to " visie " the bairn, although she was oft
and divers times sent for, both by the father and
mother of the bairn, and so by her witchcraft she
murdered the bairn.'

xiv. On Yule Eve, in '94, at three in the morning,
Janet, remaining in Gilbert Mackay's stair in the
Broadgate, perceived Bessie Schives, spouse of Robert
Blinschell, going forth of her own house to the
dwelling-house of James Davidson, notary, to his
wife, who was in travail. She came down the stair,
and cast her cantrips and witchcraft in her way, and
the said Bessie being in perfect health of body, and
as blithe and merry as ever she was in her days,
when she went out of the same James Davidson's
house, or ever she could win up her own stair, took a
great fear and trembling that she might scarcely win
up her own stair, and immediately after her up-

coming, went to her naked bed, lay continually for the space of eighteen weeks fast bed-sick, bewitched by Janet Wishart, the one half-day roasting as in a fiery furnace, with an extraordinary kind of drought, that she could not be slaked, and the other half-day in an extraordinary kind of sweating, melting, and consuming her body, as a white burning candle, which kind of sickness is a special point of witch-craft; and the said Bessie Schives saw none other but Janet only, who is holden and reputed a common witch.

xv. At Midsummer was a year or thereby, Elspeth Reid, her daughter-in-law, came into her house at three in the morning, and found her sitting, mother naked as she was born, at the fireside, and another old wife siclike mother naked, sitting between her shoulders[!], making their cantrips, whom the said Elspeth seeing, after she said 'God speed,' immedi-ately went out of the house; thereafter, on the same day, returned again, and asked of her, what she was doing with that old wife? To whom she answered, that she was charming her. And as soon as the said Elspeth went forth again from Janet Wishart's house, immediately she took an extraordinary kind of sick-ness, and became 'like a dead senseless fool,' and so continued for half a year.

xvi. She [Janet] and her daughter, Violet Leyis, desired . . . . her woman to go with her said daughter, at twelve o'clock at night, to the gallows, and cut down the dead man hanging thereon, and take a part of all his members from him, and burn the corpse, which her servant would not do, and, therefore, she was instantly sent away.

xvii. The following deposition is, however, the most singular of all:

Twelve years since, or thereby, Janet came into Katherine Rattray's, behind the Tolbooth, and while she was drinking in the said Katherine's cellar, Katherine reproved her for drinking in her house, because, she said, she was a witch. Whereupon, she took a cup full of ale, and cast it in her face, and said that if she were indeed a witch, the said Katherine should have proof of it; and immediately after she had quitted the cellar, the barm of the said Katherine's ale all sank to the bottom of the stand, and no had abaid [a bead] thereon during the space of sixteen weeks. And the said Katherine finding herself 'skaithit,' complained to her daughter, Katherine Ewin, who was then in close acquaintance with Janet, that she had bewitched her mother's ale; and immediately thereafter the said Katherine Ewin called on Janet, and said, 'Why bewitched you my mother's ale?' and requested her to help the same again. Which Janet promised, if Katherine Ewin obeyed her instructions . . . . to rise early before the sun, without commending herself to God, or speaking, and neither suining herself nor her son sucking on her breast; to go, still without speaking, to the said Katherine Rattray's house, and not to cross any water, nor wash her hands; and enter into the said Katherine Rattray's house, where she would find her servant brewing, and say to her thrice, 'I to God, and thou

to the devil!' and to restore the same barm where it
was again; 'and to take up thrie dwattis on the
southt end of the gauttreyis, and thair scho suld find
ane peice of claithe, fowr newikit, with greyn, red,
and blew, and thrie corss of clewir girss, and cast the
same in the fyir; quhilk beand cassin in, her barm
suld be restorit to hir againe, lyik as it was restorit
in effect.' And the said Katherine Ewin, when
cracking [gossiping] with her neighbours, said she
could learn them a charm she had gotten from Janet
Wishart, which when the latter heard, she promised
to do her an evil turn, and immediately her son, sucking on her breast, died. And at her first browst, or
brewing, thereafter, the whole wort being played and
put in 'lumes,' the doors fast, and the keys at her
own belt, the whole wort was taken away, and the
haill lumes fundin dry, and the floor dry, and she
could never get trial where it yird to. And when the
said Katherine complained to the said Janet Wishart,
and dang herself and her good man both, for injuries
done to her by taking of her son's life and her wort
[which Katherine seems to have thought of about
equal value], she promised that all should be well,
giving her her draff for payment. And the said
Katherine, with her husband Ambrose Gordon, being
in their beds, could not for the space of twenty days
be quit of a cat, lying nightly in their bed, between
the two, and taking a great bite out of Ambrose's
arm, as yet the place testifies, and when they gave up
the draff, the cat went away.

Some fourteen more charges were brought against

her. She was tried on February 17, 1596, before the Provost and Baillies of Aberdeen, and found guilty upon eighteen counts of being a common witch and sorcerer. Sentence of death by burning was recorded against her, and she suffered on the same day as another reputed witch, Isabel Cocker. The expenses of their execution are preserved in the account-books of the Dean of Guild, 1596-1597, and prove that witch-burning was a luxury scarcely within the reach of the many.

JANETT WISCHART AND ISSBEL COCKER.

Item. For twentie loades of peattes to burne thame	xl*sh.*
Item. For ane Boile of Coillis	xxiiii*sh.*
Item. For four Tar barrellis	xxvi*sh.* viii*d.*
Item. For fyr and Iron barrellis	xvi*sh.* viii*d.*
Item. For a staik and dressing of it	xvi*sh.*
Item. For four fudoms [fathoms?] of Towis ...	iiii*sh.*
Item. For careing the peittis, coillis, and barrellis to the Hill	viii*sh.* iiii*d.*
Item. To on Justice for their execution ...	xiii*sh.* iiii*d.*
	cliv*shillings.*

On several occasions commissions were issued by the King, in favour of the Provost and some of the Baillies of the burgh, and the Sheriff of the county, for the purpose of 'haulding Justice Courtis on Witches and Sorceraris.' These commissioners gave warrants in their turn to the minister and elders of each parish in the shire, to examine parties suspected of witchcraft, and to frame a 'dittay' or indictment against such persons. It was an inevitable result that all the scandalous gossip of the community was assiduously collected; while any individual who had become, from whatsoever cause, an object of jealousy or dislike to her neighbours, was overwhelmed by a mass of hearsay or fictitious evidence, and by the conscious or unconscious exaggerations of ignorance, credulity, or malice.

As an example of the kind of stuff stirred up by this parochial inquisition, I shall take the return furnished to the commissioners by Mr. John Ross, minister of Lumphanan:

'i. *Elspet Strathauchim*, in Wartheil, is indicted to have charmed Maggie Clarke, spouse to Patrick Bunny, for the fevers, this last year, with "ane sleipth and ane thrum" [a sleeve and thread]. She is indicted, this last Hallow e'en, to have brought forth of the house a burning coal, and buried the same in her own yard. She is indicted to have bewitched Adam Gordon, in Wark, and to have been the cause of his death, and that because, she coming out of his service without his leave, he detained some of her gear, which she promised to do; and after his death wanted [to have it believed] that she had gotten "assythment" of him. She is indicted to have said to Marcus Gillam, at the Burn of Camphil, that none of his bairns should live, because he would not marry her; which is come to pass, for two of them are dead. She is indicted continually to have resorted to Margaret Baine her company.

'ii. *Isabel Forbes.* — She is indicted to have bewitched Gilbert Makim, in Glen Mallock, with a

spindle, a "rok," and a "foil ;" as Isabel Ritchie likewise testified.

'iii. *James Og* is indicted to have passed on Rud-
day, five years since, through Alexander Cobain's
corn, and have taken nine stones from his "avine rig "
[corn-rick], and cast on the said Alexander's "rig,"
and to have taken nine "lokis" [handfuls] of meal
from the said Alexander's " rig," and cast on his own.
He is indicted to have bewitched a cow belonging to
the said Alexander, which he bought from Kristane
Burnet, of Cloak ; this cow, though his wife had
received milk from her the first night, and the morning thereafter, gave no milk from that time forth, but
died within half a year.   He is indicted to have
passed, five years since, on Lammas-Day, through
the said Alexander's corn, and having " gaine nyne
span," to have struck the corn with nine strokes of a
white wand, so that nothing grew that year but
" fichakis."   He is indicted that, in the year aforesaid
or thereabouts, having corn to dry, he borrowed fire
from his neighbour, haiffing of his avine them
presently ; and took a " brine " of the corn on his
back, and cast it three times " woodersonis " [or
" withersonis," *ut supra,* that is, west to east, in the
direction contrary to the sun's course] above the
" kill."   He is indicted that, three years since,
Alexander Cobaine being in Leith, with the Laird
of Cors, his " wittual," he came up early one morning, at the back of the said Alexander's yard, with
a dish full of water in his hand, and to have cast the
water in the gate to the said Alexander's door, and

then perceiving that David Duguid, servant to the said Alexander, was beholding him, to have fled suddenly ; which the said David also testifies.

'iv. *Agnes Frew.*—She is indicted to have taken three hairs out of her own cow's tail, and to have cut the same in small pieces, and to have put them in her cow's throat, which thereafter gave milk, and the neighbours' none. Also, she is indicted that [she took] William Browne's calf in her axter, and charmed the same, as, also, she took the clins [hoofs] from forefeitt aff it, with a piece of " euerry bing," and caused the said William's wife to " yeird " the same ; which the said William's wife confessed, albeit not in this manner. Also, she took up Alexander Tailzier's calf, lately [directly] after it was calved, and carried it three times about the cow. Also, she was seen casting a horse's fosser on a cow.

' v. *Isabel Roby.*—She is indicted to have bidden her gudeman, when he went to St. Fergus to buy cattle, that if he bought any before his home-coming, he should go three times " woodersonis " about them, and then take three " ruggis " off a dry hillock, and fetch home to her. Also, that dwelling at Ardmair, there came in a poor man craving alms, to whom she offered milk, but he refused it, because, as he then presently said, she had three folks' milk and her own in the pan ; and when Elspet Mackay, then present, wondered at it, he said, " Marvel not, for she has thy farrow kye's milk also in her pan." Also, she is commonly seen in the form of a hare, passing through the town, for as soon as the hare vanishes out of sight, she appears.'

'vi. *Margaret Rianch*, in Green Cottis, was seen in the dawn of the day by James Stevens embracing every nook of John Donaldson's house three times, who continually thereafter was diseased, and at last died.   She said to John Ritchie, when he took a tack [a piece of ground] in the Green Cottis, that his gear from that day forth should continually decay, and so it came to pass.   Also, she cast a number of stones in a tub, amongst water, which thereafter was seen dancing.   When she clips her sheep, she turns the bowl of the shears three times in their mouth.   Also, James Stevens saw her meeting John Donaldson's "hoggs" [sheep a year old] in the burn of the Green Cottis, and casting the water out between her feet backward, in the sheep's face, and so they all died. Also she confessed to Patrick Gordon, of Kincragie, and James Gordon, of Drumgase, that the devil was in the bed between her and William Ritchie, her harlot, and he was upon them both, and that if she happened to die for witchcraft, that he [Ritchie] should also die, for if she was a devil, he was too.

'There are three of these persons, Elspeet Strath-auchim, James Og, and Agnes Frew, whose accusa-tions the Presbytery of Kincardine, within whose bounds they dwell, counted insufficient, having duly considered the whole circumstances, always remitted them to the trial of an assize, if the judges thought it expedient.

'[Signed]   MR. JHONE ROS,

'Minister at Lumphanan.'

It would not be easy to find a more painful exhibition of clerical ignorance and incapacity. Probably many of the allegations which Mr. John Ross records are true, as the practice of charms was common enough among the peasantry both of Scotland and England, and is even yet not wholly extinct; but, taken altogether, they did not amount to witchcraft, the very essence of which was a compact with the devil, and in no one of the preceding cases is such a compact mentioned. And one must take the existence of the gross superstition and credulity which is here disclosed to be irrefutable testimony that, as a pastor and teacher, Mr. John Ross was a signal failure at Lumphanan.

I have already alluded to those pathetic instances of self-delusion in which the reputed witch has been her own enemy, and furnished the evidence needed for her condemnation in her own confession—a confession of acts which she must have known had never occurred; building up a strange fabric of fiction, and perishing beneath its weight. It would seem as if some of these unfortunate women came to believe in themselves because they found that others believed in them, and assumed that they really possessed the powers of witchcraft because their neighbours insisted that it was so. Nor will this be thought such an improbable explanation when it is remembered that history affords more than one example of prophets and founders of new religions whom the enthusiastic devotion of their followers has persuaded into a belief in the authenticity of the credentials which they themselves had originally forged, and the truth of the revelations which they had invented.

From this point of view a profound interest attaches to the official ' dittay ' or accusation against one Helen Fraser, who was convicted and sentenced to death in April, 1597, since it shows that she was condemned principally upon the evidence which she herself supplied :

' i. John Ramsay, in Newburght, being sick of a consuming disease, sent to her house, in Aikinshill, to seek relief, and was told by her that she would do what lay in her power for the recovery of his health ; but bade him keep secret whatever she spake or did, because the world was evil, and spoke no good of such mediciners. She commanded the said John to rise early in the morning, to eat " sourrakis " about sunrise, while the dew was still upon them; also to eat "valcars," and to make "lavrie " kale and soup. Moreover, to sit down in a door, before the fowls flew to their roost, and to open his breast, that when the fowls flew to the roost over him he might receive the wind of their wings about his breast, for that was very profitable to loose his heart-pipes, which were closed. But before his departure from her, she made him sit down, bare-headed, on a stool, and said an orison thrice upon his head, in which she named the Devil.

' ii. *Item.*—The said Helen publicly confessed in Foverne, after her apprehension, that she was a common abuser of the people; and that, further, to sustain herself and her bairns, she pretended know-

ledge which she had not, and undertook to do things
which she could not.   This was her answer, when she
was accused by the minister of Foverne, for that she
abused the people, and when he inquired the cause of
her evil report throughout the whole country.   This
she confessed upon the green of Foverne, before the
laird, the minister, and reader of Foverne, Patrick
Findlay in Newburght, and James Menzies at the
New Mills of Foverne.

'iii. *Item*.—Janet Ingram, wife to Adam Finnie,
dwelling for the time at the West burn, in Balhelueis,
being sick, and affirming herself to be bewitched, for
she herself was esteemed by all men to be a witch, she
sent for the said Helen Frazer to cure her.   The said
Helen came, and tarried with her till her departure
and burial, and at her coming assured the said Janet
that within a short time she would be well enough.
But the sickness of the said Janet increased, and was
turned into a horrible fury and madness, in such sort
that she always and incessantly blasphemed, and
pressed at all times to climb up the wall after the
" heillis" and scraped the wall with her hands.   After
that she had been grievously vexed for the space of
two days from the coming of Helen Frazer, her
mediciner, to her, she departed this life.   Being dead,
her husband went to charge his neighbours to convey
her burial, but before his returning, or the coming of
any neighbour to the carrying of the corpse, the said
Helen Frazer, together with two or three daughters of
the said Janet (whereof one yet living, to wit, Malye
Finnie, in the Blairtoun of Balhelueis, is counted a

witch), had taken up the corpse, and had carried her, they alone, the half of the distance to the kirk, until they came to the Moor of Cowhill; when the said Adam and others his neighbours came to them, and at their coming the said Helen fled away through the moss to Aikinshill, and went no further towards the kirk.

'iv. *Item.*—A horse of Duncan Alexander, in New-burcht, being bewitched, the said Helen translated the sickness from the horse to a young cow of the said Duncan; which cow died, and was cast into the burn of the Newburcht, for no man would eat her.

'v. *Item.*—The said Helen made a compact with certain laxis fishers of the Newburcht, at the kirk of Foverne, in Mallie Skryne's house, and promised to cause them to fish well, and to that effect received of them a piece of salmon to handle at her pleasure for accomplishing the matter. Upon the morrow she came to the Newburcht, to the house of John Ferguson, a laxis fisher, and delivered unto him in a closet four cuts of salmon with a penny; after that she called him out of his own house, from the company that was there drinking with him, and bade him put the same in the horn of his coble, and he should have a dozen of fish at the first shot; which came to pass.

'vi. *Item.*—The said Helen, by witchcraft, enticed Gilbert Davidson, son to William Davidson, in Lytoune of Meanye, to love and marry Margaret Strauthachin (in the Hill of Balgrescho) directly

24

against the will of his parents, to the utter wreck of the said Gilbert.

'vii. *Item.*—At the desire of the said Margaret Strauthachin, by witchcraft, the said Helen made Catherine Fetchil, wife to William Davidson, furious, because she was against the marriage, and took the strength of her left side and arm from her; in the which fury and feebleness the said Catherine died.

'viii. *Item.*—The said Helen, at the desire of the foresaid Margaret Strauthachin, bewitched William Hill, dwelling for the time at the Hill of Balgrescho, through which he died in a fury [*i.e.*, a fit of delirium].

'ix. Moreover, at the desire foresaid, the said Helen by witchcraft slew an ox belonging to the said William; for while Patrick Hill, son to the said William, and herd to his father, called in the cattle to the fold, at twelve o'clock, the said Helen was sitting in the yeite, and immediately after the outcoming of the cattle out. of the fold, the best ox of the whole herd instantly died.

'x. *Item*—The said Helen counselled Christane Henderson, vulgarly called mickle Christane, to put one hand to the crown of her head, and the other to the sole of her foot, and so surrender whatever was between her hands, and she should want nothing that she could wish or desire.

'xi. *Item.*—The said Christane Henderson, being henwife in Foverne, the young fowls died thick ; for remedy whereof, the said Helen bade the said Christane take all the chickens or young fowls, and draw them through the link of the crook, and take the hindmost, and slay with a fiery stick, which thing being practised, none died thereafter that year.

' xii. *Item.*—When the said Helen was dwelling in the Moorhill of Foverne, there came a hare betimes, and sucked a milch cow pertaining to William Findlay, at the Mill of the Newburght, whose house was directly afornent the said Helen's house, on the other side of the Burn of Foverne, wherethrough the cow pined away, and gave blood instead of milk. This mischief was by all men attributed to the said Helen, and she herself cannot deny but she was commonly evil spoken of for it, and affirmed, after her apprehension at Foverne, that she was so slandered.

' xiii. *Item.*—When Alexander Hardy, in Aikinshill, departed this life, it grieved and troubled his conscience very mickle, that he had been a defender of the said Helen, and especially that he, accompanied with Malcolm Forbes, travailed, against their conscience, with sundry of the assessors when she suffered an assize, and especially with the Chancellor of the Assize, in her favour, he knowing evidently her to be guilty of death.

' xiv. *Item.*—The said Helen being a domestic in the said Alexander Hardy's house, disagreed with one of the said Alexander's servants, named Andrew Skene, and intending to bewitch the said servant, the evil fell upon Alexander, and he died thereof.

' xv. *Item.*—When Robert Goudyne, now in Balgrescho, was dwelling in Blairtoun of Balheluies, a discord fell out betwixt Elizabeth Dempster,

24—2

nurse to the said Robert for the time, and Christane
Henderson, one of the said Helen's familiars, as her
own confession aforesaid purports, and the country
well knows.   Upon the which discord, the said
Christane threatened the said Elizabeth with an evil
turn, and to the performing thereof, brought the said
Helen Frazer to the said Robert's house, and caused
her to repair oft thereto.   After what time, immediately both the said Elizabeth and the infant to whom
she gave suck, by the devilry of the said ·Helen, fell
into a consuming sickness, whereof both died.   And
also Elspet Cheyne, spouse to the said Robert, fell into
the selfsame sickness, and was heavily diseased thereby
for the space of two years before the recovery of his
health.

'xvi. *Item.*—By witchcraft the said Helen abstracted
and withdrew the love and affection of Andrew Tilli-
duff of Rainstoune, from his spouse Isabel Cheyne, to
Margaret Neilson, and so mightily bewitched him,
that he could never be reconciled with his wife, or
remove his affection from the said harlot; and when
the said Margaret was begotten with child, the said
Helen conveyed her away to Cromar to obscure the
fact.

'xvii. *Item.*—Wherever the said Helen is known, or
has repaired there many years bygone, she has been,
and is reported by all, of whatsoever estate or sex, to
be a common and abominable witch, and to have
learned the same of the late Maly Skene, spouse to
the late Cowper Watson, with whom, during her lifetime, the said Helen had continual society.   The

said Maly was bruited to be a rank witch, and her said husband suffered death for the same crime.

'xviii. *Item.*—When Robert Merchant, in the New-brucht, had contracted marriage, and holden house for the space of two years with the late Christane White, it happened to him to pass to the Moorhill of Foverne, to sow corn to the late Isabel Bruce, the relict of the late Alexander Frazer, the said Helen Frazer being familiar and actually resident in the house of the said Isabel, she was there at his coming : from the which time forth the said Robert *found his affection violently and extraordinarily drawn away from the said Christane to the said Isabel*, a great love being betwixt him and the said Christane always thereto-fore, and no break of love, or discord, falling out or intervening upon either of their parts, which thing the country supposed and spake to be brought about by the unlawful travails of the said Helen.

'[Signed]   THOMAS TILIDEFF,
' Minister, at Fovern, with my hand.

'*Item.*—A common witch by open voice and common fame.'

I have given this 'dittay' in full, from a conviction that no summary would do justice to its terrible simplicity. Upon the evidence which it afforded, Helen Frazer was brought before the Court of Justiciary, in Aberdeen, on April 21, 1597, and found guilty in 'fourteen points of witchcraft and sorcery.'

The burning of witches went merrily on, so that the authorities of Aberdeen were compelled to get in an adequate stock of fuel. We note in the municipal accounts, under the date of March 10, that there was 'bocht be the comptar, and laid in be him in the seller in the Chappell of the Castel hill, ane chalder of coillis, price thairof, with the bieing and metting of the same, xvi*lib*. iiii*sh*.' As is usually the case, the frequency of these sad exhibitions whetted at first the public appetite for them; it grew by what it fed on. One of the items of expense in the execution of a witch named Margaret Clerk, is for carrying of 'four sparris, *to withstand the press of the pepill*, quhairof thair was twa broken, viiis. viiid.'

Among the victims committed to the flames in 1596-97, we read the names of 'Katherine Fergus and [Sculdr], Issobel Richie, Margaret Og, Helene Rodger, Elspet Hendersoun, Katherine Gerard, Christin Reid, Jenet Grant, Helene Frasser, Katherine Ferrers, Helene Gray, Agnes Vobster, Jonat Douglas, Agnes Smelie, Katherine Alshensur, and ane other witche, callit . . . .'—seventeen in all. That during their imprisonment they were treated with barbarous rigour, may be inferred from the following entries:

Item. To Alexander Reid, smyth, for *twa pair of scheckellis* to the Witches in the Stepill   ...   xxxii*sh*.

Item. To John Justice, for *burning vpon the cheik* of four seurerall personis suspect of witchcraft and baneschit ...   .   xxvi*sh*. viii*d*.

Item. Givin to Alexander Home for macking of *joggis, stapillis, and lockis* to the witches, during the haill tyme forsaid ...   .   xlvi*sh*. viii*d*.

Expense on Witches ...   ... aucht-score, xlii*li*. xvii*sh*. iiii*d*.

On September 21, 1597, the Provost, Baillies and Council of Aberdeen considered the faithfulness shown by William Dun, the Dean of Guild, in the discharge of his duty, 'and, besides this, *his extraordinarily taking pains in the burning of the great number of the witches burnt this year*, and on the four pirates, and bigging of the port on the Brig of Dee, repairing of the Grey Friars kirk and steeple thereof, and thereby has been abstracted from his trade of merchandise, continually since he was elected in the said office. Therefore, in recompense of his extraordinary pains, and in satisfaction thereof (not to induce any preparative to Deans of Guild to crave a recompense hereafter), but to encourage others to travail as diligently in the discharge of their office, granted and assigned to him the sum of forty-seven pounds three shillings and fourpence, owing by him of the rest of his compt of the unlawis [fines] of the persons convict for slaying of black fish, and discharged him thereof by their presents for ever.'

At length a wholesome reaction took place; the public grew weary of the number of executions, and, encouraged by this changes of sentiment, person accused of witchcraft boldly rebutted the charge, and laid complaints against their accusers for defamation of character. In official circles, it is true, a belief in the alleged crime lingered long. As late as 1669, 'the new and old Councils taking into their serious consideration that many malefices were committed and done by several persons in this town, who are *mala fama*, and suspected guilty of witchcraft upon many of the inhabitants of this town, several ways, and that it will be necessary for suppressing the like in time coming, and for punishing the said persons who shall be found guilty; therefore they do unanimously conclude and ordain that any such person, who is suspect of the like malefices, may be seized upon, and put in prisoun, and that a Commission be sent for, for putting of them to trial, that condign justice may be executed upon them, as the nature of the offence does merit.' No more victims, however, were sacrificed; nor does it appear that any accusation of witchcraft was preferred.

According to Sir Walter Scott, a woman was burnt as a witch in Scotland as late as 1722, by Captain Ross, sheriff-depute of Sutherland; but this was, happily, an exceptional barbarity, and for some years previously the pastime of witch-burning had practically been extinct. It is a curious fact that educated Scotchmen, as I have already noted, retained their superstition long after the common people had abandoned it. In 1730, Professor Forbes, of Glasgow, published his 'Institutes of the Law of Scotland,' in which he spoke of witchcraft as 'that black art whereby strange and wonderful things are wrought by power derived from the devil,' and added: 'Nothing seems plainer to me than that there may be and have been witches, and that perhaps such are now actually existing.' Six years later, the Seceders from the Church of Scotland, who professed to be the true representatives of its teaching, strongly condemned the repeal of the laws against witchcraft, as 'contrary,' they said, 'to the express letter of the law of God.' But they were hopelessly behind the time; public opinion, as the result of increased intelligence, had numbered witchcraft among the superstitions of the past, and we may confidently predict that its revival is impossible.

CHAPTER V.

THE LITERATURE OF WITCHCRAFT.

IT should teach us humility when we find a belief in witchcraft and demonology entertained not only by the uneducated and unintelligent classes, but also by the men of light and leading, the scholar, the philosopher, the legislator, who might have been expected to have risen above so degrading a super-stition. It would be manifestly unfair to direct our reproaches at the credulous prejudices of the multitude when Francis Bacon, the great apostle of the experi-mental philosophy, accepts the crude teaching of his royal master's 'Demonologie,' and actually discusses the ingredients of the celebrated 'witches' ointment,' opining that they should all be of a soporiferous character, such as henbane, hemlock, moonshade, mandrake, opium, tobacco, and saffron. The weak-ness of Sir Matthew Hale, to which reference has been made in a previous chapter, we cannot very strongly condemn, when we know that it was shared by Sir Thomas Browne, who had so keen an eye for the errors of the common people, and whose fine and liberal genius throws so genial a light over the pages

of the 'Religio Medici.' In his 'History of the
World,' that consummate statesman, poet, and scholar,
Sir Walter Raleigh, gravely supports the vulgar
opinions which nowadays every Board School
alumnus would reject with disdain. Even the
philosopher of Malmesbury, the sagacious author of
'The Leviathan,' Thomas Hobbes, was infected by
the prevalent delusion. Dr. Cudworth, to whom we
owe the acute reasoning of the treatises on 'Moral
Good and Evil,' and 'The True Intellectual System
of the Universe,' firmly holds that the guilt of a
reputed witch might be determined by her inability
or unwillingness to repeat the Lord's Prayer.
Strangest of it all is it to find the pure and lofty
spirit of Henry More, the founder of the school of
English Platonists, yielding to the general superstition. With large additions of his own, he re-
published the Rev. Joseph Glanvill's notorious work,
'Sadducismus Triumphatus'—a pitiful example of
the extent to which a fine intellect may be led
astray, though Mr. Lecky thinks it the most powerful defence of witchcraft ever published. And the
sober and fair-minded Robert Boyle, in the midst of
his scientific researches, found time to listen, with
breathless interest, to 'stories of witches at Oxford,
and devils at Muston.'

Among the Continental authorities on witchcraft,
the chief of those who may be called its advocates
are, *Martin Antonio Delrio* (1551-1608), who published, in the closing years of the sixteenth century,
his 'Disquisitionarum Magicarum Libri Sex,' a for-

midable folio, brimful of credulity and ingenuity,
which was translated into French by Duchesne in
1611, and has been industriously pilfered from by
numerous later writers. Delrio has no pretensions
to critical judgment; he swallows the most monstrous
inventions with astounding facility.

Reference must also be made to the writings of
Remigius, included in Pez' 'Thesaurus Anecdotorum
Novissimus,' and to the great work by H. Institor
and J. Sprenger, 'Malleus Maleficarum,' as well as to
Basin, Molitor ('Dialogus de Lamiis'), and other
authors, to be found in the 1582 edition of 'Mallei
quorundam Maleficarum,' published at Frankfort.

On the same side we find the great philosophical
lawyer and historian *John Bodin* (1530-1596), the
author of the 'Republicæ,' and the 'Methodus ad
facilem Historiarum Cognitionem.' In his 'Demono-
manie des Sorcius' he recommends the burning of
witches and wizards with an earnestness which should
have gone far to compensate for his heterodoxy on
other points of belief and practice. He informs us
that from his thirty-seventh year he had been attended
by a familiar spirit or demon, which touched his ear
whenever he was about to do anything of which his
conscience disapproved; and he quotes passages from
the Psalms, Job, and Isaiah, to prove that spirits
indicate their presence to men by touching and even
pulling their ears, and not only by vocal utterances.

Also, *Thomas Erastus* (1524-1583), physician and
controversialist, who took so busy a part in the
theological dissensions of his time. In 1577 he

published a tract ('De Lamiis') on the lawfulness of putting witches to death. It is strange that he should have been mastered by the gross imposture of witchcraft, when he could expose with trenchant force the pretensions of alchemists, astrologers, and Rosicrucians.

Happily, the cause of humanity, truth and tolerance was not without its eager and capable defenders. The earliest I take to have been the Dutch physician, *Wierus*, who, in his treatise 'De Præstigiis,' published at Basel in 1564, vigorously attacked the cruel prejudice that had doomed so many unhappy creatures to the stake. He did not, however, deny the *existence* of witchcraft, but demanded mercy for those who practised it on the ground that they were the devil's victims, not his servants. That he should have been wholly devoid of credulity would have been more than one could rightly have expected of a disciple of Cornelius Agrippa.

A stronger and much more successful assailant appeared in *Reginald Scot* (died 1599), a younger son of Sir John Scot, of Scot's Hall, near Smeeth, who published his celebrated 'Discoverie of Witchcraft' in 1584—a book which, in any age, would have been remarkable for its sweet humanity, breadth of view, and moderation of tone, as well as for its literary excellencies. One wonders where this quiet Kentish gentleman, whose chief occupations appear to have been gardening and planting, accumulated his erudition, and how, in the face of the superstitions of his contemporaries, he arrived at such large and liberal conclusions. The scope of his great work is indicated in its lengthy title: 'The Discoverie of Witchcraft, wherein the lewd dealing of Witches and Witchmongers is notablie detected, the knaverie of conjurers, the impietie of enchanters, the follie of soothsaiers, the impudent falsehood of couseners, the infidelitie of atheists, the pestilent practices of Pythonists, the curiositie of figure-casters [horoscope-makers], the vanitie of dreamers, the beggarlie art of Alcumystrie, the abhomination of idolatrie, the horrible art of poisoning, the vertue and power of naturall magike, and all the conveyances of Legierdemain and juggling are deciphered: and many other things opened, which have long lain hidden, howbeit verie necessarie to be knowne. Heerevnto is added a treatise upon the Nature and Substance of Spirits and Devils, etc.: all latelie written by Reginald Scot, Esquire. 1 John iv. 1: "Believe not everie spirit, but trie the spirits, whether they are of God; for many false prophets are gone out into the world."'

From a book so well known—a new edition has recently appeared—it is needless to make extracts; but I transcribe a brief passage in illustration of the vivacity and manliness of the writer:

'I, therefore (at this time), do only desire you to consider of my report concerning the evidence that is commonly brought before you against them. See first whether the evidence be not frivolous, and whether the proofs brought against them be not incredible, consisting of guesses, presumptions, and impossibilities contrary to reason, Scripture, and nature. See also what persons complain upon them, whether they be not of the basest, the unwisest, and the most faithless kind of people. Also, may it please you, to weigh what accusations and crimes they lay to their charge, namely: She was at my house of late, she would have had a pot of milk, she departed in a chafe because she had it not, she railed, she cursed, she mumbled and whispered; and, finally, she said she would be even with me: and soon after my child, my cow, my sow, or my pullet died, or was strangely taken. Nay (if it please your Worship), I have further proof: I was with a wise woman, and she told me I had an ill neighbour, and that she would come to my house ere it was long, and so did she; and that she had a mark about her waist, and so had she: God forgive me, my stomach hath gone against her a great while. Her mother before her was counted a witch ; she hath been beaten and scratched by the face till blood was drawn upon her, because she hath been suspected, and afterwards some of those persons were said to amend. These are the certainties that I hear in their evidences.

'Note, also, how easily they may be brought to confess that which they never did, nor lieth in the power of man to do ; and then see whether I have cause to write as I do. Further, if you shall see that infidelity, popery, and many other manifest heresies be backed and shouldered, and their professors animated and heartened, by yielding to creatures such infinite power as is wrested out of God's hand, and attributed to witches: finally, if you shall perceive that I have faithfully and truly delivered and set down the condition and state of the witch, and also of the witchmonger, and have confuted by reason and law, and by the Word of God itself, all mine adversary's objections and arguments; then let me have your countenance against them that maliciously oppose themselves against me.

'My greatest adversaries are young ignorance and old custom. For what folly soever tract of time hath fostered, it is so superstitiously pursued of some, as though no error could be acquainted with custom. But if the law of nations would join with such custom, to the maintenance of ignorance and to the suppressing of knowledge, the civilest country in the world would soon become barbarous. For as knowledge and time discovereth errors, so doth superstition and ignorance in time breed them.'

In another fine passage Scot says:

'God that knoweth my heart is witness, and you that read my book shall see, that my drift and purpose in this enterprise tendeth only to these respects. First, that the glory and power of God be not so abridged and abused, as to be thrust into the hand or lip of a lewd old woman, whereby the work of the Creator should be attributed to the power of a creature. Secondly, that the religion of the Gospel may be seen to stand without such peevish trumpery. Thirdly, that lawful favour and Christian compassion be rather used towards these poor souls than rigour and extremity. Because they which are commonly accused of witchcraft are the least sufficient of all other persons to speak for themselves, as having the most base and simple education of all others ; the extremity of their age giving them leave to dote, their

poverty to beg, their wrongs to chide and threaten
(as being void of any other way of revenge), their
humour melancholical to be full of imaginations, from
whence chiefly proceedeth the vanity of their confessions, as that they can transform themselves and
others into apes, owls, asses, dogs, cats, etc. ; that
they can fly in the air, kill children with charms,
hinder the coming of butter, etc.

' And for so much as the mighty help themselves
together, and the poor widow's cry, though it reach
to heaven, is scarce heard here upon earth, I thought
good (according to my poor ability) to make intercession, that some part of common rigour and some
points of hasty judgment may be advised upon. For
the world is now at that stay (as Brentius, in a most
godly sermon, in these words affirmeth), that even, as
when the heathen persecuted the Christians, if any
were accused to believe in Christ, the common people
cried *Ad leonem ;* so now, of any woman, be she never
so honest, be she accused of witchcraft, they cry *Ad
ignem.*'

Scot's attack upon the credulity of his contemporaries, strenuous and capable as it was, did not bear
much fruit at the time ; while it exposed him to
charges of Atheism and Sadduceeism from several
small critics, who were supported by the authority of
James I., and, at a later date, of Dr. Meric Casaubon.
He found a fellow-labourer, however, in his work of
humanity, in the *Rev. George Gifford,* of Maldon,
Essex, who in 1593 published ' A Dialogue concern-

ing Witches and Witchcraft, in which 'is layed open
how craftily the Divell deceiveth not only the Witches
but Many other, and so leadeth them awaie into
Manie Great Errours.'   It will be seen from the title
that the writer does not adopt the uncompromising
line of Reginald Scot, but inclines rather to the
standpoint of Wierus.   There is, however, a good
deal of ability in his treatment of the question ; and
some account of the ' Dialogue' reprinted by the Percy
Society in 1842, should be interesting, I think, to the
reader.

The interlocutors are named Samuel, Daniel,
Samuel's wife, M. B., a schoolmaster, and the goodwife R.

The dialogue opens with Samuel and Daniel, the
former of whom is a fanatical believer in witches.
' These evil-favoured old witches,' he says, ' do trouble
me.'   He repeats the common rumour that there is
scarcely a town or village in the shire but has one or
two witches in it.   ' In good sooth,' he adds, ' I may
tell it to you as to my friend, when I go but into
my closes, I am afraid, for I see now and then a hare,
which my conscience giveth me is a witch, or some
witch's spirit, she stareth so upon me. And sometime
I see an ugly weasel run through my yard; and there
is a foul, great cat sometimes in my barn, which I
have no liking unto.'   Having introduced his friend,
who is less credulous than himself, to his wife and
his home, he promotes an argument between him and
another friend, M. B., a schoolmaster, on this *quæstio
vexata.*

M. B. starts with a good deal of fervour:

'The word of God doth show plainly that there be witches, and commandeth they should be put to death. Experience hath taught too many what harms they do. And if any have the gift to minister help against them, shall we refuse it?'

But after some discussion he agrees, at Daniel's instance, to consider the subject in a spirit of sober argument; and the first question they take up is: 'Are there witches that work by the Devil?' The conversation then proceeds as follows:

DANIEL. It is so evident by the Scriptures, and in all experience, that there be witches which work by the devil, or rather, I may say, the devil worketh by them, that such as go about to prove the contrary, do show themselves but cavillers.

M. B. I am glad we agree on that point; I hope we shall in the rest. What say you to this? That the witches have their spirits. Some hath one; some hath more, as two, three, four, or five. Some in one likeness and some in another, as like cats, weasels, toads, or mice, whom they nourish with milk or with a chicken, or by letting them suck now and then a drop of blood, whom they call if they be offended with any, and send them to hurt them in their bodies, yea, to kill them, and to kill their cattle.

DANIEL. Here is great deceit, and great illusion; here the Devil leadeth the ignorant people into foul errors, by which he draweth them headlong into many grievous sins.

M. B. Nay, then, I see you are awry, if you deny these things, and say they be but illusions. . . . I did dwell in a village within these five years where there was a man of good wealth, and suddenly, within ten days' space, he had three kine died, his gelding, worth ten pounds, fell lame, he was himself taken with a great pain in his back, and a child of seven years old died. He sent to the woman at R. H., and she said he was plagued by a witch, adding, moreover, that there were three women witches in that town, and one man witch, willing him to look whom he most suspected. He suspected an old woman, and caused her to be carried before a justice of peace and examined. With much ado at the last she confessed all, which was this in effect—that she

25—2

had three spirits, one like a cat, which she called *Lightfoot ;* another like a toad, which she called *Lunch ;* the third like a weasel, which she called *Makeshift.* This Lightfoot, she said, one Mother Bailey, of W., sold her above sixteen years ago, for an oven-cake, and told her the cat would do her good service; if she would, she might send her of her errands. This cat was with her but a while, but the weasel and the toad came and offered their service. The cat would kill kine, the weasel would kill horses, the toad would plague men in their bodies. She sent them all three (as she confessed) against this man. She was committed to the prison, and there she died before the assizes.

Daniel then strikes into the conversation, enlarging on the Scriptural description of devils as ' mighty and terrible spirits, full of rage and power and cruelty'— principalities and powers, the rulers of the darkness of this world—and forcibly insisting that if spirits so awful and potential as these assumed the shapes of such paltry vermin as cats, mice, toads, and weasels, it must be out of subtilty to cover and hide the mighty tyranny and power which they exercise over the hearts of the wicked. And he argues that such spirits would never deign to be a witch's servant or to do her bidding. M. B. contends, however, that, although he be lord, yet is he content to serve her turn ; and the witches confess, he says, that they call forth their demons, and send them on what errands they please, and hire them to hurt in their bodies and their cattle those against whom they cherish angry and revengeful feelings. ' I am sorry,' says Daniel mildly, ' you are so far awry; it is a pity any man should be in such error, especially a man that hath learning, and should teach others knowledge.'

After some further disputation, M. B. is brought to

admit that God giveth the devils power to plague and seduce because of man's wickedness; but he asks whether a godly, faithful man or woman may not be bewitched. We see, he says, that the devil had power given him of old, as over Job. But Daniel will not admit that this is a case in point, because it is not said that the devil dealt with Job through the agency of witches. Thereupon Samuel, perceiving the drift of his argument to be that the devil has no need to act by instruments so mean and even degraded, and would assuredly never be at their command; that, consequently, there can be no witchcraft, because there is no necessity for it, suddenly interposes:

'With your leave, M. B., I would ask two or three questions of my friend. There was but seven miles hence, at W. H., one M.; the man was of good wealth, and well accounted of among his neighbours. He pined away with sickness half a year, and at last died. After he was dead, his wife suspected ill-dealing. She went to a cunning man, who told her that her husband died of witchery, and asked her if she did not suspect any. Yes, there was one woman she did not like, one Mother W.; her husband and she fell out, and he fell sick within two days after, and never recovered. He showed her the woman as plain in a glass as we see one another, and taught her how she might bring her to confess. Well, she followed his counsel, went home, caused her to be apprehended and carried before a justice of peace. He examined her so wisely that in the end she confessed she killed the man. She was sent to prison, she was arraigned, condemned, and executed; and upon the ladder she seemed very penitent, desiring all the world to forgive her. She said she had a spirit in the likeness of a yellow dun cat. This cat came unto her, as she said, as she sat by the fire, when she was fallen out with a neighbour of hers, and wished that the vengeance of God might light upon him and his. The cat bade her not be afraid; she would do her no harm. She had served a dame five years in

Kent that was now dead, and, if she would, she would be her servant. "And whereas," said the cat, "such a man hath misused thee, if thou wilt I will plague him in his cattle." She sent the cat; she killed three hogs and one cow. The man, suspecting, *burnt a pig alive*, and, as she said, her cat would never go thither any more. Afterward she fell out with that M. She sent her cat, who told her that she had given him that which he should never recover; and, indeed, the man died. Now, do you not think the woman spoke the truth in all this? Would the woman accuse herself falsely at her death? Did not the cat become her servant? Did not she send her? Did she not plague and kill both man and beast? What should a man think of this?

DANIEL. You propound a particular example, and let us examine everything in it touching the witch. You say the cat came to her when she was in a great rage with one of her neighbours, and did curse, wishing the vengeance of God to fall upon him and his.

SAM. She said so, indeed. I heard her with my own ears, for I was at the execution.

DAN. Then tell me who set her in such a devilish rage, so to curse and ban, as to wish that the vengeance of God might light upon him and his? Did not the cat?

SAM. Truly I think that the devil wrought that in her.

DAN. Very well. Then, you see, the cat is the beginning of this play.

SAM. Call you it a play? It was no play to some.

DAN. Indeed, the witch at last had better have wrought hard than been at her play. But I mean Satan did play the juggler; for doth he not offer his service? Doth he not move her to send him to plague the man? Tell me, is she so forward to send, as he is to be sent? Or do you not take it that he ruleth in her heart, and even wholly directeth it to this matter?

SAM. I am fully persuaded he ruleth her heart.

DAN. *Then was she his drudge, and not he her servant.* He needeth not to be hired and entreated; for if her heart were to send him anywhere, unto such as he knoweth he cannot hurt, nor seeth how to make any show that he hurteth them, he can quickly turn her from that. Well, the cat goeth and killeth the man, certain hogs, and a cow. How could she tell that the cat did it?

SAM. How could she tell? Why, he told her, man, and she saw and heard that he lost his cattle.

DAN. The cat would lie—would she not? for they say such cats are liars.

SAM. I do not trust the cat's words, but because the thing fell out so.

DAN. Because the hogs and the cow died, are you sure the cat did kill them? Might they not die of some natural causes, as you see both men and beasts are well, and die suddenly?

In this way the dialogue proceeds, with a good deal of ingenuity and some degree of dramatic spirit; and though the reasoning is not without its fallacies, yet it is sufficiently clear and forcible, on the whole, as a protest on the side of liberality and tolerance.

The next branch of the subject taken up for consideration is ' the help and remedy ' that is sought for against witches ' at the hands of cunning men ;' Daniel contending that, if the cunning men can render any assistance, it must be through the devil's instrumentality, and, therefore, Christian men are not justified in availing themselves of it. The alleged cures performed by witches, Daniel refers to the influence of the imagination; and in this category he tells an amusing story. ' There was a person in London,' he say, ' acquainted with the magician Fento. Now, this Fento had a black dog, whom he called Bomelius. This party afterwards had a conceit that Bomelius was a devil, and that he felt him within him. He was in heaviness, and made his moan to one of his acquaintances, who had a merry head, and told him he had a friend could remove Bomelius. He bade him prepare a breakfast, and he would bring him. Then this was the cure: he (the friend) made him be stripped naked and stand by a good fire, and though he were fat enough of himself, basted him all over with butter against the fire, and made him wear a sleek-stone next his skin under his belly, and the man had immediate relief, and gave him afterwards great thanks.'

'The conceit, or imagination, does much,' continues Daniel, ' even when there is no apparent disease. A man feareth he is bewitched; it troubleth all the powers of his mind, and that distempereth his body, making great alterations in it, and bringeth sundry griefs. Now, when his mind is freed from such imaginations, his bodily griefs, which flew from the same, are eased. And a multitude of Satan's is of the same character.'

The conversation next turns upon the danger of shedding innocent blood, which is inseparable from the execution of alleged witches ; while juries, says Daniel, must become guilty of shedding innocent blood by condemning as guilty, and that upon their solemn oath, such as be suspected upon vain surmises, and imaginations, and illusions, rising from blindness and infidelity, and fear of Satan which is in the ignorant sort.

M. B. If you take it that this is one craft of Satan to bring many to be guilty of innocent blood, and even upon their oaths, which is horrible, what would you have the judges and juries to do, when they are arraigned of suspicion to be witches ?

DAN. What would I have them do ? I would wish them to be most wary and circumspect that they be not guilty of innocent blood. And that is, to condemn none but upon sure ground, and infallible proof ; because presumptions shall not warrant or excuse them before God, if guiltless blood be shed.

Replying to observations made by the school-master, Daniel continues :

'You bring two reasons to prove that in convicting witches likelihoods and presumptions ought to be of force more than about thieves or murderers. The first, because their dealing is secret; the other, because the devil will not let them confess. Indeed, men, imagining that witches do work strange mischiefs, burn in desire to have them hanged, as hoping then to be free ; and then, upon such persuasions as you mention, they suppose it is a very good work to put to death all which are suspected. But, touching thieves and murderers, let men take heed how they deal upon presumptions, unless they be very strong ; for we see that juries sometimes do condemn such as be guiltless, which is a hard thing, especially as they are upon their oath. And in witches, above all other, the people had need to be strong, because there is greater sleight of Satan to pursue the guiltless into death than in the other. Here is special care and wisdom to be used. And so likewise for their confessing. Satan doth gain more by their confession than by their denial, and therefore rather be-wrayeth them himself, and forceth them unto confession oftener than unto denial.'

Samuel at first is reluctant to accept this state-ment. It has always been his belief that the devil is much angered when witches confess and betray matters ; and in confirmation of this belief, or at least as some excuse for it, he relates an anecdote. Of course, one woman had suspected another to be a witch. She prevailed upon a gentleman to send for the suspected person, and having accused her in his presence, left him to admonish her with due severity, and to persuade her to renounce the devil and all his works. While he was thus engaged, and she was stoutly denying the accusation brought against her, a weasel or lobster suddenly made its appearance. 'Look,' said the gentleman, 'yonder is thy spirit.'

'Ah, master!' she replied, 'that is a vermin; there
be many of them everywhere.' Well, as they went
towards it, it vanished out of sight; by-and-by it re-
appeared, and looked upon them. 'Surely,' said the
gentleman, 'it is thy spirit;' but she still denied,
and with that her mouth was drawn awry. Then he
pressed her further, and she confessed all. She confessed she had hurt and killed by sending her spirit.
The gentleman, not being a magistrate, allowed her
to go home, and then disclosed the affair to a justice.
When she reached home another witch accosted her,
and said: 'Ah, thou beast, what hast thou done?
Thou hast betrayed us all. What remedy now?' said
she. 'What remedy?' said the other; 'send thy
spirit and touch him.' She sent her spirit, and of a
sudden the gentleman had, as it were, a flash of fire
about him: he lifted up his heart to God, and felt no
hurt. The spirit returned, and said he could not
hurt him, because he had faith. 'What then,' said
the other witch, 'hath he nothing that thou mayest
touch?' 'He hath a child,' said the other. 'Send
thy spirit,' said she, 'and touch the child.' She sent
her spirit; the child was in great pain, and died.
The witches were hanged, and confessed.

Daniel, by an ingenious analysis, soon dismisses this
absurd story, which, like all such stories, he takes
to be further evidence of Satan's craft, and no dis-
proof at all of the argument he has laid down.
'Then,' says Samuel, 'I will tell you of another thing
which was done of late.

'A woman suspected of being a witch, and of

having done harm among the cattle, was examined
and brought to confess that she had a spirit, which
resided in a hollow tree, and spoke to her out of a
hole in the trunk. And whenever she was offended
with any persons she went to that tree and sent her
spirit to kill their cattle. She was persuaded to
confess her faults openly, and to promise that she
would utterly forsake such ungodly ways : after she
had made this open confession, the spirit came unto
her, being alone. " Ah !" said he, "thou hast confessed
and betrayed all. I could turn it to rend thee in
pieces :" with that she was afraid, and went away,
and got her into company. Within some few weeks
after she fell out greatly into anger against one man.
Towards the tree she goeth, and before she came at
it—" Oh !" said the spirit, " wherefore comest thou ?
Who hath angered thee ?"   " Such a man," said the
witch.   " And what wouldest thou have me do ?"
said the spirit.   " He hath," saith she, " two horses
going yonder ; touch them, or one of them." Well, I
think even that night one of the horses died, and the
other was little better.   Indeed, they recovered again
that one which was not dead, but in very evil case.
Now methinketh it is plain : he was angry that she
had betrayed all.   And yet when she came to the
tree he let go all displeasure and went readily.'

There is much common-sense, as we should nowadays call it, in Daniel's comments on this extraordinarily wild story. ' Do you think,' he is represented as saying, ' that Satan lodgeth in a hollow
tree ? Is he become so lazy and idle ? Hath he

left off to be as a roaring lion, seeking whom he may devour ? Hath he put off the bloody and cruel nature of the fiery dragon, so that he mindeth no harm but when an angry woman entreats him to go kill a cow or a horse ? Is he become so doting with age that man shall espy his craft—yea, be found craftier than he is ?'

And now for the winding-up of Parson Gifford's 'Dialogue.' 'Tis to be wished that all the parsons of his time had been equally sensible and courageous.

M. B. I could be content to hear more in these matters ; I see how fondly I have erred. But seeing you must be gone, I hope we shall meet here again at some other time. God keep you !

Sam. I am bound to give you great thanks. And, I pray you, when occasion serveth, that you come this way. Let us see you at my house.

M. B. I thought there had not been such subtle practices of the devil, nor so great sins as he leadeth men into.

Sam. It is strange to see how many thousands are carried away, and deceived, yea, many that are very wise men.

M. B. The devil is too crafty for the wisest, unless they have the light of God's Word.

Samuel's Wife. Husband, yonder cometh the goodwife R.

Sam. I wish she had come sooner.

Goodwife R. Ho, who is within, by your leave ?

Samuel's Wife. I would you had come a little sooner ; here was one even now that said you were a witch.

Goodwife R. Was there one said I am a witch ? You do but jest.

Samuel's Wife. Nay, I promise you he was in good earnest.

Goodwife R. I a witch ? I defy him that saith it, though he be a lord. I would all the witches in the land were hanged, and their spirits by them.

M. B. Would you not be glad, if their spirits were hanged up with them, to have a gown furred with some of their skins ?

Goodwife R. Out upon them. There were few !

Sam. Wife, why didst thou say that the goodwife R. is a witch ? He did not say so.

SAMUEL'S WIFE. Husband, I did mark his words well enough; he said she is a witch.

SAM. He doth not know her, and how could he say she is a witch?

SAMUEL'S WIFE. What though he did not know her? Did he not say that she played the witch that heated the spit red hot, and thrust it into her cream when the butter would not come?

SAM. Indeed, wife, thou sayest true. He said that was a thing taught by the devil, as also the burning of a hen, or of a hog alive, and all such like devices.

GOODWIFE R. Is that witchcraft? Some Scripture man hath told you so. Did the devil teach it? Nay, the good woman at R. H. taught it my husband: she doth more good in one year than all those Scripture men will do so long as they live.

M. B. Who do you think taught it the cunning woman at R. H.?

GOODWIFE R. It is a gift which God hath given her. I think the Holy Spirit of God doth teach her.

M. B. You do not think, then, that the devil doth teach her?

GOODWIFE R. How should I think that the devil doth teach her? Did you ever hear that the devil did teach any good thing?

M. B. Do you know that was a good thing?

GOODWIFE R. Was it not a good thing to drive the evil spirit out of any man?

M. B. Do you think the devil was afraid of your spit?

GOODWIFE R. I know he was driven away, and we have been rid of him ever since.

M. B. Can a spit hurt him?

GOODWIFE R. It doth hurt him, or it hurteth the witch: one of them, I am sure: for he cometh no more. Either she can get him come no more, because it hurteth him: or else she will let him come no more, because it hurteth her.

M. B. It is certain that spirits cannot be hurt but with spiritual weapons: therefore your spit cannot fray nor hurt the devil. And how can it hurt the witch? You did not think she was in your cream, did you?

GOODWIFE R. Some think she is there, and therefore when they thrust in the spit they say: 'If thou beest here, have at thine eye.'

M. B. If she were in your cream, your butter was not very cleanly.

GOODWIFE R. You are merrily disposed, M. B. I know you are of my mind, though you put these questions to me. For I am sure none hath counselled more to go to the cunning folk than you.

M. B. I *was* of your mind, but I am not now, for I see how foolish I was. I am sorry that I offended so grievously as to counsel any for to seek unto devils.

GOODWIFE R. Why, M. B., who hath schooled you to-day? I am sure you were of another mind no longer agone than yesterday.

SAMUEL'S WIFE. Truly, goodwife R., I think my husband is turned also: here hath been one reasoning with them three or four hours.

GOODWIFE R. Is your husband turned, too? I would you might lose all your hens one after another, and then I would she would set her spirit upon your ducks and your geese, and leave you not one alive. Will you come to defend witches? . . .

M. B. You think the devil can kill men's cattle, and lame both man and beast at his pleasure: you think if the witch entreat him and send him, he will go, and if she will not have him go, he will not meddle. And you think when he doth come, you can drive him away with a hot spit, or with burning a live hen or a pig.

GOODWIFE R. Never tell me I think so, for you yourself have thought so; and let them say what they can, all the Scripture men in the world shall never persuade me otherwise.

M. B. I do wonder, not so much at your ignorance as at this, that I was ever of the same mind that you are, and could not see mine own folly.

GOODWIFE R. Folly! how wise you are become of a sudden! I know that their spirits lie lurking, for they foster them; and when anybody hath angered them, then they call them forth and send them. And look what they bid them do, or hire them to do, that shall be done: as when she is angry, the spirit will ask her, 'What shall I do?' 'Such a man hath misused me,' saith she; 'go, kill his cow'; by-and-by he goeth and doeth it. 'Go, kill such a woman's hens'; down go they. And some of them are not content to do these lesser harms; but they will say, 'Go, make such a man lame, kill him, or kill his child.' Then are they ready, and will do anything; and I think they be happy that can learn to drive them away.

M. B. If I should reason with you out of the words of God, you should see that all this is false, which you say. The devil cannot kill nor hurt anything; no, not so much as a poor hen. If he had power, who can escape him? Would he tarry to be sent or entreated by a woman? He is a stirrer up unto all harms and mischiefs.

GOODWIFE R. What will you tell me of God's word? Doth not God's word say there be witches? and do not you think God doth suffer bad people? Are you a turncoat? Fare you well; I will no longer talk with you.

M. B. She is wilful indeed. I will leave you also.

SAMUEL. I thank you for your good company.

About the same time that Gifford was endeavouring to teach his countrymen a more excellent way of dealing with the vexed questions of demonology and witchcraft, a Dutch minister, named Bekker, scandalized the orthodox by a frank denial of all power whatsoever to the devil, and, consequently, to the witches and warlocks who were supposed to be at one and the same time his servants and yet his employers. His ' Monde Enchanté ' (originally written in Dutch) consists of four ponderous volumes, remarkable for prolixity and repetition, as well as for a certain originality of argument. There was no just ground, however, as Hallam remarks, for throwing imputations on the author's religious sincerity. He shared, however, the opprobrium that attaches to all who deviate in theology from the orthodox path; and it must be admitted that his Scriptural explanations in the case of the demoniacs and the like are more ingenious than satisfactory.

A violent trumpet-note on the side of intolerance was blown by King James I. in 1597 in his famous

'Dæmonologia.' It is written in the form of a
dialogue, and numbers about eighty closely-printed
pages. James, as the reader has seen, had had ample
personal experience of witches and their 'cantrips,'
and had 'got up' the subject with a commendable
amount of thoroughness. He divides witches into
eight classes, who severally work their evil designs
against mankind; then he subdivides into white and
black witches, of whom the former are the more
dangerous; and again into 'acted' and 'pacted'
witches, the former depending for their power on
their supernatural gifts, and the latter having made a
compact with Satan contrary to 'all rules and orders
of nature, art or grace.' Further, the demons have a
classification of their own; some of the higher ranks
of the demonarchy looking down contemptuously
enough on those of the inferior grades, who consist
of 'the damned souls of departed conjurers.' These
'damned souls' discharge all kinds of mean and
servile offices—bringing fire from heaven for the
convenience of their employers; conveying bodies
through the air; conjuring corn from one field into
another; imparting a show of life to dead bodies;
and raising the wind for witches to sell to their
nautical customers—who received pieces of knotted
rope, and, untying the first knot, secured a favourable
breeze, for the second a moderate wind, and for the
third a violent gale.

After describing the rites in vogue on the conclusion of a compact between witch and devil, King
James enlarges on other points of ceremonial, such

as the making of various magic circles—sometimes round, sometimes triangular, sometimes quadrangular; the use of holy water and crosses in ridicule of the papists; and the offer to the demons of some living animal. He adds that the great witches' meetings frequently took place in churches : and he says that the witches mutter and hurriedly mumble through their conjurations 'like a priest despatching a hunting masse'; and that if they step out of a circle in a sudden alarm at the horrible appearance assumed by the demon, he flies off with them body and soul.

The royal expert proceeds to indicate the means by which you may detect a witch. 'There are two good helpes that may be used for their trials; the one is the finding of their marke and the trying the insensibility thereof. The other is their fleeting on the water : for as in a secret murther, if the dead carkasse be at any time thereafter handled by the murtherer, it will gush out of blood, as if the blood were crying to the heaven for revenge of the murtherer, God having appoynted that secret supernaturale signe for triale of that secret unnaturale crime, so it appears that God hath appoynted (for a supernaturale signe of the monstrous impietie of witches) that the water shall refuse to receive them in her bosome that have shaken off them the sacred water of Baptism and willingly refused the benefit thereof: no, not so much as their eies are able to shed teares (threaten and torture them as you please) while first they repent (God not permitting them to dissemble their obstinacie in so horrible a crime),

albeit the womenkind especially be able other waies
to shed teares at every light occasion when they will,
yea altho' it were dissemblingly like the crocodiles.'

Incidentally, our witch-hunting King offers an
explanation of a peculiarity which, no doubt, our
readers have already noted—the great numerical
superiority of witches over warlocks. 'The reason
is easie,' he says ; 'for as that sex is frailer than
man is, so is it easier to be intrapped in the grosse
snares of the devil,—as was over well prooved to be
true by the serpente deceiving of Eva at the beginning, which makes him the homelier with that sex
sensine [ever since].'

As regards the external appearance of witches, he
remarks that they are not generally melancholic ;
'but some are rich and worldly wise, some are fat
and corpulent, and most part are given over unto the
pleasures of the flesh ; and further experience daily
proves how loth they are to confess without torture,
which witnesseth their guiltinesse.' He concludes
by asking, 'Who is safe ?' and replies that the only
safe person is the magistrate, when assiduously employed in bringing witches to justice. One Reginald
Scot, Esq., however, hop-grower and brewer of
Smeeth, in Kent, a persistent disbeliever in and
ridiculer of witchcraft, who had the courage to break
lances with the King and the bench of Bishops in
contemporary pamphlets, and is called by the King
an 'Englishman of damnable opiniones,' irreverently
answered this question by saying that the only safe
person was the King himself, as his sex prevented

his being taken for a witch, and the whole kingdom was satisfied that he was no conjurer.

In 1616, John Cotta, a Northampton physician, published a forcibly written attack on the vulgar delusion, under the title of 'The Trial of Witchcraft,' which reached a second (and enlarged) edition in 1624. Cotta was also the author of a fierce blast against quacks—'Discovery of the Dangers of ignorant Practisers of Physick in England,' 1612; and of a not less vehement attack on the *aurum potabile* of the chemists, entitled, 'Cotta contra Antonium, or An Ant. Anthony,' 1623.

There is a lively work by John Gaul, preacher of the Word at Great Haughton, in the county of Huntingdon—'Select Cases of Conscience touching Witches and Witchcraft,' 1646, which is worth looking into. Gaul was a courageous and persevering opponent of the great witch-finder, Hopkins.

The unhappy victims of popular prejudice found a strenuous champion also in Sir Robert Filmer, who, in 1653, published his 'Advertisement to the Jury-men of England, touching Witches, together with a Difference between an English and Hebrew Witch.' Filmer is best known to students by his 'Patriarcha,' an apology for the paternal government of kings, which does violence to all constitutional principles, but has at least the negative merit of obvious sincerity on the part of its writer. It is somewhat surprising to find a mind like Filmer's, fettered as it was by so many prejudices and a slavish adherence to prescription, openly urging the cause of tolerance and enlightenment, and vigorously demolishing the sham arguments by which the believers in witchcraft endeavoured to support their grotesque theories.

Three years later followed on the same side a certain Thomas Ady, M.A., who, with considerable vivacity, fulminated against the witch-mongers and witch-torturers in his tractate, ' A Candle in the Dark ; or, A Treatise concerning the Nature of Witches and Witchcraft : being Advice to Judges, Sheriffs, Justices of the Peace, and Grand Jurymen, what to do before they pass sentence on such as are arraigned for their lives as Witches.' The quaintly-worded dedication ran as follows :

' To the Prince of the Kings of the Earth.   It is the manner of men, O heavenly King, to dedicate their books to some great men, thereby to have their works protected and countenanced among them ; but Thou only art able by Thy Holy Spirit of Truth, to defend Thy Truth, and to make it take impression in the heart and understanding of men.   Unto Thee alone do I dedicate this work, entreating Thy Most High Majesty to grant that, whoever shall open this book, Thy Holy Spirit may so possess their understanding as that the Spirit of error may depart from them, and that they may read and try Thy Truth by the touchstone of Thy Truth, the Holy Scriptures ; and finding that Truth, may embrace it and forsake their darksome inventions of Anti-Christ, that have deluded and defiled the nations now and in former ages. Enlighten the world, Thou art the Light of the World, and let darkness be no more in the world, now or in any future age ; but make all people to walk as children of the light for ever ; and destroy Anti-Christ that hath deceived the nations, and save us the residue by Thyself alone ; and let not Satan any more delude us, for the Truth is thine for ever.'

In 1669 John Wagstaffe published ' The Question of Witchcraft Debated.' According to Wood, he was the son of John Wagstaffe, a London citizen ; was born in Cheapside ; entered as a commoner of Oriel College, Oxford, towards the end of 1649 ; took the degrees in Arts, and applied himself to the study of politics and other learning. ' At length being raised from an academical life to the inheritance of Hasland by the death of an uncle, who died without male issue, he spent his life afterwards in single estate.' He died in 1677. Wood describes him as ' a little crooked man, and of a despicable presence. He was laughed at by the boys of this University because, as they said, he himself looked like a little wizard.'

His book is illuminated throughout by the generous sympathies of a large and liberal mind. His peroration has been described, and not unjustly, as ' lofty ' and ' memorable,' and, when animated by a noble earnestness, the writer's language rises into positive eloquence. ' I cannot think,' he says, ' without trembling and horror on the vast numbers of people that in several ages and several countries have been sacrificed unto this cold opinion. Thousands, ten thousands, are upon record to have been slain, and many of them not with simple deaths, but horrid, exquisite tortures. And yet, how many are there more who have undergone the same fate, of whom we have no memorial extant? Since therefore the opinion of witchcraft is a mere stranger unto Scripture, and wholly alien from true religion ; since it is ridiculous by asserting fables and impossibilities ; since it appears, when duly considered, to be all bloody and full of dangerous consequence unto the lives and safety of men; I hope that with this my discourse, opposing an absurd and pernicious error, I cannot at all disoblige any sober, unbiased person, especially if he be of such ingenuity as to have freed himself from a slavish subjection unto those prejudicial opinions which custom and education do with too much tyranny impose.

'If the doctrine of witchcraft should be carried up to a height, and the inquisition after it should be entrusted in the hands of ambitious, covetous, and malicious men, it would prove of far more fatal consequences unto the lives and safety of mankind than that ancient heathenish custom of sacrificing men unto idol gods, insomuch that we stand in need of another Heracles Liberator, who, as the former freed the world from human sacrifice, should, in like manner, travel from country to country, and by his all-commanding authority free it from this evil and base custom of torturing people to confess themselves witches, and burning them after extorted confessions.

Surely the blood of men ought not to be so cheap, nor so easily to be shed by those who, under the name of God, do gratify exorbitant passions and selfish ends ; for without question, under this side heaven, there is nothing so sacred as the life of man, for the preservation whereof all policies and forms of government, all laws and magistrates are most especially ordained. Wherefore I presume that this discourse of mine, attempting to prove the vanity and impossibility of witchcraft, is so far from any deserved censure and blame, that it rather deserves commendation and praise, if I can in the least measure contribute to the saving of the lives of men.'

Meric Casaubon, a man of abundant learning and not less abundant superstition, attempted a reply to Wagstaffe in his treatise ' Of Credulity and Incredulity in Things Divine and Spiritual ' (1670).

At Thornton, in the parish of Caswold, Yorkshire, was born, on the 3rd of February, 1610, one of the ablest and most successful of the adversaries of the witch-maniacs, John Webster. It is supposed that he was educated at Cambridge ; but the first event in his career of which we have any certain knowledge is his admission to holy orders in the Church of England by Dr. Morton, Bishop of Durham. In 1634 we find him officiating as curate at Kildwick in Craven, and nine years later as Master of the Free Grammar School at Clitheroe. He seems afterwards to have held for a time a military chaplaincy, then to have withdrawn from the Church of England, and taken refuge in some form of Dissent. In 1653 his new religious views found expression in his 'Saints' Guide,' and in 1654, in 'The Judgment Set and the Books Opened,' a series of sermons which he had originally preached at All Hallows' Church in Lombard Street. It was in this church the incident occurred which Wood has recorded : 'On the 12th of October, 1653, William Erbury, with John Webster, sometime a Cambridge scholar, endeavoured to knock down learning and the ministry both together in a disputation that they then had against two ministers in a church in Lombard Street, London. Erbury then declared that the wisest ministers and the purest churches were at that time befooled, confounded, and defiled by reason of learning. Another while he said that the ministry were monsters, beasts, asses, greedy dogs, false prophets, and that they are the Beast with seven heads and ten horns. The same person also spoke out and said that Babylon is the Church in her ministers, and that the Great Whore is the Church in her worship, etc., so that with him there was an end of ministers and churches and ordinations altogether. While these things were babbled to and fro, the multitude, being of various opinions, began to mutter, and many to cry out, and immediately it came to a meeting or tumult (call it which you please), wherein the women bore away the bell, but lost some of them their kerchiefs; and the dispute being hot, there was more danger of pulling down the church than the ministry.'

In 1654, our iconoclastic enthusiast strongly—but not without good reason—assailed the educational system then in vogue at Oxford and Cambridge in his treatise, 'Academiarum Examen,' which created quite a sensation in 'polite circles,' fluttering the dove-cots of the rulers of the two Universities. Very curious, however, are its sympathetic references to the old Hermetic mysteries, Rosicrucianism, and astrology, to the fanciful abstractions and dreamy speculations of Paracelsus, Van Helmont, Fludd, and Dr. Dee. One cannot but wonder that so acute and vigorous an intellect should have allowed itself to be entangled in the delusions of the occult sciences. But his study of the works of the old philosophers was, no doubt, the original motive of the laborious research which resulted in his 'Metallographia; or, A History of Metals' (1671). In this learned and comprehensive treatise are declared 'the signs of Ores and Minerals, both before and after Digging, the causes and manner of their generations, their kinds, sorts, and differences ; with the description of sundry new Metals, or Semi-Metals, and many other things pertaining to Mineral Knowledge. As also the handling and showing of their Vegetability, and the discussion of the most difficult Questions belonging to Mystical Chymistry, as of the Philosopher's Gold, their Mercury, the Liquor Alkahest, Aurum potabile, and such like. Gathered forth of the most approved Authors that have written in Greek, Latin, or High Dutch, with some Observations and Discoveries of the Author Himself. By John Webster, Practitioner in

Physick and Chirurgery. " *Qui principia naturalia in seipso ignoraverit, hic jam multum remotus est ab arte nostra, quoniam non habet radiam veram super quam intentionem suam fundit.*" Geber, Sum. Perfect., lib. i., p. 21.'

In 1677, Webster, who had abandoned the cure of souls for that of bodies, produced the work which entitles him to honourable mention in these pages. According to the fashion of the day, its title was almost as long as a table of contents. I transcribe it here *in extenso:*

' *The Displaying of supposed Witchcraft,* Wherein is affirmed that there are many sorts of Deceivers and Impostors. And Divers persons under a passive Delusion of Melancholy and Fancy. But that there is a Corporeal League made betwixt the Devil and the Witch, Or that he sucks on the Witches Body, has Carnal Copulation, or that Witches are turned into Cats or Dogs, raise Tempests or the like, is utterly denied and disproved. Wherein also is handled the Existence of Angels and Spirits, the Truth of Apparitions, the Nature of Astral and Sidereal Spirits, the Force of Charms and Philters; with other Abstruse Matters. By John Webster, Practitioner in Physic. " *Falsæ etenim opiniones Hominum præoccupantes, non solum surdos sed ut cæcos faciunt, ita ut videre nequeant, quæ aliis perspicua apparent.*" Galen, lib. viii., de Comp. Med. London. Printed by I. M., and are to be sold by the Booksellers in London, 1677.'

Webster, who was evidently a man of restless and inquiring intellect, and independent judgment, died on June 18, 1682, and was buried in St. Margaret's, Clitheroe, where his monument may still be seen. Its singular inscription must have been devised by some astrological sympathizer :

> Qui hanc figuram intelligunt
> Me etiam intellexisse, intelligent.

Here follows a mysterious figure of the sun, with several circles and much astrological lettering, which it is unnecessary to reproduce. The inscription continues :

> Hic jacet ignotus mundo mersus que tumultus
> Invidiæ, semper mens tamen æqua fecit,
> Multa tulit veterum ut sciret secreta sophorum
> Ac tandem vires noverit ignis aquæ.
>
> Johannes Hyphantes sive Webster.
> In villa Spinosa supermontana, in
> Parochia silvæ cuculatæ, in agro
> Eboracensi, natus 1610, Feb. 3.
> Ergastulum animæ deposuit 1682, Junii 18.
> Annoq. ætatis suæ 72 currente.
> Sicq. peroravit moriens mundo huic valedicens,
> Aurea pax vivis, requies æterna sepultis.

In 1728, Andrew Millar, at the sign of The Buchanan's Head, against St. Clement's Church in the Strand, published 'A System of Magick : or, A History of the Black Art,' by Daniel Defoe ; a book which, though it by no means justifies its title, is one of more than passing interest, partly from the renown of its author, and partly from the light it throws on the popularity of magic among the English middle classes in the earlier years of the eighteenth

century.   As it has not been reprinted for the last
fifty years, and is not very generally known, some
glimpses of the stuff it is made of may be acceptable to
the curious reader.*

In his preface Defoe lavishes a good deal of contempt on contemporary pretenders to the character of
magician, who by sham magical practices imposed on a
public ignorant, and therefore credulous.   Magicians,
he says, in the first ages were wise men; in the middle
ages, madmen ; in these latter ages, they are cunning
men.   In the earliest times they were honest ; in the
middle time, rogues ; in these last times, fools.   At
first they dealt with nature ; then with the devil ;
and now, not with the devil or with nature either.
In the first ages the magicians were wiser than the
people ; in the second age wickeder than the people ;
and in this later age the people are both worse and
wickeder than the magicians.   Like many other
generalizations, this one of Defoe's is more pointed
than true ; and it is evident that the so-called magicians could not have flourished had there not been an
ignorant class who readily accepted their pretensions.

Defoe's account of the origin of magic is so vague
as to suggest that he knew very little of the subject he was writing about.   'I have traced it,' he says,
' as far back as antiquity gives us any clue to discover it by : it seems to have its beginning in the
ignorance and curiosity of the darkest ages of the
world, when miracle and something wonderful was

---

* Some authorities doubt the authorship; but the internal
evidence seems to me to justify the claim made for it as Defoe's.

expected to confirm every advanced notion ; and when the wise men, having racked their invention to the utmost, called in the devil to their assistance for want of better help ; and those that did not run into Satan's measures, and give themselves up to the infernal, yet trod so near, and upon the very verge of Hell, that it was hard to distinguish between the magician and the devil, and thus they have gone on ever since : so that almost all the dispute between us and the magicians is that they say they converse with good spirits, and we say if they deal with any spirits, it is with the devil.'

Here the greatness of his theme stimulates Defoe into poetry, which differs very little, however, from his prose, so that a brief specimen will content everybody :

> 'Hail ! dangerous science, falsely called sublime,
> Which treads upon the very brink of crime.
> Hell's mimic, Satan's mountebank of state,
> Deals with more devils than Heaven did e'er create.
> The infernal juggling-box, by Heaven designed,
> To put the grand parade upon mankind.
> The devil's first game which he in Eden played,
> When he harangued to Eve in masquerade.'

Dividing his treatise into two parts, our author, in the introduction to Part I., discusses the meaning of the principal terms in magical lore ; who, and what kind of people, the magicians were ; and the meaning originally given to the words 'magic' and 'magician.' As a matter of course, he strays back to the old Chaldean days, when a magician, he says, was simply a mathematician, a man of science, who, stored with knowledge and learning, was a kind of walking dictionary to other people, instructing the rest of mankind on subjects of which they were ignorant ; a wise man, in fact, who interpreted omens, ill signs, tokens, and dreams ; understood the signs of the times, the face of the heavens, and the influences of the superior luminaries there. When all this wisdom became more common, and the magi had communicated much of their knowledge to the people at large, their successors, still aspiring to a position above, and apart from, the rest of the world, were compelled to push their studies further, to inquire into nature, to view the aspect of the heavens, to calculate the motions of the stars, and more particularly to dwell upon their influences in human affairs—thus creating the science of astrology. But these men neither had, nor pretended to have, any compact or correspondence with the devil or with any of his works. They were men of thought, or, if you please, men of deeper thinking than the ordinary sort ; they studied the sciences, inquired into the works of nature and providence, studied the meaning and end of things, the causes and events, and consequently were able to see further into the ordinary course and causes both of things about them, and things above them, than other men.

Such were the world's gray forefathers, the magicians of the elder time, in whom was found ' an excellent spirit of wisdom.' There were others— not less learned—whose studies took a different direction ; who inquired into the structure and organization of the human body; who investigated the origin, the progress, and the causes of diseases and distempers, both in men and women; who sought out the physical or medicinal virtues of drugs and plants; and as by these means they made daily discoveries in nature, of which the world, until then, was ignorant, and by which they performed astonishing cures, they naturally gained the esteem and reverence of the people.

Sir Walter Raleigh contends that only the word 'magic,' and not the magical art, is derived from Simon Magus.   He adds that Simon's name was not Magus, a magician, but Gors, a person familiar with evil spirits; and that he usurped the title of Simon the Magician simply because it was then a good and honourable title.   Defoe avails himself of Raleigh's authority to sustain his own opinion, that there is a manifest difference between *magic*, which is wisdom and supernatural knowledge, and the witchcraft and conjuring which we now understand by the word.

In his second chapter Defoe classifies the magic of the ancients under three heads : i. *Natural*, which included the knowledge of the stars, of the motions of the planetary bodies, and their revolutions and influences; that is to say, the study of nature, of philosophy, and astronomy; ii. *Artificial* or *Rational*, in which was included the knowledge of all judicial astrology, the casting or calculating nativities, and the cure of diseases—(1) by particular charms and figures placed in this or that position ; (2) by herbs gathered at this or that particular crisis of time ; (3) by saying

such and such words over the patient ; (4) by such
and such gestures ; (5) by striking the flesh in such
and such a manner, and innumerable such-like pieces
of mimicry, working not upon the disease itself, but
upon the imagination of the patient, and so affecting
the cure by the power of nature, though that nature
were set in operation by the weakest and simplest
methods imaginable ; and, iii. *Diabolical*, which was
wrought by and with the concurrence of the devil,
carried on by a correspondence with evil spirits—
with their help, presence, and personal assistance—and
practised chiefly by their priests.   Defoe argues that
the ancients at first were acquainted only with the
purer form of magic, and that, therefore, sorcery and
witchcraft were of much later development.   The
cause and motive of this development he traces in his
third chapter ('Of the Reason and Occasion which
brought the ancient honest Magi, whose original
study was philosophy, astronomy, and the works of
nature, to turn sorcerers and wizards, and deal
with the Devil, and how their Conversation began').
Egyptologists will find Defoe's comments upon
Egyptian magic refreshingly simple and unhistorical,
and his identifications of the Pyramids with magical
practices is wildly vague and hypothetical.   Of the
magic which was really taught and practised among
the ancient people of Egypt, Defoe, of course, knows
nothing.   He tells us, however, that the Jews learned
it from them.   He goes on to speculate as to the time
when that close intercourse began between the devil
and his servants on earth which is the foundation of

the later or diabolical magic, and concludes that his
first visible appearance on this mundane stage was
as the enemy of Job. Thence he is led to inquire,
in his fourth chapter, what shapes the devil assumed
on his first appearances to the magicians and others,
in the dawn of the world's history, and whether he is
or has been allowed to assume a human shape or no.
And he suggests that his earliest acquaintance with
mankind was made through dreams, and that by this
method he contrived to infuse into men's minds an
infinite variety of corrupt imaginations, wicked desires,
and abhorrent conclusions and resolutions, with some
ridiculous, foolish, and absurd things at the same
time.

Defoe then proceeds to tell an Oriental story, which,
doubtlessly, is his own invention :

Ali Albrahazen, a Persian wizard, had, it is said,
this kind of intercourse with the devil. He was a
Sabean by birth, and had obtained a wonderful reputation for his witchcraft, so that he was sent for by the
King of Persia upon extraordinary occasions, such as
the interpretation of a dream, or of an apparition, like
that of Belshazzar's handwriting, or of some meteor
or eclipse, and he never failed to give the King satisfaction. For whether his utterances were true or
false, he couched them always in such ambiguous
terms that something of what he predicted might
certainly be deduced from his words, and so seem to
import that he had effectually revealed it, whether he
had really done so or not.

This Ali, wandering alone in the desert, and

27

musing much upon the appearance of a fiery meteor, which, to the great terror of the country, had flamed in the heavens every night for nearly a month, sought to apprehend its significance, and what it should portend to the world; but, failing to do so, he sat down, weary and disheartened, in the shade of a spreading palm. Breathing to himself a strong desire that some spirit from the other world would generously assist him to arrive at the true meaning of a phenomenon so remarkable, he fell asleep. And, lo! in his sleep he dreamed a dream, and the dream was this: that a tall man came to him, a tall man of sage and venerable aspect, with a pleasing smile upon his countenance; and, addressing him by his name, told him that he was prepared to answer his questions, and to explain to him the signification of the great and terrible fire in the air which was terrifying all Arabia and Persia.

His explanation proved to be of an astronomical character. These fiery appearances, he said, were collections of vapour exhaled by the influence of the sun from earth or sea. As to their importance to human affairs, it was simply this: that sometimes by their propinquity to the earth, and their power of attraction, or by their dissipation of aqueous vapours, they occasioned great droughts and insupportable heats; while, at other times, they distilled heavy and unusual rains, by condensing, in an extraordinary manner, the vapours they had absorbed. And he added: 'Go thou and warn thy nation that this fiery meteor portends an excessive drought and famine; for

know that by the strong exhalation of the vapours of
the earth, occasioned by the meteor's unusual nearness
to it, the necessary rains will be withheld, and to a
long drought, as a matter of course, famine and
scarcity of corn succeed. Thus, by judging according to the rules of natural causes, thou shalt predict
what shall certainly come to pass, and shalt obtain
the reputation thou so ardently desirest of being a
wise man and a great magician.'

'This prediction,' said Ali, 'was all very well as
regarded Arabia ; but would it apply also to Persia ?'
'No,' replied the devil ; for Ali's interlocutor was no
less distinguished a personage—fiery meteors from
the same causes sometimes produced contrary events ;
and he might repair to the Persian Court, and predict the advent of excessive rains and floods, which
would greatly injure the fruits of the earth, and occasion want and scarcity. 'Thus, if either of these
succeed, as it is most probable, thou shalt assuredly
be received as a sage magician in one country, if not
in the other ; also, to both of them thou mayest
suggest, as a probability only, that the consequence
may be a plague or infection among the people,
which is ordinarily the effect as well of excessive
wet as of excessive heat. If this happens, thou shalt
gain the reputation thou desirest ; and if not, seeing
thou didst not positively foretell it, thou shalt not
incur the ignominy of a false prediction.'

Ali was very grateful for the devil's assistance, and
failed not to ask how, at need, he might again secure
it. He was told to come again to the palm-tree, and

to go around it fifteen times, calling him thrice by
his name each time : at the end of· the fifteenth cir-
cumambulation he would find himself overtaken by
drowsiness ; whereupon he should lie down with his
face to the south, and he would receive a visit from
him in vision.   The devil further told him the magic
name by which he was to summon him.

The magician's predictions were duly made and
duly fulfilled.   Thenceforward he maintained a constant communication with the devil, who, strange to
say, seems not to have exacted anything from him in
return for his valuable, but hazardous, assistance.

Defoe's fifth chapter contains a further account of
the devil's conduct in imitating divine inspirations ;
describes the difference between the genuine and the
false ; and dwells upon signs and wonders, fictitious
as well as real.   In chapter the sixth our author
treats of the first practices of magic and witchcraft
as a diabolical art, and explains how it was handed
on to the Egyptians and Phœnicians, by whom it was
openly encouraged.   He offers some amusing remarks
on the methods adopted by magicians for summoning
the devil, who seems to be at once their servant and
master.   In parts of India they go up, he says, to the
summit of some particular mountain, where they call
him with a little kettledrum, just as the good old
wives in England hive their bees, except that they
beat it on the wrong side.   Then they pronounce
certain words which they call ' charms,' and the devil
appears without fail.

It is not easy to discover in history what words

C. Think! nay, I did not think; I was dead, to be sure I was dead, with the fright, and expected I should be carried away, chair and all, the next moment. Then it was, I say, that my hair would have lifted off my hat, if it had been on, I am sure it would.

D. Well, but when they were all gone, you came to yourself again, I suppose?

C. To tell you the truth, master, I am not come to myself yet.

D. But go on, let me know how it ended.

C. Why, after a little while, my old man came in again, called his man to set the chairs to rights, and then sat him down at the table, spoke cheerfully to me, and asked me if I would drink, which I refused, though I was a-dry indeed. I believe the fright had made me dry; but as I never had been used to drink with the devil, I didn't know what to think of it, so I let it alone.

In his third chapter (' Of the present pretences of the Magicians; how they defend themselves; and some examples of their practice') Defoe has a lively account of a contemporary magician, a Dr. Bowman, of Kent, who seems to have been a firm believer in what is now called Spiritualism. He was a green old man, who went about in a long black velvet gown and a cap, with a long beard, and his upper lip trimmed ' with a kind of muschato.' He strongly repudiated any kind of correspondence or intercourse with the devil; but hinted that he derived much assistance from the good spirits which people the invisible world. After dwelling on the follies of the learned, and the superstitions of the ignorant, this lordly conjurer said: ' You see how that we, men of art, who have studied the sacred sciences, suffer by the errors of common fame; they take us all for devil-mongers, damned rogues, and conjurers.'

The fourth chapter discusses the doctrine of

spirits as it is understood by the magicians ; how far it may be supposed there may be an intercourse with superior beings, apart from any familiarity with the devil or the spirits of evil ; with a transition to the present times.

And so much for the ' Art of Magic ' as expounded by Daniel Defoe.

In 1718 appeared Bishop Hutchinson's ' Historical Essay concerning Witchcraft,' a book written in a most liberal and tolerant spirit, and, at the same time, with so much comprehensiveness and exactitude, that later writers have availed themselves freely of its stores.

Reference may also be made to—

John Beaumont, ' Treatise of Spirits, Apparitions, Witchcrafts, and other Magical Practices,' 1705.

James Braid (of Manchester), ' Magic, Witchcraft, Animal Magnetism, Hypnotism, and Electro-Biology' (1852), in which there is very little about witchcraft, but a good deal about the influence of the imagination.

J. C. Colquhoun, ' History of Magic, Witchcraft, and Animal Magnetism,' 1851.

Rev. Joseph Glanvill, ' Sadducismus Triumphatus; or, A full and plain Evidence concerning Witches and Apparitions,' 1670.

Sir Walter Scott, ' Letters on Demonology and Witchcraft,' 1831.

Howard Williams, ' The Superstitions of Witchcraft,' 1865.

It may be a convenience to the reader if I indicate some of the principal foreign authorities on this subject. Such as—Institor and Sprenger's great work, ' Malleus Maleficarum ' (Nuremberg, 1494); The monk Heisterbach's (Cæsarius) ' Dialogus Miraculorum ' (ed. by Strange), 1851 ; Cannaert's ' Procès des Sorcières en Belgique,' 1848 ; Dr. W. G. Soldan's ' Geschichte der Hexenprocesse ' (1843) ; G. C. Horst's ' Zauber-Bibliothek, oder die Zauberei, Theurgie und Mantik, Zauberei, Hexen und Hexen processen, Dämonen, Gespenster und Geistererscheinungen,' in 6 vols., 1821—a most learned and exhaustive work, brimful of recondite lore; Collin de Plancy's ' Dictionnaire Infernal ; ou Répertoire Universel des Etres, des Livres, et des Choses qui tiennent aux Apparitions, aux Divinations, à la Magie,' etc., 1844 ; Michelet's ' La Sorcière ' is, of course, brilliantly written ; R. Reuss's ' La Sorcellerie au xvie. et xviie. Siècle,' 1872 ; Tartarotti's ' Del Congresso Notturno delle Lamie,' 1749 ; F. Perreaud's ' Demonologie, ou Traité des Démons et Sorciers,' 1655 ; H. Boguet's ' Discours des Sorciers,' 1610 (very rare) ; and Cotton Mather's ' Wonders of the Invisible World,' 1695—a monument of credulity, prejudice, and bigotry.

BOOKS ON MAGIC.

It may also be convenient to the reader if I enumerate a few of the principal authorities on the history of Magic, Sorcery, and Alchemy. A very exhaustive list will be found in the ' Bibliotheca Magica et Pneumatica,' by Graessel, 1843; and an 'Alphabetical Catalogue of Works on Hermetic Philosophy and Alchemy is appended to the 'Lives of Alchemystical Philosophers,' by Arthur Edward Waite, 1888. For ordinary purposes the following will be found sufficient: Langlet du Fresnoy, 'Histoire de la Philosophie Hermétique,' 1742; Gabriel Naudé, 'Apologie pour les Grands Hommes faussement soupçonnès de Magie,' 1625; Martin Antoine Delrio, 'Disquisitionum Magicarum, libri sex,' 1599; L. F. Alfred Maury, ' La Magie et l'Astrologie dans l'Antiquité et au Moyen Age,' etc., 1860; Eus. Salverte, 'Sciences Occultes,' ed. by Littré, 1856 (see the English translation, 'Philosophy of Magic,' with Notes by Dr. A. Todd Thomson, 1846); Abbé de Villars, 'Entretiens du Comte de Gabalis'('Voyages Imaginaires,'tome 34), Englished as ' The Count de Gabalis: being a diverting History of the Rosicrucian Doctrine of Spirits,' etc., 1714; Elias Ashmole, 'Theatrum Chemicum Britannicum;' Roger Bacon, 'Mirror of Alchemy,' 1597; Louis Figuier, 'Histoire de l'Alchimie et les Alchimistes,' 1865; Arthur Edward Waite, ' The Real History of the Rosicrucians,' 1887; Hargrave Jennings, 'The Rosicrucians,' new edit.; William Godwin, 'Lives of the Necromancers,' 1834; Dr. T. Thomson, 'History of Chemistry,' 1831; 'Encyclopædia Britannica,' in locis; Dr. Kopp, 'Geschichte der Chemie;' G. Rodwell, 'Birth of Chemistry,' 1874; Haerfor, 'Histoire de la Chimie,' etc., etc.